P9-DNN-039

Kudos for Paul Levine, Jake Lassiter,
and
FLESH AND BONES

"PAUL LEVINE IS GUILTY OF MASTER
STORYTELLING IN THE FIRST DEGREE."
Carl Hiaasen

"LEVINE'S PROSE GETS LEANER, MEANER, BETTER
WITH EVERY BOOK . . . There's something
inherently lovable about Jake Lassiter . . .
He echoes that most famous of all fictional
South Florida heroes, Travis McGee . . .
Levine peoples *Flesh and Bones* with the oddities
that South Floridians take for granted and
the rest of the country can't quite believe . . .
Lassiter's self-deprecating wisdom is
endearing . . . And Jake has a lot more charisma
than Perry [Mason] ever did."
Miami Herald

"JAKE LASSITER [IS] IN FINE FORM . . . The action-
packed Levine tale is liberally sprinkled with dark
humor, great dialogue and vivid characters . . .
There are enough courtroom shenanigans to
please even the most stalwart John Grisham fan."
Lansing State Journal

"JAKE LASSITER IS MY NEW FAVORITE
PERSON IN FICTION."
Larry King

"ABSORBING . . . A TIGHTLY WRITTEN, VERY READABLE BOOK, WITH SOME GREAT PLOT TURNS."
Florida Times-Union

"JAKE LASSITER IS [THE] NEW TRAVIS McGEE."
San Diego Union-Tribune

"ANOTHER WINNER IN THE REFRESHINGLY UNPRETENTIOUS JAKE LASSITER SERIES . . . [Levine's] a wily and spirited practitioner of ripe plotting and big-time narrative excess."
Publishers Weekly

"THE AUTHOR KEEPS THE SUSPENSE HIGH WITH INNOVATIVE TWISTS while accenting *Flesh and Bones* with an insider's view of Miami and Coconut Grove and a dry humor that spices up the courtroom scenes . . . Levine has managed to imbue Jake with an appealing combination of strength and sensitivity."
Tampa Tribune & Times

"LEVINE CAN WRITE."
Washington Post Book World

"LASSITER IS SMART, TOUGH, FUNNY, AND VERY HUMAN. He's coming on fast as one of the most entertaining series characters in contemporary crime fiction."
Booklist

"PAUL LEVINE WON THE JOHN D. MacDONALD
FICTION AWARD, NAMED IN HONOR OF
[TRAVIS] McGEE'S CREATOR. *FLESH AND BONES*
IS PROOF THAT THE AWARD WAS WELL-DESERVED."
Detroit Free Press

"A CRIME NOVELIST WHO ISN'T JUST PROMISING—
HE'S PRODUCING . . . I suspect we will hear a lot
from Levine in the coming years."
Sacramento Bee

"A NEW DIRECTION FOR AUTHOR LEVINE . . .
In *Flesh and Bones*, Levine adds more depth
to his hero while mining a plot that is distinct."
Fort Lauderdale Sun-Sentinel

"A SKILLED STORYTELLER WITH
AN INSIDER'S KNOWLEDGE."
St. Louis Post-Dispatch

"PAUL LEVINE IS A TRUE ARTIST . . . He obviously
knows the law, he knows people, and
he knows Miami."
Muncie Star

"LEVINE'S JAKE LASSITER NOVELS CAN'T
COME FAST ENOUGH."
Kirkus Reviews

Other Jake Lassiter Mysteries by
Paul Levine
from Avon Books

FOOL ME TWICE
MORTAL SIN
SLASHBACK

Avon Books are available at special quantity discounts for bulk purchases for sales promotions, premiums, fund raising or educational use. Special books, or book excerpts, can also be created to fit specific needs.

For details write or telephone the office of the Director of Special Markets, Avon Books, Dept. FP, 1350 Avenue of the Americas, New York, New York 10019, 1-800-238-0658.

FLESH & BONES

A JAKE LASSITER MYSTERY

PAUL LEVINE

AVON BOOKS ◆ NEW YORK

AVON BOOKS
A division of
The Hearst Corporation
1350 Avenue of the Americas
New York, New York 10019

Copyright © 1997 by Paul Levine
Published by arrangement with the author
Visit our website at **http://www.AvonBooks.com**
Library of Congress Catalog Card Number: 96-35364
ISBN: 0-380-72591-6

All rights reserved, which includes the right to reproduce this book or
portions thereof in any form whatsoever except as provided by the U.S.
Copyright Law.

Published in hardcover by William Morrow and Company, Inc.; for information address Permissions Department, William Morrow and Company, Inc., 1350 Avenue of the Americas, New York, New York 10019.

First Avon Books Printing: May 1998

AVON TRADEMARK REG. U.S. PAT. OFF. AND IN OTHER COUNTRIES, MARCA
REGISTRADA, HECHO EN U.S.A.

Printed in the U.S.A.

WCD   10   9   8   7   6   5   4   3   2   1

If you purchased this book without a cover, you should be aware that
this book is stolen property. It was reported as ''unsold and destroyed''
to the publisher, and neither the author nor the publisher has received
any payment for this ''stripped book.''

For Luisa

ACKNOWLEDGMENTS

I acknowledge the assistance of numerous individuals who have been generous with their time and expertise.

My courthouse brigade includes attorneys Roy Black, Donald Bierman (and his wife, Rosetta), Ted Klein, Ira Loewy, Pamela Perry, Howard Rosen, Richard Sharpstein, Edward Shohat (and his wife, Maria), and Dade County Circuit Court Judges Stanford Blake and Paul Siegel.

I also thank Dade County assistant medical examiners Dr. Emma Lew and Dr. Bruce Hyma, who have guided me through the morgue and taught me forensic medicine. Other physicians lending substantial help include Dr. Joel Kallan, Dr. Charles Kalstone, Dr. Eric Prystowsky, Dr. Robert Rosenthal, and Dr. Brian Weiss.

E. Jack Donohue introduced me to the modeling world on South Beach. I also thank the models who shared their experiences with me: Liz Aron, Tracy Bond, Chrissy Cornell, Sherry Harper, and Asha Mollier.

Special thanks to Lisa St. John Dority of the South Florida Water Management District, psychologist Carolyn Robins for her jury-selection expertise, Judi Smith for her incisive research, and Karen Fierro for her nutrition advice.

We are each the sport of all that goes before us.

—Clarence Darrow

1

Loaded Dice

I was sitting at the end of the bar sipping single-malt Scotch—eighteen-year-old Glenmorangie at nine bucks a shot—when I spotted the tall blond woman with the large green eyes and the small gray gun.

Not that I knew she had a gun. Not that I even saw her at first, even though she was five feet eleven barefoot, and at the moment was wearing black stiletto heels. According to the A-Form later filled out by a bored female cop, the tall blond woman wore three items of clothing that night, and the Charles Jourdan shoes were two of them. The third was a scooped-back, low-cut, black tank minidress. Nothing more. No rings, necklaces . . . or underwear. She did carry a beaded black Versace handbag, which apparently held the gun, until she pulled it out and . . .

But I'm getting ahead of myself. When she walked in, I was twirling a snifter, admiring the golden liquid inside, trying to catch the smoky scent that had the Yuppies all atwitter, and likewise trying to figure out why I wasn't home drinking beer, eating pizza, and watching ESPN, as is my custom. Life in the no-passing lane.

"Do you sense the reek of the peat?" Rusty MacLean asked me, while twirling his own glass. "Do the pepper and the heather transport you to the Highlands?"

At the moment we were five feet above sea level, two blocks from the ocean on South Beach, with palms swaying and a Jamaican steel band playing, so you'll pardon me if the outdoor club called Paranoia didn't feel like Inverness or the Isle of Skye. "Can we drink it now, or are you going to keep blowing smoke up my kilt?" I asked.

"Patience, Jake, patience. Did you clear your palette of the Royal Lochnagar?"

"Palette clear, throat dry. Can we drink it now?"

"Did you appreciate the Lochnagar's muscular, oaky flavor? The hint of sherry?"

"Okee? As in Okefenokee? As in swampy?"

Rusty gave me his exasperated, why-do-I-put-up-with-you look. "Jake, I'm trying to civilize you. I've been trying for years."

Rusty MacLean had been my teammate on the Dolphins about a thousand years ago. He was a flashy wide receiver with curly red hair flapping out of his helmet. A free spirit, the sportswriters called him. Undisciplined, the coaches said. Used to drive Shula crazy. Rusty loved to baby himself, nursing small injuries, sitting out Tuesday practices. It is a given in pro football that by midseason *everyone* is hurt. I've played—though not very well—with turf toe, a broken nose, and a separated shoulder, once all at the same time. Rusty, who had far more natural ability, could make a hangnail seem like a compound fracture.

Rusty MacLean raised his glass and said something that sounded like "*Slanjeh*. To your health, old buddy."

I hoisted my glass. "Fuel in your bagpipes."

He sipped at his Glenmorangie, while I swilled mine, letting it warm my throat. Damn good, but I wouldn't admit it. No need to spoil my image as a throwback and relentlessly uncool, unhip, and out of it. I am so far behind the trends that sometimes I'm back in fashion, just like the Art Deco buildings in the very neighborhood where we now sat, drinking and swapping lies. I wore faded jeans, a T-shirt from a Key West oyster bar advising patrons to EAT 'EM RAW, and a nylon Penn State windbreaker. I thought I was underdressed until I saw a skinny guy in black silk pants, no shirt, and an open leather vest that couldn't hide his navel ring. Or his nipple ring. Rusty wore a black T-shirt under a double-breasted Armani suit, his hair tied back in a ponytail.

He savored his drink, eyes closed, a beatific smile on his face. "Mmmm," he purred. "I've screwed girls younger than this Scotch."

"And *you're* trying to civilize *me*?"

Rusty was signaling the bartender, pointing to another bottle of the single-malt stuff. We were going in some sort of ritualized order, from Lowlands to Highlands to islands, and The Glenlivet was next. "Not Glenlivet," Rusty had instructed me, "*The* Glenlivet."

"I know. Like the Eiffel Tower, The Donald, The Coach."

"Robust with a long finish," Rusty said as the bartender poured the liquid gold into fresh snifters. "The marriage of power and finesse."

A waitress slinked by, offering canapés from a silver tray, smoked salmon curled around cream cheese, caviar on tiny crackers. A long way from the trailer park in Key Largo. I remembered a tavern song my father used to warble after he'd had a few, none of them sips of single-malt Scotch aged in oak casks.

> Rye whiskey, rye whiskey,
> Rye whiskey, I cry.
> If I can't get rye whiskey,
> I surely will die.

Funny thinking about my father at that moment, a knife plunged into his heart, dying on a saloon floor.

I watched her approach the bar, not from some sixth sense that trouble was brewing, though in my experience, tall blondes are trouble indeed. I watched because Rusty MacLean, using the peripheral vision that had always let him know where the safety was lurking, had just gestured in her direction and compared her knees to Dan Marino's. Unfavorably to Dan's, I might add.

A few minutes earlier, I had asked him why he'd given up being a sports agent to open SoBeMo, a modeling agency. His answer competed in volume with the Dolby-enhanced nihilistic baritone poetry of Leonard Cohen. *Everybody knows that the dice are loaded. Everybody rolls with their fingers crossed.*

"Forty percent," Rusty said.

Everybody knows the fight was fixed; the poor stay poor, the rich get rich.

My look shot him a question, so he continued. "Twenty percent from the model, another twenty percent from the company booking the shoot. Compare that to four percent for representing some sixth-round, preliterate prima donna from Weber State, and I'll take the babes every time."

"We don't call them babes anymore," I corrected him, having been dragged into the nineties, just in time for the millennium.

Now, as I followed his gaze, Rusty said, "Here's another reason. Whose knees would you rather look at it, Dan Marino's or Chrissy Bernhardt's?"

If they'd asked similar questions on the Bar exam, I would have passed the first time.

I watched Chrissy Bernhardt walk the walk, hips rotating with that exaggerated roll forward, the arms swinging gracefully so far back she could have been waving at someone behind her. A stroll down the runway in Milan. Her bare shoulders had the rounded, developed look of hundreds of hours in the gym. Her ash-blond hair slid across those shoulders with each stride, and in her black stiletto heels, she was as tall as me, though a hundred pounds lighter.

Twenty feet away now, headed right for us, Chrissy Bernhardt seemed to look at Rusty. He always got the eye contact before I did. I am not a bad-looking man, despite a nose that goes east and west where it should go north and south. I have shaggy, dirty-blond hair, blue eyes, broad shoulders, and a waist that is just beginning to show the effects of numerous four-Grolsch nights. Rusty has a different look, sleek and feral, and women love it. He always seems to send out sonar waves that bounce off attractive women and back to him. This time, though, when he smiled, she didn't smile back.

Now I saw she was looking past Rusty at the beefy man on the next barstool. About sixty, a pink well-fed face, a nose that seemed too small for the rest of him, and thick arms with a golfer's tan peeking out from beneath the short-sleeved guayabera. Earlier, the man had twice asked the bartender for the time. Then he had given me a look and grinned. "I know you. Number fifty-eight for the Dolphins, right?"

"Long time ago."

"I remember a game against the Jets, you made a helluva hit on the kickoff team, recovered the fumble . . ." He smiled again, then continued in a deep, gravel-voiced rumble, "Then went the wrong way. You ran toward the wrong end zone."

"I got turned around when I made the hit," I explained, as I have so many times over the years.

"Lucky for you, your own kicker tackled you."

Yeah. Garo Yepremian couldn't tackle me if I was drunk and blindfolded. He had, however, fallen on me after I tripped on the twenty-yard-line stripe.

Everybody knows the war is over. Everybody knows the good guys lost.

Now the woman reached into the little beaded black

handbag she was carrying. The deep-voiced man next to us seemed to recognize her, too, and a thin smile creased his face. When it disappeared, I glanced back at Chrissy Bernhardt, who now was holding a Beretta 950, a silly little handgun that shoots .22 shorts out of a two-inch barrel. It's a lousy weapon for killing someone, but it weighs only ten ounces and leaves room for cigarettes and makeup in a tiny handbag.

With a single tear tracking down her face—navigating the contours of those granite cheekbones—Chrissy Bernhardt held the small pistol in both hands and squeezed off the first shot. The pop was no louder than a champagne cork's, and anyone in the bar who heard it probably thought it was just another celebratory bottle of the middling California hiccupy stuff the management was serving to the SoBe, chi-chi crowd of opening-night freebieglomming party freaks.

Of course, the beefy man with the pale, thinning hair didn't think it was a champagne cork. Not after the red stain appeared on the right side of his chest, armpit high. He sat there a second in disbelief, watching the blood dribble down the front of his creamy guayabera. Then, speechless, he looked up toward the tall young woman.

And so did I.

A second tear rolled down her lovely face, now illuminated by the spotlights set into the recessed ceiling of the outdoor bar. Potted palms rustled gently in the soft evening breeze, carrying the scent of the ocean mixed with jasmine and a hint of locally grown high-grade marijuana. There was something faintly Hollywood about the whole scene, except if this were a movie, I would have dived from my barstool and knocked the gun from the woman's hand, after which she would have fallen in love with me.

But I didn't. And she didn't. Or did she?

Mouth agape, like the cop holding on to Lee Harvey Oswald as Jack Ruby plugged him, I just watched as she fired the second shot, this one lower, plinking the tip of the man's pelvis and ricocheting toward the dance floor, where the police would later find it and slip it into a little plastic bag, as they are inclined to do.

Everybody knows that the boat is leaking. Everyone knows the captain lied.

Frozen to my barstool, I watched Chrissy Bernhardt lower the gun slightly, aiming at the man's crotch.

Everybody got this broken feeling like their father or their dog just died.

The man tried covering his groin with his hands, and the third bullet slipped between his spread fingers, nicked his penis, then entered his thigh, lodging in but not breaking his femur.

All of this took just a few seconds. Rusty never moved, except to lean toward me and away from the line of fire. In games, he'd always head for the bench during brawls, and I'd be out there busting my knuckles against the top of some gorilla's helmet.

As she took aim again, I finally leaped from the barstool and dived for the gun, knocking it away. Chrissy Bernhardt fainted, and I caught her, just scooped her up and held her there, her cheek resting on my shoulder, her flowing hair tickling my neck. Which is how my picture came to be plastered on page one of *The Miami Herald*, a beautiful, unconscious woman in my arms, a dumb, gaping look on my face. Beneath the photo, the caption "Lawyer disarms gun-toting model—too late."

Story of my life: a step too slow.

2

Concussion Zone

"Patricide," Doc Charlie Riggs said with distaste. "A crime of biblical dimensions."

"And mythical," I added.

"Oedipus, of course," Charlie said. "And let's see now . . ."

Talking to the retired coroner is like playing poker with ideas, and today it was my turn to deal. "Orestes," I told him. It isn't often I get the upper hand on Charlie, so I milked it. "Orestes beheaded his mother, Clytemnestra, for plotting the death of his father, Agamemnon."

"Yes, of course. Very good, Jake. Very good, indeed."

He gave me his kindly teacher look. It's fun proving that I didn't spend five years at Penn State for nothing, if you'll pardon the double negative. My freshman year, I was drafted by the Thespian Club to play Big Jule in a student production of *Guys and Dolls,* mostly because the other actors had the physique of Michael J. Fox. It was fun, and it prompted me to switch my major from phys. ed. to drama, where I specialized in playing large, dumb guys. Yeah, I know, type casting. My favorite part was Lennie in *Of Mice and Men,* and I still remember hearing sobs in the audience when I asked George to tell me about

8

the little place we'd get, and there was George pulling the gun out of his pocket. "And I get to tend the rabbits," I said, and George was pointing the gun at the back of my head, and the people in the audience were sniffling and bawling. I wish Granny could have been there.

Anyway, here I was—two careers later—still acting, but this time for judges and juries. At this precise moment, I was listening as my old friend told me about the autopsy report, which his friends at the county morgue had slipped him last night.

The gunshots should not have killed Harry Bernhardt, Doc Riggs told me. Would not have killed him if he hadn't had a heart condition. Seventy-five percent blockage of two coronary arteries due to a lifetime of Kentucky bourbon, Cuban cigars, and Kansas beef.

"The shock of the shooting set loose a burst of adrenaline," Charlie said, leafing through the report. "Combined with the blockage, that could have killed him instantly."

"But it didn't," I protested. "He survived. The surgery was supposedly successful."

"Sure, the bullets were removed, the bleeding stopped. But, between the shooting and the surgery, the system had taken some brutal shocks, especially for a man with damaged arteries. While recovering in the ICU, the unfortunate Mr. Bernhardt went into spontaneous ventricular fibrillation. The muscle fibers of the heart weren't getting enough oxygen." Charlie opened and closed his fist rapidly to demonstrate. "The heart was literally quivering, but no blood was being pumped. Cardiac arrest followed. The Code Blue team attempted to resuscitate and defibrillate but was unsuccessful. Death was imminent."

"But he was fine when they put him into the ambulance," I said.

"Fine?" Charlie raised a bushy eyebrow. It was a look he'd used hundreds of times to tell jurors that the lawyer questioning him was full of beans. Charlie Riggs had been medical examiner of Dade County for twenty-five years before retiring to fish the Keys and drink Granny Lassiter's moonshine. Now, he was sitting in my office high above Biscayne Boulevard, giving me the benefit of his wisdom, without charging me a fee, except for a promised Orvis graphite spinning rod. A small bandy-legged man with an unruly beard, he wore eyeglasses fastened together with a bent fishhook. A cold meerschaum pipe was propped in the corner of his mouth. "Fine?" he repeated. "Mr. Harry Bernhardt was leaking blood from three bullet wounds. Four, if you count both the thigh and the penis, which were hit with the same bullet."

"Let's count the penis. I would if it were mine." I riffled through the paramedics' report and the hospital records. "But he survived the surgery, which stanched the bleeding and removed the bullets. He was in critical but stable condition in the ICU for two hours after he was patched up."

"What are you getting at, counselor?"

"The heart attack could have been independent of the shooting. Maybe I can get Socolow to charge her with aggravated assault, instead of—"

"You can't represent her! You're a witness."

"Me and a hundred others, plus a security videotape that caught the whole thing. I already talked to Socolow. He said he'd rather have me as an opposing lawyer than a witness."

"If I were you, I wouldn't take that as a compliment."

"Socolow's been wrong before. Besides, Ms. Christina Bernhardt asked me to represent her."

"What'd you do, slip your card into her bra when she was passed out?"

"Wasn't wearing a bra, Charlie. Panties, either."

"Good heavens!"

"It's a model thing. Interferes with the smooth flow of fabric on skin."

Charlie Riggs looked at me skeptically. "Just when did you become an expert on models?"

"Rusty MacLean taught me a few things. Actually, he's the one who retained me. He's her agent, promises to pay the tab."

"Better get a hefty retainer from that weasel," Charlie advised, "or you'll never see a dollar."

"Hey, Rusty's an old friend. He introduced me to every after-hours watering hole in the AFC East and many of the women therein."

"Even in Buffalo?"

"Especially in Buffalo. What else is there to do?"

Charlie harrumphed his displeasure. "I never trusted a receiver who didn't like going over the middle."

Like coaches and generals, Doc Charlie Riggs had remarkable tolerance for other people's pain.

"Charlie, believe me, no one likes going over the middle. It's a concussion zone."

It's true, of course. No one wants to run full speed into Dick Butkus, Jack Lambert, or even little old me, Jake Lassiter, linebacker with a tender heart and a forearm smash like a crowbar to the throat.

"It's not just that he short-armed it," Charlie said. "It's that he never gave a hundred percent. With you, Jake, it was different. You had no business being out there. You just gave it everything and overachieved."

"It was either that or drive a beer truck," I said. In those days, I hadn't thought about law school, still confining myself to honest work. But Charlie Riggs was right about one thing. Rusty had talent he never used.

Rusty MacLean was a natural. A four-sport star at a Chicago high school, he was an All-American at Notre Dame and a first-round draft choice with the Dolphins. I was a solid, if unspectacular, linebacker at Coral Shores

High School in the Florida Keys, a walk-on at Penn State, and a free agent with the Dolphins. I hung on as a pro because of a willingness to punish myself—and occasionally an opponent—on kickoff teams. I played linebacker only when injuries to the starters were so severe that Don Shula thought about calling Julio Iglesias to fill in.

Rusty could do anything—pole-vault, high-jump, play tennis with either hand. The first time he touched a golf club, he shot a 79. But he hated practice and loved parties. Blown knee ligaments ended his career when he didn't have the discipline to suffer through a year of painful rehabilitation. My career ended differently. I fought back after knee surgery, numerous fractures, and separated shoulders, but was simply beaten out by better, younger players. I enrolled in night law school because it left days free for windsurfing.

Charlie grumbled something else about my old teammate, then went back to the autopsy report, pausing once to tap tobacco into his pipe and then light it. I stood up and paced, stopping in front of the floor-to-ceiling windows that overlooked the bay, Key Biscayne, and the ocean beyond. From the thirty-second floor, I could make out tiny triangles of colorful sails on the waters just off Virginia Key. Windsurfers luxuriating in a fifteen-knot easterly. Beats murder and mayhem any day.

"What about it, Charlie? Will you testify that the heart attack was an intervening cause?"

"But it wasn't!" he thundered. "The shooting was the proximate cause of the coronary."

"Not so fast," I cautioned. "At his age, with the condition of his arteries, Harry Bernhardt could have had a coronary at any time, right?"

"But he didn't have it *any* time. He went into cardiac arrest three and a half hours after your client—if that's what she is—plugged him, her own father, for God's sake."

"How about just helping me out at the bond hearing, Charlie? Maybe give a little song-and-dance to get her out of the can."

Charlie raised his bushy eyebrows at me. "Are you suborning perjury?"

"No, I was just saying—"

"That I lie at the bond hearing, as if that would be a lesser evil than at the trial." His look was a dagger. "Jake, an oath is an oath."

I remembered what a writer once said about another lawyer, the disgraced and now deceased Roy Cohn: "He only lies under oath." Well, why not? That's when it counts.

"*Veritas simplex oratio est,*" Charlie said. "The language of truth is simple. But lies, prevarications, calumnies, they'll catch you in their web."

I hate arguing with Charlie Riggs because he's always right, and he keeps me semihonest with his damned Yankee rectitude. "The grand jury meets tomorrow," I said. "I was hoping to talk Abe Socolow into a plea to a lesser—"

"Jake, how long have you known Abe?"

"Since he was prosecuting shoplifters and I was a rookie learning how to obfuscate the facts, confuse the jury, and obstruct justice."

"You mean when you were in the PD's office."

"That's what I said."

"So you've known Abe your entire career."

"Such as it is."

Doc Riggs cocked his head to one side and gave me his disappointed-mentor look.

"Okay, Charlie, I know what you're saying. Abe's a hard ass, and I should know it. I just thought we had a special case here. A woman with no prior record who's no threat to the community . . ."

"Right. She's got no other fathers to kill."

"Charlie, all those years working for the state have warped your sense of fairness. You've become a real shill for the prosecution."

"A shill?" He growled and jabbed his pipe at me. "I'm just objective, and you're not."

"Of course not!" Now it was my turn to raise my voice. "I'm Christina Bernhardt's lawyer, her shield against the powerful forces of the state or anyone else who would do her harm."

"So what is it you want? Probation, counseling, community service?"

My shrug asked, Why not?

"Face it, Jake. You've got yourself a murder trial, and a loser at that."

"Don't underestimate me, Charlie."

"I never have. I just think that sometimes you don't know when you're in the concussion zone."

I was chomping a cheeseburger at my desk when Cindy, my secretary, walked in, made a face, and twirled a finger through her burnt-orange curls. "If the nitrites and benzopyrene don't give you cancer, the pesticides and heavy metals will."

"What?" A drop of grease splattered a slip-and-fall file that was open in front of me.

"That disgusting fat-laden animal flesh you're eating will kill you. The excess protein will cause kidney failure, and the antibiotics actually lower your resistance to infection."

"Bon appétit," I said, hoisting my dripping burger toward her.

"Do you know that the production of animal foods consumes twenty percent of our energy supply? Do you know that seventy-five percent of our water is devoted to raising animals for food?"

"And worth every drop." I belched. "Where do you get these numbers, anyway?"

"The Vegan Society," she said, plopping down in one of the two matching client chairs, the oak armrests stained by years of sweaty palms.

Oh, the vegans. No animal products whatsoever, including dairy, eggs, and honey. I pictured a bunch of skinny busybodies, eating their tofu and raising hell with your basic steak-and-lobster guys such as my very own carnivorous self.

"What do you have for me?" I asked.

She consulted her pad. "Roberto Condom is in the waiting room," she said, stifling a laugh. "With all the legal work you do for him, you'd think he'd ask for a name change, too."

"What's wrong with 'Roberto'?"

She wrinkled her nose at me. Droll wit is so seldom appreciated. "Anyway, you gotta get moving," Cindy ordered. "You've got Rusty MacLean at three, his place. Then Christina Bernhardt at five, her place."

"Very funny, Cindy."

Chrissy's place was the Women's Detention Center, where she was being held without bond. At least for now.

"Bobby, you look great!"

"*No sé*, Jake. They want to revoke my probation."

"What? Are you looting lobsters again?"

My client gave me his pained look. "Jake, *mi amigo,* I was setting them free from their traps. Don't you remember our defense?" He let his voice slip into a pretty fair impression of my impassioned closing argument. "Roberto Condom, protector of the environment, friend of flora and fauna, mammal and crustacean alike."

"We might have won," I reminded him, "if the Marine Patrol hadn't found three hundred deceased lobsters iced down in your pickup truck."

Roberto shrugged. That's life. He was in his mid-thirties, toreador thin, with slicked-back black hair, a pencil mustache, and long curving sideburns that resembled the blade of a scythe. He wore a bird's-egg-blue linen shirt with puffy sleeves, and pleated white slacks. Though he looked like a gigolo in a 1940s movie, Roberto Condom was more at home in a swamp than in St. Moritz.

As a thief, Roberto was a specialist, and his *especialidad* was stealing living things. He never boosted a car, but he had rustled cattle from ranches near Ocala. He never rifled a cash register, but he had once broken into a pet store and stolen every tropical fish in the place. He poached sea turtle eggs, which he could sell for a hundred bucks a pop to *botánicas* in Little Havana where they were believed to be aphrodisiacs, water spider orchids from Fakahatchee Strand State Preserve, and live ostrich chicks from Lion Country Safari. At this very moment, Roberto Condom was wearing hand-sewn ostrich-skin cowboy boots that would run you a thousand bucks, unless you brought your own ostriches to the bootmaker.

Roberto disdained mundane crime, especially drug dealing. Which was how I'd gotten him off when a partner double-crossed him and stuffed condoms—yeah, I know—filled with cocaine inside seven hundred boa constrictors Roberto was smuggling into the country. Before the boas left Bogotá, someone had jammed the packets of cocaine inside their rectums, then sewed the orifices shut, a job I have never seen advertised in the "Help Wanted" section. When the constipated and ornery snakes were discovered by Customs, Roberto was charged with drug importation as well as cruelty to animals. Roberto showed up for trial with Bozo, his pet six-foot boa, curled around his neck, pleading that he loved snakes and would never do such a thing. The jury was out only twenty minutes, and Roberto walked. At Christmas, I was rewarded with a snakeskin jacket that looked familiar, but it took me three months to figure out that I hadn't seen Bozo in a while.

"So if it's not lobsters, what?" I asked. "Stone crabs, sponges, starfish, wood storks? You're not stealing live coral from Pennekamp Park, are you?"

"Jake!" Again feigning insult. Then he fingered his necklace of alligator teeth, and I knew.

"Gators. You're poaching in the Everglades."

"*Chíngate!* I'm no poacher. I have a license."

"Which limits you to six gators a season."

"Six," he sniffed. "How can a man make a living? I get two hundred dollars a hide, then some fancy store in Bal Harbour sells one purse for twenty times that."

"Nobody said life is fair."

"*Verdad.* Even if you shoot a big *caimán* right in the eye, it'll flop around in your boat for hours. You gotta stick a wire in its spine to kill it, and then you'll be up to your knees in gator shit."

"If that's an invitation to your next hunt, forget it."

"I'm just saying that your everyday working guy like me has it tough."

"Okay, so you're Lunch-Bucket José. How many hides they catch you with?"

"*Solamente* fifty-seven."

"Jeez, a serial poacher."

"Three days' work. This time of year, it should be more like a hundred. I tell you something funny. The water level's been down in the Glades for six months."

" 'Course it has. It's the end of the dry season. Wait a few weeks, and it'll rain every dog day afternoon."

"Yeah, but the dry season hasn't been that dry this year. Something's screwy. The gator holes are parched. Damn few turtles and ducks for them to eat, and fishing's shot to hell. I called the Water Management Office, pretended to be one of those Audubon Society types. They said they'd look into it, but you know how government is."

I filed the information away in one of the dusty recesses

of my mind, wondering how we would use it. As usual, my client was a step ahead of me.

"So I'm thinking, Jake, maybe I was doing the gators a favor."

"How, by plugging them through the eye with a three hundred Weatherby?"

"Beats starving to death, *verdad*? Jeez, I'm just speeding evolution along. Natural selection, survival of the fittest. In a way, I'm a visionary, ahead of my time."

I remembered what Charlie had said about Chrissy's case. "So what do you want, Bobby—probation, community service?"

"Hell, no! I'm a goddamn hero. They should give me a medal."

3

Cheekbones and Chic Bones

"So-Be-Mo," Rusty MacLean said, giving each syllable a little push. "South Beach Models. Catchy, no?"

"Catchy, yes," I agreed.

We were sitting in his office on the third floor of an Ocean Drive Art Deco building. The facade of the 1930s structure had recently been repainted seafoam-green with flamingo-pink racing stripes. The windows were topped by cantilevered shades that looked like eyebrows, and the lobby was framed in keystone and decorated with ornamental friezes that seemed to celebrate leaping sailfish.

Rusty's office walls were decorated with covers of magazines that were not on my regular reading list: *Mondo, Grazia, Esprit, Vogue,* and *Elle.* Each cover displayed a beautiful young woman in fancy duds, some of the models displaying enough cleavage to distract a guy who wouldn't know Ralph Lauren from Ralph Cramden.

"The Wall of Fame," Rusty told me. His girls who had made good. I recognized Chrissy Bernhardt's pouting lips on a cover of *Marie Claire.*

An interior window looked into an adjacent office where one of Rusty's talent scouts, a chain-smoking middle-aged woman with eyeglasses on a chain of imitation pearls, interviewed a mother and her two teenage daughters. All three were dressed identically in tank tops, black miniskirts, knee socks, and high-heeled white sneakers.

"Mom's living through her daughters," Rusty had said when he escorted me to his office past the glass-enclosed room. "They waltz in here on open-audition day, girls who aren't five-six on their tippy-toes, with mashed potatoes where their cheekbones should be. Eileen Ford used to say there's no such thing as a model with a short neck, but nobody gave the word to these moms."

I looked outside through the other window, across Lummus Park to the ocean. The beach was dotted with blue umbrellas, and a mile or so offshore, a cruise ship was making its way through turquoise water with a thousand happy tourists aboard.

"Not a bad view, eh?" Rusty asked. He gestured toward a telescope at the corner of the room, its barrel pointed due east toward the water. "The Tenth Street beach is topless these days. Wanna take a look?"

"Another time, Rusty. I've got to get to the women's jail and—"

"Brazilians," he said.

"What?"

"They started it. Just took off their tops. Didn't wear much of a bottom, either. Then the local girls started doing it. Pretty soon you had a topless beach. Go farther north, up to Haulover, and it's totally nude."

"Rusty, do you think we could talk about Chrissy?"

He shrugged and pulled a large scrapbook from a shelf. "She walked in here with a first-rate book about a year ago. I knew right off she was a winner, a real gravy train for an agent. Maybe not what the French call the *top du top des top models,* but in the upper echelon. Hard worker who paid her dues in Italy, France, New York, the usual stops. Started doing real well about the time tits came back in.''

"I never knew they were out."

"She had the raw material. You ever hear the expression 'cheekbones and chic bones'?''

"Don't think anyone at the Quarterdeck Saloon ever says that," I admitted.

"Well, Chrissy has it. Straight, thin nose, full lips, flawless complexion, long legs, and those shoulders. You gotta have shoulders to work the runway or the clothes look like shit. She's got an expressive face and great hair and can be ultrasleek and sophisticated or a California beach girl, whatever the client wants. Her body's perfect, everything in proportion, but a lot of girls have that. There's something else that's hard to define, a kind of spark that ignites in front of the camera, an energy that makes you watch. The best models are full of life, even when they're perfectly still. They're not passive unless the shot calls for it. You understand, Jake?''

"Not a word of it."

He was thumbing through the pages of her book, Chrissy in a swimsuit and high heels, in a striped silk blouse and miniskirt, in an ankle-length dress from a magazine ad. Then a couple of moody black-and-white shots taken in the woods. Sunlight filtered through leafy branches and Chrissy lay nude on her back on a fallen tree, her knee coyly raised to shield her groin, both hands hovering over, but not quite covering, her breasts.

"She had a reputation in Europe as pretty wild, but in this business, that's par for the course. She could party all night and still make an eight A.M. call. Took the work seriously. Used to give hell to the crews. The lighting, the makeup, the clothes. Everything had to be right and never was. In France, her nickname was Casse-Couille, 'Ballbreaker.' ''

Rusty ran a hand through his long hair, giving his ponytail a little pat. "When she got back here, I landed one national commercial for her. Iced tea. She was in a white tennis outfit, and by the time she gulped down the tea, every man in America wanted to fuck her, marry her, or adopt her. Maybe a hundred fifty grand in residuals. Did some international spots, Latin America, a couple in the Far East, and a lot of fashion, five thousand a day for catalog work, some very classy editorial, too. The only negative, she wouldn't fuck me."

"Talented and smart, too," I said.

"Yeah, now that you mention it, she's pretty sharp. More than most *mowdells*. You know what they call a model with half a brain?"

"I have a feeling I'm going to find out."

"Gifted."

"That's dated, Rusty. Chauvinist, too."

"What does a model say when she's screwing?"

"What?"

" 'Are all you guys on the same team?' "

"Sometimes, Rusty, I think your emotional development stopped at about age twenty-two."

"Rookie year. A thousand yards in receptions, a babe in every city in the conference, two in Baltimore."

"The prosecution rests."

Rusty put down the book and walked to the window. He squinted through the telescope and fiddled with the focus knob. "Chrissy's different than most of the girls, 'cause she grew up rich. A lot of them come from farms in the Midwest, trailer parks in Georgia. They go off to New York or Milan when they're sixteen, and they don't read a book for the next ten years."

"Whereas you're a regular Edmund Wilson, right?"

"Who?"

"Never mind. What's the point?"

He thought about it a moment. Next door, the mother and daughters were gone. In a corridor, a booking agent was watching a female model step onto a doctor's scale. It reminded me of a jockey weighing in at the track, only the model was a foot taller and wasn't carrying a saddle. She looked fine to me, even a bit too thin, but the booking agent scribbled something on a clipboard and mouthed the words *three pounds,* her scowl making it seem like a capital offense.

Finally, Rusty said, "The point is that Chrissy had all the advantages. Do you know who Harry Bernhardt is?"

"Was," I reminded him. "From now on, Harry Bernhardt is purely past tense. Didn't he do some farming?"

Rusty barked out a laugh. "Yeah. And Johnny Unitas did some throwing. Harry Bernhardt is . . . *was* a goddamn conglomerate. Sugarcane, cattle, real estate, you name it. Houses in Palm Beach, Aspen, and London. Well connected both politically and socially, major contributor to both political parties at the state and national levels. The only red on that old boy's neck came from the afternoon sun in Monaco."

"Chrissy ever talk about him?" I asked.

"Not a word. She left home when she was a teenager. Damn few people even knew the connection 'til she aced him."

"Any other acts of violence? Ever see her threaten anyone?"

"Chrissy? Hey, Jake, listen to me. Chrissy Bernhardt might not be an angel, and she sure as hell has a past, but I've never known her to hurt anyone, with the possible exception of herself. So if she killed her old man, which you and I saw with our very own eyes, she had a damn good reason."

4

Am I Getting Warmer?

I learned how to interview clients from Jimmy Stewart and José Ferrer.

Okay, so maybe watching old movies isn't quite the same as earning an Ivy League law degree or even toting Edward Bennett Williams's briefcase, but we all work with what we've got. So as I exited the Dolphin Expressway—honoring the likes of Griese, Buoniconti, Csonka, and Warfield, not Flipper—I couldn't help playing the scenes.

Jimmy Stewart is smoking a cigar while interviewing his jailed client, Ben Gazzara, in *Anatomy of a Murder*.

"What's your excuse, Lieutenant, for killing Barney Quill?"

Ben Gazzara paces around the sheriff's office, noodling it. "What excuses are there?" he asks, and right away you know this is a savvy client. Not some blabbermouth, but a thinking man's defendant.

"How should I know?" Jimmy Stewart answers in his aw-shucks drawl. "You're the one who plugged Quill."

Ben Gazzara paces some more, then mumbles, half to himself, "I must have been mad."

"No," Jimmy says. "Bad temper's no excuse."

You can see the light bulb blink in Gazzara's head.

24

"I mean, I must have been crazy. . . . Am I getting warmer?"

That's the right way to do it. Hint a little, but don't come right out and coach your client.

The other night, I was watching television with my nephew Kip, a twelve-year-old who doesn't do his homework but has total recall of the newsreel voice-overs from *Citizen Kane*. Kip had asked me the secret to being a good lawyer. First, I told him, you've got to win your client's confidence by expressing optimism. Then we sat down to watch José Ferrer meet his clients in *The Caine Mutiny*.

"I don't want to upset you too much," José Ferrer tells the nervous defendants, "but you have an excellent chance of being hanged."

"So what's your excuse for shooting your father?" I asked Christina Bernhardt. I am nothing if not a good student by rote.

"My excuse?" She shook her head in that way women have of clearing the hair out of their eyes. I always thought it was an unconscious gesture, but maybe they do it only when men are watching.

"Ms. Bernhardt—"

"Chrissy," she said, "and I'll call you Jake."

"Fair enough. Chrissy, what's your legal justification for what would otherwise be cold-blooded murder?"

"I have my reasons."

"I'm sure you do. I just hope they constitute a lawful defense."

"Such as?"

Good question. Maybe she'd seen Ben Gazzara, too. "Self-defense, defense of others, accident, insanity. For insanity, we'd have to prove that you didn't know right from wrong at the time of the shooting."

"Right from wrong," she repeated. "Oh, how I know the difference."

"Let me stop you right there," I said. We were sitting on hard wooden chairs designed by Torquemada in the attorneys' conference room at the Women's Detention Center. Chrissy Bernhardt wore a blue jailhouse smock, matching loose-fitting pants with a drawstring, and the paper slippers they give inmates so they won't bash each other with leather shoes. It was an outfit never seen in *Vogue* or *Elle,* but still she looked . . . well, like she'd stepped out of the pages of a magazine. Her ash-blond hair fell across her shoulders. Her green eyes were clear and bright, no evidence of crying. No makeup, but her skin glowed, a good trick under the fluorescent jail lights where everyone looks jaundiced and some probably are.

I looked straight into those bright eyes and said, "Before you say anything else, remember this. If you tell me something now, I can't let you testify differently." This is the ethical lawyer's way of telling a client to be circumspect, even when talking to your very own mouthpiece. I won't lie to a judge or let a client do it. But I'm not adverse to advising my presumably innocent client to tell me what the hell happened only *after* I explain what makes a better story in the eyes of the blindfolded lady with the scales.

"You're charged with first-degree murder," I told her. "It's a capital crime requiring premeditation. There is no question as to identity. You walked into a crowded bar and shot your father, not once, but three times."

"It would have been four, but I fainted," she said.

"I think we can rule out accident."

She gave me a little smile, dimples showing under the prominent cheekbones. "Do you know what Rusty says about you?"

"Probably that I was a sucker for the play-action fake."

"He says you're not the brightest lawyer in town, but that you have the biggest heart, and that if you believed in me, you'd bleed for me. I liked that. And I liked the way it felt when you carried me out of the club."

Through the interior window, a male jail guard watched us. Actually, he watched Chrissy. Most of the women inmates were drug addicts and hookers, plus an occasional poor soul who'd blown away an abusive spouse or lover. Most were not Chrissy Bernhardt.

"You were unconscious," I said.

"I was woozy and seeing stars, but I remember feeling your heartbeat against me. You're very strong, and I felt secure, protected in your arms."

"That was before I dropped you in the police car."

"Do you remember what you said to me?"

"Something about not saying a word to anyone until you had a lawyer. Standard advice."

"Then you brushed a tear from my face and squeezed my hand. You were very gentle and very caring. You had this look. I can't describe it, exactly. Sympathy, sorrow, empathy, and something that said you cared about me, even though you didn't know me."

I cleared my throat, embarrassed. What had I felt? That she was a beautiful young woman in terrible trouble. A damaged woman in great need. I'd been down that road before and had found only pain. "You did have an effect on me," I said. "Now all I have to do is get the jury to feel the same thing, and maybe we have a shot."

Yeah, and all Hannibal had to do was cross the Alps, and he still never got to Rome.

"Why don't I just tell you why I did it," Chrissy said, "then you figure out if I was legally justified?"

It's not the way Jimmy Stewart would have done it, but I said, "Shoot," and immediately regretted my choice of words.

"Where do you want me start?"

I'm no expert on the Bible, but I do remember the first three words of Genesis. "In the beginning," I said.

* * *

"I was a tomboy," Chrissy told me. "Tall and athletic. I'd wrestle with the boys, play football, go tarpon fishing with my father. We had the big house on the ocean in Palm Beach, a weekend place in Islamorada, a ranch outside Ocala. I raced horses, did some jumping events, even played polo." She stopped and let a memory drift by. "When I was fourteen, I started sneaking into the barn with a stableboy who worked for the family. My father caught us and chased him off the property with a pitchfork. Would have killed him if he'd caught him."

"Tell me about your father."

"A powerful man. My earliest memories are of his booming voice. He could rattle the windowpanes ordering coffee. He was so . . . competent at everything, so in charge. I admired him, respected him. Loved him."

Her eyes grew watery, and a tear trickled down her cheek just as it had when she nailed her beloved father with three .22 shorts. Unless there was a darker side to powerful, competent, deceased Harry Bernhardt, the jury would be out about fifteen minutes before convicting my lovely and lethal client.

This time, Chrissy wiped away her own tear and said, "Do you have a cigarette?"

"No. They don't let you smoke in the jail anymore."

"Even on Death Row?"

I like clients with a sense of humor, even gallows humor.

"All models smoke," she told me. "We spend a lot of time waiting, at castings, at shoots, everyplace. Plus, it's a great way to control weight."

"Your father," I said, trying to bring her back. "Tell me more."

And she did.

Harry Bernhardt grew up poor but ambitious near Indiantown, east of Lake Okeechobee. Chrissy's mother, Emily Castleberry, grew up rich and privileged in Palm Beach, only child of Flagler T. Castleberry, banker, landowner, and sugarcane baron. Young Harry was a bass fishing guide on the lake, and old Flagler fancied himself quite a fisherman. He hired the husky young man, then brought him home to do odd jobs around the mansion.

When he wasn't pruning the hedges or replacing broken roof tiles, Harry would spend his time surf casting in the waters behind the oceanfront mansion. Which is where young Emily, a tall, slender teenager, would play volleyball and drink rum-and-Cokes with her equally rich Palm Beach friends. Always rebellious, Emily astonished her friends by running off with Harry to Georgia, where they were married by a justice of the peace.

The young and apparently mismatched couple lived in a hunting cabin for a year before old Flagler forgave them both, offered Harry a job, and established a trust fund that would make Emily a very wealthy young woman. Then he had the good taste to die of a spontaneous aortic aneurysm, leaving Harry to run the businesses, all of which were in Emily's name.

It was a childless marriage for six years until Christina was born, Emily having had three miscarriages along the way. Christina was an only child, or so it seemed until eight years later when Harry brought home a surprise. He was Guy Bernhardt, a surly seventeen-year-old, the unhappy product of a one-night stand in a fishing shack when Harry had been little more than a child himself. Guy's mother had either run off or had been sent to a state mental hospital, no one knew for sure, and now Guy inherited what had been his father's position at the mansion, handyman and not quite a member of the family.

"Did you have a happy childhood?" I asked.

Chrissy gave me an enigmatic smile before answering. "That's the way I always remembered it. I was Daddy's little angel, and he spoiled me. Whatever I wanted, I got.

For a long time, he seemed embarrassed about Guy, like just looking at him brought back bad memories, reminded him who he was and where he came from. They weren't close, but then how could they be? Guy was practically grown before they even met. Of course, that changed over the years. Daddy brought Guy into the business, made him start at the bottom, shoveling shit, both literally and figuratively, just like my grandfather had done with him. But Guy is a lot like Daddy. He's not afraid of hard work and has great patience. It took over twenty years, but Guy pretty much runs everything now."

"And your mother?"

"So elegant and beautiful. I wanted to be just like her, at least until I went into my rebellious stage. Body piercing, drinking, drugs when I was twelve. Mom died of a heart attack when I was thirteen."

"I'm sorry."

"She was so young. She had always been frail, and she drank too much, especially the last two or three years. She was a lonely, unhappy woman."

"So your father raised you?"

"He tried. I was pretty wild as a teenager, and it horrified Daddy. He would have locked me in my room if he could."

There was a knock at the door. Chrissy reached across the table and took my hand. "Are we out of time? I really don't want you to go."

I took her hand between both of mine. "Relax. There's only a time limit in the movies. I'm your lawyer, and I can stay all day."

The door opened, and an enormous female jail guard toddled in, carrying a brown paper bag, a set of keys jiggling on her wide belt. She had cocoa skin and dreadlocked hair, and her nametag read "D. Scruggs."

"Hello, Do-lo," I said. "Chrissy, this is Dolores. If you have any problems—"

"You just call me, honey," Dolores said, smiling at my client. "One look at you, and I know you're in the wrong place."

"Thank you. I . . ."

Dolores was unloading takeout containers from the paper bag. The small room filled with the aroma of spicy pork.

"Chinese?" Chrissy asked. "You can order out here?"

"Jake can," Dolores said. "Anything he wants for his clients."

"How about bolt cutters with the moo shu?" I suggested.

"Don't be funning me," Dolores said, then turned to Chrissy. "Jake tell you about the last client he had who sat in that chair?"

Chrissy looked concerned. "No."

"Jake always advises his clients to show up in court clean and well dressed, ain't that right?"

"Do-lo, is this necessary?"

"So, this sister comes into the arraignment in a fancy suit, sort of avocado-colored, by one of your designers, like a . . ."

"Chanel?" Chrissy helped out.

"Yeah, something like that, with a double strand of pearls, the real thing. And Jake had just pleaded her not guilty to a home burglary, when there's this scream from the gallery. I mean, a woman screams bloody murder. Am I lying, Jake?"

"Actually, she screamed, 'Thief!' She was the victim, and she ran down the aisle yelling, 'That's my suit, my pearls!' "

"So, honey," Dolores said, "you be careful when you follow this mouthpiece's advice." Cackling with laughter, she headed out the door.

After a moment, Chrissy asked, "What was your defense?"

"The suit looked better on my client," I said.

"No, seriously."

"A wise old friend of mine taught me that lawyering is like playing poker. One of the first things you learn in poker is when to fold your cards. We pled guilty."

"Oh," Chrissy sighed, and I could tell she was wondering about my competence. Why should she be any different from anyone else? I opened the containers and peeled the chopsticks out of their paper. "Dolores seems very fond of you," Chrissy said. Probably wondering just how many of my clients end up in jail.

"Her name means 'sorrow' in Latin. My same wise old friend told me that. Do-lo put three of her own kids through college and is a foster mom to about a dozen more. Incorrigibles, kids nobody wants. When they get in trouble, which is often, I handle their cases."

"For free?"

"For some of Dolores's home-cooked ribs or special considerations for a hungry client."

Chrissy was already digging into the shredded cabbage and wood mushrooms of the moo shu pork. "God, this is good. Do you know what the food's like in this place?"

"Yeah, the Donner Party ate better in the winter of 1846."

We sat a moment in silence before I got us back on track. "Your father would have locked you in your room. . . ."

"And I would have done anything to get out. Out of the mansion, out of Palm Beach. When a talent scout spotted me on Worth Avenue and said I could be a top model, I told Daddy I was going to Paris, and he yelled, 'You're only sixteen!' So I said, 'Mom married you when she was seventeen.'"

"Touché."

"Yeah, but Daddy said he doubted she would have done it if she had a second chance."

I gobbled a spring roll. "So you went to Europe."

"I was so-o-o-o naive. I had a book of photos shot by an amateur in Lauderdale. They were laughable, really hideous. Poorly lit, dumb, stilted poses like a kid pretending to be a model, my hair sprayed into place like concrete."

"Did you get work?"

"Not at first."

Chrissy opened a plastic cup of hot tea and took a sip. "I took my book into the office of one of the scouts for a big Parisian agency. They call them *rabatteurs,* the men who beat the bushes to flush out the prey. Only in this case, instead of rabbits . . ."

"Young girls who want to be models."

"Right. He was right out of Central Casting, a little mustache, a lewd twinkle in his eye, and he wore a white silk scarf in the office. Anyway, he offers me a glass of wine and starts looking through the book. He laughs, says something to himself in French, laughs again. 'Do you know what a go-see is?' he asks me. I tell him, 'Sure, it's when a model takes her pictures to a client to get work.' Then he puts the book in his lap, unbuttons his fly, and lays out his dick, right at the fold. '*Oui,* but for you to get work, *chérie,* a go-see is a go-suck.' "

"This guy must have gone to prep school with Senator Packwood. What did you do?"

"I smiled sweetly, reached over, and grabbed the book by each side, then slammed it shut as hard as I could."

"Good for you!"

"Yeah, well, my morals didn't hold up as well after I ran out of money and was hungry."

"Didn't your father help you?"

"He would have if I'd asked."

"But you didn't."

"I didn't even tell him where I was."

"Why not?"

She stared off into space. A shadow crossed her face for

just a second, and there it was again, that vulnerability and need. I am not a white knight bedecked in armor, mounted on a gallant steed. But if I were, I would have scooped her up, tugged at the reins, and spirited her away to a refuge in a forest of high pines.

"I didn't know at the time," she said finally, "but I do now."

Why? I wanted to ask, but sometimes the best questions are left unspoken. I knew Chrissy would get around to it, so I let her tell the story in her own time, in her own way.

"For the next two years, I was more of a party girl than a model. I went to Milan to build my book and fell in with a fast crowd. *Figli di papà,* Daddy's boys, Italians with trust funds. Some of them just want a beautiful girl on their arm; most want to fuck you and pass you off to a friend. When I started working, I lived in a models' apartment building the Italians called Principessa Clitoris."

"Cute."

"We just called it the Fuck Palace."

I dragged a piece of pork through the rice and tossed the mixture into my mouth. Outside our enclosed room, three male guards looked in through a window. If there had been a curtain, I would have pulled it. Behind them, a stream of female inmates lined up on their way to the cafeteria. Stringy hair, sallow faces. I wondered what Chrissy would look like after a year behind bars. Or twenty.

"I did the whole party scene," she said, "licking coke off hundred-dollar bills in rest rooms, skinny-dipping in fountains, parties for Arab sheiks, hanging with the disco droids. Amazingly, I was doing well, professionally at least. The makeup covered the dark circles under my eyes and I had a look that was hot, or so they said. I was traveling, making good money, but my personal life was chaotic and destructive."

"The men?"

"The *wrong* men. Playboys, married men, abusive men, starving actors, untalented painters. I was having nightmares, flashbacks that made no sense. I was bulimic one month, anorexic the next, then stuffed myself like a pig the third. I binged, gained weight, starved and lost weight, got depressed, got sick and was a total wreck. When I was fat, which was like a hundred twenty-eight pounds, the photographers would call me 'Flesh.' And when I was skinny, they'd call me 'Bones.' Finally, they combined the two."

"Flesh and Bones," I said.

"I really hated the name. One day, I'm walking up Fifth Avenue in New York, and one of those street-corner preachers with a filthy beard is ranting and raving, and he starts following me, right past St. Patrick's, heading toward the park, and he's waving his Bible and shouting, 'Flesh and bones cannot inherit the kingdom of God.' "

"I think it's 'flesh and *blood,*' " I said, trying to remember Granny's Bible lectures.

"That's what made it so creepy. It was like he knew me, like he was telling me I was gonna die for my sins of the flesh and—I don't know—go to the boneyard and straight to hell."

"But you straightened yourself out."

"It was either that or die. A few months later in Paris, I had a very bad trip on acid. Hallucinated I was jumping off a bridge into the Seine, and guess what, I almost was. I had climbed onto a railing and was model-walking above the water. The same week, my roommate, Pia, died of a heroin overdose. I was down to about a hundred five pounds, had these big dark circles under my eyes. Kept getting all this editorial work, the French photographers into their doomed-beauty stage."

"What did you do?"

"I came home."

"To your father?"

"No. To therapy. I went to Dr. Schein. Lawrence Schein. He'd treated my mother, became her friend when she and Daddy had nothing left to say to each other."

I shoved the food cartons aside and made a note on my pad. At last, a witness. "A psychiatrist?"

"Yes, and a good one. He said my problems had to be rooted in my childhood. We talked and talked and talked, but I couldn't remember anything more traumatic than falling off a horse. He insisted the memories were there but buried, 'sublimated' he called it, so we did hypnotic regression and repressed-memory therapy."

I tore open the little plastic bag with a fortune cookie inside. "And it worked?"

"He shined a light into dark corners I didn't know existed. It all came back to me. I owe him so much."

She let the thought hang there a moment and I didn't grab it. I saw where we were going and it occurred to me that she might owe him even more than she knew. She might owe him life in prison.

Chrissy looked around the barren little room. "I wish I could have a cigarette."

"What, Chrissy? What came back to you?"

Her eyes filled with tears. "My daddy. My daddy."

I waited but she didn't go on. "Did he molest you?"

No answer.

"Chrissy, tell me," I whispered. "Did he rape you?"

"No. He loved me."

The tears streamed down her face.

"Chrissy."

"No!"

She wrung her hands together on the table, her fingers entwined like restless snakes.

"Chrissy, trust me. Tell me."

Sobs stopped her. I waited. Her eyes were tightly closed. She put her head down between her arms and sobbed, keeping the sound and the pain inside as her body shuddered. I stood and moved around the table, wrapping my arms around her, tears dripping from her cheek to my shoulder. After a moment, she lifted her head and dabbed at her eyes with the sleeve of her smock.

"I'm sorry. I can't talk. Not now. Not yet."

I sat down again and looked into her puffy eyes, seeing the same doomed beauty the photographers found so compelling. She shook her head, as if arguing with herself. I waited. She would tell me; if not today, tomorrow.

"You look terrible," Chrissy said after a moment, forcing a laugh. Then neither of us said a word. We sat that way a moment. The only sound in the room was the tick of an old schoolroom clock on the wall, its second hand jerking along. From somewhere on the other side of the window, a buzzer sounded and an electronic door banged shut.

"A man raped me once," she said. "In Paris."

Another sound then, too, the crack of the fortune cookie splintering in the palm of my hand.

"I suppose you'd call it date rape. I was coked out at a party filled with Mexican drug dealers, French playboys, American models. Some combination, huh? Today, I don't even remember his face. He owned some shitty line of ready-to-wear, had pomade in his hair. At the time, I wanted to kill him. I wanted to kill all of you."

I reached out and took both her hands in mine. "All of who?"

"You, Jake. Men! I wanted to kill you all."

5

Guilty as Sin

I aimed my ancient but amiable chariot south on Useless 1, passing endless fast-food emporiums, gas stations, and strip shopping centers in Kendall and Perrine. The old engine was humming, all 400 cubic inches of the Olds 442 convertible, vintage 1968. Canary-yellow with a black canvas top, a four-speed stick, a four-barrel carburetor, and twin exhausts. Four-four-two, get it?

I picked up the turnpike extension and passed through mango groves and tree farms near Homestead, then got off and found the old highway again, entering Monroe County where bait and shell shops joined the burger joints as roadside attractions. I cruised through Key Largo, which now has all the charm of Altoona but ten times the traffic.

At a little past six P.M., I turned into the sandy driveway on the gulf side of Islamorada and parked in the shade of a coconut palm. The TV blared through the open windows, Granny Lassiter still believing that air conditioning caused arthritis. Doc Charlie Riggs sat in a rocker on the porch of the old cracker house with the slanted tin roof. He was snoozing, a book folded across his chest. *Medico-Legal Investigation of Death.* Sleep well, Charlie. You already know everything about the subject.

I opened the screen door and walked inside. Tom Cruise and Jack Nicholson were yelling at each other in the Florida room.

"You want answers?" Nicholson shouted with the impatience of a Marine colonel not used to being cross-examined.

"I want the truth!" Cruise demanded, all decked out in his Navy JAG uniform.

"You can't handle the truth!" Nicholson fired back from the witness stand.

"Hello, Kip," I said to the towheaded twelve-year-old boy sprawled on the floor watching the tube.

" 'Lo, Uncle Jake," the kid mumbled, without looking away from the screen.

I wandered into the kitchen just as Jack Nicholson was launching into a diatribe about a world with walls and the men who guard them. Granny Lassiter hovered over the stove, slicing cabbage palm—called swamp cabbage hereabouts—into a frying pan filled with sizzling bacon. Supposedly, the native Calusas taught Ponce de León's Spaniards all about this delicacy. I'll have to ask Granny. She was probably there.

"Well, look what the cat drug in," she greeted me, as always.

"Hello, Granny," I said, and just to embarrass her, I gave her a peck on the cheek.

"Don't be making a fuss," she said, waving me off with a spatula.

Granny wore khaki shorts, climbing boots, and a T-shirt with the slogan I STILL MISS MY EX, BUT MY AIM IS IMPROVING. Her hair was jet-black, except for a white stripe down the middle, but the last guy who called her "Skunky" got brained with a tarpon gaff.

"You hungry, Jake?" she asked. She checked on a pot, boiling with hopping John, black-eyed peas, and rice. In the sink, a bucket held several pounds of fresh frog legs soaking in beer.

"Had a late lunch. Chinese. But I can always eat."

"Chinese," she sniffed. "All that mono-sodium pollutamate will shrivel your testicles." She gestured toward the bucket of marinating frog legs. "Give me a hand here."

I grew up in this house, hanging on to Granny's apron strings, so I didn't need instructions or a second invitation. I just dipped a pair of legs into a bowl of milk and eggs, sloshed them through a dish of flour, then dropped them onto a hot griddle.

"Seen your pit-cher in the paper," she said, pointing toward the refrigerator. Indeed, the clipping was held there by a magnet shaped like a stone crab. Some wit had added a mustache and hat so that I looked like a villain in a silent movie, the heroine unconscious in my arms.

"I see Kip's been practicing his artistry again."

"Don't stifle the boy, Jake." She looked into the sizzling pan. "And not so much flour! Those hoppers lose their taste with all that breading."

I hadn't even known I had a nephew, or a half sister, until Kip was arrested for spray-painting graffiti on a movie theater that had changed the advertised showing of *Casablanca* to *Revenge of the Nerds III*. I got him probation and became his semilegal guardian, though Granny helped out considerably.

On cue, Kip's bare feet padded onto the linoleum floor of the kitchen. "All righty then!" he proclaimed with a goofy Jim Carrey grin.

"Kip, did anybody ever tell you that you watch too many movies?"

"Yep. And Uncle Jake, did anyone tell you that you look guilty?"

"What?"

"In the paper. Doesn't he, Granny?"

"Guilty as sin," she agreed.

"Neat, Granny," Kip said, laughing. "That was a movie. Rebecca De Mornay's a lawyer who defends Don Johnson on charges he killed his wife. 'Course she falls for him."

"Ain't that a conflict of interest?" Granny asked, looking at me. "Litigating by day, fornicating by night."

"Sure is," I allowed.

"You'd never do that, would you, Jake?"

"Am I under oath?" I asked.

"The same thing happened to Glenn Close and Jeff Bridges in *Jagged Edge*," Kip said. "He's a rich guy accused of killing his wife. She defends him, and they get it on."

"Kippers," Granny warned, "watch your mouth!"

"Does Hollywood always copy itself like that?" Kip asked.

"Like a virus," I said.

I took a long look at Kip, still in wonder that the same blood flowed through our veins. Razor-thin, blond hair, pale complexion with a light blue vein visible on his temple, he was almost fragile. Nothing like his thick-necked and thick-headed uncle.

Kip opened the refrigerator door and grabbed a container of Granny's smoked mackerel. He dipped a finger in and licked it off. Closing the door, he gestured at the photo. "Look at yourself, Uncle Jake. Just like *North by Northwest* when a guy gets knifed at the UN, and a photographer shoots a picture of Cary Grant holding the dying man."

"Jake doesn't look like Cary Grant," Granny chimed in. "More like Harrison Ford if somebody had broken his nose."

"Hey, you two! I didn't kill anybody. Chrissy Bernhardt did."

Granny took over at the stove, yanking a frog leg from

my hands. "So how can you represent her if you know she's guilty?"

" 'Cause she's a babe," Kip volunteered. "Just like Madonna in *Body of Evidence*. Willem Dafoe's defending her on charges she killed her husband by"—he lowered his voice—"screwing him to death."

"Kippers!" Granny shouted.

"Hey, Kip, why don't you do your homework?"

"Don't have any."

I looked at him skeptically. "Is that the truth?"

He curled a lip at me and raised his voice into a twelve-year-old's snarl. "You don't want the truth!"

"What?"

"Because deep down in places you don't talk about at parties, you *want* me on that wall, you *need* me on that wall!"

"Kip, I'm going to toss the VCR in the gulf and put my foot through the TV screen."

"It's true, Uncle Jake. School ended yesterday."

"Oh."

Granny was rooting around in her walk-in pantry, where she puts up pickles and preserves. In a moment, she came out carrying three mason jars of her moonshine, or "rye likker," as she called it. "So why represent this no-count party girl what killed her father?"

"What makes you think she's a party girl?" I was already thinking about jury selection and the impression my client makes.

"I seen her pit-cher. I can tell."

I made a mental note to have Chrissy the Model dress like Marian the Librarian when we picked a jury. "Just because she admittedly shot her father doesn't mean she's guilty," I told my assembled kinfolk.

Granny poured the bacon-fried swamp cabbage from a pan into a serving platter and shoved it at me. "Just like an obfuscating, prevaricating, fast-talking shyster. Just like the so-called Dream Team that made me want to scream, lying through their teeth. 'It's not O. J.'s blood, but if it is, the cops planted it.' Now why would they do that? Seems to me the cops gave him all the breaks every time he slammed the bejesus out of his wife. It's not his glove, it's not his shoe, it's not his hair, it's not his cap, it's not his blood. I suppose the disguise in the Bronco wasn't his neither. So why the hell was he running away? Explain that one to me.''

"Granny, don't ask me. I'm just—"

"A lawyer! 'Course you're not as good as Johnnie Cochran, who's slick as owl shit, so I don't expect you to get that party girl off.''

"Johnnie has his style, I have mine.''

It's true. My style is straight ahead, both hands wrapped around the ball. No ninety-yard touchdowns, but not many fumbles either.

"Didn't you tackle that fellow when you were a so-called athlete?'' Granny asked.

"I *missed* a lot of tackles, including one in Buffalo, where I ended up with a snowdrift in my face mask and he got a touchdown.''

"Well, it just seems to me that you lawyer fellows are getting too damn good at making excuses,'' Granny went on, haranguing me as always. "You got your so-called battered wives slicing off their husbands' John Henrys. You got those rich boys in Beverly Hills shotgunning their parents. The Abuse Excuse, I seen it on *Oprah.* You attack the victim and then haul out some phony-baloney eggheads to mix up the jury with syndromes and traumas and irresistible impulses. They got a reason for everything,'til it seems nobody takes responsibility for their own actions.''

"Remind me not to seat you on one of my juries,'' I said.

"I wouldn't do it unless I could get conjugal visits from Charlie,'' Granny said, winking.

"What's conjugal?" Kip asked.

"Never you mind," my licentious granny told him. She put a pitcher of limeade on the table, then turned to me. "Would somebody please tell that old goat that supper's on?"

Just then Charlie Riggs appeared in the doorway, rubbing his eyes. "Did I hear the word 'supper'?" he asked.

Dr. Lawrence Schein let a stream of water play against the leathery green leaves of a wild coffee shrub and said, "Xeriscape landscaping. Environment-friendly and drought-resistant."

After just a few moments, Schein turned the hose on a wild tamarind tree, its purple puffball flowers in full bloom. "You don't see any palm trees, hibiscus hedges, or blooming impatiens in my yard, do you?"

Figuring it was a leading question, I could have objected, but instead I just listened.

"They just swallow up the water. You know the town of Manalapan?"

"Sure, up in Palm Beach County. Big houses, big yards, a Ritz-Carlton hotel."

"Until they put a stop to it, that little town was using six hundred twenty-seven gallons of water a day per resident, most of it watering lawns and flowers. Can you imagine it?"

We were in the yard of Dr. Schein's ranch house in the Redlands section of southern Dade County. I had spent the night at Granny's, eating her food, drinking her moonshine, and losing to Kip in gin rummy. At one point, in the cinematic equivalent of a mixed metaphor, he told me, "You play a mean game of gin, fat man."

Now, on a steamy June morning, I was trying to determine just how useful Dr. Schein would be to the defense of Chrissy Bernhardt. He was a thin man in his late fifties with a shaved head and a small goatee. I had somehow pictured him in a herringbone sports coat with leather elbow patches, but today he wore bib overalls and L. L. Bean rubber boots as he watered his plants.

"You know what's happening to the Biscayne Aquifer, don't you?" Dr. Schein asked.

"Water level goes down a little every year."

"And the salt level comes up! We're headed for a disaster unless we change our ways."

He moved a few steps to the house and turned off the spigot, giving an extra tug to stop the dripping. Then he picked up pruning shears and clipped some dead leaves from a bright red bougainvillea vine.

"You knew the Bernhardts, Chrissy's parents," I said, trying to move the discussion from landscaping to the law.

"I did, and I've known Chrissy since she was a child."

"Tell me about Chrissy and her father."

"She didn't tell you?"

"Not yet."

"But surely you've surmised . . ."

"Yeah, but I need to hear it. From you and from her."

"May I be blunt?"

"I prefer it."

"Harry Bernhardt raped Chrissy when she was eleven. He committed incest, a crime of unspeakable ugliness." The doctor seemed pained. He didn't look at me, but snipped a branch of the bougainvillea with such vigor, he might have thought he was castrating old Harry. "He continued coming to her bed—oh, damn the euphemisms— he continued fucking his little girl until she was fourteen and he found her in the barn with a stableboy. He called her a dirty slut, said her mother was frigid and she was a whore, something like that."

I tried to picture Chrissy as a child, burdened with the secret, living in fear and pain. I had to force myself to keep a professional distance. Clients need logic and clarity from their lawyers, not emotions and pity.

"During these years, you spent a lot of time in the Bernhardt home, didn't you?" I asked.

"Yes."

"But you never suspected her father of abusing her?"

"Unfortunately, no. Looking back, of course, you see things differently. Christina in her father's lap, something that seemed so innocent, takes on a different connotation. He doted on her, was jealous of others' attentions to her. At the time, I thought he was just being overly protective, but in retrospect, that wasn't Harry's way at all."

"What was his way?" I asked, thinking of Granny's complaint: *Attack the victim.*

"Harry Bernhardt was a hard man. Insensitive to Emily, Christina's mother, who was a lovely woman, as refined and sophisticated as Harry was crude. Still, who could have known, this hideous thing, incest . . ." He let the ugly word hang there a moment, then said, "I have to confess that it caught me completely by surprise."

He picked up a rake and smoothed some mulch around the roots of a wild coffee plant. "Holds the moisture in, prevents evaporation," he explained.

"So Chrissy shot her father because she remembered what he had done to her?"

"Oh, that's an oversimplification. Christina suffers from posttraumatic stress disorder. I'm sure you're familiar with the term."

"Yeah. I saw it on *Geraldo*."

"Vietnam syndrome, we called it a generation ago. And that was just an offshoot of shell shock from World War I and combat fatigue from the Second World War. But psychiatry's come a long way. We know so much more now. You don't have to be a soldier to have sublimated the horror in your life."

Dr. Schein was talking to me, but he was examining the leathery green leaves of the coffee plant. I wondered what a shrink would say about his failure to make eye contact.

"When Christina came back from Europe and I first treated her," he said, "she had great difficulty controlling her emotions. Her history was an encyclopedia of clues. She overreacted to stress, misdirected her anger, and had problems with alcohol, drugs, even food. Classic symptoms right down the line."

"Classic?"

"For the survivor of incest. Migraines, nightmares, feelings of dread without reason. She had huge blocks from her childhood that were missing. She couldn't, or wouldn't, remember them, another indication that she was in denial. She simply locked out the memories."

"And you unlocked them?"

He cocked his head and showed a little smile. "Let's just say I handed her the key. She still had to turn it."

I gave him back his little smile just to show my appreciation at how gosh-darned clever he was. "You're confident the memories are real?"

"Unquestionably. The little girl in Christina, her inner child, was talking, and she had no reason to lie."

"Could she have been mistaken?"

"Not a chance. Christina had repressed her memories of childhood incest. I helped her recover those memories, which were always there, buried under layers of shame and denial. When they returned, they were clear and vivid and real."

"And they couldn't have been dreams or something she just imagined?"

"Counselor, you're looking the proverbial gift horse in the mouth. I'm handing you your defense."

"No, you're not. You're handing the prosecution its motive. Here's how Abe Socolow will see it. Once Chrissy turned the key you handed her, she hated her father for abusing her years ago. Harry Bernhardt posed no current threat to Chrissy, so the shooting couldn't be self-defense or justifiable homicide. It was pure revenge, and that's walking straight into a first-degree murder conviction.''

"I see," the doctor said, somewhat subdued.

"Look, maybe you could help at a sentencing hearing, but that happens only after she's been convicted, and if it's murder one, the only two options are death and life without parole, no matter what you say."

Dr. Schein stopped fooling with the mulch and leaned on his rake. "Would it make a difference if Christina shot her father while suffering a blackout or a flashback to the abuse itself?"

"Did she?"

"Quite likely."

"You'd be willing to testify to that?"

"Of course."

I thought about it. If Chrissy had blacked out, she wouldn't have the requisite criminal intent to support a murder charge. Manslaughter, maybe, but not murder. With a plea, maybe ten years, out in six. Better than life without parole. Of course, I'd have to ask Chrissy about the blackout. Better yet, I'd get Jimmy Stewart to ask. "I'll need her complete file to get ready for the bond hearing," I said.

"Already copied it for you." He gestured toward a red-wood picnic table just behind me.

I picked up a file six inches thick, then sat down to examine it. One folder contained handwritten notes of the therapy sessions; another seemed to be transcripts. "You taped the sessions?" I asked.

"Only the hypnosis. You'll find the transcripts to be quite complete."

"Good. But I'd like to have the tapes, too."

His arched eyebrows shot me a *Why?*

"If they're helpful, we play them for the jury," I said.

"If they're not, wouldn't it be better if you didn't have them?"

It took me a second to figure that out. Schein was a

slippery shrink. First, he was handing me my defense. Now, he was playing hide the evidence. What was on those tapes anyway? "You're worried about me having to turn over the tapes to the prosecution?"

He began raking the mulch again, though as far as I could see, it was evenly spread. "Once I testify, your client will have waived the physician-patient privilege, will she not?"

"Yeah."

"And wasn't the psychiatrist's tape recording of the Menendez brothers admissible?" he asked.

"Sure was."

"So . . ."

"So, you can't destroy them, no matter what's on them. That'd be obstruction of justice."

"I see," he said.

"But I do appreciate the gesture."

I looked through the folder, checking the dates along the left margin of the therapy notes. "You were seeing her three days a week."

"At one point, five days a week."

I thumbed through several pages in a file labeled simply MEDICATION. "I had no idea she was taking so many drugs. Xanax and Ativan . . ."

"For anxiety related to depression."

"Mellaril . . ."

"To control flashbacks." He carried a potted fern to the picnic table and sat down across from me.

"Any idea whether she was taking them the day of the shooting?"

He shrugged. Another question for Chrissy.

"Prozac and Desyrel . . ."

"For depression." With a small clipper, he cut away some brown stems of the fern. For some reason, the gesture reminded me of a woman plucking her eyebrows.

"Restoril, Darvocet, and lithium."

"To help her sleep, for headaches, and mood swings."

"Better living through chemistry," I said.

"The proper use of drugs is an essential part of therapy."

"Uh-huh. What about now?"

"I beg your pardon."

"Does she need drugs, therapy, anything?"

"Oh, no. Christina has confronted her demons and exorcised them."

"By remembering . . . or by killing?"

Dr. Schein put down his clippers, briefly scanned his environmentally friendly, xeriscaped yard, then looked me in the eye for the first time. His smile was just this side of smug. "In one sense, the killing of Harry Bernhardt was quite unfortunate."

"Especially for Harry Bernhardt," I agreed.

"But in another sense, what Christina did was finally take control of her own life, and that was therapeutic. Quite therapeutic indeed."

6

A Perfect World

I approached the intersection of *Calle Ocho* and Twelfth Avenue in Little Havana, intending to turn left and head north. But the city *padres* had changed the street signs again and, momentarily confused, I missed the turn to the bridge on my way to the sadly misnamed Justice Building.

Oh, we *seek* justice in the building, just as we seek holiness in a house of worship. Both goals are difficult to achieve and seldom witnessed by mortals. Which is not to say that the building doesn't dispense "law" by the bucketful. Law is the product that spews out of the building's courtrooms, hundreds of times each day. Guilt, innocence, suspended sentences, pretrial intervention, *nolle prosequi*, time served, mistrials, adjudication withheld. The product comes in a dozen brands. But justice is an ideal, a vague concept we strive for but can barely define, much less master.

Justice requires lawyers who are prepared, witnesses who tell the truth, judges who know the law, and jurors who stay awake. Justice is the North Star, the burning bush, the Holy Virgin. It cannot be bought, sold, or mass-produced. It is intangible, ineffable, and invisible, but if you are to spend your life in its pursuit, it is best to believe it exists, and that you can attain it.

So there I was, going farther east on *Calle Ocho,* or Eighth Street, or Olga Guillot Way, according to the new sign that threw me. I don't know why the bolero singer got the honor, unless it was because a few blocks away, Celia Cruz, the salsa singer, has the same street named for her, and a few blocks from that, so do Carlos Arboleya, Felipe Valls, and Loring Evans. If that's not baffling enough, a stretch of Twelfth Avenue, near here, is called Ronald Reagan Avenue.

Our city and county commissioners, ever desirous of licking the boots of their constituents, once named a street Leomar Parkway after a major campaign contributor who turned out to be a major drug dealer. There are streets named for Almirante Miguel Grau, a Peruvian admiral in the 1800s, and Francisco de Paula Santander, a Colombian general. There's even one named for José Canseco, the baseball slugger, who has been fined repeatedly for driving his sports cars at more than one hundred miles an hour. Maybe a lane at the Daytona Speedway would be more appropriate.

Eventually, I doubled back and found General Máximo Gómez Boulevard—no, I don't know who the hell he was—and made my way north to the Justice Building, which houses criminals and other miscreants such as judges, prosecutors, and defense lawyers.

It was just before nine A.M. when I slipped into a parking place next to the jail. Overhead, prisoners were being taken across an enclosed walkway directly into holding cells on the fourth floor. Chrissy would already be inside, having arrived by bus from the Women's Detention Center a few blocks away.

I hurried down a narrow alley toward the back entrance of the building, nearly running into Curly Hendry, who was leaning on his rolling trash bin. Curly, who was bald, had spent several stretches in the county jail, plus a couple of years upstate. I represented him once, when cops found an ATM machine all trussed up in a towing chain, the other end of which was attached to a winch on his heavy-duty Dodge pickup. These days, he pushed a broom for the county.

"*Qué pasa,* Curly?"

"Don't talk no Espan-oley to me, Jake. I'm just a cracker who's got to clean up after them crazy island fuckers." He pointed into the trash bin and held his nose. "So far this morning, three dead chickens and a goat's head. Now what's this?"

He bent down and looked at a cake with frosted icing.

"To sweeten a judge's disposition," I told him.

"Damn voodoo."

"More like Santería."

"Makes me want to move to Georgia. Yesterday, had some damn broken eggs out here. The sun got to 'em before I did, could smell 'em all the way to Hialeah."

"They're to make the case collapse."

He scooped up the cake and tossed it into the trash bin. "Last week, a dead lizard with its mouth tied shut."

"That's—"

"I know. To shut up a snitch."

"Right."

"So, Jake, what brings you out here with all these witch doctors and Third World types?"

"Bond hearing. Say, Curly, you find anything that'll get me bond in a murder one?"

"To hell with cakes and lizards, Jake. Just pray for a judge whose brother-in-law is a bondsman who needs the work. If not, slip some Ben Franklins in an envelope and call it a campaign contribution."

"Curly, you know I don't play the game that way."

He went back to his broom. "No damn wonder I did twenty-seven months at Avon Park."

* * *

"If a bad childhood were an excuse for murder, our prisons would be empty," Abe Socolow said gravely. "I'm quite sure every inmate on death row had a perfectly atrocious childhood. Far worse than that of Ms. Christina Bernhardt in her oceanfront mansion, I daresay."

He daresay?

Abe Socolow had a tendency toward pomposity, but for a prosecutor, he was almost human. A little rigid, a little self-righteous, but honest and fair. He was tall and lean and sallow and preferred undertaker-black suits with white shirts and blood-red ties. His cuff links were miniature silver handcuffs.

At the moment, Honest Abe was ridiculing my assertion that the state had overcharged my client, going for murder instead of manslaughter.

"Recovered memories," Socolow sniffed. "Posttraumatic stress disorder. Judge, these silver-tongued defense lawyers come up with more syndromes than a dog's got fleas."

Damn, it sounded like Abe had been talking to my granny. Either that or he was just trying to be folksy, something that didn't come naturally. Judge Myron Stanger peered down from the bench, his eyes hidden behind tinted glasses so we couldn't tell when he dozed off. He had a bulbous nose lined with tiny blue veins and a white fringe of hair on his egg-shaped head. His Honor was fond of the Bolívar brand of Cuban cigars, and at this moment was chewing on a cold Corona Gigantes, in violation of both courtroom protocol and the federal Embargo Act. The judge was flanked by the American flag and the Florida flag. A set of *Florida Statutes* sat, still in shrink wrap, on his desk. Only a few spectators were on the long wooden benches that resembled church pews. I was sitting at the defense table on a heavy mahogany chair whose brown leather seat had cracked with age and taken on the shininess of cheap trousers.

Abe rambled on, "Battered-spouse syndrome supposedly lets a woman kill her husband, though she's in no immediate danger. A white man guns down two black teenagers and says he's been traumatized by urban survival syndrome and ought to be excused. A woman who shot her husband on Super Bowl Sunday says she suffers from football widow syndrome. A fellow charged with tax evasion has failure-to-file syndrome. Abused-child syndrome, black rage, mob psychosis—where's it going to end? I ask Your Honor, where will it all end?"

Judge Stanger seemed startled, perhaps wondering if Socolow really wanted an answer. Then he said, "Let's not argue the case today, gentlemen. This is merely a bond hearing, and under *Arthur* v. *State,* the defense has the burden of showing that the proof is not great and that a presumption of guilt is not evident. As I understand the proffered testimony of Dr. Schein and Mr. Lassiter's argument, there's no factual dispute. The defendant shot her father."

The judge nodded toward the defense table, where Chrissy, in a jailhouse smock, sat next to me. We'd get her dressed up prim and proper by the time a jury was called. She seemed dazed, out of place, in the controlled chaos of the courtroom. To those of us who work there, it's a second home. Same for my customers, those recidivists who know as much law as I do. But to someone from east of the highway, as we call those who grew up near the ocean, it's a frightening new world.

The judge waved his giant cigar in my direction and said, "While conceding that the shooting occurred, Mr. Lassiter argues that the defendant may not have had the requisite criminal intent to be charged with premeditated murder. Is that about it?"

"All the elements of the crime having been established, the grand jury indicted her for first-degree murder," Socolow said, raising his hands, as if it were out of his control.

"The grand jury would parade naked down Biscayne Boulevard if Abe asked them to," I piped up.

"Your Honor," Socolow said, shooting me a murderous glance, "even assuming all this psychiatric mumbo-jumbo is true, it's not a defense. Just because criminal behavior is *caused* doesn't mean it's *excused*."

I got to my feet and approached the lectern for the second time that morning. "May it please the court," I said, in the lawyer's traditional line of fealty, "Mr. Socolow ignores the fact that we have raised a substantial issue as to one of the elements of the crime. If the state cannot prove intent, it cannot secure a conviction. The court must instruct the jury that, to be found guilty of murder one, my client must have killed the decedent with premeditation, which the law defines in these terms . . ." I picked up the manual of jury instructions that Judge Stanger would eventually read to the jurors. " 'Killing with premeditation is killing after consciously deciding to do so. The decision must be present in the mind at the time of the killing, and the intent to kill must be formed before the killing.' "

I put down the manual and did a little sidestep toward the defense table, forcing the judge's gaze toward the lovely defendant. She looked as helpless and innocent as an angel without wings. "If Christina Bernhardt was suffering from flashbacks or blackouts which coincided with the shooting, she made no conscious decision to shoot the gun and could not be guilty of murder one. If she's been overcharged, bond should be granted."

"Blackouts," the judge mused. "Flashbacks. Is that your case, Jake?"

Using my given name. A little familiarity, asking me to cut the bullshit and level with the court. What's the trial going to be all about? I had already summarized Dr. Schein's opinion, right down to Sigmund Freud's view of repression as a defense mechanism used to suppress psychic trauma.

"That is the proffer of Dr. Schein's testimony," I said, and out of the corner of my eye, I saw Socolow shoot me a look. He doesn't miss much, and he didn't miss this. I hadn't answered the question.

Just before the bailiff called our case, I had huddled with Chrissy in the jury room, our courthouse being woefully insufficient in meeting space. "I look terrible," she said, fiddling with her hair, which was held back in a ponytail with a simple rubber band.

"You look beautiful," I told her, violating another of my rules, the one about maintaining a professional distance from the clients. I don't go fishing with the guy customers and I don't go to bed with the gals.

"Am I going to testify?" she asked.

"Not today. But before we go in there, I need to tell you something. Dr. Schein is prepared to testify that you may have suffered a blackout before the shooting, that you were in a trancelike state when you shot your father."

She looked at me with those bright green eyes. "You're asking me a question, aren't you? Like, is that the way it happened?"

I held my breath and nodded.

"Do you want the truth?" she asked.

"Yes," I said.

No, I thought. *I can't handle the truth.*

"I didn't black out. I wasn't in a trance. I saw Daddy sitting there, so pleased with himself. I wanted to hurt him. I wanted to hear his screams. I wanted him to hurt as much as he had hurt me. But did I want to kill him? I don't know. I really don't."

"Doesn't matter. If you understood that your actions created a strong likelihood of death, you're guilty of premeditated murder."

Her eyes opened wider, seemed to ask a pleading question: *What are we going to do?* I didn't know. I came into the courtroom drowning in my dilemma, the ethical conflict of a lawyer who owes the highest duty of loyalty to his client and a somewhat more vague duty to the legal system.

Now, I was doing a high-wire act, portraying our defense in terms of "if." If there had been a blackout, blah, blah, blah. At trial, it becomes more difficult. I wouldn't be able to put Dr. Schein on the stand to testify to something Chrissy couldn't corroborate. And now that she told me she had known very well what she was doing, I couldn't let her take the stand to say she had blacked out, even if she wanted to. I've never lied to the court or let a client do it. I like to win, but I like to win fair and square. I know it's old-fashioned, but that's the way I am. I like the low-scoring, smash-mouth, frozen-field Big Ten game, not the lah-de-dah, point-a-minute passing of touch football in the SEC. I hate guys who jitterbug in the end zone after scoring a touchdown. Celebration of self, dirty dancing, and taunting opponents have no place in the game I love.

When I was at Penn State, Joe Paterno ordered us to hand the ball to the official should we ever be so fortunate as to cross the goal line while carrying the leather spheroid. "Act as if you've been there before," he said. I hadn't, but in a game against Pitt, I blocked a punt in the end zone, not with my hands, but with my head. The ball stuck in my face mask and gave me a concussion. I thought I should have had a touchdown, but the officials ruled it a safety because I never had possession of the ball . . . my helmet did. It took two equipment managers to get the ball out of the mask, and I saw double for a week. But I had scored. Two points for my career.

"So, to paraphrase your argument," Judge Stanger said, spitting out a few fibers of Cuban tobacco, "you're seeking bond as if this were a second-degree or manslaughter case."

"That's what they should have charged," I responded, "but let there be no mistake, Your Honor. Our plea is *not* guilty. We'll be seeking an instruction under 782.03 on excusable homicide."

"That's outrageous!" Socolow thundered. "This wasn't an accident. That's the most absurd argument I've ever heard in a courtroom."

"You've lived a sheltered life," I whispered to Abe, then turned back toward the judge. "Accident is not the only statutory excuse for homicide, Your Honor." Again, I picked up the book. Even when I've memorized the statute, it somehow seems more authentic if I read it to the court. "A killing is excusable and therefore lawful when done by 'accident *or* misfortune in the heat of passion, upon any sudden and sufficient provocation.' "

"Where's the heat of passion?" Socolow demanded, his face reddening. "Where's the provocation? Harry Bernhardt was sitting at the bar sipping mojitos, for crying out loud."

"The provocation could very well have been the flashback," I said, choosing my words carefully. "A flashback of the decedent raping my client could have been just as real as if it were happening now."

Could have been. Maintaining my integrity by hedging.

"What's the precedent for this?" Socolow demanded.

"It's a simple application of the law," I said. "A woman is lawfully justified in using deadly force to resist a rape. Therefore, if Christina Bernhardt thought she was being raped at that moment, then—"

"Nonsense!" Socolow thundered. "That's not the intent of the statute." I listened a few minutes as Socolow railed against the newfangled theories under which the wily Jake Lassiter was trying to wrangle bond.

Finally, the judge cut him off with a wave of his cigar,

an orchestra conductor with his baton. "Okay, that's enough from both of you. Save it for trial." He made a note on the jacket of the court file. "This court has never before granted bond in a first-degree murder case. However . . ."

I loved that *however*.

". . . I find that the defendant has no prior criminal record or history of violence, and Mr. Lassiter raises a substantial defense, albeit a novel one. Motion for bond granted. Cash or surety in the amount of one million dollars."

A million bucks? Ouch! That's like no bond at all.

"Defendant is to surrender her passport and not leave the confines of Dade and Broward counties without notice to the prosecution and leave of the court."

Judge Stanger banged his gavel, stood up, and left by the rear door to his chambers. His cigar was lit before the door closed behind him.

Socolow gave me a wry smile and a raised eyebrow. "Flashbacks and blackouts, Jake? I can hardly wait."

Chrissy Bernhardt hugged me and gave me a peck on the cheek. "Am I getting out of jail?"

"Only if you have a guardian angel. A very rich guardian angel."

From the gallery, a man I didn't know approached the defense table. He was about forty, stocky, with black hair slicked straight back, a brown western-style suit with shoulder piping, a gold ring in one ear. And a checkbook in his hand.

I knew who he was as soon as he opened his mouth. The same gravelly rumble of a voice I'd heard that deadly night. And now that I studied him, Guy Bernhardt looked a lot like his father. Thin-lipped, thick-necked, small piggy eyes. Seeing Chrissy's half brother made me realize how lucky she was to carry her mother's genes or, as Granny would say, favor her mama.

Guy gave Chrissy a hug and a look of either genuine concern or rehearsed sincerity, I couldn't tell which. "I don't know why you did it, Sis," he said, "and I'm heart-broken to lose Pop. But I'll do whatever I can to help."

"Thank you, Guy," Chrissy said. "I'm sorry. I know you loved him. I'm sorry for you, but not for him."

Guy nodded as if he understood. "Anything you need, just ask. If I'm not in the office, have them track me down. All hell's broken loose with Pop gone; I'm trying to keep things together while we sort through all the companies. He let me run the day-to-day operations, but he kept a lot of the business in his head."

Chrissy hugged him and thanked him again. Then Guy Bernhardt took me by the arm and steered me away from the defense table. "The bond's no problem," he said in a whisper. "I'll pay the premium, put up some property as collateral if that's okay."

"It's fine. It's better than fine. There aren't too many defendants who can put up a million-dollar bond."

He signed his name to a blank check and handed it to me. "Anything I can do to help your case, you just ask."

"Sometime soon, I'm going to want to sit down with you, ask what you know about Chrissy and your father."

"It's hard for me to believe he molested her, if that's what you mean. I knew Pop better than anyone in the world, and . . . it's just not like him."

"I've been taking a cram course on the subject, and that's what everyone always says."

"Who's everyone?"

"Family members always say 'Not him' when a loved one is charged with incest. It's gotten to be a real cliché, like the neighbors saying the serial killer next door was real quiet and liked to keep to himself."

His look hardened. "Look, Lassiter, I'm on your side.

I don't want Chrissy to go to prison. Sis is **a** delicate thing, has been since she was a little girl. Her mother spoiled her, so did Pop. I've been talking to Larry Schein, and my advice is, plead insanity, work out some deal for confinement and treatment. I'll pay the bills, the best damn place where they handle this sort of thing. I've already looked into it. There's a private hospital just outside Seattle that's supposed to be first rate. Expensive as hell, but so what?''

A ringing came from inside his coat pocket, and he pulled out a cellular phone, punched a button, and looked at me apologetically. After a couple of short ''yeahs,'' he covered the phone with a meaty hand and said to me, ''I gotta take this. Whenever you want, call me to set up a meeting. I mean it. Anything you need, just ask.''

He headed back down the row of pews toward the door, speaking in hushed tones into the phone, and in a moment he was gone.

A female bailiff took Chrissy back into a holding cell where she'd wait until I could get the bond processed. So I stood there alone in the empty courtroom.

Thinking.

Twice he had said it: ''Anything you need, just ask.''

Here's what I wanted to ask: Why this talk about insanity? Dr. Schein hadn't said anything about it, at least not to me. Insanity means confinement and treatment. Maybe you get out, and maybe you're John Hinckley.

And Seattle? There are a lot of institutions that are first rate, to use Guy's term. So why choose the one that's farthest from home?

7

Tracks of the Monster

If you're a lawyer in a TV show, you handle only one case at a time, wrap it up by the last pitch for Pepto-Bismol, after which you're toting your briefcase down the courthouse steps with a beautiful client congratulating you for a wonderful job.

Real life is different.

After lunch, I avoided three phone calls from Roberto Condom, who was leaving messages with Cindy on how to plea-bargain his gator-poaching case, the gist being that he would give the Wildlife Commission fifty-seven live gator eggs to replace the grown animals he'd killed. Next time he called, I'd ask him just where he'd get the eggs without stealing them or hatching them himself.

I also spent an hour not answering my mail, not drafting pleadings, and not attending a partners' meeting intended to choose new artwork for the office. The choice was between Winslow Homer sailboats and Pablo Picasso nightmares. I once suggested that the conference room be decorated with several Jacques Cousteau shots of sharks in a feeding frenzy. No one took me seriously, except the managing partner, who slashed my bonus in half at the annual meeting where we devour thirty-two-ounce porterhouse steaks and carve up the profits. Firm motto: We eat what we kill. The spoils are divided (and eaten and drunk) at the Fiscal Year Banquet, as the firm brochure describes it. Pig Pool is a better description.

Cindy was away from her desk, so I inadvertently accepted a call from Silvio Sánchez at the jail. He'd taken a fall as a serial diner, eating in expensive restaurants, just to get room and board on the county when he couldn't pay the tab. Now he wanted to sue because they don't serve decaffeinated coffee behind bars. All the caffeine was keeping him up, and surely that must violate his constitutional right to a good night's sleep.

I interviewed a new client, a man wearing leather pants, loafers without socks, an open-necked silk shirt, and a gold chain. If they were doing a remake of *Saturday Night Fever,* maybe Morris Gold could get a part, even though he was fifty-three years old and his shiny black toupee was out of kilter.

After he plopped down in the client chair, he asked, "Can I show you my dick?"

"Let's get to know each other first," I said. "Now, how did you come to visit Dr. Pedro Cordeón?"

"I saw his ad on TV. Right after *American Gladiators.*"

I nodded appreciatively, as if this were an act of great diligence worthy of praise.

"So then I called the toll-free number, 1-800-BIG-COCK, for more information." Morris Gold pulled out a clipping and handed it to me.

"Circumferential Autologous Penile Engorgement," I read aloud. "What the hell is that?"

"CAPE. They liposuction fat from your stomach, then inject it into your dick. Makes it thicker." He winked and added with a little tune, "It takes two hands to handle the Whopper."

"Clever," I said. "What seems to be the problem?"

"You wanna see?"

"Later we'll take photos, put you on *Hard Copy,* whatever you want. For now, just tell me what's wrong. Have you become impotent? Is it misshapen? Why do you want to sue for malpractice?"

"It looks shorter."

"Looks? Is it or isn't it?"

"No, it's an optical illusion. By getting bigger around, my dick looks shorter. The doc should have warned me."

Should have warned.

Sure, we need to be warned not to stand on the top rung of a ladder, or not to crawl under the wheel when changing a tire, or that objects are closer than they appear in a rear-view mirror. We are a fundamentally stupid people in the eyes of the law, and if we are surprised by perfectly logical risks in our lives, well . . . sue the bastards.

I buzzed Cindy, interrupting her weekly routine of painting her toenails fuchsia. At my request, she ushered Morris Gold out of the office, but not before taking him up on the offer of a sneak peak. She also advised him to eat more legumes and cut out all lactose, but I haven't the slightest idea why.

Having cleared my desk by simply placing everything on the floor, I opened Dr. Lawrence Schein's file and began reading. The notes corroborated what he had told me about Christina Bernhardt. Complaints of headaches, nightmares, feelings of dread. Bouts of insomnia alternating with patterns of lethargy and excessive sleep. Bulimia while a teenager, booze and cocaine by the time she hit twenty-one. A general, indefinable malaise for as long as she could remember. Blocks of missing memories from childhood.

I slipped a cassette into a portable player on my desk, pushed the Play button, stood, and walked to the window. From the thirty-second floor, I could see the beach at Virginia Key. A steady line of whitecaps, corduroy to the horizon. Twenty knots from the southeast. A few board-sailors were on the water, their outhauls pulled taut. I imagined the multicolored sails crackling in the wind, the whistle of a steady breeze through the boom. But the next sound I heard wasn't the wind at all.

"Do you feel you have to control your emotions?" Dr. Lawrence Schein asked.

A pause. Then Chrissy's voice. "Doesn't everyone?"

"No, not really. Do you overreact or misdirect your anger when you're frustrated?"

"I suppose so. Sometimes."

The scratch of pen on paper. Then, "Do you space out or daydream inappropriately?"

Another pause, and I found myself daydreaming about windsurfing. Maybe inappropriately, who the hell knows?

"Yes, I think so. I drift off sometimes."

The questions kept coming. "Do you feel different from other people? . . . Do you feel you have to be perfect? . . . Do you use work or achievements to compensate for inadequate feelings in other parts of your life?"

Chrissy answered tentatively but affirmatively, and so did I. And so would a large portion of the American public, I was reasonably sure. Still, I had an open mind. I am tolerant of what I don't understand, and even if it sounded like a *Cosmo* self-help quiz, maybe there was a defense to murder hidden in these tapes.

It took several sessions to get down to it. From daydreams, the discussion turned to nightmares. Chrissy was having trouble remembering her dreams, and Dr. Schein was helping her out. "Can you recall any locked doors or hidden passageways?"

"I don't think so," she said, her voice small and distant.

"Waterfalls or rivers with dangerous rapids?"

"No." In my mind's eye, I could see her shaking her head, a strand of blond hair falling across a cheekbone.

"What about snakes?"

Silence. Then, "No."

"Does he ever come into your bedroom and do things to you?"

"No. I don't remember anything like that at all."

"Christina, memory is a funny thing. There are memories we recall and some we just feel. What do you feel?"

"I don't know. Strange things."

"Ah, that may be the beginning. Do you know what sex is?"

"Yes."

"Did you ever have sex with your father?"

Another sob. "I don't remember that."

"But you're crying. Why are you crying?"

"I don't know."

"Christina, have you ever seen the tracks of a wild animal in the woods?"

"Not in the woods, but I've seen turtle tracks on the beach."

"And did you see the turtle, too?"

"Not always. Sometimes just the tracks."

"But you knew the turtle had been there."

"Yes."

"I can see the tracks of the animal all through your life. The monster has been there. I think you see it, too, but you've covered it with layers of dirt. Can we scrape through that dirt, can we uncover the monster?"

"I don't know."

Click. What the hell was that? The faint sound of the recorder being turned off.

Then Schein's voice. "Let's talk about your father."

Wait a second! I stopped and rewound the tape. The same *click,* and then Schein continued. How long was the gap? A second, a minute, eighteen and a half minutes? Who knows? And what happened then? What did Schein say in the darkness of his office to the troubled young woman, groggy under hypnosis? And what was he saying now?

"Let's talk about your father."

"I always loved my daddy. Always."

"Good Chrissy. That's a good girl."

"And my daddy always loved me."

"Did he?"

"Daddy told me I was his best girl, and now that Mommy's sick, I . . ."

"What, Christina?"

"I remember now. I remember."

"Very good, Christina. Very good. What do you remember?"

"I make Daddy happy. I pretend I'm Mommy."

"Does he come to your bedroom?"

"Yes."

"Do you have sex with your daddy?"

"Of course I do, silly. I'm his wife."

I listened to the rest of the tapes. The memories became more vivid and graphic. Chrissy's little-girl voice re-created the nighttime whispers with her father. "Our little secret," he had told her. Her adult cries reflected her anger. She was in and out of a hypnotic trance. I heard her sobs when she described the pain she had felt in her "peepee." I heard her voice waver between the innocent confusion of a child and the angry cries of a woman.

The male of the species. His chromosomes tuned for survival of the fittest, he wages war and slaughters his fellowman. His soul shriveled, he defiles the earth, mocks his Creator, and lives by no code other than his own. At the low end of the evolutionary scale, he lords his physical superiority over women, beating and raping. At the very bottom, this reptilian cousin of *Homo sapiens neanderthalensis,* this horned beast of hellish evil, is the father who would rape his own child.

I felt sick and angry and, for a moment, felt like killing Harry Bernhardt myself. Which made me think. Whether the memories were real or not, they sounded authentic. And though I knew that the prior abuse was not a defense to murder, I wondered if a jury might not be persuaded to come back on a lesser charge of manslaughter or even to acquit.

On the final tape, Chrissy wasn't hypnotized at all. She was telling Dr. Schein about her adult life, the failed romances, the drug and alcohol abuse, and thanking him for opening the door to her past. "I've thought more about what we discussed yesterday," she said.

"The need for goals?" he asked.

"No. What we talked about afterward."

There was a pause. "Oh, that."

"I've made a decision that you're not going to like."

"Maybe you shouldn't tell me," he said.

What the hell was this all about? What were they dancing around?

"But I've told you everything else. I can't imagine not telling you first."

"All right then. But first, let me . . ."

I heard papers rustling and the sound of a chair squeaking.

Click.

Again. Damn! I waited, but this time, nothing. Just a faint mechanical hum as the tape wound out. I looked for another tape, but there was none. I checked the date on the plastic box: June 14, 1995.

I considered all the things Chrissy might have said to her psychiatrist two days before shooting her father, and I didn't like any of them one bit.

8

Like Father, Like Son

A short, stocky Nicaraguan woman in a white uniform dipped a ladle into a bowl and served me chilled gazpacho. I tasted some without slurping or leaving a tomato stain on my blue oxford-cloth shirt. Refreshing on a steamy July day, but a tad too heavy on the cayenne pepper for my taste.

"I hope you like mangoes," Guy Bernhardt said. He was wearing jeans and a red-plaid western shirt with the sleeves rolled up to the elbows. His forearms were work hardened and cabled with veins, but his face was soft, his cheeks pudgy, giving his little eyes a permanent squint.

"Love them. Have a tree in my backyard. Kents."

Guy gestured to another servant, who began pouring mango iced tea from pitchers into tall glasses. "You must live in Coconut Grove."

"How'd you know?"

"Leith Kent planted the first mangoes there in 1932. Just about the best eating ones, but so fragile they don't ship well. We grow Cushmans, Hadens, and Glenns, plus some Nam Doc Mais brought over from Thailand. Sweet as can be and no fiber."

We were sitting at opposite ends of a table of Dade

County pine on the patio of a ranch house at Bernhardt Farms near Homestead, thirty miles south of Miami. A cedar overhang kept us in the shade and paddle fans waved at the soggy air. Sitting between us on one side of the table was Guy's wife, Loretta, a woman in her mid-thirties with dyed red hair and some extra weight around the hips. Across from her sat Dr. Lawrence Schein, who wore a Florida Marlins ball cap, khaki shorts, and a matching shirt with epaulets. Loretta had already consumed three mango daiquiris, thick as milk shakes, which left a creamy mustache on her upper lip.

"Guy's a nutcase when it comes to mangoes," Loretta said, a trace of Georgia in her voice. "He's got 'em on the brain."

"Pop grew them even before he had the Castleberry money," Guy said. "I use the same fertilizer mix he formulated thirty years ago. If it ain't broke, why fix it? Mangoes are in my blood, that's all."

"Sure, darlin'," she cooed. "And thank God I love them, too." She turned to me and winked. "Guy won't admit it, but he divorced Mary Ann because she wouldn't eat mangoes."

"She was allergic," Guy said, finishing his gazpacho.

"Could have been psychosomatic," Dr. Schein said. "If Guy and Mary Ann were having other problems, the mangoes began to represent Guy."

"Oh, fiddle!" Loretta nearly shouted. "No more head-shrinking talk, Larry."

"Think about it," the doctor continued, a little smile forming. "Were not the mangoes the fruit of Guy's labor, both figuratively and literally? So Mary Ann rejected him by refusing to eat his mangoes."

"That ain't all she refused to eat, if Guy's telling the truth," Loretta said, with another wink and a laugh, followed by a burp.

"Mangoes would make her break out in a rash," Guy

said. "Stomach cramps, headaches. Didn't have anything to do with me."

Loretta leaned back in her chair. "Seven years we've been married and I've never had a headache, have I, honey?"

"No, Loretta. You're a real trouper."

"My mama raised me that way. I don't cause a man any trouble." She shot me a look to make sure I was listening, then turned toward her husband. "Not like that half sister of yours. Spoiled rotten from day one, just getting by on her long legs and pouty lips. Now look at her." Loretta Bernhardt sounded downright pleased that her sister-in-law, or maybe her *half* sister-in-law, was getting her comeuppance. "And if you ask me—"

"Nobody did, Loretta," Guy interrupted.

"Your daddy never touched that girl," she continued, now looking across the table at me. "Harry was a dear man, never once got out of line with me or anyone else I heard of. That girl's got you all fooled. I'll bet she planned to kill Harry and cooked up all that abuse talk after seeing some TV show."

"Why?" I asked.

Loretta looked at me. "Why what?"

The Nicaraguan woman was clearing away the soup bowls, while another served grilled yellowtail snapper covered with mango salsa. At the head of the table, Guy was digging into a platter of fried sweet plantains.

"Why would she want to kill her father?" I asked. "What was her motive?"

"Money, honey. Ain't it always?"

"What about the estate?" I asked, turning to Guy. "What did the will provide?"

"Fifty-fifty," he said. "Chrissy and I split everything."

"But if she's convicted of murder, she forfeits the inheritance," I said, munching a bite of tender white snapper. "Everything would go to you if she takes the fall."

"That's why she cooked up that cockamamy story," Loretta announced triumphantly. "You're supposed to get her off, and my bleeding-heart husband's helping you, though for the life of me, I don't know why. She killed his father, for goodness' sake. And if she gets away with it, Guy has to share the estate with her. It doesn't seem right."

"Actually, I don't even have to get her off," I said. "If Chrissy is convicted of manslaughter instead of murder, she'll get her share of the estate."

"Why?" Loretta demanded.

"It's the law," I said. "If someone pulls a Menendez, acing his parents to hurry up the inheritance, he'll go directly to jail, without collecting the two hundred bucks."

"Not in California," Dr. Schein said. "At least not without a circus."

"Send in the clowns," I said in partial agreement. "But manslaughter is different than murder. It's almost considered an accident."

Loretta scrunched up her face in a look of inebriated contemplation. "So, why help her at all?" She shot a look at her husband. "What kind of man would be so damned . . ."

She let it hang there, so I said, "Giving?"

"More like stupid!" Loretta gave a helpless shrug and looked toward her husband. "I'm sorry, darlin'. I love you to death. I just don't understand you. If it was me, I'd turn the first spadeful of dirt to bury her."

Guy placidly sliced his snapper and gave no indication of wanting to engage his wife in conversation. Married men have a surefire way of changing the subject: Simply ignore the wife. After a moment, Guy gestured toward me with his fork. "The food okay, Jake?"

"Great. The snapper's good, the salsa even better."

Guy smiled. "It's my own recipe."

"Quite a combination: sweet mangoes, mild onions—

Vidalias, I'd guess—then the strong jalapeño.''

"You got it."

"There's another taste I can't quite identify."

"Cilantro."

"Right. And a little olive oil?"

"Very good," Guy said. "You pay attention. That's a fine attribute in a man."

"And a lawyer," Lawrence Schein said.

I nodded and finished eating, damn proud to be a culinary sleuth. Now if I could only figure out these characters.

After the servants cleared the plates, they brought mango sorbet to clear the palate, followed by a small course of barbecued mango chicken, where I easily identified the brown sugar and vinegar but completely missed the chopped chipotle chiles in adobo sauce. Then came the mango-passionfruit crème brûlée, and finally espresso, which, best I could tell, did not have a trace of mango.

Loretta was right. Guy had mangoes on the brain.

And Guy was right about something. I *do* pay attention. I had been wondering the same thing as sweetly drunk Loretta. Just why was Guy Bernhardt helping a half sister he hadn't even known the first seventeen years of his life? Why help this spoiled, pampered favorite child when anything less than a murder conviction would cut his inheritance in half?

But I didn't agree with Loretta.

Guy Bernhardt wasn't stupid.

So why didn't I think he was giving either?

I was shoulder to shoulder with Dr. Schein in the back of a Jeep Wrangler. Guy Bernhardt sat in the passenger seat, and a uniformed security guard was driving. A second Wrangler was in front of us, and a third one was right behind. A guard with a shotgun sat in each of our two escort Jeeps . . . well, riding shotgun.

We were bouncing through ruts and drainage ditches

between rows of gnarly mango trees, and Guy Bernhardt was lecturing on the fertilizers, yields per acre, and every other damned bit of minutia you probably didn't want to know about *Mangifera indica,* including the fact that the fruit is related to the cashew.

I was inhaling the musky aroma of the field, half listening to Guy, half wondering what the hell was going on with the odd couple of Guy Bernhardt and Larry Schein. I couldn't shake the feeling that Guy was more complicated than a good-ole-boy mango grower and Schein had more secrets than Freud's Wolf Man.

"You have a problem with varmints?" I asked, and Guy seemed puzzled for a moment, then saw I was looking at a 12-gauge mounted between the front seats.

"Oh, that? Yeah, the two-legged kind. It's to protect the water, which is more valuable than the fruit—hell, more valuable than oil. We've got our own well fields out here, and some of the neighboring farmers claim we're sucking their wells dry. Then the state cited us for supposedly lowering Little Bass Lake a foot or so."

We passed under a forty-foot irrigation tower that resembled an oil derrick, and I watched a rainbow form in the parabola of a giant stream of water that shot from the gun assembly at its peak. Mist drifted into the Jeep, cooling us.

"You do any environmental law, Jake?" Guy asked.

Seducing me with the hint of future business.

"Don't know the first thing about it."

"You oughta learn. It's a real lawyers' relief act, all those regulations. They want to fine us ten thousand dollars a day, can you believe that horse crap? I told them it's the drought, go sue God."

"What about your neighbors?"

"Hell, when their wells went dry, I sold them water. Got a special act through the legislature—Pop had some clout up in Tallahassee—so they treated us like a mini-utility. Some of the locals, the lime and avocado growers, didn't like my price and didn't like me, so the bastards complained to the state, to the Department of Environmental Resources Management, to the Army Corps of Engineers, to their congressmen, who wouldn't know a well field from . . .''

"A hole in the ground," I helped out.

"Yeah. So I said, screw you. No more water for you at any price, and we'll pump as much as the Water Management District lets us, and maybe a little more." He laughed, and we crossed a wooden bridge into a different section of the field. "Now we have some hardcases who sneak out here at night and cut our irrigation pipes."

After about fifteen minutes, we turned onto a road of crushed seashells and into the tree farm, where palms of a dozen different varieties were growing from seed. Here, too, irrigation towers shot long graceful arcs into the air, which misted into kaleidoscopes of color.

"Pop loved to grow things," Guy said. "Jake, you ought to come up to Palm Beach sometime, see Pop's work at the house on A1A. Shouldn't he, Larry?"

Next to me, Dr. Schein's ball cap nodded in assent.

"Flowering trees were Pop's favorites. Jacaranda, mahogany, pigeon plum, wild tamarind. Planted some for old man Castleberry, kept planting them after he owned the place. Liked to dig the holes himself, get his hands dirty."

"Like father, like son," Dr. Schein said, taking off his cap and running a hand over his gleaming scalp.

"It's true," Guy said, laughing. "The mango doesn't fall far from the tree."

"I'd like to see the place someday," I allowed.

"Anytime," Guy said, fiddling with his gold earring.

It seemed out of place on him, this husky son of a farmer. I don't wear an earring, carry a purse, or say "ciao," so men with pierced ears seem as out of place to me as a nun shooting the bird.

The Jeeps crossed a narrow irrigation stream where water rippled through a shallow gully. Guy said something in Spanish to the driver, and I turned to Schein. "You're pretty close to the family, aren't you?"

"Oh, I've been making house calls—to all their houses—for twenty years. I'm more of a friend than a doctor."

To Guy Bernhardt, he meant. To Chrissy, he was still a doctor, I figured. And despite Guy's apparent attempts to help Chrissy, I couldn't help but wonder which was stronger, Schein's relationship with his patient or that with his friend.

"I need to ask both of you some questions about Chrissy's case."

"Shoot," Guy said. Then he laughed. "No pun intended."

I sat there a moment, trying to keep from looking startled. A trial lawyer never wants to appear surprised, in or out of court. The man's father had been shot dead two weeks ago, and he was making a little joke. Okay, we all react to loss differently, but it just struck me as a discordant note.

Turning to the doctor, I said, "The tape recorder you use on your office sessions, does it take batteries?"

"Well, it can. But I use the jack to a wall outlet, or else I'd be changing batteries twice a week."

"Uh-huh. There seemed to be a gap on the tape of the hypnotic regression session when Chrissy remembered the abuse."

"A gap?" Sounding innocent enough. "I could have run out of tape and inserted a new one."

"No. The tape was about two thirds of the way through. You had just asked Chrissy about her father, and the tape went dead. Then it picked up again, but of course I can't tell how long it was off."

The doctor shrugged. "Sometimes my secretary buzzes

me if there's an emergency call I have to take, and I'll hit the Stop button. Or maybe I had to sign for a package. Who knows?''

Not me, that's for sure. I hadn't heard a secretary buzzing or a UPS driver toting packages into the room. All I'd heard was the *click*, and next thing I knew, Chrissy was recovering lost memories.

"Then on the last tape, June fourteenth, she was going to tell you something, some decision she made, but you turned off the recorder.''

"No. I wouldn't do that. Did you look at my office notes of the session?''

"Yeah. They just say Chrissy's agitated and anxious. She's to continue medication and see you on the seventeenth.''

"But on the night of the sixteenth . . .'' he said, and he didn't have to finish.

"Do you have any idea how long Chrissy was in your office on June fourteenth?''

"Not offhand.''

"But your appointment book would tell us.''

"Yes. I mean, it could. But if there wasn't an appointment right after hers, it might appear she was there longer than she was.''

"Uh-huh. How long was she usually there?''

"It varied. The hypnosis sessions could last two or three hours, some even longer.''

"Three hours,'' I repeated.

The team's orthopedic surgeon hadn't taken that long rebuilding my knee. Five days a week. Chrissy wasn't a patient; she was a career.

"Hey, Jake, what's the big deal?'' Guy Bernhardt broke in. "If it took an hour or a year, Chrissy came up with it. I didn't want to accept it, but Larry says that Sis is telling the truth, so I have to live with the knowledge that my old man was a miserable letch, and you can make hay with it in court.''

"Yeah, maybe. Let me ask you something, Guy. In court the other day, you mentioned an insanity plea. But our defense is lack of intent due to posttraumatic stress disorder, and that's not insanity.''

We passed over another road and into a stand of tropical fruit trees. Surinam cherry, carambola, and banana. The air was sweet with ripening fruit.

"I was just giving you another option,'' Guy Bernhardt said. "Larry and I talked about insanity as another way to go.''

Great, the inmates were running the asylum. And trying to send my client there.

"Thanks for the help,'' I said evenly.

"According to Larry, you weren't jumping for joy over the defense he handed you.''

He handed me? Funny, that was the same term Schein had used the other day. These guys did talk a lot. Now what were they handing me? Manure for the mangoes?

The doctor cleared his throat. "We're not trying to interfere. You're the lawyer. We're just members of your team.''

"You're the captain,'' Guy Bernhardt said.

They seemed so sincere. Why couldn't I just take what they were offering? Why did my Dream Team have nightmare written all over it?

"You don't do much forensic work, do you, Doctor?'' I asked.

"No. I have a private practice, and thankfully, my patients don't often end up in court. A divorce once in a while, but nothing like this.''

"Then let me clue you in, so you can give me informed advice, teammate to teammate. I filed a written not-guilty plea yesterday. If we're going to rely on insanity, I have two weeks to notify the state. Then the judge will appoint three psychiatrists to examine Chrissy. I have no control over who the judge picks or what they'll say at trial. So even if you're willing to venture an opinion that Chrissy was insane at the time of the shooting—which I've yet to hear you say—you might be outvoted three to one.''

"Oh, we wouldn't want that, would we?" Schein asked rhetorically.

"Hell, no," Guy said. "Don't let any other shrinks go poking around."

Why not? I wondered. What might they find?

"I won't, at least not any the state can call to testify," I said. "I was thinking about hiring my own, though, as backup."

"Is that necessary?" Schein said. "I mean, I'm the treating physician. I don't know what anyone could add who's just coming in cold."

Objectivity, I thought.

"You may be right," I said. "If it ain't broke, why fix it?"

We were almost back to the house, having made a circle of the tree farm and listened to Guy's soliloquy on the Senegal date palm, thatch palm, queen palm, fishtail palm, and sago palm. While his father had loved the trees, Guy's favorites were the tropical fruits, which he claimed had medicinal properties. The Haitians use the Surinam cherry to soothe a sore throat, he told me. The papaya, or *fruta bomba*, is a digestive aid, and the Jamaicans squeeze the tamarind to cure stomachaches. Guy Bernhardt had a real pharmacy growing out here.

The Jeeps were digging ruts in a dirt perimeter road on the mango fields when a radio on the dashboard crackled with static followed by some rapid-fire Spanish that I didn't catch.

"Go!" Guy shouted to the driver, who blew his horn twice at the accompanying Jeeps.

The driver stomped on the accelerator, and we jolted through muddy potholes off the road and into a row of blooming mango trees. In the Jeep ahead of us, the guard in the passenger seat stood and leveled his shotgun across the top of the open windshield.

Guy spoke excitedly in Spanish into the radio, then turned to me. "You must be psychic, my friend."

"Huh?"

"We got a problem with varmints."

When we rounded a corner, close enough to a tree to rattle the branches and have a couple one-pounders fall into the Jeep, I saw what he meant. A heavy-duty pickup truck with no license plate, its bed filled with mangoes, was racing down the row ahead of us. A shotgun blast reverberated from the Jeep in front of us, and the pickup swerved but stayed on the road. Another shot, and I heard the ping of buckshot off the rear gate of the pickup.

"Son of a bitch! We'll head them off," Guy shouted, and again the driver blew the horn.

The Jeep in front peeled off to the left, the one behind to the right. We gained on the pickup. Guy reached under his seat and came up holding a Glock nine-millimeter handgun. He stood and held the gun in both hands, reminding me of his half sister in the club, though this weapon was bigger and packed more punch. The *pop-pop-pop-pop* was followed by Guy's grunt, then, "Damn! Can't steady it." He braced himself, then fired off several more rounds. Another shotgun blast from the Jeep to the left. The aim must have been high, because in a second, a tree was dripping with eviscerated fruit.

As we approached a T-intersection at the end of the grove, the pickup swung to the right, but one of the Jeeps was headed straight at it. The pickup swerved back to the left, but the third Jeep was coming from that direction. The truck tried to straighten out, slid in the mud, and flew straight across the road and up and over an earthen levee.

We heard the splash as our Jeep skidded to a stop at the base of the levee. Guy was the first one out, and he tromped up the slope, pistol in hand. I followed, and by the time I reached the top, two guards were aiming shotguns at the overturned pickup truck. Three men tumbled out of the cab and stood with their hands over their heads in the shallow water. A thousand pounds of freshly picked mangoes were dribbling into the water and slowly floating down the irrigation channel.

Guy Bernhardt pointed the Glock in the general direction of the mango rustlers. "Bastards! Chickenshit thieving bastards! I ought to kill you."

His face was red, and his little eyes were slits in his porcine face. "You know what I do to shitheads who steal from me! I kill them! Who would even miss you, buried under a jacaranda tree, you jerk-offs!" He aimed at one of the men, who trembled visibly. "What about it, Lassiter?"

"What?"

"You're my lawyer. If you can get Sis off, what about me? If I kill these pukes, do I have a problem?"

"Are you in imminent fear for your life?"

"Hell, no! But they are."

"Then you'd better not shoot them."

"Fucking poachers! And fucking lawyers! Everybody wants something for nothing. But nothing worth having is free. Not water. Not mangoes. Not nothing. I've worked for everything I've got, Lassiter."

He fingered his earring with one hand and held the gun with the other. "You ready, poachers? You ready to die?"

"Guy, I think that's enough venting for today," Schein said placidly. "I believe the gentlemen get the point."

Guy Bernhardt shot Schein an angry look, then swung the gun toward the channel. He emptied the magazine, killing several innocent mangoes as they floated toward Biscayne Bay.

As the echoes died down, my mind wandered. Had Chrissy worked for everything, too? Or had it all come too easily? The career. And now the inheritance. I was still thinking about red-faced Guy and his half sister when I noticed that there was something vaguely familiar about the pickup. Just then the driver, knee-deep in the channel, spoke for the first time.

"Jake, *mi amigo,* am I glad to see you," Roberto Condom said, hands high over his head, blood dripping from his nose.

9

Sirens' Song

Step into the lobby of the Fontainebleau, and it's 1959. You can almost hear Bobby Darin singing "Mack the Knife," and you expect to see Sammy Davis, Jr., walking out of the Poodle Lounge, maybe chatting up Frank Sinatra. The architecture—all gilt and marble—is a combination of faux French and Miami Beach kitsch. We've lost a lot of our local landmarks in recent years. Gone is the Coppertone sign on Biscayne Boulevard with the puppy pulling off the little girl's bikini bottom. Gone are Eastern Air Lines, Pan Am, and the *Miami News*. But the Fontainebleau is still here, and I love the place. It has no pretensions about its pretensions and is off limits to the South Beach terminally trendy crowd.

From the lobby, I took the escalator down to the ground floor, strolled past the obligatory sunglasses and sundries stores, and found something new. A spy shop. In the window were voice-activated tape recorders to catch a cheating spouse or business partner, bionic binoculars with earphones, telephone scramblers, bomb suppression blankets, and ninety-thousand-volt stun guns. A nice touch, I thought, but the hotel could do even more. With rampant mayhem against tourists, shouldn't the Fontainebleau offer a modified American plan: breakfast and dinner plus a bulletproof vest and transportation from the airport in a Humvee?

The Season was over, and summer is still an afterthought here, so the pool deck was mostly deserted, except for a few Chileans escaping their cold season. The day was sweltering, but a breeze from the ocean rattled the palm fronds and kept things bearable.

It wasn't hard to find Chrissy. She wore a white one-piece swimsuit cut low in front and high on the sides. She slouched in one of those canvas-backed director's chairs under an umbrella, a queen bee, while the drones buzzed around her. A makeup artist—a pale young woman sans makeup—dusted her forehead. A hair stylist—a skinny guy with unruly shoulder-length curls—used a portable dryer to comb out her hair. A barefoot male assistant in khaki shorts fanned Chrissy with a magazine.

A scrawny young man I took to be the director hovered over her, gesturing with a rolled-up script toward the free-form pool, where a waterfall tumbled over Disneyesque rocks. He looked about twenty-five and was lost inside a huge gray T-shirt that claimed to be the property of the Chicago Bears, though I doubted the guy had ever heard of Mike Ditka, much less sweated through a nutcracker drill.

"Chrissy, you look positively fab," he gushed. "Perfecto! Next, scene three, catching rays in the lagoon."

Okay, so it wasn't *Gone With the Wind.*

Sitting in a matching chair was another model, a dark-haired, deeply tanned young woman in a green bikini. She seemed to be pouting, maybe because Chrissy was getting all the attention, or maybe it was just her normal look. A photographer toted a video camera to the edge of the pool while an assistant took readings with a light meter. Several technicians and production people busied themselves around the pool with lights, reflectors, and assorted accoutrements of their trade. The place hummed with serious activity, Mission Control before a launch. Everyone wore shorts and T-shirts, except this big lug of a lawyer, whose blue oxford-cloth shirt was already beginning to show sweat stains.

I headed toward Chrissy when a young woman with a stopwatch hanging from her neck held up her hand. "Whoa! Crew only."

"I'm with Chrissy," I said.

She looked at me dubiously, but I was saved by my client. "Jake! Over here. We'll just be a minute."

I gave the stopwatch woman my best crooked grin. "Making a commercial is pretty intense, I guess."

"An advertorial, not a commercial." She sounded offended.

"Sorry." I walked past her and into the little circle around Chrissy. My social standing had just improved by several strata.

The director was talking to Chrissy and gesturing with his hands. "It's not merely suntan oil. It's an attitude, a way of life. It makes you glow on the inside, as well as outside."

"Only if you drink it," I said.

Chrissy suppressed a grin. Annoyed, the director looked up then continued talking to this stunning young woman who, at this precise moment, was facing a murder charge but looked ready for a relaxing week in Barbados. "Let them see your *joie de vivre*. Let your beauty radiate outward like the rays of the sun, warming you with its breath, a lover's kiss. The sun gives us hope, renewal . . ."

"Cancer," I added helpfully.

The budding Spielberg turned to me and scowled. "If you're here about the insurance, it's been taken care of."

"The insurance?"

"Yes!" he said petulantly. "The liability policy. Aren't you the hotel risk manager?"

"Is that what I look like?"

Chrissy giggled as the director squinted at me. "No, not really. I'd cast you as a security guard, maybe an ex-boxer with a broken nose and a checkered past."

"I'm a lawyer."

"Maybe in real life, but on the screen, never! Too solid." He smacked me on my right shoulder, the one with the steel pin inside. "Not shifty enough. Too All-American."

"Not even third team," I told him, but he didn't get it.

Chrissy bounded out of the chair, a strand of blond hair curled across her forehead. The hair stylist put his hands on his hips and glared. "Don't blame me if you end up with the Hurricane Andrew look."

"Jake, thanks for coming," Chrissy said, hugging me. "Just wait a minute and we can talk."

A minute.

Maybe it's a modeling term that means "until we lose the daylight." Because it took six hours.

They shot video of the two models in the pool, the waterfall pouring over them. Why the fuss about the hair? Don't ask me; it stayed wet most of the day. They took more footage at the cabana, rubbing lotions on each other's backs while a deeply tanned actor in white slacks and a blue blazer said, "Even our attitude is sunny on a sunny day. Let's see how Chrissy and Sofia enjoy the sun." Then he said something about aloe, vitamin E, and healthy color. I don't think Brando could have done a better job.

The whole crew moved from the pool deck down to the beach, where the photographer took some footage of the models building sand castles, running into the water, frolicking in the miniature surf, snorkeling, knee boarding, Jet Skiing, playing kadima and Frisbee, and smacking a volleyball with two male models who mysteriously showed up, pecs glistening, pearly teeth grinning.

Generic stuff. It could have been one of those beer commercials with such impossibly beautiful people you hope somebody tears an anterior cruciate ligament diving for a ball or a brew. But this wasn't an ad for one of those piss-weak American beers. It was, pardon me, an *advertorial* for Pineapple Pete's suntan oil.

I waited a while, then moseyed over to Coconut Willie's for a Grolsch and a six-dollar burger. I had no choice but to chill while Chrissy earned her five-thousand-dollar daily fee, which was precisely five thousand more than I was making today.

By the time I got back to the beach, they were shooting the last segment, which the stopwatch woman told me was called "hanging out." Indeed, Chrissy and Sofia simply chatted as they strolled leisurely along the waterline. A few octogenarians toddled by, including one gent wearing a yarmulke and baggy boxer trunks that hung to his knees. He stopped and stared at the two women, a cute shot— the contrast of age and youth, and all that artistic stuff— until he ruined it by scratching himself in a place you'd never use suntan oil.

I hoped Don Shula didn't come walking along the beach. Or Joe Paterno. Or my granny.

I was wearing a fluorescent orange thong that was barely large enough to hold a roll of quarters much less . . . well, a linebacker's gear. Chrissy had asked one of the male models for a spare so I could get out of my charcoal pin-stripes and black wing tips. Usually, on the beach, I wear cutoff jeans or boxer trunks of the Lloyd Bridges/*Sea Hunt* era. But here I was, awkward, uncomfortable, exposed.

"Who does your casual attire?" the male model had asked, serious as could be. "Calvin would seem right for you, though cut perhaps too small in the shoulders."

"My *attire* is early locker room," I'd told him. "Old

jerseys, faded warm-up gear. If I need something new, I call 1-800-PRO-TEAM.''

Now, as Chrissy and I walked down the beach at the end of the day, I said, ''I listened to the tapes.''

''Do we have to talk about it?'' she asked. Her head was down, and she seemed to be watching her toes squishing into the wet sand.

''We do, and then you do. You're going to have to tell the judge and jury.''

''It's very hard for me.''

''I know, but you have to. It's all we've got.''

''It brings back the anger.''

''Prior to the hypnosis, did you have any idea?''

''No. But afterward, it made so much sense.''

''Did you ever confront your father, accuse him of raping you?''

''No. I couldn't face him.''

''Did he ever threaten you as an adult? Were you in fear of him?'' Hoping for something, some shred of evidence that could move us closer to the battered-women cases.

''No. Once I learned what really happened, all I had was hate for him. It burned inside me. I wanted to kill him. That's all I thought about.''

Just great. Premeditation and malice all wrapped up together.

''And now, how do you feel? Any regrets, any remorse?''

''No!'' Her face reddened. ''I still hate him! He deserved to die. People will understand it.'' She raised both hands in front of her, as if holding the little Beretta, and aimed at a tern hovering over our heads. ''Bang!''

The tern took off, and Chrissy turned to me, the imaginary gun still in her hands. ''It wasn't hard to do, Jake. Isn't that eerie?''

Yeah, but not the way she meant. Just now, I wondered

about the lack of remorse, the apparent inability to relate to anyone's pain except her own.

"Did Dr. Schein tell you to shoot your father?"

"No. Why would he do that?"

"I don't know. Tell me more about Guy and Schein."

"Like what?"

"What's their agenda? What's in it for Guy if you get off?"

It was still hot, even though the sun had moved over the city and was headed toward the Everglades. An easterly breeze blew Chrissy's hair across her face. She smoothed it back with a hand and said, "Nothing, except I'm his sister."

"No. You're his *half* sister. You killed his father, and he's busting a gut to help you."

A dozen ring-billed gulls hovered over the wave crests, dipping down to feed on small fish near the surface. Chickenhearted, they don't dive like the smaller terns.

After a moment, Chrissy said, "I don't know what you're looking for."

"Neither do I. This case is so screwy. When someone's been killed and you don't know who did it, Doc Charlie Riggs always asks, *Cui bono?* Who stands to gain? Here, you did the killing, but what does Guy have to gain from your getting off?"

"If he's helping, what difference does it make?"

"Because if I don't know, I can't tell if he's really helping. I have to know his stake in all of this. Schein's, too."

We walked another few minutes in silence, leaving two sets of footprints in the wet sand. Sea oats waved in the breeze on the restored dunes. Joggers plodded along the boardwalk. Finally, Chrissy said, "There's something I didn't tell you."

Isn't there always?

"What?"

"Larry Schein was in love with my mother."

"You mean she had an affair with him."

"I think so. Daddy thought so, too."

"Did he accuse her?"

"Not exactly. More like, he ridiculed her." Chrissy let her voice go husky: " 'Is the good doctor coming over to rub your psyche or your back today, Emily?' That sort of thing."

"Did Guy know?"

"I think everybody knew."

"Did Schein ever talk about it?"

"Not in so many words. But I remember at the funeral, he cried as much as I did. Daddy didn't cry at all, but he was dead drunk most of the week."

We kept walking, passing a family picnic on the beach. The aroma of grilled chicken floated on the sea breeze. "Jake, I'm famished," Chrissy said. "We worked right through lunch."

"All right. Dinner's on me. Let's head back."

I looked at her in the pink glow of the setting sun, the makeup scrubbed off, her hair flying free. She had picked up some color during the day. For the first time, I noticed a sprinkling of freckles across the bridge of her nose. A young and innocent look. Beauty takes so many forms. The beauty of nature, the beauty of the spirit, and, just now, the utter physical beauty of this woman.

But I was looking at the superficial, and as Doc Riggs says, things are seldom what they seem; skim milk masquerades as cream. What was there below the surface? I already had seen Chrissy with a gun in her hand. Twice, if you count here on the beach with the make-believe pistol.

And now, so icy. Cold-blooded revenge is not a defense to murder. If it was revenge at all. She sounded so convincing on the tapes. The tears, the wrenching sobs. I remembered going over Chrissy's card and one-sheet at Rusty's modeling agency. Three years of acting lessons.

Okay, I heard an imaginary teacher tell the class, *you've just learned that you were sexually abused by your father as a child. What emotions can you bring up from your gut?*

It would not be the first time I had confused beauty with innocence. Now I wondered if I could be the pawn in an elaborate conspiracy. Murder and cover-up by Guy Bernhardt, Larry Schein, *and* Chrissy. Could that be it? Arranged from the start, with fabricated tales of abuse. But why?

I looked back at Chrissy and chased the ugly thought.

"I respect you, Jake," she said, suddenly.

"What?"

"You're really trying to help me, aren't you?"

"Of course; it's my job."

"Uh-huh. You're a very attractive man, Jake."

"I'm your lawyer," I said stiffly.

"Are the two mutually exclusive?"

I watched a tiny four-eyed horseshoe crab scuttle along the shore break, then burrow into the sand. "Actually, they are. At least while the case is pending. Afterward . . ."

I let it hang there. Afterward, barring a miracle, she'd be in prison.

"So you're just doing your job?"

Teasing me.

"Okay, it's more than that. I like you. A lot. I'm not going to stand here and tell you how beautiful you are, because every man you've ever met has told you that. I'm not going to make a pass at you, because that would only foul me up and it wouldn't help the case any."

"Are you going to win for me?"

"I'm going to try to win."

Don't ask me how, I thought. *I don't know.*

"Do you believe me, Jake?"

"I believe you think your father abused you, and I'm going to use it because it's all I've got. But it's more complicated than that. Life always is. I've got to pick up some rocks and look underneath.''

''What do you expect to find?''

''Same as always. Snakes.''

''Snakes,'' she repeated.

I thought about the therapy sessions and her nightmares. Perhaps she did, too.

We walked several more minutes before the Eden Roc and Fontainebleau came back into view. Chrissy turned to me, leaned over, and gave me a peck on the cheek.

''What's that for?'' I asked.

''For being a man I can look up to without lying on my back.''

''It's a deal,'' I said. ''For now.''

''Good. Now, feed me before I starve to death.''

She took off running, her heels kicking up sand. I watched a second, then headed after her. Her motion was smooth, her calf muscles undulating at every step, her bottom rolling with each stride. I was never the fastest linebacker in the AFC East, but I could still catch a beach bunny model.

If I wanted to.

At the moment, I was happy to be right where I was. Okay, okay, I know. The modern man is not supposed to react like he's just descended from tree apes. I try, I really do. But I'm a throwback in lots of ways. Obsolete by today's standards. I still hold the elevator door for women, say ''Thank you, ma'am'' to waitresses, and pick up the check when I take a lady (yeah, I still use the term) to lunch. I prefer Tony Bennett to Tupac Shakur, Norman Rockwell to Andy Warhol, and Gene Kelly to Michael Jackson. I wasn't around at the time, but I am plagued by the notion that the 1940s, war and all, were somehow better than the 1990s.

We were no more than fifty yards from the rows of hooded chaise longues that marked the Fontainebleau property when Chrissy seemed to stumble. I caught up with her as she stopped and turned, her body going limp.

Déjà vu. Only this time, she hadn't shot anybody.

I caught her just as I had before, sweeping her up in my arms. She breathed my name as I held her against me. Then, for a long moment, the only sound was the familiar slap of waves against the shore.

Chrissy came to, tired, disoriented, and hungry. We were in my Olds 442, headed toward Coconut Grove. She dozed off, and I made a call on the cellular, one of my few concessions to modern technology. My friend, legendary trial lawyer Stuart Z. Grossman, once said the cellular is the greatest advance of the twentieth century. No way, I told him. Not greater than the Wonderbra.

By the time we got to my little coral-rock house, my brain trust was there. I carried Chrissy inside, banging open the humidity-swollen door with my good shoulder. Waiting in the kitchen was everyone in the world I loved: my granny, my nephew, and my mentor.

Granny took a look and said, "That gal needs some meat on her bones."

Doc Riggs measured Chrissy's pulse, temperature, and blood pressure and pronounced her vital signs strong.

Kip sauntered by, sneaked a peak at Chrissy, then winked at me, guy to guy.

Granny had shown up with a wicker basket filled with food and home remedies, from essence of cherry plum flowers to essence of rye whiskey. In the next fifteen minutes, Chrissy downed three bowls of conch chowder, half a loaf of Bimini bread slathered with smoked swordfish, and a pot of chicken and dumplings, all washed down with a half jar of Granny's moonshine.

"A week of my cookin', and you'll be fit as a fiddle," Granny told Chrissy as she ate.

"I have a gargantuan appetite," Chrissy said between

bites, "but I have to watch it. The camera puts on five pounds."

"And I'll put on another ten," Granny promised. "You like country ham with biscuits and sausage gravy, maybe some corn chowder with heavy cream, bread pudding for dessert?"

"Sounds great. Usually I eat bean sprouts and tofu with black coffee."

"Ye gods! No wonder I can see your hip bones."

I cleared my throat. "Granny, I think the fainting is due to stress, not malnutrition."

"Stress! You been listening to them shrinks again? You didn't hear anything about stress when I was a girl."

"When you were a girl, Freud wasn't old enough to masturbate."

"Don't sass me, Jacob, or I'll put you across my knee. And don't talk dirty around Kip."

"Kip? When I asked if he was ready for my lecture on the birds and the bees, he told me—"

"I'd seen the director's cut of *Basic Instinct,*" Kip interrupted. "Plus a double feature of *Showgirls* and *Kids.* Next question."

"Jacob, what kind of a uncle are you?" Granny asked, grilling me with her black-eyed glare.

"A totally awesome one," Kip said, in my defense.

"A child shouldn't learn about sex from the movies," Granny said in a stern Dr. Joyce Brothers tone.

"I didn't," Kip said. "When Uncle Jake was dating that stripper from the Organ Grinder, I used to listen to them."

"Kip!" I shouted, trying to shut him up. "She was an exotic dancer, not a stripper. And you shouldn't eavesdrop. It's an invasion of privacy."

"Jeez, Uncle Jake. You two were so loud, I had to sleep on the back porch."

"She was teaching me Spanish," I said.

"I'll bet," Granny fumed.

"Uncle Jake's telling the truth," Kip said defending his Tío Jacobo. "I kept hearing her yell, '*Ay, Dios! Ay, Jesús, María, y José!*' Then, after a few minutes, she'd get real quiet and sing 'Ave Maria.' "

"Criminy!" Granny stomped around the living room for a few moments, getting her ornery look. "We'll talk about this later, Jacob." Then she turned to Charlie. "What do you think, Doc? Why's this sweet young girl always fainting?"

"How would Charlie know?" I asked in my smart-ass tone. "He's never had a patient who lived."

"Jacob Lassiter!" Granny was fuming now. "You didn't get that smart mouth from my side of the family."

"No, ma'am. I get my law-abiding nature from those moonshining, tax-evading, cousin-marrying kin of yours."

"That does it! One more word, and I'll brain you with a rolling pin!"

I retreated from the kitchen, taking Chrissy with me to the living room. Fifteen minutes later, she was asleep on the sofa, an old quilt pulled up under her chin. I sat on my haunches against the wall, just below an aerial photograph of South Dade, torn apart by Hurricane Andrew in 1992. Kip sank into a beanbag chair, circa 1971. Charlie Riggs paced in front of the sofa, puffing on his pipe, waves of sweet cherry smoke drifting toward me.

"She's real pretty, Uncle Jake," Kip said. "Kind of like Elle Macpherson in *Sirens*."

"What in tarnation is that?" Granny demanded, carrying some coconut cake from the kitchen.

"The Sirens sang songs that lured ancient sailors to their deaths on the rocks," I said.

"Sounds like the women you're usually involved with," Granny replied. "There was that Gina Florio, who married rich and fooled around poor. There was that English psychiatrist who was crazier than her patients, then there was that Baroso persecutor woman."

"*Prosecutor,* Granny. She was an assistant state attorney."

"Same difference. Sirens all of them."

"We could fill Jake's ears with wax," Charlie Riggs suggested.

Granny gave him a sideways glance.

"Odysseus had his men fill their ears with wax so they couldn't hear the Sirens' song," he explained.

"Better blindfold him, too," Granny said. "You watch yourself, Jake. Every time you get involved with these birds with the broken wings, you find trouble with a capital *T.*"

"And that rhymes with *P*, and that stands for 'pool,' " Kip sang out.

"Indeed," Doc Charlie Riggs said. "*Ubi mel ibi apes.* Where there is honey, there will be bees."

"I asked you folks over here to help me, not trash me," I said.

"I'll order a blood work-up on her," Charlie said, looking down at the sleeping Chrissy. "It may be as simple as hypoglycemia, and Granny's advice would be right. A better-balanced diet would help. But, while you're at it, get a drug screen done."

"Why?"

"No reason. No reason at all. But if you ask for my advice, follow it!"

"Okay, okay. Why is everybody on my case today?"

"Because we love you, Uncle Jake," Kip said.

"Good. I feel like a hug."

Kip came over and jumped into my arms. He was tall and gangly, and I hoisted him up so he could wrap his legs around me. "I love you, too."

Charlie harrumphed his displeasure at the display of emotion and said, "I already have the hospital records and I've talked to the doctors and nurses."

"Yeah?"

"Nothing special. They had Harry Bernhardt hooked up to an EKG. The ventricular fibrillations are clearly visible in the squiggles. Looks like a nine on the Richter scale. No doubt about the cause of death. Lethal dysrhythmia."

"Maybe we ought to have a cardiologist take a look," I said.

"Sure, if you want. I've double-checked everything in the autopsy report. Harry Bernhardt's heart was soft and flabby, four hundred five grams. Microscopically, there was some separation of myocardial fibers. His grossly fatty liver weighed three thousand one hundred twenty-five grams, suggesting excessive alcohol consumption. His blood alcohol at death was point nine. He had a four point five percent carbon monoxide hemoglobin saturation, which could be expected in a cigarette smoker."

"The son of a bitch would still be alive if he took better care of himself," I said. "He would have survived the shooting."

"Don't start whining about that again," Charlie said. "The cause of death may have been a heart attack, but the heart attack was caused by your client shooting him."

"Walk me through it."

"What?"

"Harry's last moments on earth. Would he know he's dying? Would he be conscious?"

"When the ven fibs start, the heart muscle quivers, and no blood is being pumped. He'd suffer cerebral anoxia almost immediately. Figure about ten seconds of consciousness."

"Enough to say something," I said.

"Like Mel Gibson in *Braveheart,* just before they chop off his head," Kip blurted out.

We all looked at him, waiting.

"Free-dom!" he shouted, loud enough that Chrissy stirred on the sofa.

"Then what?" I asked.

Charlie shrugged. "Harry's heart monitor starts ringing like a slot machine hitting jackpot. The Code Blue team gets there in a matter of seconds. They work on him. He has some agonal reflexes, maybe a few audible gasps, some limb and axial skeletal contractions, regurgitation of the gastric contents into the upper airway. They can't revive him."

"Did he say anything to the doctors or nurses?"

"Not a word. I asked them. He was just trying to breathe and dying in front of their eyes."

I was picturing the scene, Harry dead in the ICU, Chrissy on her way to jail, and me heading home, the aroma of Chrissy's perfume on my clothing.

"Why did she shoot her own father?" Kip asked innocently.

Charlie and I exchanged looks. What do you say to a kid?

"Years ago, when Chrissy was a child, about your age, her father . . ." I tried to figure out how to explain it.

"Did he rape her?" Kip asked.

As usual, he was way ahead of me.

"Yeah. She says so."

"So why did it take all these years for her to kill him?"

A kid's question. And a juror's.

"She forgot," I said, realizing how stupid it sounded.

"Forgot?"

"Actually, it's more like she pushed the memory aside so she wouldn't have to remember. Then the memory came back."

Kip looked at me skeptically. "That's your case? She forgot something that awful and then remembered years later, and that's why she killed her father?"

"A lawyer can't make up the facts, Kip. You play poker with the hand you're dealt."

"I know, Uncle Jake. Granny taught me to play. She said never to draw to an inside straight, and fold your cards when you know you're beat."

10

Slippery When Wet

The paddle fan above my bed was making its endless circles with a sleepy *whompeta-whompeta*. Outside, a mockingbird sang its lonely song in the chinaberry tree, calling for a mate. The TV in Kip's room was turned low, but I could still hear its metallic drone. I was sitting up in bed, rereading a Travis McGee novel, envying the life of that "big brown loose-jointed boat bum." No matter how tight a jam he was in, he could think and fight his way out. Me, I'm just a second-string jock turned night-school lawyer who tries to do the right thing but usually ends up leading with his chin.

I got out of bed and walked to the head of the stairs. The door to Kip's room was closed, so I didn't bother him. He'd fall sleep when he was ready, and if he wanted to watch TV all night, let him. After a couple of days, he'd be so tired that he'd adjust his schedule without any help from me. I belong to the hands-off school of child rearing, because that was how Granny raised me after my mother ran off and my father was killed.

"We are each the sport of all that goes before us," Clarence Darrow once said. That's an argument a lawyer makes when trying to spare the life of a ruthless killer who had a lousy childhood, but it applies to more mundane matters, too. We unconsciously pick up the habits and attitudes, likes and dislikes, biases and tolerances of those who raise us. Maybe I missed out on some things, but Granny taught me never to pick on anyone weaker and to help those who deserve it. She taught me to have a healthy disrespect for authority and to make my own path through the woods. She would have been just as happy if I'd been a shrimper like my father, or a trucker, bartender, or fishing guide, like the men who passed the time with her over the years. Ever since my teenage years, I've tried to follow her credo of going through life doing the least damage possible.

Wearing my red-plaid boxer shorts, I padded barefoot down the stairs. Chrissy was still asleep on the sofa, purring softly into a pillow. Her face was in such peaceful repose, she was almost childlike in her beauty and innocence. I stared at her a moment and felt a stirring, then a pang of guilt at being a voyeuristic satyr.

I walked into the kitchen and pulled a piece of Granny's peanut butter pie from the fridge. The first bite was melting in my mouth when it hit me. Granny. I hadn't heard her leave. Or Charlie.

They weren't upstairs. They weren't downstairs. Where were they? My house is a compact two-story box with a backyard overgrown with junglelike trees and vines.

The yard.

I looked out through the jalousie windows. The yard was illuminated by an eerie glow from my neighbor's sodium-vapor anticrime lights. There, in the hammock slung between a live oak and a poinciana tree, was my mentor. And my granny. All curled up on this warm, humid night scented with jasmine, sleeping soundly, arms wrapped around each other. Crazy kids.

I finished my pie with a glass of cold milk and headed

back up the stairs. The TV still hummed in Kip's room, and as I passed the door, I heard his voice.

Then another voice. And a giggle.

What the hell?

I tapped gently on the door and opened it.

Kip was in bed, a pillow propped behind him. Jim Carrey was on the tube, trying to rescue Dan Marino from an insane cross-gender kidnapper. Frankly, Dan's a better quarterback than actor.

Someone else was in bed, too, also propped up on a pillow.

"All righty then!" Kip said. "Uncle Jake, this is Tanya."

"Hello, Tanya," I said to the girl, because it's more polite than saying, *What are you doing in my nephew's bed, harlot?*

"Tanya lives across the street," Kip said.

Of course. "Tanya! You're Phoebe's daughter."

"Hello, Mr. Lassiter," she said sweetly. She was a dark-haired, petite girl of about twelve. The last time I noticed, she'd been maybe six years old, riding a bike with training wheels. Now she wore cutoff jeans and a T-shirt that blossomed with her budding womanhood. Oh, Lord.

"How's your mom?" I asked.

"Great," Tanya said.

"Does she know you're here? This late, I mean." I didn't like the sound of my own voice, old and uptight.

"Sure. She's spending the weekend doing the smoke-house and fire-walking shtick at the Miccosukee village, so I'm sort of on my own."

"I see," I said, my voice filled with disapproval. I had already concluded that Phoebe's mothering didn't measure up.

"Mom's into a lot of neat stuff," Tanya said. "She has her own shaman who teaches naturopathy, herbalism, psychic healing."

No wonder she didn't have time to trim the hedge.

"I asked Tanya to sleep over," Kip said.

"Uh-huh," I said, as if this were as natural as mosquitoes following a rain.

"But if there's a problem," Kip said, "we could stay at her place."

"No!" I responded, a little too quickly, the volume a little too high. "Tanya can stay here. Of course, we don't actually have another bedroom."

They both giggled, and I knew I was the object of adolescent ridicule. I considered having her mother arrested for conduct unbecoming a parent. I remembered Phoebe had a tattoo on her shoulder and wondered if Tanya did, too, and whether Kip would see it before the night was out.

Now I was getting angry at myself. Just when had I become so judgmental? All this time, I'd thought I was such a hip surrogate dad, and it turned out I was really Ward Cleaver.

"It's okay, Mr. Lassiter," Tanya said. "I brought my sleeping bag." She gestured toward the corner of the room, where indeed a sleeping bag was stretched across the carpet between piles of videotapes and Sega game cartridges.

"I see," I said for the second time, because I was utterly speechless.

"Hey, Uncle Jake, you're not going to get all freaky on us, are you?" Kip said.

"No. Why? I mean, of course not."

" 'Cause just now you seem like a major goober."

Tanya's voice managed to be both soothing and mature. "Kip and I just hang out. We're not, you know . . ."

I looked at my nephew, trying to remember what I'd been like when I was twelve. I seem to recall thinking a lot about girls but never doing anything icky like kissing them.

"All right," I said. "But don't stay up too late, and . . ."

And what?

"And don't forget to brush your teeth."

That set them to giggling again.

I left the room, closing the door behind me, feeling like a major goober indeed. Back in bed, I got back to my book, following Travis across the Gulf Stream toward Bimini, chasing a very bad character named Junior Allen. I remembered my own trip across the stream, where I'd followed a beautiful but lethal boardsailor named Lila Summers.

I was feeling sad and alone when there was a soft knock at my bedroom door. If Kip was going to ask permission to share a sleeping bag, the answer was a firm—

"Jake," came the woman's voice from the other side of the door, "are you awake?"

Chrissy and I sat on my bed, not unlike the twelve-year-olds across the hall. Except, if Kip was thinking what I was thinking, I was going to ground him for the next dozen years.

Chrissy arched her long neck and exhaled a puff of cigarette smoke toward the overhead paddle fan. I would try to get her to quit. Orders from her boy scout lawyer: no more shooting, no more smoking.

We sat there, side by side, talking. She told me everything she liked. Stone crabs and hash browns, Paris in the rain, snorkeling over tropical reefs. Yeah, and walks on the beach with somebody she cared about. We talked about plays and movies and even football. She had a decent understanding of the game and thought Troy Aikman was cute. I always thought quarterbacks were pampered, overpaid sissies, the rock stars of the business, but at least Aikman could take a hit.

We played a word association game we made up as we

went along, and we laughed at each other's jokes. We talked about those who had sailed through our lives and examined each other's psychic scars.

I was quiet a moment, and she just looked at me.

"What?" I asked.

"No man has ever cared for me."

It was such an outrageous statement that I laughed. Her look told me she was serious.

"That's hard to believe," I said. "Impossible, in fact."

"Oh, men have bought me things, taken me places. They've used me, and I've used them. But they never *cared* for me."

She let the line dangle there. I circled it but didn't bite.

"You do, though—don't you, Jake?"

"I do," I said.

"So you don't have to pretend that this is just another case."

"I won't. I can't."

"Then talk to me. Tell me what you're feeling."

"That's not easy for me. Never has been."

"All right. You have the right to remain silent. Anything you say may be used against you in a court of . . ."

Court of what? She didn't say. Law? Last resort? Love?

"Tell me how you feel," she ordered.

How do you wrap words around feelings? I didn't know.

"It's complicated," I said. "I have a duty to you. You're relying on me, not as a man, but as a—"

"Knight in shining armor."

I shook my head. "No, as a lawyer."

She ground out her cigarette in a Super Bowl commemorative plate on the nightstand. "Aren't you going to rescue me?"

"I want to. Believe me, I want . . ."

Outside, the mockingbird was at it again, and in the distance, a police siren wailed. "What do you want, Jake?"

"I want to wrap my arms around you and carry you off somewhere. Someplace safe where no one can hurt you."

"Ah, you are my knight."

"No. The armor's rusted, the knees are creaky, and my steed has thrown a shoe. Besides that, I've always been a step too slow."

She leaned over and kissed me. Smoky and sweet. "Not for me," she said.

Softly, tentatively, she kissed me again. Waiting for me to kiss her back. But I didn't. I stalled.

"It's important that we maintain some distance," I said. "At least until the case is over."

"You mean geographical distance?" She scooted closer on the bed, gave me a playful smile, and ran a hand through my hair. "Or emotional distance?"

"Both. I find the two are usually related."

"Oh, I don't know. I've been physically close to lots of men. But not emotionally close."

"Everyone's done that," I said. "But it's so meaningless. So . . ."

"Empty."

"Exactly."

"You don't want to get involved with me, do you?" she asked.

"It's not that I don't want to. I can't."

"What are you afraid of?"

"You. Me. I've been down this road before."

"Would it be unethical?"

"Technically, yeah. The Bar passed a rule that prohibits lawyers from sleeping with their clients."

"Really?"

"Unless they were involved before the case. Then the lawyer's grandfathered in."

"Nice choice of words," she said.

"But that's not the point. I didn't learn my ethics from

a book. I just try to do what's right. And if we're involved, it'll cloud my judgment.''

''And we wouldn't want that,'' she said, wriggling close enough that we were breathing the same oxygen.

''Chrissy, I'm serious.''

''So am I.'' She stripped the T-shirt off over her head, and then the shorts that covered her bikini bottom, and then the bottom, too. She stood and stretched, and though there was something practiced in it, back arched, breasts thrust forward, a pose she may have struck a thousand times, it was also so completely natural and innocent as to be even more provocative. Which, of course, was exactly what she intended. Some beautiful women may be unaware of their effect on men. Others, particularly those whose living depends on their looks and the moods they can create, know precisely the effect of every tilt of the head, every turn of the hip, every shadowy smile. There is neither pride nor shame in their display of naked flesh. It is just a fact, and in the perfection of details, the symmetry of features, the combination of physical strength and robust health that emanates from such a creature, there is always the knowledge that it will fade. Next year's model will soon replace it, so if you possess such beauty, the time to use it is now.

Chrissy turned toward the door, giving me a view of her tapered back, the slope of her ass. She flicked the light switch, then whirled and came back to the bed, moving gracefully, silhouetted in the darkness, a lithe, willowy sexual animal totally aware of her powers. She sat down, tucked her legs under her, and leaned toward me, her breasts pressed against my chest.

I'm sure some man exists somewhere on this planet who could have resisted. But Pope John Paul II wasn't in bed with Chrissy Bernhardt. That poor excuse for a chivalrous knight, Jake Lassiter, was there, all six feet two, 223 pounds of him, blood pumping, imagination soaring. I needed a stern warning. Caution, libido loose. Dangerous curves. Slippery when wet.

She tilted her head and kissed me again. This time, I kissed back. Slowly, then deeply. I cradled her head in my hands, and we kissed some more, our tongues fencing; then she dug her teeth into my lower lip.

I wanted to save her and savor her, taste her and devour her. I wanted a thousand things, and all of them now. A yearning moan rose from her, and we clutched at each other, hands roaming.

She reached down and pulled off my boxers, which I kicked across the room. She let a hand run down over my chest to my stomach, to my crotch. I was so hard it hurt.

We kissed some more, hungrily, biting each other's lips, sucking, searching, finding. Our hands explored each other, stroking and grasping. I cupped a hand around a firm round breast and took a nipple between forefinger and thumb.

''Harder, Jake. It won't break.''

I squeezed, and she gasped, and I took the nipple into my mouth like a ripe red cheery. My hand swept down across her flat stomach and found the wet heat of her. As I touched her, she gasped, then grabbed me by the back of the neck and put her lips to my ear. ''Love me, Jake. Love me, please.'' Her voice heavy with yearning and sadness and a crushing physical need. The sounds reverberating like a bass chord deep inside me. I wanted to cover her with my shield, to protect her from harm, to carry her away to a place where no one could hurt her again.

She spread her long legs and whispered again. ''Love me now, Jake.'' The same desperate longing.

I pressed myself against her pubic bone, which ground into my shaft. I slid lower and she was open to me, steamy, waves of heat rising from her. I entered her, and she locked herself around me, and we fell into the same rhythm, our bodies moving to the same beat, ever so slowly. I let her set the pace, and as it quickened, she bit at my chest, clawed at my back with her nails, then grabbed my head with both hands and tore at my hair. Her breath came in short, hot blasts against my neck, and half in pain, half in delirious pleasure, I quickened my pace, thrusting harder and faster, until a growl came up from deep inside her and then me, and her eyes rolled back, and she gave a low, wolflike wail, and then she thrust her wrist into her mouth and bit down hard, as if she could not stand to hear her own pleasure.

I pounded harder, coming then, too, and she wrapped even tighter around me, and I held her there, my face pressed against hers, until finally I tasted a salty drop and saw that her tears were mixed with mine.

11

Fruit of the Earth

"Let's see if I got this straight," Roberto Condom said. "You got some babe who's charged with murder out on bond, but me—who maybe was in the vicinity of a larceny involving some fruit—me, I got to sit in this shithole."

"If you're convicted, it's three first-degree felonies," I said, "and they'll have you under the habitual offender law. Life in prison."

"*Carajo!*"

"My sentiments exactly."

"It's 'cause I'm Cuban, isn't it, Jake? I'm an oppressed minority."

"Sorry, Roberto. In Miami, you're the majority."

We were sitting in a tiny lawyers' visiting room in the Dade County Jail. I had elbowed my way past throngs of relatives on the sidewalk, a polyglot of mothers, wives, girlfriends, and screaming babies. Overhead, men leaned out through barred windows, their women yelling up at them, screaming they'd like to suck them or shoot them, howling about unpaid rent, forgotten birthdays, and a variety of domestic ills not usually aired at mega-decibels on public streets.

From inside the visitors' room, I could hear men shouting and steel doors clanging. I am always claustrophobic inside a jail, even when I have a pass that gets me out the door. With the incessant racket and the metallic disinfectant smell, I imagine myself crunched inside a fifty-five-gallon barrel as someone bangs on the lid with a baseball bat.

"Maybe you can give the judge a little present," Roberto said.

"I don't bribe judges."

"Not a bribe. I got a friend who'll send him a human skull with red and black beads and fourteen pennies. Give the judge leprosy."

"C'mon, Roberto. You should have more faith in your lawyer."

"I'll put my faith in *brujería* and *palo mayombe*."

"The judge could come down with Ebola virus, but you'd still be in the can. Let me work on it, okay?"

"Yeah, but it ain't fair. First of all, they got nothing on me. *Nada*. Maybe trespassing, which is what, a misdemeanor? How they gonna prove I *took* the mangoes? Maybe they fell into my truck. Maybe it's not even a crime to pick the fruit of the earth, which belongs to all of God's creatures, right?"

I just love it when clients devise my strategy.

"They wouldn't prosecute a possum for stealing mangoes, would they, Jake?"

"No, they'd shoot it, which is what Guy Bernhardt wanted to do to you."

"That *puerco*! Stealing from Guy Bernhardt ain't stealing at all," Roberto said.

From somewhere above us, one inmate yelled at another to turn down his radio. "What do you mean by that?"

"The *hijo de puta* steals water from half the farmers in South Dade. My cousin Xavier has thirty acres two miles from the Bernhardt farm, and his wells have gone dry."

"Bernhardt told me about the battle over water down there."

"Bet he didn't tell you everything."

"It's an old story, Roberto. The rich get richer. The poor die of thirst."

"Yeah, but did you know Bernhardt dumps most of the water he's pumping?"

"What do you mean?"

"His irrigation ditches flow into a canal that goes straight into Biscayne Bay. When his trees have had enough, Bernhardt's wells keep pumping, but he dumps the water. I seen it with my own eyes. Three nights in a row, before we did the mango heist, I cased the place, crawled all over that property on my belly. Water was five feet deep in the irrigation ditch, flowing like a river, due east."

"That doesn't make any sense. He sells the water. Why waste it?"

"How should I know?"

Outside the room a buzz, and a security door clicked open, then clanged shut. "You're pulling a scam on me, aren't you, Roberto? You're cooking up some defense. You weren't out there to steal mangoes. You were working undercover for the Water Management District."

"Jake, *mi amigo,* you gotta believe me." Sounding hurt, which a con man can do to make you feel guilty for mistrusting him. "Guy Bernhardt's dumping water into the bay. I swear it. Have you ever known me to lie?"

"Only under oath," I said, thinking of Roy Cohn.

"Well, I'm telling you I seen it with my own eyes."

But why? I kept wondering. I thought about it but didn't come up with any bright ideas. Mango-loving, sister-helping, trigger-happy Guy Bernhardt was getting more mysterious by the moment.

"So, like I was saying, Jake. They shouldn't arrest me for stealing mangoes from that *cabrón*. They should—"

"I know. I know, Roberto. They should give you a medal."

12

Memories

"What can I do for you, Mr. Lassiter?" she asked.
"You can call me Jake."

"Fine, and you can call me Dr. Santiago." She belted out a hearty laugh. "Actually, you can call me Millie."

Dr. Milagros Santiago was a heavyset woman in her fifties, with glasses perched on top of her forehead. Her office was on the second floor of a three-story stucco building on Coral Way, a crowded street lined with banyan trees and small shops. It was a hot June day, but inside, the air conditioning was booming full blast. A rubber tree sat in one corner of the room, looking forlorn and in need of therapy. The wallpaper was beige grass cloth. A couch and matching chairs were in muted, soothing earth tones.

"Charlie Riggs told me you might help me with a case," I said.

"*Mi querido hombre!* Are you Charlie's friend?"

"He's like a father to me."

"What a dear man. We worked together on psychological profiles of serial killers when I was with the Behavioral Science Unit."

"Charlie didn't tell me you were an FBI agent."

"I wasn't. I had a fellowship, wrote a bunch of papers

nobody read. I spent three years listening to death row inmates describe their sexual fantasies, then opted for a change of venue.''

"Private practice," I said.

"Yeah. Now, I listen to housewives tell me how they dream Clint Eastwood will park his pickup truck in front of their house and pick flowers for them.''

She slid the glasses down from her forehead and studied me a moment. Then she stood up and walked to a counter where an espresso machine was humming. She turned a lever, and thick black liquid fizzed into two thimble-sized containers. "If I give my patients a full cup," she said, "they talk so fast I can't take notes.''

She handed me the steaming rocket fuel, which, for reasons my Cuban friends cannot fathom, I drink without sugar. "I saw a shrink a couple of times," I said.

"Good for you. Some men would never do that, or admit it if they had.''

"I'd just been cut by the Dolphins, sacked by a girlfriend, and rejected by three law schools.''

"Your life seemed to be at its nadir, and I suspect your self-esteem had taken a tumble.''

"You would think so, but I went to the shrink to find out why I didn't seem to care. I spent all my time partying and windsurfing and hanging out. Drinking too much, sleeping too late, and settling into an unmotivated life of unrelenting fun. I was a rebel without a clue, and I needed to find out why.''

She seemed to think it over while she sipped at the syrupy drink. "Your indifference may have been a defense mechanism to failure. You really *did* care, but you couldn't admit to yourself that you did.''

"Yep. And once I figured that out, I set some goals and changed my life.''

"And you've stayed off the couch ever since.''

"No. Once, a few years ago, a woman died. A woman

I cared about. I thought I could have saved her, should have saved her, so I had some things to work out.''

''Did you?''

''No. I still feel guilty, and I still have nightmares. So I'm batting five hundred with your profession.''

''Better than most. What can I do for you, Jake?''

''Charlie says you've done some research on repressed memory.''

''*Ay!* Don't tell me you have a client who wants to sue a parent for sexual abuse twenty years go.''

''I wish she'd taken that route,'' I said, then sipped at the espresso. I told her everything I knew, starting with the night at the club, Chrissy's gunning down her father, the recitation of her memories, and Dr. Schein's notes and tape recordings, including the gap I couldn't explain. When I was done, I pulled copies of Schein's file out of my brief-case and gave them to her.

''I'll go through everything,'' she said, ''but I can tell you right now that I'm skeptical.''

''About what part of the story?'' I asked.

''Everything.''

Then she told me why.

''Memory isn't neatly stored away in files waiting to be called up like bytes on a computer disk,'' she said. ''Human memory is labile, dynamic, and . . .'' She searched for the word. ''Malleable.''

''By therapists, you mean.''

''By anyone in a position of control.''

''What about recovering repressed memories?''

''Oh, that!'' She waved her hand in the air, seeming to dismiss the notion. ''We can thank Freud for the theory that all our experiences are stored away somewhere in the brain, just waiting to be recovered by therapy. Of course, even he changed his mind about that. A huge number of his patients seemed to recall terrible memories of child-hood incest. Initially, Freud accepted the stories as true.

Later, he concluded they were what he called screen memories, fantasies hiding primitive wishes. Others believe they're just false memories.''

"So what's the truth?"

She shrugged. "Who knows? But I can tell you that I despise the emotional strip-mining that therapists use to recover so-called repressed memories.''

"Millie, you're losing me. Is it the method you object to or is it the underlying concept of repressed memory?''

"Oh, memories may be repressed and then recovered, but does that make them true? I'm sure you remember many events in your life that are absolutely false.''

"I don't get it. If I remember them, they're true.''

"Not necessarily. You may try to store memories like a librarian shelving books. But each of us constructs a personal myth about what we think is true. We may exaggerate. Good times in the past become even better, hard times even worse. Individuals who were bad become outright demons. And some of our memories might simply be dreams that never took place at all.''

My face must have given it away. Millie asked, "What's wrong?''

"I was just thinking how much Abe Socolow would love to have you on his witness list.''

"But he can't.''

"No, not after I retained you.''

"Look, Jake, I don't want to kill your case, but you should know the truth.''

"That's why I came here.''

"Good. Then I'll tell you.''

She told me how memory resembled a blackboard with lots of chalk and lots of erasers. Whatever was written last tended to stick. A witness to a crime would remember it differently—erroneously—after reading an inaccurate account in the newspaper. She told me there were two kinds of truth. "Historical truth really happened. Narrative truth is what we remember. There are true memories with false details, and false memories with true details.''

I followed most of what she said, my mind zooming along on two cups of Cuban coffee. I'm always encountering new disciplines in my practice—DNA testing, blood-splatter evidence, voiceprinting—and I always reach the same conclusion. At first, a new field seems simple enough, but the more you learn, the more complicated it becomes. The more rules, the more exceptions. The more experts, the more debates.

I know my own limitations. ''Brilliant'' is not an adjective usually associated with my name. ''Dogged,'' perhaps. Same as in football. I was never a fancy high-stepper like Rusty MacLean, who could hip-fake a tackler and wink at a cheerleader at the same time. I was never called ''flashy'' or ''spectacular,'' not even in high school, where I was a fullback who wrapped two hands around the ball, lowered my head, and ran north and south. In college, I was a bread-and-butter linebacker who liked to take on the tight end, and as a pro, I was second string. I don't miss the glory, because you can't miss what you never had.

So here I was trying to figure out whether Lawrence Schein had handed me a sophisticated scientific defense or a smoke-and-mirrors sham that Abe Socolow would destroy in front of a jury. Another thought, too. What if it was a sham, but Socolow didn't know it? What if I could win with it? Would I?

After a moment, I said, ''Dr. Schein told me that psychological trauma is like a karate chop to the brain that interrupts the normal process of memory encoding.''

''How colorful,'' Millie Santiago said, shaking her head.

''He told me Chrissy could have put herself into a trance when the abuse was going on, so that the images of what happened were recorded, but without the whole story, in far-flung parts of the brain. The images never got transferred to the part of the brain where stories dwell. All he had to do was open the gateway to the parts where the images were stored, and they could re-create the memories.''

''Re-create or create?'' she asked, standing up and walking to the shaded window. Outside, horns honked as rush hour traffic crawled west toward Coral Gables and Westchester. ''I'm sure neurologists would be fascinated. We know damn little about thought processes. We know the nerve cells of the brain, the neurons, transmit information by electrical impulses. We know the cells release chemicals called neurotransmitters into synapses, gaps between the neurons. But we don't know where memories are stored and how they're recalled. Your Dr. Schein is part of the recovered-memory movement, which relies on feelings and images and theories that can neither be proved nor disproved. If it *feels* real, it must be real. The memories must be there if we can only dig them up. But doesn't it make more sense that traumatic memories are clearer, more detailed, and longer-lasting than any others?''

''Yeah, I would have thought so, but I'm not a doctor.''

She came back to her desk and sat down. ''How long did it take Schein to uncover these alleged memories?''

I smiled ruefully as I imagined Abe Socolow asking the same question. ''Several months. He wasn't getting anywhere until he started the hypnosis.''

She slammed a hand onto her desk. ''Of course. Hypnosis simply enhanced her suggestibility. In fact, the more easily someone is hypnotized, the more amenable to suggestion and manipulation they are.'' The doctor thumbed through Schein's medical records. ''Did he have her on any medication?''

''Yeah. Chrissy was ingesting enough drugs to make Cheech think he was Chong.''

She came to a page and stopped. ''Here it is. Xanax, Ativan, Mellaril, Prozac, Desyrel, Restoril, Darvocet, and lithium. Anything on her own? Was she smoking pot, dropping acid?''

''She says not. Charlie had a drug screen done and it didn't turn up anything.''

''Let me see it.''

I found the report and handed it to her.

''She had traces of barbiturates.''

''I know. The lab says they're from the sedatives.''

''Not this mix. She's got 3-hydroxyamobarbital, N-glucosylamobarbital, and 3-carboxyamobarbital.''

''Yeah, so what?''

''It all adds up to sodium amytal. It releases inhibitions, makes people more voluble. It's often used in hypnosis therapy. Schein would probably tell you it's a truth serum. I think it's just as likely to warp memory.''

''Why didn't Schein put it in his records?'' I asked.

She threw up her hands. ''You're the lawyer. You figure it out.''

''So, Millie, what are you saying? Schein secretly drugged Chrissy, then implanted memories of abuse that never happened?''

''Are you asking what I can testify to under oath?''

''Use the legal standard. What can you say to a reasonable degree of medical certainty?''

She shrugged. ''Who the hell knows? Should I tell you what I suspect?''

''I think I know that, Millie.''

''Look, memory fades with time, making it more susceptible to postevent information.''

''Like a therapist's suggestions.''

''Exactly.'' She sat down on a corner of the desk. ''How will you deal with the tapes in court?''

''I don't know. Schein's questions weren't so much leading as 'pushing.' Chrissy denied being raped. Then the recorder was turned off. When it came back on, she remembered.''

Millie Santiago was shaking her head.

I kept talking. "We'll have to produce the tapes, and Socolow will have a field day. He'll probably move to strike all the testimony about the abuse, and if that fails, he'll be happy to get the tapes in front of the jury."

"Heads you lose, tails you lose. Dr. Schein hurts you as much as he helps you."

Now it was my turn to stand and pace. "The problem is, I need Schein. I have no defense to a murder one charge except what he gave me."

"I'm sorry," Dr. Santiago said. "I didn't mean to clobber you like this."

"No. That's all right. I have to know the truth."

"Maybe another therapist would agree with Schein. I could recommend a couple if you want to try them."

"You mean someone who'll say what I want?"

"That's the way the game is played, isn't it?"

"I guess. I had a blood-spatter expert on the stand in a case not long ago. The state attorney is cross-examining, trying to be tough. He asks, 'Did Mr. Lassiter pay you to lie for him?' And the witness says, 'No, he doesn't have that kind of money.' "

"A little cynical, are we, Jake?"

"Yeah. You know the acronym for an expert?"

"Tell me."

"*Witness Having Other Reasonable Explanation.*"

"Don't get hostile, Jake, or I'll have to suggest therapy."

"Sorry. It happens whenever I have a woman about to take a fall."

"A woman?"

"Did I say 'woman'? I meant 'client.' "

Her eyes twinkled at me. "Uh-huh."

"Hey, Millie, cut me a break."

"You left something out of the story, didn't you, Jake?"

The drone of the air conditioning was the only sound in the room. "Yeah, I left something out."

"You want some free advice?"

"Sure."

"Pull back. Don't get emotionally involved. There's only pain where you're headed."

"I know. I've been there before."

She cocked her head and studied me. "You want to talk about it? No charge."

An image flashed by, Susan Corrigan facedown in a swimming pool. "I've let someone down before."

"Someone?"

"A woman. I thought I could help her, but I botched it." Another image, Lila Summers looking out to sea, then the flash of an explosion, the boat tearing itself apart. "Maybe we can talk sometime."

"Anytime you say. If you're Doc Riggs's friend, *mi casa es su casa.*"

I gathered my briefcase and stood up. "Thanks, Millie. Send me a bill."

"Don't worry. I will." She walked me to the door. "Oh, Jake, one more thing."

I turned around. "Yeah?"

"I'm not saying that memories can't be repressed and then later recovered. I can't say it's impossible. But suggestions can implant phantom memories that look like they're repressed, or they can shape real memories into something else."

"Dammit, Millie! What are you saying? What did Schein do?"

Her look was filled with regret, as if she'd like to help me but didn't know how. "Maybe Schein implanted your client's memories of abuse."

"Yeah, I already figured that out."

''But maybe he didn't.''

''Meaning what?''

''Maybe *she* did it, Jake. Maybe she concocted these memories to fool her shrink. And to fool you, too.''

13

Water Wars

Harrison Baker was yelling over the roar of the airplane engine, but I couldn't hear a thing. The old man tried again, then mouthed a word I couldn't quite pick up. He pointed to the cloudless sky above a cypress hammock and I saw the big black birds.

"Buzzards," he was saying.

Behind us, Jimmy Tiger eased back on the throttle and the airboat glided to a stop about two hundred yards from the higher ground. Jimmy's black hair was tied back in a ponytail, his eyes hidden behind aviator sunglasses. He wore the traditional Miccosukee jacket of bright red with multicolored stripes.

As the engine idled, Baker said, "We get buzzards during floods, and we get them during drought. The damn shame is that man causes both. Feast or famine, we're to blame."

Baker sat next to me in the small airboat. He wore khaki pants, a bush jacket, and a Boston Red Sox cap. He had a white mustache, a sun-creased face, and a patrician bearing. Twenty years ago, Baker had retired from an insurance company up north and discovered the Everglades. Now he devoted his life to saving what was left of it.

In the water next to us, an alligator carried its baby on its back. Nearby, a scrawny deer waded through shallow water toward the hammock, but the leaves of low-hanging branches had already been stripped clean, leaving nothing edible on the little island. Through binoculars, I could see the skeletons of small animals on the shore. We floated in a shallow channel, but on both sides, the earth was dried into a cracked mosaic of parched soil. It was in the nineties and humid. This time of year, Miamians with the wherewithal head for the mountains. The deer apparently hadn't gotten the message or didn't know the route.

Baker pointed toward a stretch of land near the hammock. "There ought to be two feet of water right there. There ought to be plenty of vegetation for the deer, tiny fish for the wading birds, and water holes for the gators to lay their eggs. But look at it."

"Dry as my granny's rye toast," I said.

Jimmy Tiger leaned down from his perch above us. "They're taking all the water for the farms and the cities. Then, in the rainy season, they flood us."

Tiger gunned the engine, and we took off again down the channel in the east Glades, through patches of green water lettuce and lilies. To my untrained eye, there seemed to be plenty of flora and fauna as we sped over the shallow water, crunching through yellow sawgrass. But then, I didn't know what it was like a century ago. We roared past hardwood hammocks with live oak and royal palm trees, scattering half a dozen egrets into the air. A predatory osprey flew overhead, searching for lunch, reminding me that I was hungry. A turtle swam slowly by, and two black snakes gracefully slithered through the water. Earlier, on wetter ground near the Shark Valley Slough, I had spotted the unique pink feathers of a roseate spoonbill carrying twigs in its spoon-shaped beak and, not far away, a black-and-white wood stork.

When I pointed out all the birds, Baker gave me a bitter

laugh. "Not long before you were born, Jake, there was an area called Rookery Branch west of here that was packed with white ibis, tricolored herons, and snowy egrets. Between half a million and a million of them in a strand of trees a hundred yards wide and three quarters of a mile long. Can you even imagine the sound they made?"

"Yeah, and the birdshit, too," I said.

"Their songs could be heard for miles," Baker continued.

It made me think of the banyan trees near the public tennis courts on Florida Avenue in the Grove. Two dozen green parrots roost there in the winter, chirping their hearts out. "What happened?" I asked.

"The Army Corps of Engineers built the canal south of Tamiami Trail. The water turned brackish. No more birds, no more music."

I am not an environmental nut, believing in moderation in all things except consumption of Dutch beer. I am more pained by an inner-city child without a home than a heron without a nest. I don't understand people who treat a man sleeping in a cardboard box as if he were invisible but race across the street to curse at a woman wearing a fur. Sorry, but I care more about people than minks, which I always considered uptown rats.

At the same time, I am opposed to fat-cat business-industrial types, such as a certain rotund, cigar smoking radio host who calls people like Baker "environmental Nazis." There is a balancing to be done between the needs of a growing populace and the preservation of the wild. If I had to choose between Baker and those who would pave the wetlands, drill for oil on the reefs, and ravage the forests, count me with the tree huggers.

Harrison Baker had already given me a history lesson. The Everglades, that wide, slow river flowing from Lake Okeechobee on the north to the Gulf of Mexico on the south, has been straitjacketed by fifteen hundred miles of canals and levees, two-hundred water control structures, and eighteen pumping stations. A man-made plumbing system tries to accommodate the water needs of farmers, industries, and ten million people in the southern half of the state. The environment comes last. The Glades is half its original size, and the number of endangered species grows each year.

"South Florida is an environmental disaster," Baker told me. "We've got one-tenth the wading birds we had at the turn of the century. We've cut the flow of fresh water through the Glades, so Florida Bay is dying. Algae has killed the shoalgrass and turtle grass and turned the water brown. The mullet, trout, and tarpon have been devastated. The Glades is polluted with mercury and phosphorus and pesticides. Beaches are eroding, mangroves are fouled with garbage, reefs are dying, and every week new developments are started, moving west from Miami, Fort Lauderdale, and West Palm Beach right into what's left of the wetlands."

"What about water?" I asked him. "Fresh water?"

"Ah," he said, a sad smile crinkling his eyes. "Water is the real story. Water is where it'll all come home to roost. We're bleeding ourselves dry, and no one seems to care."

Tiger skidded the airboat to a stop next to a squat metal building on stilts. Here in the wilderness, it looked so out of place it could have been from Mars. "Water control station," he said, pointing at the invader. "Another feeble attempt by man to control nature. We always muck it up!"

Tiger let the engine idle, and Baker looked toward the horizon. "Give me a weather report, Jake."

I followed his gaze. A thick thunderhead was boiling up in the west. "It's going to rain," I said.

"Damn right!" Baker replied, laughing. "The rainy season is starting. That's the delicious irony. Two hundred years ago, pirates didn't even come ashore to get fresh water. It bubbled up in the middle of Biscayne Bay—that's how high the water table was. So what's the problem now? It doesn't rain any less. Hell, we had ninety inches in 1994! We get sixty to seventy inches most years, and we're running out of water. Why?''

"The canals," I said, having been a good student earlier in the day.

"Right. We shoot most of the water to the ocean. Whoosh!" He made a flowing motion with a hand. "We get too much in the summer and not enough in the winter, and once they chopped up the Glades, which was a natural storage area, the aquifer couldn't get enough. We don't have melting snows or giant mountain lakes. Our rain barrel is a limestone-and-sand sponge underground which stores water for us. But statewide, we've lost half the wetlands, over three million acres, and every year they lay more asphalt and build more malls, and every year the water level drops and the saltwater intrusion moves in farther from the sea.''

We passed a nearly dry mangrove creek, where wading birds stomped through the shallow water looking for tiny fish. Above us the sky was darkening, and in the distance lightning flashed.

"So why not just knock down the damn things and go back to the way it was?" I asked.

That brought another laugh. "I'd love it!" Baker turned around to face Jimmy Tiger. "How 'bout you, Jimmy?"

"Sure. Drown all the white men."

"It surely would," Baker said, "at least the short ones. On Jake, here, the water would only be up to his chin." He turned back to me. "They could restore the Glades by letting the natural ebb and flow of the water take over. Of course, everything west of I-95 would be flooded up and down the coast. The sad truth is, man wasn't intended to live in South Florida, at least not in the millions. Maybe a few thousand of Jimmy Tiger's people could do it, living in the slough with the natural floods and droughts. But not the rest of us.''

"So what's the solution?'' I said.

"We could start with conservation. We use about two hundred gallons of water per person per day. In Europe, the average is closer to sixty gallons.''

"But we like big cars and long showers and green grass.''

"Sure, it's our God-given right,'' he said with a rueful smile. "Well, God's got a surprise for us. One day we'll run out of water.''

"What can be done?''

"The federal government has promised to restore some of the Glades. The Army Corps of Engineers is going to divert water back into the Shark River Slough, which will flow into the national park.''

"That's good,'' I said. "You should be happy about it.''

"I am, but you city folk shouldn't be. Farmers, either. It means less water for you. There won't be enough to go around. We could be like some of the Caribbean islands— just turn off the water until it rains. Can you imagine that? Folks come down to their three-hundred-dollar-a-day hotels and can't take a shower or brush their teeth. No new sewer hookups, no lawn watering, rationing of water to maybe one fourth of what each family uses now. Most farmers will lose everything, though it's their own damn fault. Jake, have you ever seen one of those irrigation guns up on a tower, shooting water in a big circle like some kind of fountain?''

"Yeah. Guy Bernhardt's farm must have dozens of them.''

"Bernhardt! That son of a bitch is worse than his father. He's the biggest water abuser in South Dade. Each of those guns shoots a thousand gallons of water a minute, and they lose half to evaporation and just plain misplacement. We try to get them to use the new drip technology and retain moisture with mulch, but water's been cheap and plentiful so long, they won't do it. They get permits from the Water Management District to pump a certain amount, but it's all free. 'It's my land, and it's my water.' That's what Bernhardt and his kind say. And the district is powerless to stop them. There are no meters, no inspectors to prevent overpumping. It's all an honor system, but men like Guy Bernhardt have no honor. He's a pig who's..." He searched for a phrase.

"Bleeding us dry," I said.

"Exactly. But the day of reckoning is coming. Jake, I'll bet you that before the millennium, we'll have full-fledged water wars down here."

"Water wars? That sounds like something from a B-western."

"Nope. It's already happened over in Tampa–St. Pete. Some law-abiding folks from Hillsborough and Pasco counties were tired of having their lakes and wetlands sucked dry just so the people of St. Petersburg could grow impatiens in the winter."

"What happened?" I asked.

"They became vigilantes, blew up a pipeline running from a well field down to Pinellas County."

That reminded me of Guy Bernhardt's story about his neighbors. "I don't get it," I said, and not for the first time in my life. "If there's a war, where are the battle lines drawn?"

"Simple, Jake. It's between those who control water and those who don't. In the past, land was money and power. Today, or in the very near future, it'll be water. Damn few people realize it, but our whole world has changed. Everything is water, and water is everything."

14

Road Kill

I was gnawing my third ear of corn when Roberto Con-dom showed up and sat down across from me at the picnic table outside the ribs joint on South Dixie Highway. It was dusk and still rush hour, a steamy heat rising from the pavement. Plumes of carbon monoxide mixed with the tang of smoking ribs as traffic clogged the north-south road, horns bleating.

I offered to buy Roberto a pork sandwich or a slab of ribs, but he declined, shooting nervous glances from side to side and whispering anxiously, "I can't get busted, Jake. You gotta know that. You, of all people, gotta know that."

"I need you, Roberto. You have to trust me. I did get you out on bond."

"Yeah, well, if I'm busted—"

"I know. I know. I'll handle the case for free."

"Hell with that! I'll flip on you. You're gonna need your own lawyer."

At the next table, a truck driver with tattooed forearms shot us a look. I slathered my ribs platter with barbecue sauce—heavy on the vinegar with a touch of cayenne—slopping some onto the fries.

I decided to play the guilt card. "They always talk about

a lawyer's loyalty to a client. What about the other way around?''

"*Chíngate!*" Roberto Condom said.

"I guess playing the guilt card only works with someone who has the capacity to feel guilty."

"Fuck you," he told me, in case I hadn't gotten it the first time.

I was wearing an old Oakland Raiders jersey, one of the black ones, turned inside out so the silver numbers wouldn't glow in the moonlight. It belonged to a left-handed quarterback who had left it behind at my house following a Super Bowl to which neither of us had been invited. My recollection is hazy, but I seem to recall the QB leaving the party with a blonde who had started the evening as my date, leaving me with his jersey and several empty tequila bottles. And you wonder why I hate quarterbacks.

Roberto Condom was wearing an army camouflage outfit, his pant legs neatly bloused into paratrooper boots, his face greased with eye black. A bit overdone, I thought, but with his Latino good looks, he could have been a recruiting poster for the Panamanian Defense Force.

We were crawling on our bellies through a muddy field fragrant with the scent of ripe mangoes. I had left the Olds at the ribs joint, and Roberto had driven us to the edge of the Bernhardt farm in a Ford Taurus with Manatee County plates.

"You rented a car?" I had asked him.

"No, I borrowed it."

"What?"

"I'm a valet parker at Flanigan's Quarterdeck Saloon, so I just—"

"Flanigan's doesn't have valet parking," I said.

"How many tourists you think know that? I stand there at the front door, a guy gets out of his car, I rush over and take his keys."

"Doesn't he want a receipt?"

"I give him a used trifecta ticket from jai alai, he gives me his new Taurus."

A three-quarter moon was rising in the east, darting in and out of a thin layer of scudding clouds. We continued moving along in what the marines call the high crawl, weight on the forearms and legs, knees behind the butt to keep close to the ground without belly slithering. A swarm of tiny gnats the locals call no-see-ums buzzed around my ears and invaded my nostrils. The night was moist with the fecund bouquet of growing things. We crept past a fragrant bush of white ginger, what Granny calls the butterfly lily. I remember its scent on a lei worn by Lila Summers in Maui. Not far away was a wild blooming jasmine, the fragrance heavy and overpowering.

"*Cristo!* Smells like a funeral parlor out here," Roberto muttered.

The earth itself gave up the fertile aroma of freshly plowed soil, and the night was alive with the sound of feeding birds and singing crickets.

Suddenly, I caught the scent of a woman.

Or of perfume.

Eerily like Chanel No. 5.

"Do you smell that?" I asked Roberto.

"Ilang-ilang trees. They're planted along the irrigation ditch, so we must be getting close."

"Intoxicating. I've never smelled a tree like that."

"Jake, you gotta learn to appreciate nature more."

"Like you, the thief of palms?"

"Among other things," he admitted.

To the west, heat lightning reflected off clouds billowing over the Everglades. The only other illumination came from sodium-vapor lights on poles spaced every fifty yards or so. Along with the cawing of the night birds, there was the crickety noise of insects and the incessant whine of a rodent named Roberto Condom.

"Jeez, Jake, I'm telling you, if I see any of those *chichi cabrón* guards with shotguns, I'm gonna shit my pants.''

"C'mon, Roberto. We're almost there.''

Suddenly, a whirring as one of the giant irrigation towers' guns came on, spraying us with a mist from a hundred yards away. "Shit, now I'm gonna catch pneumonia,'' Roberto complained.

As we headed toward the house, Roberto kept up his patter. "If you get disbarred for this, Jake, where does it leave me?''

"Stop worrying.''

"If you go down, I don't want some ca-ca lawyer representing me,'' Roberto said.

"Not politically correct, Roberto, making fun of the Cuban-American court-appointeds.''

"Yeah, well, I don't want an *abogado* just off the boat from Mariel. I want you, Jake.''

"And you're my favorite two-time loser,'' I said, trying to reciprocate.

A moment later, I silently raised an arm, signaling Roberto to stop. "Do you hear something?''

"Yeah. I hear my probation officer calling the state attorney.''

"Water. Running water.'' Rising up on one knee, I saw what looked like the outline of a mountain on the horizon. "There's the levee along the irrigation channel.''

"Jeez, look at that!''

His tone startled me, and I whirled around but saw nothing except a clump of small trees.

"Sago palm,'' Roberto said. "Smart to hide them in the middle of a mango field. I could get a thousand bucks easy for a six-footer. Damn things only grow an inch a year.''

"C'mon, Roberto.''

"You think we could fit one in the trunk of the Taurus?''

"Roberto!''

* * *

The sound of rushing water grew louder, and in a moment we were slogging up the soggy levee and looking down into a river. Glowing silver in the moonlight, the water tumbled down the channel, gurgling merrily, rippling over rocks, tree branches, and clumps of dirt.

"The well field's a mile to the west," Roberto said. "They're pumping God knows how much water into the channel. Some is siphoned off for the irrigation towers, some for drip irrigation, but most of it just flows, west to east, toward the open bay."

"Why?" I asked. "Why waste all that water?"

"*No sé,* man, and I don't want to know. I just want to get out of here."

We were five hundred yards from the farmhouse when Roberto started bellyaching again. "Ain't gonna add B and E to trespassing, no way."

"We're not going inside," I assured him. "Just a little surveillance."

The house was surrounded by rows of rosebushes. I hadn't thought about it before, but now, working through them, they were a pretty good perimeter defense. Not as good as a minefield maybe, but still . . .

"Ouch!" Roberto winced and pulled a thorn from his shoulder. "Jake, I'm telling you, this is crazy."

"Quiet down."

Two Jeeps were parked in the driveway. So were Guy Bernhardt's Land Rover and Lawrence Schein's Jaguar. Another house call.

"Roberto, stay here. If there's any trouble, take off. I'll meet you at the car."

"Like I'd really wait for you. It ain't Hershey's Kisses they got in those shotguns."

As I crawled toward the house, I thought I heard him praying in Spanish.

The jalousie windows to the den were cranked open,

and inside, paddle fans spun. The walls were Dade County pine, varnished to a gloss. A boar's head was mounted on one wall, a rack of antlers on another. I squatted in a bush of Spanish bayonet, and every time I moved, another thorn pierced my skin. Through the louvered windows, I could see about half the room. I was staring at the back of Lawrence Schein's bald head, which appeared above a leather sofa. Somewhere out of sight was Guy Bernhardt.

"Regrets? Hell, no!" It was Guy's voice from a corner of the room. There he was, standing at the bar, dropping ice cubes into a Manhattan glass. "We both got skeletons in the closet from way back, so trust me when I tell you to look ahead. Don't look back."

"My life's been devoted to opening those closets, shaking those skeletons," Schein said.

"Spare me the Hippocratic horseshit, okay?"

I strained to get a closer look, pressing my cheek to the glass. Bernhardt walked toward Schein, carrying two drinks. "Will he figure it out? Before the trial, I mean."

"I suspect he will," Schein answered. "Like his buddy said, he's smarter than he looks."

Bernhardt handed one drink to Schein, then sat down on a leather chair that faced the sofa. Though I knew he couldn't see me through the darkened window, from this angle it seemed as if he was looking right at me, and I caught my breath.

"Then what? What the hell will he do?" Bernhardt asked.

"He'll have an ethical dilemma."

"And . . . ?"

A pause before Schein spoke. "Who knows? MacLean says he's honest."

Somewhere in the distance, a dog barked. And somewhere inside my head, cymbals were clanging. "So we're better off than if she had a top-flight lawyer," Bernhardt said.

I was trying to process the information.

The "he" was definitely me.

The "top-flight lawyer" was definitely not me.

What "ethical dilemma" would I have?

"You know what I was thinking?" Bernhardt again. He didn't wait for an answer. "Pop would be proud of me."

"That is a transparent rationalization, Guy."

"No, hear me out. Pop took Castleberry's money and multiplied it tenfold. What I'm doing ... well, it's even bigger."

"Your methods, Guy. What about your methods?"

Bernhardt snorted a mirthless laugh. "They're okay. I checked them out with my inner child."

"Go ahead, mock me."

Bernhardt laughed again.

What the hell were these guys up to? What methods? The dog barked again, and a second later, *splat.* A clod of mud landed in the bushes, startling me, and giving me a crown of thorns as I leaped backward. *Ping,* a pebble this time, banging off the window. Shit. I turned around and saw Roberto's silhouette, arms waving madly.

"What was that?" Bernhardt said, from inside the house.

I flattened myself into the soft earth as Guy Bernhardt walked over to the window. My head buried in my arms, I could sense him above me, barely inches away.

The dog barked louder, then stopped. Maybe it was the Hound of the Baskervilles. Or the Bernhardts.

Guy Bernhardt turned away from the window. I lifted my head and saw that Roberto Condom was gone.

"... water."

Bernhardt's voice again.

"Are the permits in order?" Schein asked.

"All the *i*'s dotted and *t*'s crossed."

"You're a man ahead of your time."

"You got that right," Bernhardt said. "Twenty years

from now, they'll be writing books about me."

Now what the hell were they talking about? Too many questions, too few answers. I didn't have time to think about it, because I heard a husky voice somewhere behind me. "Whoa, girl! Slow down."

Near the corner of the house, not thirty feet away, I caught a glimpse of a man with a German shepherd tugging at a leash. A shotgun was cradled in the man's arms. A radio crackled, and he said, "B-two, I'm at the house. Blossom's got a straw up her ass. Got the scent of something, probably a possum."

Blossom. I liked that way better than Killer.

"Okay." The radio clicked off. "Go on, girl, but don't be bringing back any road kill."

Why did "road kill" sound like a lawyer joke, a dead lawyer joke, just now?

I heard him open the collar latch, and then Blossom headed straight for me, head down, shoulders low, panting hard. Maybe a German shepherd's impression of the high crawl.

I burst out of the bushes, the thorns clawing at me.

"Shit!" the guard cried. "Halt! Freeze!"

I zigzagged away from him, through the rosebushes, giving him a moving target. Yapping loudly, Blossom was at my heels.

The shotgun blast echoed over my head. Way high.

Of course. He wouldn't risk killing his dog. The shot was meant to scare me into stopping. Instead, it sped me up. Maybe all those years of gassers after practice were worth something after all.

I was into the mango grove when the spotlights came on. I was still cutting back and forth, making like Emmitt Smith, when it occurred to me that Blossom was alongside, running in stride. She could have taken me down with a firm crunch to the calf, but there she was, barking loudly.

Happily keeping pace with me. Much more fun than being tethered to a guard.

I slowed to a trot, and so did she. I put my hand out and she licked it, then started barking again. In the distance, I saw the headlights of a Jeep, heard men shouting.

"Quiet, Blossom," I told her.

She barked louder.

I reached up, pulled a mango from a tree, and rolled it a few feet away. Blossom trotted over and picked it up in her mouth. No more barking. Then she brought the mango to me, dropped it at my feet, and barked some more.

I picked up the mango and hurled it as far as I could. Barking happily, Blossom took off that way, and I ran the other.

I was nearly to the levee when I heard an engine kick up. A second Jeep was there, waiting. The headlights came on, freezing me. Engine growling, it headed straight for me. I pivoted and ran up the levee, scrambling on all fours in the soft dirt. I heard the Jeep slam to a stop, heard the men yelling behind me.

At the top of the levee, my knee buckled, the one with the railroad track scars, and I tumbled down toward the water. A shotgun blast kicked up mounds of dirt alongside me. With no Blossom running interference, I was in their line of fire now.

I either dived into the water or fell into it. Either way, it was deep enough and fast enough to carry me off. I took a breath and went under, going with the flow. I came up, heard another shotgun blast, and went under again. I held my breath as long as I could and came up again. The shouts were well behind me now. I was gone, body surfing down this channel of clear, fresh water, so recently sucked up from the aquifer.

In a few minutes, the water grew deeper, the current faster. I tried to touch the bottom but couldn't. I slid onto my back and floated farther still. It is not easy to judge the passage of time when your adrenaline is pumping. Maybe it was ten minutes, maybe it was forty, but it wasn't long before the water slowed. A tree branch floated alongside me, and I grabbed it. A black mangrove. Then I caught the scent of brackish water and knew I was nearing the bay.

A mist rose from the moist soil into the night air and then, shining eerily above me, a light. And then another. I was passing through the orange glow of a string of high-intensity lights, and above me, through the ghostly mist, I saw the silhouette of a building. Or at least the skeleton of one, under construction. Girders and framing a dozen stories high, rising like a spooky dreamscape. Bigger than anything in these parts, power-plant-sized, with a concrete smokestack poised like a missile next to the building.

And then it was gone. The gleam of the lights grew weaker, then disappeared, too. As I floated along, a strange thought worked its way into my consciousness. Had I seen anything at all rising out of the mist, or was it the product of my imagination, my fears, my dreams? *Dr. Millie Santiago, where are you when I need you?*

The water picked up speed again, and when I tried to swim toward the side of the levee, I was so exhausted I just let it carry me on. In a moment, the current slowed again, then stopped. The water was suddenly warmer. And salty. And endless. I was in Biscayne Bay. Keep swimming east and I'd hit the coast of Africa.

A gentle tide was headed out to sea, and so was I. Floating on my back again, I turned over and did a slow crawl, angling north along the shoreline. Just offshore, the lights of a shrimp boat twinkled in the night. I swam in that direction. A fish jumped from the water, silvery in the moonlight.

I swam some more, picking up strength, cutting smoothly through the flat, warm water. Suddenly I was thirsty, and I thought of Harrison Baker and his tale of fresh water spouting up in the middle of the bay. I thought of the coral reef not far south of here, alive with fish. I thought of all that lay beyond the horizon, so much of it unknown. As a boy, I had wanted to run away to the sea. Now, here I was, wanting to come back to land. There, too, to face the unknown.

15

Ready to Wear

The policeman knocked on the door and waited. So did I.

Water dripped from my clothing onto the dark wood of the hallway. Blood trickled from a dozen scratches on my forehead, legacy of the thorns. Even worse, my nose itched, and with my hands cuffed behind my back, I couldn't scratch it.

Through a window at the end of the hall, I could see the orange glow of the sun rising over the ocean. It had been a long night.

The cop knocked again, louder. A muffled voice came from the other side of the door. A moment later, Chrissy Bernhardt, dressed in a black-and-red silk kimono, cracked open the door, the chain still attached. She didn't seem surprised to see a cop at her door at dawn.

"Sorry to bother you, ma'am," the Miami Beach cop said. Yeah, he actually said "ma'am," just like in the movies. The cop was in his fifties, probably a year or so away from a retirement watch and juicy pension. He pushed me toward the door. "Do you know the subject?"

"Subject?" I asked, offended. "I always thought of myself as more of a verb."

"Let me get a good look at him," Chrissy suggested. She pursed her lips and studied me through sleepy eyes. "He has a certain animalistic charm, don't you think, officer?"

"I wouldn't know."

"Could we strip-search him?"

"Chrissy!" I protested.

"So you do know him," the cop said.

"Intimately," she said, pursing her lips.

"Can you state with certainty whether he's an American citizen?"

She shrugged her shoulders.

"*Sí, jefe,*" I answered in a really bad imitation of the Frito Bandito. "I love thees country very much."

" 'Cause he floated up the beach this morning, landed near South Pointe, just like one of those Cuban rafters. I was ready to turn him over to Immigration, get him a deportation hearing."

"I was sort of hoping for France," I broke in, "though I'm told the Costa del Sol is nice this time of year."

The cop shook his head. "He claimed he was swimming, then was picked up by a shrimper who dropped him just offshore. Says he was on his way to see you, but he's got no ID, no money . . . and just look at him."

I was standing in a puddle of water. My face felt swollen, and my back ached.

"He is a mess," Chrissy agreed.

"A warm bath ought to help," I suggested.

"Maybe you should leave those cuffs on, officer," Chrissy said.

The cop was already fishing for his key. "No can do. City property."

The hot water trickled down my chest as Chrissy squeezed the sponge, a real one that used to float in the gulf off Tarpon Springs. She leaned forward and I leaned back. She was behind me in the big old tub with the claw feet, her legs wrapped around my waist, her soapy breasts pressed against my back.

Chrissy had already dabbed my cuts with hydrogen peroxide and scrubbed seaweed from various crevices and orifices. Now she was letting the warm water lull me into a fuzzy state of sleepiness and semi-arousal.

Which was when her breasts began pressing against me, and her nipples hardened.

And so did I.

She was moving the sponge lower now. Down my chest, down the washboard abs, not quite as tight as they used to be, down, down, down. And then back up again.

"Tease," I complained.

"Just relax, Jake. We have all day."

I leaned back against her again. I closed my eyes and sank lower into the water, inhaling the sweet, soapy fragrance of her wet hair. She hugged me tight and said, "It feels good to take care of you. You've done so much for me."

"I haven't done anything yet, and I'm worried about—"

"Shhh. Not now."

I let myself drift, still feeling the ocean swells rising beneath me. A feeling of calm. But not peace. The nagging questions hung over me. I would ask Chrissy. Later.

A little plop in the water, and Chrissy said, "Whoops, dropped the soap."

Her hands moved down my chest again, and lower still. Once underwater, she latched onto me. "Whoa, Jake. Did you bring an oar with you?"

"Yeah. I thought I might row your boat."

"Precisely what I had in mind."

She gracefully slid out from behind me, swung around, and sat down facing me, her legs spread. We slid closer, and her long legs wrapped around my hips. Warmed by

the water and the wet friction of body parts, we kissed—
a long, sweet, soft kiss. The second kiss was harder, more
urgent. The third kiss, or maybe it was an extension of the
second, was filled with gasps and the biting of teeth on
lips. I opened my eyes to see Chrissy open hers, a startled
look on her face. In that moment, as she wriggled closer,
lifting her hips and lowering herself onto me, I looked into
her eyes and saw something I wanted to believe no other
man had ever seen. She had felt something, something
new, I was sure.

A man's conceit.

Making love to a woman.

Believing it had never been like that for her before.

I've had women *say* it. Once in a while even scream it.
But I never believed it. Hell, no one's that good. Chrissy
didn't say a word. But her look, as if she were in an altered
state; her sounds, the guttural urgency that rose from
within her; and the movement of her body against mine—
finally led to an explosion that rocked us both and settled
me deeper into her.

After a moment she said, "I love you, Jake. God, how
I love you."

Chrissy was looking for something to wear.

One hand fanned through her closet; the other clutched
a liter bottle of French water. Four bottles a day, she told
me. For the complexion. A cigarette dangled from her
mouth. For the lungs.

The closet was filled with clothing. Packed tight. Dis-
organized. Tasteful suits that Audrey Hepburn or Grace
Kelly might have worn, jammed next to beaded, see-
through bodysuits that could get you arrested in Tupelo,
Mississippi. Skirts that stopped just below the knee, just
above the knee, way above the knee, and some so short
they were hardly there at all. Sculpted stiletto-thin dresses,
shapeless tentlike dresses, ribboned dresses, embroidered

dresses, chained dresses, one held together with a dozen brass safety pins, all for show.

When she couldn't find anything in the closet, Chrissy swung open a six-foot-high cardboard closet, the kind movers use. There were two of these boxes in the bedroom, another three in the corridor. Inside, structured jackets, destructured jackets, crepe trousers, leather trousers, dresses with tie-up corsets and others that looked like bustiers, and lots of black and red.

"This is going to take a while, isn't it?" I said.

"Sorry, Jake, but I just don't have a thing to wear."

"Hey, we're just getting a burger at the News Café. Gianni Versace isn't going to be there."

"He was last week."

"Oh."

My sweatpants and Raiders jersey had just finished tumbling in her dryer. I was wearing Chrissy's kimono, but it looked a hell of a lot better on her. She was scattering assorted articles of clothing across her bed but seemed on the verge of selecting some Levi's with holes in the knees when I brought it up. "What is it you're not telling me?"

"About what?"

"Water. What do you know about Guy's water wells?"

She exhaled a puff of smoke and looked puzzled. "Nothing. He's a farmer, he's got wells. So what?"

"What about an industrial building under construction on the eastern edge of the tree farm?"

"I don't know. What does it have to do with me?"

"That's what I'm trying to find out. Tell me about you and your brother and Dr. Schein. What secrets does Guy have in his past?"

"How should I know? I was in Europe modeling. I barely even know Guy."

"What about Schein? There's a gap on the tape in the session where you recovered the memories."

"A gap?"

"Yeah, like the recorder was turned off and then back on."

"I don't remember that. Maybe Larry took a phone call. Maybe he gave me another injection."

"When the tape was off, did he tell you what to remember, what to say?"

"Jake, I just said I don't remember the recorder being turned off, so how would I remember what—"

"I thought when you're hypnotized, you remember everything."

"Well, maybe I don't!"

Rattled now. I do that to clients sometimes. Challenge them. Anger them. Push them into telling the truth. It comes with the territory, and usually it's easy. But usually I don't share a bathtub with my murder clients.

"What about the last session, June fourteenth?" I asked. "You told Schein you'd made a decision he wasn't going to like. Then he turned off the recorder and never turned it back on. Two days later, you shot your father."

She waited, though my next question had to be obvious.

"What had you decided?"

She seemed to think about it before answering. "To stop therapy. That's all right, isn't it? I mean, it doesn't hurt the case."

"No, it's fine."

It's a helluva lot better than having decided to be judge, jury, and executioner, I thought. And it made sense, didn't it? Quitting therapy, a decision Dr. Schein wouldn't like. But who knows what she really told the shrink behind the closed blinds of his office? I wanted to believe her. But could I? With clients and lovers, either you trust them or you don't.

I studied her for a moment, then asked, "How did you get to me in the first place?"

She stopped fiddling with the clothes and turned around to face me. "Why are you cross-examining me?"

"It's my job."

"Really? And in the bathtub just now, was that your job, too? Will Guy get billed for the time?"

"I told you it would be a problem if we got involved."

"No, *you're* the problem."

"Just bear with me, please. Why did you choose me as a lawyer?"

"You know why." Exasperated with me. "Rusty MacLean recommended you."

"I've known Rusty a long time, and he never sent me legal work before, other than his own miscues, which I handled for free. Why now? Why you?"

"I don't know!"

"Does Rusty know your brother?"

"How should I . . . Wait, yes, Rusty told me that Guy agreed to pay your fees."

"When? Before the bond hearing?"

"Yes. Right after you visited me in jail the first time."

"So Rusty knew about it before I did." I turned to her, anger rising in my voice. I was angry at Guy Bernhardt and Lawrence Schein and Rusty MacLean, and angry at myself, too, but it probably sounded as if I were angry at Chrissy. "What else does Rusty know that I don't?"

"Jake, why are you doing this? What's going on?" She seemed to be on the verge of tears.

"I don't know! That's what's going on! I'm about to defend you in a murder trial, and I don't know the truth. I know that Schein and your brother have something cooked up, but I don't know what."

She walked over, leaving a trail of smoke in her wake. She stood just out of reach. "And you think I do?"

"No. I think they're keeping something from you, something they don't want you to find out. But you may know a bit of it. You may have picked up some clues."

"If I had, I'd tell you. Jake, after getting this close to you, do you think I could lie to you?"

My heart said no, but my head wasn't sure. "I don't know."

She slapped me. Hard. "You bastard! I just told you I loved you. Do you think that's something that comes easy to me? It's not just the case you don't know about. You don't know me."

"Then tell me. Chrissy, God knows I care about you . . . deeply. I want to be with you, but I can't let that interfere with the case. Tell me everything!"

"I have. My father had sex with me when I was eleven. I repressed the memories. When the memories came back in therapy, the hatred just overcame me. I killed him, Jake. I killed him because of what he did to me, and that's the truth."

"Then we're going to lose," I said.

Rusty MacLean didn't see me coming toward his sidewalk table at the Booking Table Café. If I'd had a little gun in a beaded purse, I might have plugged him just to get his attention. Instead, I ran a Z-pattern around a ponytailed, earringed waiter and approached Rusty head on. He was sitting with two young women, one a freckled redhead, the other a blue-eyed blonde. Their books were spread open in front of them, eight-by-ten glossies spilling out. They were tall and young and freshly scrubbed, and their Caesar salads were barely picked over.

When Rusty finally saw me, he smiled broadly, winked, and nodded his head, first toward one of the women, then the other. "Jake, c'mon. Make it a foursome."

I didn't take the empty chair. Instead, I grabbed Rusty by the lapels of his aloha shirt and yanked him to his feet. I am blessed with strong wrists and forearms, the legacy of fighting big fish on little lines, and I lifted my old teammate cleanly into the air. Wide receivers can run with the wildebeests, but they have no iron in their bones.

"Jake!" His smile was frozen into place. "I love you, but I don't want to kiss you."

I pushed him backward into the open restaurant until he was pressed against the bar. Then I leaned him over, putting some pressure on his lower spine.

"I'm feeling very loved, Rusty. You and Chrissy on the same day."

"Hey, you're hurting me. I got a bad disk. Remember, I missed a play-off game in Pittsburgh."

"You sat out the game because it was ten below zero and you had a hangover."

"Look, Jake, I don't know what you're so mad about. Are you nailing one of these honeys? Which one, Tracy? 'Cause it's just business with me. You say the word, and I'll keep it in my pants."

"Shut up, Rusty."

He shut up.

"Tell me about Guy Bernhardt," I ordered.

"What do you mean?"

"Was it his idea or yours to hire me?"

He didn't answer, so I bent him farther across the bar. His arms flailed and he knocked over an empty margarita glass, which shattered on the tile floor. Two waiters eyed me but didn't move in my direction.

"His idea. So what?"

"When did he call you?"

"The night it happened. Maybe two A.M. Said his old man croaked in the hospital. He knew I was Chrissy's agent, knew I was a witness. He's got some friends who are Miami Beach cops. Saw their reports before the homicide chief did. Anyway, he asked me if I knew you, the guy on barstool number three on the police reports. I told him we were like brothers."

I released my grip a little.

"He asked if you were a good lawyer," Rusty continued, "and I told you you were the best lawyer to ever play linebacker for the Dolphins, better than Buoniconti, though he was a helluva lot better on the field. So he said, 'Hire him.' He'd pay the tab, and that was it.''

''Why didn't you tell me?''

''Guy said it would be better to keep it quiet for business and personal reasons. Like his wife wouldn't understand him helping his half sister or something.''

I looked at my old teammate and let him go.

Like brothers?

No. Rusty was too self-absorbed to be anyone's brother. On the team, opinon had been divided. Half the guys disliked him; the other half hated him. Sure, Rusty and I had gotten drunk together and chased women together. We'd celebrated wins and bitched about losses, but we weren't really friends, much less brothers. We had been thrown into the same pit, like foxhole buddies. That war was over. This one was just beginning.

16

Desal

This is how I broke my hand.

The second time.

The first time, I took a wild swing at the head of a big-bellied Notre Dame offensive lineman, a head encased in a helmet. After the third crackback block of a bitterly cold, trash-talking, eye-gouging afternoon, he went for my knees, which were already held together with baling wire and spit. I lost it and launched a roundhouse right he never felt. I wound up with a cast on my hand, a fifteen-yard penalty for unnecessary roughness—a term I find quaintly amusing, given the sport—another fifteen for unsports-manlike conduct for accusing the referee's mother of un-natural acts, and a seat so far down Joe Paterno's bench my feet were in Wilkes-Barre.

The second time, just an hour after leaving Rusty MacLean on Miami Beach, I was standing at the counter of the Dade County Building and Zoning Department, star-ing through a Plexiglas window. There are three windows, and if they're not bulletproof they should be, just to protect indolent, slothful clerks from irate, ignored taxpayers.

No one manned or even personed my window. Or the other two.

Three clerks sat at their desks, a dozen feet or so behind their little windows, doing their best to ignore the broad-shouldered taxpayer leaning on the counter who, luckily for them, was not armed. "Hey there," I cooed at the enormous black woman directly in line with my window, the middle of the three.

In her thirties, she was wearing an orange muumuu and had a telephone cradled on her shoulder. At the moment, she was loudly declaring that if Spike didn't get his rag-gedy-ass, lazy bones out of her house by six o'clock, she would haul his flea-bitten, egg-sucking worthless self half-way across the Everglades and feed him to the gators.

So I turned my attention to the window on the right. A middle-aged Hispanic man sat at his desk, drinking Cuban coffee from a thimble-sized paper cup. He had a beard that needed trimming and wore an off-white guayabera. Maybe there was paperwork on his desk, but I couldn't tell. A carton of pastries took up most of the surface. *"Hola!"* I called out.

"Estoy en mi hora de descanso," he said.

"Now? It's ten past nine. You just started work."

He took a bite of a pastelito, and guava filling oozed out onto his beard. *"No hablo inglés,"* he said.

"Really? So I'd be wasting my time telling you how much you look like Fidel Castro."

"Fuck you," he said crisply.

I turned to my left and looked through the third window. An Anglo kid of maybe nineteen with an earring and pony-tail sat at his desk, feet propped on a stack of cartons. His eyes were closed, a Sony Walkman was plugged into his ears, and his feet kept time with undoubtedly clamorous music.

"Hey, you!" I yelled.

He didn't hear me.

"You!" I tried again. "The brain-dead kid. Wake up!"

Still no luck.

I took heart that the utter indifference of our public servants was dispensed in an ethnically diverse, evenhanded
manner. It also was a source of my civic pride that these
well-paid, barely worked, juicy-pensioned paper shufflers
were entitled to their birthdays off with pay, courtesy of
property owners such as my very own taxpaying self.

Still, yearning for some attention, I punched the Plexiglas window. Hard.

A straight right hand.

Which made a hell of a racket.

Causing the Hispanic man to spill his coffee, the black
woman to drop her phone, and the Anglo kid to pry open
his eyes.

The window didn't crack, but my third metacarpal did.

"Hey, stupid. Destruction of county property is a misdemeanor," the black woman said in a bored tone that
made me think she'd said it before. "I'm gonna call a
cop."

I was hopping on one foot, squeezing my right hand
into my left armpit, trying to strangle the pain. "The only
time I was arrested," I said grimacing, "it was a case of
mistaken identity."

She gave me a cross-eyed look.

"I didn't know the guy I hit was a cop."

"I don't understand, Carmody," I said, leafing through
stacks of zoning permits and building plans. "It's got to
be here."

"Don't be stupid," Carmody Jones said.

The huge woman clerk and I had progressed to first
names. I called her Carmody and she called me Stupid.

She thumbed through a file of her own. "That farm is
in what's called a special taxing district. It's almost like a
little city. Like what Disney World did. Constructs its own
sewers and roads."

"And buildings," I said, thinking of the giant structure

rising along the irrigation ditch. "Just when did Guy Bernhardt get himself a special taxing district?"

"Last November twelfth," she said, pulling out a blue-backed document with a gold seal. "A resolution followed by special ordinance of the county commission. It was unanimous. Recommended by the staff of Building and Zoning, also the Department of Environmental Regulation, the Planning Commission, the South Dade Master Plan Council. A special agenda item at the end of the meeting. No debate, no protesters."

"No publicity," I said, looking at the file. My right hand was tucked into a Baggie filled with ice, courtesy of Carmody. I started reading aloud: "Whereas Bernhardt Farms, Inc., a Florida corporation, intends to pursue the public purpose of furnishing water both for itself and for other users, including Dade County; whereas Bernhardt Farms, Inc., has pledged to undertake this activity on its own without resort to public funds; whereas South Florida suffers the clear and present danger of drought and a falling water table; and whereas Bernhardt Farms, Inc., has pledged to use the latest technology in desalination . . ."

Desalination.

Now there was a new one for me. Confusing as ever. First good old Guy Bernhardt outrages his neighbors by sucking their wells dry. And now he's going to turn salt water into gold.

"Desal," Charlie Riggs said.

"He's going to take salt water from the ocean and make fresh water?" I asked.

"More likely he's going to draw up brackish water from the Floridan Aquifer."

Doc Charlie Riggs knows most of what's worth knowing and a lot that isn't.

"I would agree," said Harrison Baker, fiddling with his mustache. I was in the presence of two old coots, and that didn't include my granny, who was filling mason jars with a clear liquid that surely did not come from the aquifer. We were on the porch of her old house in Islamorada. The sun was setting in the gulf, the palm fronds were slapping the tin roof, and all of us were a tinge overheated from the white lightning, which only stoked the fires of a tropical July day. "Salt water is too expensive to treat," Baker went on, "except when there's no other choice. On desert islands, that sort of thing."

"Then there's the salt byproduct and the question of disposal," Charlie Riggs added.

"Quite right," Baker said, taking a sip of Granny's moonshine. "Produce ten million gallons of water a day and you'll end up with over two million pounds of salt. You can't leave it on the ground or it will pollute the groundwater. You can't put it back in the ocean or it will destroy all life for a hundred miles."

He paused a moment, his eyes tearing, either from the thought of dying coral or the sting of Granny's liquor.

"But with the new technology," Charlie Riggs said, "once you recovered capital costs for construction, you could probably treat brackish water for the same price as fresh groundwater and produce far less brine than with seawater."

Baker nodded. "Reverse osmosis would be best."

Charlie sipped at his mason jar and seemed to agree.

I asked a few questions. I learned that reverse osmosis, like distillation, takes the water out of the salt, whereas electrodialysis and ion exchange take the salt out of the water. To oversimplify it, Charlie said with a look that implied I needed all the simplification I could get, all you need for osmosis is a lot of electricity, some high-pressure pumps, and a filter. And lots and lots of brackish water.

We get our drinking water, Baker had already told me, from the Biscayne Aquifer, the layer of porous rock that sits just under the ground. Go deeper and you'll run into sediments about seven hundred feet thick. Below that is the Upper Floridan, containing brackish, highly mineralized water not suitable for drinking unless you remove the salt.

"Some cities have done it," Baker said, turning to me, "but no private party ever has, not with a plant like you're describing, not on that scale."

"So what's Guy Bernhardt going to do with all the water he's going to produce?" Charlie Riggs asked.

I knew, of course, but my granny was quicker. "Unless he's a dang fool," she said, "he's gonna sell it."

17

I Am a Man

I didn't tell Chrissy Bernhardt where we were going. I didn't want her to have time to call Dr. Schein, or her brother, or anyone else who might have told her what to do.

Like take a pill raising her blood pressure.

I figured she wouldn't know the other tricks the cons are so good at. Biting the tongue. Sticking a nail in the shoe.

So I wasn't playing straight with her. Because I was afraid she wasn't playing straight with me.

A lawyer needs to know the truth.

No, strike that. I can't speak for my brethren. *I* need to know the truth.

Maybe it's a failing. Maybe I'd be better off not knowing. Maybe I should just take whatever gift horse Schein was riding. But I couldn't. I don't know why, I just couldn't.

With the top down, I aimed the Olds 442 west on the MacArthur Causeway, caught the connector north onto I-95, then swung west again on the Miami Dolphin Expressway. Though I didn't pour the asphalt, I always took a bit of pride in the highway, especially when passing the Orange Bowl, the faded lady on our left.

"Where are we going?" Chrissy asked.

"To see an old friend."

I got off at Le Jeune Road, just east of the airport, and headed north to Okeechobee Road, turning left along the old Miami Canal. West of the canal was Miami Springs. East was Hialeah, once a haven for Georgia crackers and now overwhelmingly Hispanic. I hung a right on Palm Avenue, drove a few blocks into a neighborhood of single-story stucco homes, many with statues of the Virgin Mary planted along with the hibiscus, and pulled up in front of a pink house with an orange barrel-tile roof.

"Here?" Chrissy asked.

"Here."

"Your friend has an odd sense of color combinations."

"The house belongs to an ex-cop," I said, as if that explained it.

Tony Cuevas was a lifelong bachelor. He had bought the house when he retired from the Sheriff's Department, and if you asked him the color, he probably wouldn't have a clue.

On the way to the front door, Chrissy stopped and looked at me. "So why are we here?"

She was wearing spandex shorts and a halter top, and when I grabbed her shoulders, her skin was warm from the sun. I pulled her close to me and looked into those green, luminous eyes. "It's important that I treat you like a client, and not like . . ."

"A lover, a woman . . . a person," she helped out.

"Yeah, sort of. If we hadn't gotten involved, this would be easy."

"What, Jake? What would be easy?" Exasperated now.

"In preparing for trial, in planning strategy, lawyers sometimes ask their clients to . . ."

I couldn't say it.

The door opened before we could knock. Tony Cuevas stood there, a little paunchier than when he'd worked Internal Affairs. He still wore the short-sleeved shirt and tie. "Hello, Jake," he said. "You look like shit."

"Thank you, Tony."

He smiled pleasantly at Chrissy. "Hello, Miss Bernhardt. Let me tell you what you need to know about your polygraph exam."

Chrissy sat in a hard wooden chair, her eyes blazing at me. A blood pressure cuff was wrapped around her right arm, pneumograph tubes circling her chest and abdomen. Electrodes were attached to two fingers of her left hand. She sat on an inflatable rubber bladder and leaned back in the chair against another one.

"Just relax," I said.

"Go to hell!" Chrissy responded, and Tony's eyebrows shot up as he watched five pens on the chart scrawl a steep mountain.

"Actually, it is important that we stabilize your blood pressure," Tony said.

"Get him out of here," she commanded.

Him was me.

I wanted to say something. Something about how I needed to know the truth and how my feelings for her wouldn't change even if she was a cold-blooded murderer. But the words didn't come. Retreating in silence, feeling cowardly and deceptive, I walked into the screened Florida room, where a paddle fan clunked out of plumb over my head.

We are not all smart in all things. Left brain, right brain. A writer of sonnets may not be able to adjust a carburetor. A physicist may be incapable of constructing a simple sentence with subject and verb. I am moderately proficient in a number of fields. I can sense the location of the lurking bonefish. I can lead a hostile, perjurious witness into a humiliating mass of contradictions. I can predict run or pass from whether the offensive tackle leans forward or backward in his three-point stance.

But with a woman, my wiring shorts out. My senses respond to the physical and the chemical, the scent and sheen of her. Evil could not possibly reside in the form of this angel, could it? Sure, I'm politically incorrect. I'm retro, a caveman.

I admit it.

I confess.

Nolo contendere. Guilty as charged. I am, Your Honor, the lowest of the species, still wet from the swamp, tracks of webbed feet fossilized in the mud. I am a Man.

Through the open door, I could hear Tony's soothing voice. "Let's just chat a while."

He asked several innocuous questions about Chrissy's background and schooling, the names of her pets, whether she enjoyed skiing or surfing. At the same time, he fiddled with the cardioamplifier and the galvanic skin monitor. Chrissy doubtless thought the test hadn't even begun, but it had.

The neutral questions set the parameters for the lower range of blood pressure, respiration, and perspiration. They also set the stage for the control question, an attempt to elicit a lie.

"Have you ever smoked marijuana?" Tony Cuevas asked.

"Sure."

"Have you ever used cocaine?"

"That, too."

Tony paused, and I knew he was still searching for the little lie that could help uncover the big one.

"Did you ever have sex with more than one person at a time?"

"I worked in Paris," Chrissy said. "Surely you've heard of ménage à trois."

"Is that a yes? Did you ever have sex with more than one person at a time?"

"Does a schizophrenic boyfriend count?"

"Miss Bernhardt." Firmly now.

"All right, yes! I had sex with two people, and it wasn't twice the fun. I was playing with nose candy at the time, a couple of bumps a night. It was Paris, and I was nineteen."

"Have you ever had sex with a woman?"

"I've tried a lot of things."

Calmly, never changing his inflection, "Is that a yes?"

"Yes! I've had sex with a woman. That's related to your *last* question. In fact, it's redundant."

Whatever her responses to the big questions, it was hard as hell to get Chrissy to lie about the little ones.

"Have you ever had sex in return for money?"

"Modeling's a form of prostitution."

"Ms. Bernhardt, please answer the question."

"One time on a test shoot, an Italian photographer stripped naked. We were in his hotel room. As he shot me, he jerked off. He was very famous. You would know his name. Well, maybe *you* wouldn't, but believe me, he was big-time, and all the girls knew he liked to get off during a shoot, but he'd never touch you."

"Ms. Bernhardt, have you ever had sex in return for money?"

"No, but I've been offered. A lot!"

"Please confine your answers to yes or no."

"Sure."

"Have you ever used heroin?"

A pause. "I thought we were done with the drug questions."

"Have you ever used heroin?"

After a moment, "No."

A longer pause from Tony, and I knew he had his control question. He was letting the physiological reactions die before getting to the heart of it. I was thinking about her lie. She had told me she had been a ''chipper'' in Paris, occasionally smoking a potent combination of heroin and cocaine, but she'd given it up without becoming addicted. Still, the stigma prevented her from admitting it to a total stranger. The sexual improprieties, I guessed, were mere peccadilloes compared to smoking smack.

Tony started up again. ''Did your father have sexual relations with you when you were a minor?''

A soft ''Yes.''

I knew Tony was watching the squiggles. If the reaction to the little lie about not using heroin was greater than the reaction to the question about her father, she was telling the truth. If the reaction to the relevant question was greater, her concern about it meant she was probably lying.

''Did you kill your father?''

''Yes.'' An obvious answer to a neutral question.

''Did you kill him because he had sex with you as a child?''

''Yes.''

''Did you tell Jake Lassiter the truth about everything?''

''Does anybody tell the truth about everything?'' she said, and I heard the sound of the tape tearing off skin, then tubes crashing against the terrazzo floor as Chrissy stood and ran for the door.

18

Hell on Earth

The winds shifted to the southeast, bringing the humid Caribbean air, then died altogether. Days were broiling, nights stifling, and my little house felt like a hamper filled with sweat socks. The temperature soared, thunderheads formed over the Glades, and afternoon squalls rolled in from the west, a hard, pounding rain that did not cool the air. Steam rose from the pavement. Hell on earth.

Summer in South Florida starts early and ends late. This year, a dozen tropical storms and hurricanes chugged through the Atlantic and Caribbean, swirling up clouds, then breaking off to the northwest, skimming the coast, or heading due west across the Yucatán. Each time a storm came within a thousand miles, our breathless TV reporters stirred up memories of Andrew's flattened buildings, scaring the bejesus out of us. Just as gullible as my neighbors, I stood in line at the supermarket for bottled water and flashlight batteries, and because I had read that chick-peas are an excellent source of protein, my cupboard was now chock-full of them.

My little house in the South Grove is made of coral rock two feet thick, and it has withstood every hurricane from 1926 onward. If it is blown down, there won't be anything left standing in Dade County, and don't crack wise by saying that's not such a bad idea.

With the summer, the southeasterly breezes are too light for windsurfing, especially if you weigh more than a ballerina. I carted the board out to Key Biscayne a few times to catch the tail ends of gusty thunderstorms, but I've never been entirely comfortable on the water with a sixteen-foot-high mast that doubles as a lightning rod.

One day in August, the water slate-gray in a pelting rainstorm, I cruised on a broad reach off Virginia Key. I was hooked into the harness, leaning back against the weight of the sail, enjoying the sheer pleasure of speed, tasting the salty spray as the board chop-hopped past the reef. A disk-shaped Atlantic ray swam alongside, looking like some prehistoric beast, its winglike pectoral fins undulating, propelling it just below the waterline. I watched until the ray disappeared in the foam of a roller.

A few years ago, when I missed a jibe and landed ass-over-elbows next to the board, I was trying to waterstart, lying under the sail on my back like a beached turtle, when my arm caught fire. At least that's what it felt like, the spiny tail of a southern stingray wrapping itself around my wrist. The venomous sting left me with a scar that looks like a bracelet melted into my skin.

Then there are the sharks. It's hard to windsurf any distance from shore and not see a few. The Tourist and Convention Authority doesn't advertise it, but schools of tiger sharks, lemon sharks, and many of their cousins feed in schools just a few hundred yards off our beaches. I've enjoyed swimming and boardsailing in the Miami Beach surf for years, and it's still a thrill to paddle over a nurse shark lying motionless on the bottom in five feet of water.

With our sea creatures—barracuda, sharks, morays, jellyfish, Portuguese men-of-war, sea urchins, and stinging corals—it's a wonder more tourists don't end up in the emergency room.

So this day, as the ray squooshed by me and vanished in the vast, deadly sea, I thought about the other dangerous creatures in my life. Guy Bernhardt was paying the bills on time, calling me with pep talks about the case, doing everything except sending me notes with little smiling faces. Dr. Schein answered all my questions as I prepared for trial. He seemed eager to testify to the veracity of Chrissy's repressed memories, as well as the likelihood of her diminished mental state when she pulled the trigger—three times. Chrissy wouldn't talk to me at all, except in the most perfunctory way about the case. The personal relationship was over, tanked by the polygraph exam.

"I've never felt so betrayed," she told me as we sat across from each other in my conference room, separated by a mountain of files and a gulf of wounded feelings. I thought the statement was a bit overdone, especially from someone who claimed she'd been sexually molested by her father. Still, who was I to tell her what she should be feeling?

Tony Cuevas called to say what I already knew. Chrissy had passed the polygraph test. "So her father sexually abused her," I said.

"She thinks he did," Tony said. "She remembers it."

All right, she wasn't lying. But memories can be wrong. I remembered everything Dr. Millie Santiago had told me. Or was it everything?

By day, I prepared for trial—interviewing witnesses; gathering boxes of exhibits; deposing cops, bystanders, paramedics, doctors, nurses, and the assistant medical examiner. By night, I wandered around the Grove, avoiding Cocowalk with its teens and tourists, its guys with boa constrictors around their necks or macaws on their shoulders. In my time, I have gone to great lengths to attract women, but being strangled by a reptile or shit on by a bird is not my idea of foreplay. I'd head to the Taurus, the only bar in the Grove that's older than I am. It's a brew-

and-burger place in a quiche-and-cappuccino world, and I like it there. I'd have a couple of drafts, shoot some blow darts on the patio, tell harmless lies to various women, all the time wondering just what the hell was going on. Swimming through the surf of the upcoming murder trial, I had the gnawing feeling that I had yet to see the shark lurking on the ocean floor.

Summer turned to fall, not that you would know it. Tropical depressions still formed in the Atlantic. Our news boys and girls still went agog at the prospect of every gale. The night air in the Grove was heavy with the scents of jasmine and hibiscus. An occasional cold front made its way south, always petering out in northern Florida, but clocking the winds around and reducing our humidity.

I spent interminable days in the sadly misnamed Justice Building, a seven-story structure attached to the county jail by an overhead tunnel, an umbilical cord through which prisoners were force-fed into the so-called justice system.

We get the idea from books and television that the courthouse is a theater, the trial a play. The better analogy is a huge tent with a three-ring circus inside. The judge is the ringmaster, wielding his chair, cracking his whip, forcing the lions onto their haunches in mock-serious poses of respect. We rise when the judge enters and exits, and we beg for permission before we speak. The judge feeds us when we are good, chastises us when we are bad, and either way we bow our heads in meek gratitude.

In any given courtroom on any given Monday morning, the performers are not preparing for O. J. Simpson or the Menendez brothers. Not a trial of the century or even of the week. Hundreds of everyday cases flow along the conveyor belt of justice, dozens of bored inspectors picking them off, tossing them into this box or that for handling.

The system, both civil and criminal, intervenes when society has broken down. A wrong has been committed, or at least alleged. Offended at this breach of order, the system devises ways to make the offender pay, with either money or liberty. Like watching sausages or laws being made, observing the grist being milled in the courthouse is not an appetizing sight.

If we could peel off the outer wall of the Justice Building, as Hurricane Andrew did to several condos just south of here, we would see a beehive buzzing with activity. Defendants stream into courtrooms from their holding cells; dark-suited lawyers slouch against the bar, whispering their deals or their golf scores; cops bleary-eyes from the graveyard shift sip coffee in the corridors, their holsters emptied in respect to this place of constitutional reverence; robed judges in their high chairs listen as the endless flow of humanity streams by them: victims, witnesses, defendants, and the prosecutors and defense lawyers, engaged in an obligatory conspiracy to dispose of cases with dismissals, plea bargains, and reduced sentences, lest the entire system crunch to a halt.

In a dozen governmental offices, other anonymous functionaries push the paper and store the bytes that record the comings and goings of a world run amok. Stenographers, probation officers, bailiffs, translators, clerks, plus the girlfriends, mothers, and wives of the defendants themselves, bit players in the sagas that unfold under the pretentious and misleading sign that adorns each courtroom: WE WHO LABOR HERE SEEK ONLY TRUTH.

If we moved our camera close to the shaved-off walls, if our microphone picked up the whispers and cries, what would we see, what would we hear? The rap of a guard's nightstick on the holding cell's bars, the muttered curses of the inmates, the whining entreaty to a prosecutor of a defense lawyer (''No way we agree to three years minman'') refusing to accept the consequences of a plea with a minimum mandatory sentence, the mechanical drone of the judge accepting a guilty plea, finding a defendant "alert and intelligent," which, if true, would probably preclude his being there in the first place.

I have spent too much time in this building, too much time listening to the presumably innocent, hearing fanciful tales of alibis, of being in the wrong car at the wrong time, of guns that fire without triggers being pulled, of lying cops, thieving partners, and cheating wives. My clients are the put upon, the wrongfully accused, victims themselves, and they have an excuse for everything.

Now I had a client I desperately wanted to believe, wanted to help.

But did I? Could I?

19

I Hate Surprises

I was doing what I always do the day before trial, trying to figure out what I'd forgotten to do. I thumbed through the pleadings, skimmed the deposition summaries, looked for the tenth time at the state's exhibit list, and sketched out some ideas for my opening statement. I was so lost in the file that I didn't notice Cindy slip into my office until she dropped a three-page faxed document under my nose.

"Just came in from the state attorney's office," she said.

I took a look. "What the hell's Abe doing?"

On cue, the phone rang on the private line. I picked it up, and Abe Socolow barked his name. Life is like that sometimes. But this was no coincidence.

"Jake, you're gonna get a supplemental witness list, if you haven't already," he said.

"I'm looking at it right now," I told him. "What bullshit! It's the eve of trial."

"Only two new names, and I'll make them available for depo during recesses," he said quickly.

I scanned the document. Two witnesses I'd never heard of, one with a Rome address, the other Hampshire, England. "Who the hell are Luciano Faviola and Martin Kent?"

174

"Ex-boyfriends of your client. Four years ago, she ran over Kent in his own Jaguar, or at least tried to. Pulled a gun on him, too, but never fired. Faviola she tried to kill with a handgun two years ago in Italy. Fired twice, missed both times."

"So what?" I said, angry at Abe, but twice as angry at Chrissy for not telling me. "I punched out a tight end for the Jets. You gonna bring that up, too?"

"Under the *Williams* rule, Jake, we've got a pattern of misconduct."

"The hell you do! This isn't a case where a wife killed five husbands in a row with arsenic in the omelets. This is a bullshit attempt to prejudice the jury with irrelevant facts, if they're facts at all."

"It's all true. I'll get you the police reports by courier."

I wanted to say a few choice expletives to my old buddy Abe, but Cindy was signaling me that I was wanted on another line.

It was Guy Bernhardt. Something had come up. Something important. Could I get there right away?

I had never been in Guy Bernhardt's den. Oh, I had *looked* into the den through the jalousie windows. Now I peeked out the window into the rosebushes and Spanish bayonet shrubs where I had once lurked. Sensing Bernhardt's glance, I looked guiltily back at the boar's head mounted on the wall.

"You like to hunt?" I asked pleasantly.

"No, that was Pop's hobby. Nailed that one up in the forest north of Sopchoppy. Big bastard had already gutted two hounds." Guy winked at me. "The boar, that is. Not my pop."

Dr. Lawrence Schein sat on a leather sofa next to me, holding a glass of bourbon, idly swirling the ice cubes around in his glass.

"Those antlers came off a buck Pop shot up in Mon-

tana,'' Guy said, pointing at the buck on the other wall.
''Me, I never cared much for guns or killing living things.
I'm a grower. I create life.''

''Like a god,'' Lawrence Schein said. His loopy smile
was the giveaway. He'd been putting away bourbon long
before I arrived.

''You're a man who likes a beer, aren't you?'' Guy
asked, looking my way.

''Sometimes two or three,'' I answered.

He bent down at the bar, opened a little refrigerator, and
pulled out a large green bottle with a porcelain stopper.
''Grolsch, right?''

''How'd you know?''

He laughed. ''I do my research.''

Guy brought my beer and settled down on the sofa with
his own bourbon, straight up. No mango daiquiris tonight.
Bourbon and beer for the menfolk. He was chewing on an
unlit cigar, a fat Bolívar from Havana. I recognized the
Belicosos Finos, a 52-gauge number my teammates and I
used to smoke Sunday nights after victories. Hell, after
losses, too. Overhead, the paddle fan swished through the
air. Outside, the trees were bare, stripped of their fruit, and
bedding down for the coming winter.

''Did you two ask me down here to help me pick a jury
or just to have a drink?''

''Neither one, actually,'' Guy Bernhardt said, fiddling
with the stitching on his pale gray guayabera. ''Larry
wants to share some new evidence with you.''

''New evidence? The night before trial, and you've
found some new evidence?''

''The missing tape,'' Schein said matter-of-factly.

''What missing tape?'' I asked, louder than I intended.

''Oh, it wasn't missing, really. I'd turned off the recorder on the last session. But the backup continued rolling.''

''You didn't tell me about a backup.''

He sipped at the bourbon. "No, that would have spoiled the surprise." He giggled. It must have been a four-lap head start with the liquor.

I hate surprises. There was no sound in the room but the incessant whoosh and whir of the paddle fan. I studied Lawrence Schein. His shaved head was showing black bristles above the ears, and his goatee needed trimming. I was going to have to tell my star witness to clean up his act and lay off the bourbon. But first I had to figure out if he was still my star witness.

"You want to tell me about it?" I asked finally.

"Actually," Guy Bernhardt said, "we thought you'd like to hear it. What's the expression, something like a picture is worth a thousand words?"

"*Res ipsa loquitur,*" I said, thinking of Charlie Riggs. "The thing speaks for itself."

"Oh, it does," Bernhardt said. "It surely does."

"I've thought some more about what we discussed yesterday." Chrissy's voice.

"The need for goals?" Schein. I'd heard all this before.

"No. What we talked about afterward."

There was a pause.

"Oh, that."

"I've made a decision that you're not going to like," Chrissy said on the tape.

"Maybe you shouldn't tell me."

This time, it sounded even more ominous.

"But I've told you everything else. I can't imagine not telling you first."

"All right then. But first, let me . . ."

The sound of papers rustling and a chair squeaking and a *click*. I'd heard that all before. But then, something new.

"Is it off?" Chrissy's voice.

"It's off," Schein said.

"Well, like I said, I was thinking . . ."

"Yes?"

"I've bought a gun."

"I thought you were just going to visualize it."

"No. That's not enough. I've got to kill him."

"Figuratively? As part of therapy?"

"C'mon, Larry. That isn't what you meant. It couldn't be."

"I didn't mean anything. I raised certain hypothetical actions, all intended to be therapeutic."

"I decided last night. I couldn't sleep. I haven't slept through the night in weeks. I'm having nightmares and migraines."

"It's all part of the process. The pain is coming out."

"No, it's not. Maybe it will after . . ."

"After?"

"I'm going to kill my father for raping me. I'm going to kill him for ruining my life and for ruining Mom's."

"What would that solve?"

"I don't know. But I'm going to do it." A sob and then the sound of her sniffling. "You've shown me what the bastard did to me. Now I know why everything in my life has been so—"

"You'll be caught."

"I saw on *Oprah,* the other day, a woman who shot her husband after he'd beaten her. She got off."

"I don't know."

"Oh, Larry, don't look so depressed." A laugh that was mixed with a sob. "That's funny, isn't it? I mean, you're treating me, and I say you're depressed."

"You know I can't endorse what you're planning."

"You can't stop me either."

"I'm not even sure you're serious. Most people never act on their revenge fantasies."

"You've helped me so much," she said. "I'll just be so glad when it's over."

"What, therapy?"

"No, Larry, when the bastard is dead."

There was the clink of ice against glass. Guy Bernhardt took a sip of bourbon and waited for me to say something. Larry Schein cupped his glass between his trembling hands. Bernhardt studied me with a wry smile. "What do you think of your precious client now?"

I couldn't speak. I couldn't move. A dozen cinder blocks sat on each shoulder.

She'd lied to me.

How many times had I caught a witness in a lie, then turned to the jury? *If she lied about one thing, she's lied about others. How can you trust anything she told you?*

What else had Chrissy lied about? What whispers in my darkened bedroom were part of a grand plan?

After a moment, I said, "You'll go to jail, Schein. The DPR will pull your license, and you'll go straight to jail."

Schein laughed nervously. "For what?" I wanted to jam those ice cubes down his throat.

"Conspiracy to commit murder, obstruction of justice, perjury, and a few other things Socolow will come up with."

"Let's examine that," Bernhardt said in a condescending tone. It was clear who was calling the shots. "Larry, what about it?"

"I haven't testified yet, so there's certainly no perjury," he said carefully. "I may have misled you by not producing the tape earlier, but misleading a defense lawyer is hardly obstruction of justice."

"Hell, no!" Bernhardt barked out a laugh. "It furthers justice."

"As for the conspiracy," Schein continued, "I never dreamed my patient would act out her fantasy of killing her father, and I certainly didn't encourage it."

"Fantasy? She said she bought a gun. She said she would kill him."

"Role playing. Chrissy as avenging angel. That was merely part of the therapy. At least, that's what I considered it. Unfortunately, it would appear that Chrissy played me for the fool. She planned the murder all along."

"Surprising the shit out of you two, right?"

"Truly, I'm shocked at the outcome," Schein said in a performance that would have gotten him tossed out of a high school drama class. "I had thought the therapy was coming along so well. Perhaps the estate could sue me for not warning Harry that Chrissy was threatening him. But the law is murky in that area, isn't it, Jake? In a conflict between a therapist's duty to his patient and to third parties, the evidence has to be quite overwhelming to justify a betrayal of a patient's confidence. I believe I'm on firm legal ground both criminally and civilly. The state attorney won't seek to prosecute after convicting your client. They do like to close their files, don't they?" He turned to Guy Bernhardt with a little smile. "And I don't think Guy's going to sue me."

Bernhardt grinned back and downed his drink.

"Of course he won't!" I yelled. "He's going to *pay* you!"

It was coming into focus now. How could I have been so stupid? All this time it had troubled me that Guy Bernhardt was helping the woman who had killed his father. But of course, he wasn't helping her at all.

"You planned to kill your father, and you tricked poor Chrissy into doing it," I said.

"Poor Chrissy?" Guy mused. "Poor little rich girl. Everyone was always so worried about her."

"Is that what this is about, your jealousy, your hatred of her?"

"That isn't it at all," Schein said.

"Shut up, Larry." Bernhardt pointed his cigar at his

buddy, and then at me. "Lassiter, you don't have any proof to back up these wild accusations. In fact, the only proof is that my darling half sister shot and killed my father in front of a couple hundred witnesses after being tape-recorded as saying she would do just that."

"You set her up!" I thundered. "You had this fleabag shrink plant false memories in an emotionally troubled young woman, then you had her do your dirty work. And you set me up, too. You had Rusty MacLean invite me to Paranoia that night. You wanted me there, to see her, maybe even to fall for her. But you wanted something else, too. You wanted me to lose her case."

Bernhardt allowed himself a little smile. "Do you know what Rusty said about you?"

"Probably that I was too slow to cover the flanker over the middle and I was dumb enough to fall for that repressed-memory garbage."

Bernhardt poured himself another bourbon and came back to his chair without offering me a second beer. "Actually, he said you were smarter than you look."

"No, I'm dumber than dogshit. You suckered me. It's the night before trial and I've got no defenses. Not temporary insanity, not posttraumatic stress disorder, not some blackout. I've got nothing, and even if I wanted to plead Chrissy to manslaughter, Socolow wouldn't take it. Why should he? He's got murder one, so he's not gonna offer a deal. And you figured all that out. Because with a manslaughter conviction, Chrissy could still inherit from her father's estate. But murder's different. It would all go to you, just like you planned all along. You got her to do your dirty work and then tanked her case."

"To the contrary. On the one hand, I am enraged that Christina killed Pop. On the other hand, I love her as my blood kin and pity her. I am conflicted. I am suffering from . . . what is it, Larry?

"Cognitive dissonance," Lawrence Schein said.

"Cognitive bullshit!" I said.

"Your problems, on the other hand, are more immediate, your options more limited," Bernhardt said. "Especially since Rusty also told us you were an essentially honest lawyer."

"If that's not an oxymoron," Schein said.

Bernhardt ignored the doctor and kept going. "When Rusty was a sports agent, he got in a dispute with an athlete over commissions. There was a rough draft of a contract that the athlete had signed by mistake. Rusty wanted to testify it was the operative contract. You tore it up."

"It would have been a fraud," I said. "I don't lie to the court or let a client do it."

"How noble," Bernhardt said. "Subsequently, you lost. Without the phony contract, you had no case."

"Just as you'll lose this one," Schein said. I was beginning to think Bernhardt kept him around as a Greek chorus.

"Plead her to second degree," Bernhardt said, making it sound like an order. "Twenty years, out in twelve. Of course, she still forfeits her share of the estate."

"And if I don't?"

"Socolow gets the tape," Bernhardt said evenly. "Christina will be convicted of first-degree murder, life without parole."

"You really have no choice," Schein said, his courage bolstered by his bourbon. "Once the tape is played, it's over. I couldn't help you even if I wanted to. God couldn't help you. Just like with Rusty, you've got no case."

"There's one difference," I said with just enough hostility to make Schein sit up a little straighter. "I never loved Rusty."

20

Her Lawyer and Her Lover

A tear streaked down my cheek as I drove north from Bernhardt's farm toward Miami Beach.

Then another tear.

I wasn't embarrassed. I wasn't ashamed.

I am a big tough guy. I have bricklayer's shoulders and an acre of chest. I played the game with the oblong spheroid in knickers and plastic hats at the highest level, even if my talent was less than my desire. When I broke my nose on an opening kickoff—catching an elbow through the face mask—I stuffed cotton in each nostril to stanch the blood and hustled downfield on the punt return team three plays later.

I am used to physical pain and accept it without complaint.

Emotional pain is different.

My father was killed in a barroom brawl when I was ten. He was a shrimper, and I remember his strong, coarse hands and the smell of his clothes, caked with salt and fish guts. We would wrestle in the shallow water of Buttonwood Sound off Key Largo. He could hold a fishing rod in one hand and toss me over his shoulder with the other. I marveled at his strength and took comfort in his arms.

He was not afraid to show emotion and told me—more than once—that he loved me. I miss him terribly.

One day, I saw my father sitting alone on the porch of our weather-beaten cracker house with the tin roof. The sun was setting in the gulf, the flat water shimmering orange with bursts of silver. Dad was sipping Granny's moonshine from a mason jar, and at first I thought the alcohol was wringing tears from his eyes. But it wasn't the booze. It was something with Mother, and though it was left unsaid, I knew. A few moments later, the screen door banged open, and my mother darted out of the house and flew off the porch, a blur of bleached-blond hair and a tight sleeveless dress with a pattern of red hibiscus, a look Granny called "all tramped up." A moment later, the old Plymouth kicked up shells in the driveway, then tore down U.S. 1. I crawled onto my father's lap, and he wrapped his arms around me, his chin resting on top of my head, and I heard him sob.

About a year later, a man in a tavern shoved a knife through my father's heart. Granny never told me, but I always suspected Dad was defending my mother's honor, such as it was. But that could be my imagination. It could have been an argument over a poker debt, a football game, or who had the right to shrimp Card Sound.

My mother took off for Oklahoma with a roughneck who had wintered in a trailer park near Marathon. His name was Conklin, and though he left without marrying my mother, he was kind enough to leave her something to remember him by: a daughter, Janet. Mom is long dead, Janet is somewhere in drug rehab, and her son, Kip, now bunks with me. Granny also pitches in, figuring if she raised me from a pup, she can do it again.

I tried to tell Kip about my mother, his grandmother, and even though I sugar-coated it—"a real friendly blonde with a big laugh who loved to play Elvis on the jukebox of the Poachers' Inn and Saloon"—Kip pegged her.

"Sounds like Jessica Lange in *Blue Sky*," he said.

I told him about my father, too. How a good, strong man can weep, too.

"I never cry," Kip said, and it was true. He had been abandoned and hurt, and now he had erected a wall to protect himself from more pain.

"Don't you ever get sad?" I asked him.

"Nope. Never."

"When I was your age, I read a book that made me cry," I told him.

"A book?"

"Yeah, lots of pages with two covers on it."

"I know what books are, Uncle Jake. They must have been great before the Internet and a hundred movie channels on the satellite."

"It was called *The Diary of a Young Girl,* by Anne Frank."

"I know it, Uncle Jake. I saw the movie. I thought the TV was fried until I figured out it was in black and white." The shadow of a thought wrinkled his forehead. "It was real sad."

"The saddest story ever."

"Okay, is that the uncle-gram for today?"

"Not just that. One time, on the practice field at Penn State, a row of thunderheads moved into the valley. Big steel-gray clouds were just hanging over the field, but toward the mountains, it was clear and sunny. It started raining, pouring on us, and in the distance was the brightest rainbow I've ever seen."

"Yeah?"

"It brought tears to my eyes."

"Why?"

"I'm not sure. Maybe because it made me think of my father. I wished he could have seen it. He loved natural beauty. Dolphins jumping together, a waterspout on the bay, sunset in the gulf."

"What's your point, Uncle Jake?"

"It's okay to cry. It's okay to show your emotions." I tried to think of an example. "Let's say you're watching a sad movie—"

"Like *Terms of Endearment* where Debra Winger dies."

"Yeah. It's okay to bawl your eyes out if you want to."

"Uh-huh."

"Or if something makes you sad, you can talk about it with your uncle Jake."

It was all he could do to keep from rolling his eyes. "Sure."

"Anything you want to talk about right now?"

"No thanks, Uncle Jake, but I'm glad we had this little talk."

My ancient convertible navigated the interstate, exited in downtown Miami, then picked up the MacArthur Causeway to Miami Beach. As I sped north on Alton Road, passing kosher delis, funeral homes, and Rollerblade shops, the wind finally dried my tears. I turned right on Eleventh Street, passed Flamingo Park, and headed toward Ocean Drive.

The apartment building had rounded corners, porthole windows, a porch with terrazzo floors, and decorative nautical pipe railings. The walls had recently been painted a color I would call Pepto-Bismol pink but the renovation artist probably described in more decorous terms. Concrete eyebrows hung over the casement windows, and a spire stuck out of the roof like the mast of a fine sailing ship. Tour guides would call the place Art Deco, or Streamline Moderne, but to us locals, it's just an old stucco building with a fresh coat of paint.

I pounded on the door for a full minute before a light came on. "Chrissy, it's me, Jake."

She opened the door and peered at me, sleepy-eyed. "Do you know what time it is?"

"Why do people always say that when you wake them up? Why not 'It's three-thirty-seven A.M. Do you know where your brains are?' "

"Jake, aren't we due in court this morning?"

I pushed through the door and grabbed her. She was wearing a Dolphins jersey and nothing else. Number 13. I was relatively certain that Dan Marino, a solid family man, was not hiding in the closet. I had her by the shoulders and pulled her close. She had lied to me. Maybe Schein had implanted false memories or maybe the memories were real. It didn't matter. She had lied to me, her lawyer and her lover.

Now I wanted to look into those flinty green eyes. I wanted to see her blink when she lied again. I wanted to see her cry.

"Your eyes are bloodshot," she said. "Have you been drinking?" She looked frightened. Good.

"We have about five hours," I said. "I want the truth." I thought about Jack Nicholson and Tom Cruise. Could I handle the truth?

"What do you mean?"

"I want to know why you killed your father and what that slimy half brother of yours had to do with it. I want to know everything about Schein."

"Guy's not involved in this. Neither is Larry."

I squeezed her upper arms and pulled her close.

"Jake, you're hurting me."

"I've never hit a woman. I hate the cowardly cretins that do. But if you were a man, right now I'd knock you through that wall and kick your ass across Ocean Drive."

"Jake, you're acting crazy!"

I let her go and she pulled away.

"You thought you were being so smart," I said. "Well, your pal Schein taped you when you thought he wasn't.

He's got proof you planned to kill your father. No black-outs, no irresistible impulses. No nothing but a life behind bars.''

She blinked but she didn't cry.

"And here's another little surprise. Two characters named Faviola and Kent are getting expenses-paid vacations to Miami.''

"Luciano doesn't need the money," she said quietly. "Martin would do anything for a dollar.''

My look asked the question, which she quickly answered. "Luciano Faviola is an Italian playboy. He tried to rape me at a party when I was stoned.'' She shook her head and said bitterly, "I wish I'd killed him.''

"Perfect trial demeanor," I said sarcastically, "showing your tender, remorseful side. I'm sure the jury will have a lot of sympathy for a coke-snorting, spoiled bitch princess who carries a gun and cries rape at every opportunity.''

"Is that what you think I am?''

"It doesn't matter what I think.''

"It does to me," she said, her eyes tearing. She walked to the window and stared out at Ocean Drive. "Martin Kent was a playboy without a bankroll. He stole from me. He was just another one of my incredibly poor choices where men are concerned.''

She was talking about Kent, but was she thinking about me?

"Can they really testify?'' she asked.

"It's up to the judge. I'm more concerned about the tape. It's clearly admissible, and it's damning.''

For a moment she was silent. Then, speaking softly, she said, "If I tell you the truth, will you still help me?''

I didn't answer. I couldn't. I didn't know.

"My father did rape me, Jake. You must believe that.'' We sat at her kitchen table. Chrissy reached for a cigarette and lit it. "I had blocked it out and couldn't remember it.

I always had these vague feelings of uneasiness around my father. I knew he'd done something, but I didn't know what. Larry Schein brought it out under hypnosis. It's all true. All I lied about—left out, really—was that I planned to kill him. I planned it, and I told Larry.''

"Who has it on tape," I said. "He's the one who can send you away. If you'd told me, maybe there's something I could have done.''

"What would you have done?'' She exhaled, and a plume of cigarette smoke drifted toward the ceiling.

"I don't know. Something!''

Chrissy poured a second cup of coffee for each of us. Outside the kitchen window, the sun was blinking through thin streaks of clouds where the horizon touched the ocean. "I wanted to kill my father. I wanted to be cleansed, but I didn't want to go to prison. I'd done some reading. I knew about posttraumatic stress disorder. Damn it, Jake, I had it! I was just able to rationally decide what to do.''

"Rationally?''

"Yeah. What difference should it make if a woman blows away her abusive husband while he's beating her, or if she does it after sitting down and thinking about it? That's the only difference here. I thought about it for a while, then did it.''

"The difference,'' I said, "is between manslaughter and first-degree murder.''

"Then they should change the law.''

"Great, write your legislator.'' Chrissy's coffee was burning a hole in my gut and my mood wasn't improving. "Did Schein ever encourage you in this rational plan to kill your father?''

"Not in so many words. He did say something like my father's death could be therapeutic, but phrased real vaguely. He never used the word 'kill' or 'murder.' ''

"What about Guy? Did he know?''

"I certainly didn't tell him.''

"But Schein did! Don't you see? They wanted you to kill your father. They set you up with a phony defense, then trashed it the night before trial. They want you convicted."

"Why?"

"Money! Guy gets the entire estate and you spend the rest of your life in prison."

She wasn't rattled, and she still didn't cry. "That doesn't make any sense. Guy's rich enough."

"Some people never are. And there are other reasons, too. Guy never got over the fact that you were the pampered child. He probably hated your father for it."

"No. The first few years were tough on Guy—he was treated like hired help—but Daddy made it up to him. He brought Guy into the business, turned it over. It can't be that."

"Then what is it, Chrissy? If it's not money, if it's not anger, what's his motive?"

"I don't know."

"You have to know!" Losing my patience.

She angrily tossed the cigarette stub into her coffee cup. "You don't believe me. You never have. That's why you tricked me into taking the lie detector test."

"On a relative scale, that should rank somewhat lower than tricking you into committing a first-degree murder." She glared at me and I added, "If they really did trick you."

"Bastard! How can you defend me if you don't believe me?"

"I do it every day. It's my job."

"That's not the way I want it to be," she said, her tone more sad than angry.

"Fine, I'll ask the judge for permission to withdraw. If he grants it, you'll get a continuance. Maybe another lawyer can figure out—"

"No! I want you. I trust you, even if it's not reciprocal."

"I don't know how to try the case. I don't know how to win."

"Don't change anything. Play the tapes. I'll tell the jury I damn well planned it, and I'd do it again. Let Schein testify I planned to kill Daddy. Let's tell the truth."

"The truth?" The idea was so preposterous I just laughed.

"Isn't that what you wanted? Isn't that what you demanded in your holier-than-thou tone? Okay, Mr. Self-righteous. Let's take the truth and go with it."

"There are times," I said sadly, shaking my head, "when the truth will not set you free."

21

I Wanted Me

I sat in the cushioned chair in front of Judge Myron Stanger's desk. Freshly shaved, my hair still wet from the
shower, packaged in my sincere blue suit and burgundy
power tie, I almost looked like a lawyer, even with my
neck bulging out of my collar. Abe Socolow sat in the
leather chair next to me, his sallow complexion set off
nicely by his funereal black suit. A young woman sat next
to the judge, perched over her stenograph, awaiting the
words of jurisprudential wisdom, or at least semigram-
matical English, that are occasionally spoken in chambers.

On the sofa behind us all, beneath dozens of plaques
proclaiming His Honor's civic high-mindedness, sat
Chrissy, her legs demurely crossed. She was dressed in a
charcoal-gray suit over a white silk blouse that she once
wore in a TV commercial while playing a business executive with intestinal gas.

"Let me get this straight, Jake," Judge Stanger said.
"A hundred prospective jurors are cooling their heels in
the courtroom right now and you're asking to withdraw
from the case."

"That's correct, Your Honor."

"And you will not state the grounds for your motion to
withdraw?"

"I cannot, Your Honor, without prejudicing my client's case."

The judge fingered the latch on a cedar cigar box that occupied a prominent position on his desk. At Christmas, trial lawyers with spirit of giving delivered smuggled Cuban cigars to the judge. "That's not good enough, Jake."

"All I can say is that my client and I have irreconcilable differences as to the handling of the case."

"Hell, Jake, my wife and I have had irreconcilable differences for thirty years, but neither of us has cut and run."

Next to me, Abe Socolow tried to suppress a smile. He enjoyed seeing me squirm.

"It's not in the best interest of my client for me to represent her," I argued.

"That so?" The judge removed his yellow-tinted glasses from his bulbous nose and looked toward Chrissy Bernhardt. Myron Stanger had been a personal injury defense lawyer, representing the Southeast Railroad Company, which had an unfortunate habit of hiring alcoholic and color-blind engineers. After thirty-five years of wrongful-death and quadriplegia cases from railroad crossing collisions, Stanger, an avid Democratic party fund raiser, had called in a marker from the governor and been appointed to the bench. Trial lawyers generally liked him because he let them try their cases without too much interference. "How about it, Ms. Bernhardt? Would you be better off with a new lawyer?"

Chrissy seemed to pout, or was that her usual look? "No, Your Honor. I want Mr. Lassiter. I can't imagine anyone else defending me."

"Well, that's that," the judge announced, turning to the court reporter. "Motion to withdraw denied. Anything else before we pick a jury?"

"The defendant moves for a continuance," I said. "There is newly discovered evidence which I have not had an opportunity to fully investigate."

The judge scowled. "You really don't want to try this case, do you, Jake?" Without waiting for an answer, he turned to Socolow. "What's the state's position?"

"I don't know what can be so new," Socolow said with his barracuda's smile. "There is no issue as to the identity of the killer. Mr. Lassiter's had several months to prepare his psychobabble defense, and—"

"I resent that! Your Honor, would you admonish—"

The judge waved me off. "C'mon, Jake, you know that's just Abe's way of saying good morning. Now, why can't you try the case today?"

"Again, Your Honor, I cannot be more specific without prejudicing my client's case. I'll simply say that our main expert witness is . . ." I searched for the right word. "Unavailable."

Socolow snorted. "Unavailable or unhelpful?" He was enjoying this so much, I wanted to strangle him with his black silk tie.

"If forced to go to trial today," I said, "we may call Dr. Schein as an adverse witness because of his hostility to the defense. This is a new development, and we need time to prepare for this turn of events."

I hadn't seen Socolow smile so broadly since the last time one of the miscreants he had prosecuted was strapped into the hot seat at Raiford. "Sounds like Jake hasn't done his trial prep," he said, "but that's no grounds for a continuance."

"That's not fair, Your Honor," I protested. I hated displaying my wounds prior to trial, but I didn't have any choice. Besides, Socolow's case was so straightforward, it wouldn't matter. He'd put on the bartender and a couple of witnesses to the shooting, then a forensics guy who would discuss the prints on the gun and the powder marks on Chrissy's hands, the paramedics who'd taken Bernhardt to the hospital, the surgeon, the nurse, and an assistant medical examiner as to cause of death.

The state rests.

Call your first witness, Mr. Lassiter.

The defense calls Dr. Lawrence Schein. On second thought, just let me fall on my sword.

"You know, Jake, I tried a lot of cases in my day," the judge began. Like a lot of jurists, Myron Stanger enjoyed reminding the lawyers that, before he became Caesar, he'd been a gladiator. "And I know everything doesn't go the way you plan it. Hell, *nothing* goes the way you plan it. So you've got to prepare for the unexpected."

I nodded my deep appreciation of the old fart's hoary cliché.

"Witnesses disappear, die, or change their minds," the judge continued. "But I can't let the jury venire sit out there on its collective ass while I try to scrape up another trial for today. Now you boys were specially set, and—"

"But, Your Honor—" I interrupted, sounding whiny even to myself.

"No, listen up, both of you. When you two walk into the courtroom and see the venire, you're thinking jurors. But when I hand them certificates for doing their constitutional duty, do you know what I see?"

"Voters," I suggested.

The judge gave me a cautionary look. "Neighbors. Good honest citizens with a sense of values. I'm not going to mistreat them. Motion for continuance denied. Gentlemen, let's pick a jury."

Juries.

I've read books on how to pick them. I've hired psychologists, sociologists, and psychics. I've relied on Marvin the Maven, a retired shoe store owner from Pittsburgh, who told me to avoid men in polished wing tips—too conservative and respectful of authority—and go for women in sandals with red-painted toenails. "Their minds will be as open as their shoes," Marvin advised.

For Chrissy's case, I hired a psychologist to run a community attitudes survey. Without revealing the name of the case, Dr. Lester (Les Is More) Weiner mailed a questionnaire to several hundred demographically correct households. We learned to stay away from parents, especially those estranged from their adult children. We learned that accountants, marine biologists, meteorologists, and other scientific types would scoff at our defense. Not surprisingly, we learned that jurors who had gone through therapy would be preferable to ones who ridiculed mental health treatment. Anyone who derided psychiatry was out. Dr. Weiner advised that women would be more sympathetic to our case, but I disregarded the advice. Call me a chauvinist pig, but in my experience, women jurors are unkind to younger, thinner, sexier women litigants.

I wanted men who would fall in love with my client. In other words, I wanted me.

I am a regular guy. I don't wear an earring or a gold chain. I don't carry a pager or a purse. I don't belong to a private club or a mystic cult. I don't go to La Voile Rouge to smoke fancy cigars, and the next time some overweight stockbroker in suspenders and French cuffs drops ashes on me at a bar, I will jam his stinking stogie down his throat. There is no one so intolerant as a reformed sinner.

I consider myself a decent judge of character and knowledgeable in human relations, but I am constantly surprised in jury selection. I have a standing bet with the old bailiff, Clyde Thigpen—a pot of his conch chowder for a jar of Granny's swamp cabbage—as to the foreperson. I always pick the guy in the dark suit, but Clyde has seen thousands of trials, and he doesn't rely on clothing. He can sense the authority figure.

Sometimes prospective jurors are nervous. Just this morning, a member of the panel sought to be excused from our case. "My wife is about to become pregnant," he told the judge.

"I think he means she's about to deliver," I said.

"You're excused," Judge Stanger said. "Either way, you should be there."

Of course, we don't really select jurors. We try to eliminate those we don't want. Once, in a civil case, I ran out of peremptory challenges and couldn't evict a young guy with a Fu Manchu mustache who glared at me all through voir dire. He cleaned septic tanks for a living, which was the only thing we had in common. Whenever I looked at him, he cupped his chin in his hand with the middle finger extended. For a week, every time I glanced at the jury box, there he was in a work shirt emblazoned WE'RE THANKFUL FOR YOUR TANKFUL, shooting me the bird. When the jury came back in and he stood up as foreman, I started planning my appellate brief. But then the jury ruled for us, and when I shook his hand on the way out of the courtroom, I noticed the finger was frozen stiff. A construction accident, he said, when he caught me looking down at his hand. Things are not always as they seem, or, as Doc Riggs says, *non semper* something or other.

So now, with Chrissy sitting next to me, appearing demure and nonlethal, I looked at the panel of several dozen prospective jurors. It was the usual collection of schoolteachers, government workers, *Miami Herald* pressmen, American Airlines mechanics, housewives, and retirees, with an occasional college student thrown in. I've had juries with a lobster pot poacher, a nipple ring designer, a *santero* who chanted prayers to Babalu Aye during recess, and a cross-dressing doorman from a South Beach club, so today's group looked pretty normal.

I went through the motions of asking personal questions that I assured the panel were not meant to embarrass them. After determining that nearly everyone had been the victim of a crime but very few admitted to seeing a psychiatrist,

I started paying attention to body language, or kinesics, as Dr. Weiner calls it.

I watched for hands clasped in tension or arms crossed, closing me out. I watched for crossed ankles and hands squeezing the chair in a death grip. At the same time, I paid attention to my own gestures. ''Keep your palms open and friendly,'' Dr. Weiner always reminded me. ''Watch your proxemics, your space usage. You're too tall to get close to the rail. Your vertical power will intimidate the jurors. And don't put your hands on your hips. Taking up too much horizontal space is simply too authoritarian.''

Thanks a lot. Before hiring the ponytailed, tinted-lensed Dr. Les Weiner, I was content just to know my fly was zipped up.

So I did my friendly big-guy act, not getting too close, not taking up too much space, smiling, shucking and jiving, and trying to find six honest, sympathetic souls who would hear us out, whatever we might have to say. In the front row of the gallery, Marvin the Maven sat impassively, frowning at me whenever I leaned over to talk to my expensive hired gun. As I questioned the jurors, Dr. Weiner took notes when he wasn't thumbing through the latest yachting catalog. He kept his trawler, a forty-two-foot Krogen named *The Pleasure Principle,* docked at Dinner Key Marina in what he called his Freudian slip. The Krogen is a lot like me, a widebody that is slow but steady in rough seas and high winds. It is finished in rich teak and impresses the doc's women companions, who tend to be young, blond, and susceptible to strong margaritas and salty breezes.

It took all day to seat a jury. Then Judge Stanger gave the group his spiel, telling them not to talk about the case with each other or anyone else. They all nodded knowingly. They'd seen it all on TV a thousand times. In our courthouse, we call it Ito-izing the jury.

I stood and bowed slightly, trying to make eye contact,

as the jurors filed out of the courtroom. I would do the same at every recess and adjournment until the trial was over. Some looked at me and some didn't.

Then I took Chrissy Bernhardt by the arm and steered her out of the courtroom. I needed a drink, a good night's sleep, and a trial strategy, and at the moment I would have taken two out of three.

22

Chrissy, Chrissy, Chrissy

First thing in the morning, Judge Stanger gave his preliminary instructions, and the jurors leaned forward, listening intently. They're like that at the beginning. On edge,
wanting to do their duty. As the surroundings become
more familiar, as the lawyers wear out their welcome with
repetitious questions and obstreperous objections, jurors
kick back and daydream or doze. Sometimes I imagine
them as cartoon characters, scenes of bass fishing or sexual
liaisons filling little bubbles over their heads. Why not?
That's what occupies my mind when Abe Socolow is strut-
ting in front of the jury box or the judge is endlessly re-
peating his admonitions.

"The indictment is not evidence," Judge Stanger said,
"and should not be relied on by you as evidence of guilt."

He told the jurors that they were not permitted to infer
guilt if the defendant didn't testify. It's a standard instruction, and many times I won't put a client on the stand,
since most defendants will only muck it up. In one of my
first trials as an assistant public defender, the prosecutor
asked my client, "You say you're innocent, yet five people
swore they saw you steal a watch."

"So what?" my saintly client said. "I can produce a

hundred people who didn't see me steal it.''

When your client remains silent, the prosecution isn't permitted to comment on the failure to testify, and the judge repeats his Fifth Amendment instruction after closing argument. Still, I wonder what the jurors think. Even if they don't discuss it, aren't they saying to themselves, *If I was innocent, I'd sure as hell put my hand on the Good Book and tell the whole dang world*?

The judge ordered the jurors not to speculate about why the lawyers make their objections and what the answers would have been if the objections had been overruled. So silly. Try not thinking of a pink elephant. Whoops, can't do it. He told them that opening statement was not evidence, but rather each lawyer's version of what the evidence would show. He advised them not to discuss the case with anyone, including their families, friends, and presumably their pets. And then Honest Abe got up to talk.

''This is a simple case,'' Abe Socolow said. ''A man sits at the bar at the opening of a Miami Beach nightclub. His name is Harry Bernhardt, and he is minding his own business, enjoying the fruits of his labors. Harry is a hardworking man who has accomplished much with his life but has so much more to do. As he sips his drink, Harry has no idea it will be the last beverage he ever consumes.''

A little B-movie dialogue, I thought, and not strictly accurate if you count the Ringer's lactate IV at the hospital.

''Now, picture this, if you will,'' Abe continued. ''A young woman enters the club, and in front of dozens of witnesses pulls a gun from her Versace handbag.''

Versace. Abe's way of saying ''spoiled rich bitch.''

''And as Harry sits there, here comes this woman with the gun, walking toward him.''

Harry. Humanizing the victim. Making the jurors hold their breath, waiting as Abe cuts back and forth cinematically between villain and victim.

"The woman aims the gun at Harry, a Beretta 950, which was hidden in her handbag. Hidden from the security guard outside, hidden from Harry, hidden from the world, so that she could carry out this premeditated assassination. Harry has had no time to put his affairs in order, to say good-bye to friends and loved ones. He has not lived his three score and ten, and no voice has asked him, as Job was asked, 'Hast thou seen the doors of the shadow of death?' "

Job? A reminder that the prosecution has God on its side.

"The woman, *this* woman sitting here . . ."

Abe approached the defense table and pointed, his index finger a foot from Chrissy Bernhardt's nose. She didn't blink. She just sat there in her three-piece Calvin Klein suit, a big-buttoned V-neck jacket in steel-blue crepe and matching skirt, and a gray washed-silk blouse.

"This woman, Christina Bernhardt, aimed the gun at Harry Bernhardt, her *father,* and with malice and premeditation, she pulled the trigger. Not once, not twice . . ."

Thrice?

". . . but three times. Bang! Bang! Bang!"

Two jurors winced at the sound effects. The others didn't, perhaps because Abe's perpetual sinusitis muffled the shots like a silencer on a barrel.

"Harry was rushed to Mount Sinai Hospital, where heroic measures were undertaken to save his life. But two hours after surgery, he suffered cardiac arrest and died, his death the proximate result of the shooting. Unlike most trials, in this one there is no doubt as to any of this. You will hear testimony of eyewitnesses who will state under oath that Christina Bernhardt did, in fact, shoot her father. You will hear the testimony of the paramedic, the surgeon, a treating nurse, and the assistant medical examiner. You will hear that the cardiac arrest suffered by Harry Bernhardt was inextricably linked to and caused by the shooting, and therefore you will be compelled to find that Christina Bernhardt killed her father, and that she is guilty of murder in the first degree."

Abe went on for a while, advising the jury to pay keen attention to the witnesses, to follow all of Judge Stanger's instructions, and to listen carefully to Mr. Lassiter when he stood up for his opening statement. By raising his eyebrows and his voice just a bit, Abe made "carefully" sound like "skeptically." He thanked the good folks for their time, told them he'd move the case along quickly— implying that any delays were my fault—then sat down with a warm and gracious smile.

I stood and bowed slightly toward the judge. Behind me, I heard a press camera click, the sound not quite deadened despite the elaborate apparatus designed to silence it. The courtroom door creaked open, then banged shut. Shoes squealed on the tile floor, and someone in the first row coughed. I heard it all, just as I'd always heard the few cheers and many boos that greeted me in the stadium.

"May it please the court," I began, paying homage to five hundred years of English common law. Then I turned toward the jury. "Yesterday, I asked each of you if you would wait until all the evidence is in before making up your minds as to whether the state has proved its case beyond a reasonable doubt. You all said yes."

Jurors are an honest bunch. Remind them of their promises.

"That is important in every case, but crucial here, for this is *not* a simple case, though certain facts *are* undisputed. Chrissy Bernhardt did shoot her father, who did die later that night. But there will be issues as to Chrissy's intent and her mental state, issues that Mr. Socolow did not discuss with you."

And I won't either. Not in any detail anyway, because I still don't know what the hell to say.

"These issues are important because you cannot find

Chrissy guilty of first-degree murder without finding that she had the specific intent to kill, and that she formed that intent before acting and had that intent when she did act.''

"Objection, Your Honor." Socolow got to his feet. "Opening statement is no place to argue the law."

"I'm not arguing, Your Honor," I replied. "I'm just previewing a jury instruction."

"Overruled as long as the law is not misstated. But, Mr. Lassiter, the function of opening is to discuss the evidence, so move it along. I'm quite capable of telling the jurors the law at the appropriate time."

I decided to walk the fine line the judge drew for me. "When all the evidence is in, Judge Stanger will instruct you on the law. He will read you the legal definition of first-degree murder, and you will apply that legal standard to the evidence. The judge will tell you that to find Chrissy Bernhardt guilty, you must find that she killed her father with premeditation. And then the judge will define that term. 'Killing with premeditation is killing after *consciously* deciding to do so.' I suggest to you now that the evidence will show that my client did not *consciously* form such an intent."

The jurors looked puzzled. Who could blame them? I sounded like a hairsplitting pettifogger. Better to play to my strength, my beautiful and presumably innocent client.

"You will learn much about Chrissy Bernhardt in the course of this trial. You will learn about her upbringing and about her invalid mother, about why Chrissy left home as a teenager, refusing to ask her father for support, even refusing to tell him where she was."

Chrissy, Chrissy, Chrissy. Making her sound like a child, even now.

"You will learn that there are two victims of this tragic incident."

Making it sound like an accident.

I moved close to the jury box and gave its occupants

my sincere look. "This is a hallowed proceeding, the ultimate in our democracy." I turned and rested a hand on the back of the witness chair. "Here, truth and nothing but the truth is acceptable. Nothing less than complete, unvarnished, untainted truth should be acceptable to you. If lies, fabrications, and falsehoods come from this chair, this throne of truth, if any doubts are raised as to the guilt of Chrissy Bernhardt, you must acquit."

If the glove doesn't fit . . .

"Objection," Socolow said. "This isn't closing argument."

The judge waved him off without a word. I seldom object during opening statement or closing argument. In my old game, when you throw the ball, three things can happen, two of them bad. Same thing here. Object during opening, the judge is likely to overrule you or ignore you.

I rambled on for a while, telling the jurors I was their taxi driver, and we were going to take a trip of discovery, learning the facts as we went. But it was a bumpy road filled with potholes and dangerous curves. I spoke in vague terms, hinting at the sexual abuse without saying it. I never mentioned Dr. Lawrence Schein by name, but as I stood there, skimming my notes, watching for jurors' eye contact, occasionally scanning the gallery where crime reporter Britt Montero was taking notes, it occurred to me that I didn't have a choice. I had to put Schein on the stand. He had become the enemy. He could cast doubt on the memories he had uncovered, hurt us with the tape that showed premeditation, and toss out any number of lies I wouldn't be prepared for. But I didn't have anything else. If I could prove he'd had a motive to kill Harry Bernhardt, I could put the gun in his hands. To have a chance, I had to destroy him. Anything less, and he would destroy us.

23

Javert and Finch

A good prosecutor is a careful carpenter building a bookshelf. He saws a sure cut, hammers the nails straight, and hangs the shelves in plumb. Nothing fancy. The goal is to build the case slowly, competently. No razzle, no dazzle. No missing pieces.

A good prosecutor does not ask questions without knowing the likely answers. He does not ask a defendant to try on a pair of gloves that may not fit. He is a solid fullback, not a dipsy-doo wide receiver. The path to the end zone is a straight line if you don't fumble.

Abe Socolow is a master of his craft. His strength is his burning desire to win. He is fueled by a righteous indignation toward those miscreants who dare violate the law, and he takes seriously his role as representative of the people.

As a career prosecutor, Abe is not looking for a cushy job in private practice or an appointment to the bench. He wants to do what he always has done: get in early, work like hell, eat a brown-bag lunch, work some more, and, by the end of the day, ship another criminal upstate.

Abe sees the world in stark contrasts. Good and evil are painted in white and black, to hell with shades of gray. A defendant had a shitty childhood. Tell it to the prison chaplain. Drugs made you a robber or a rapist. Fine, we've got the cure, and it's not hugs and therapy. When the law has been broken, justice demands a penalty. It's as simple as that, and most folks in this great land of ours would agree.

Even me. Unless I'm representing the lawbreaker. Then my duty is different. It's not to society as a whole, or to the victims, or to abstract notions of justice. My loyalty belongs solely to my client, and I'll ford the deep rivers where the current is swift if it will save the poor soul whose fate is entrusted to me.

So our roles are clearly defined, Abe's and mine. From my days as a drama student and woeful actor, I sometimes cast friends and foes in various productions. If you were casting *Les Miz,* Abe Socolow would be a perfect Javert, the relentless arm of retributive justice. And me?

All defense lawyers see themselves as Atticus Finch, standing tall before a jury, pleading for—no, demanding— justice. But few of us look like or sound like Gregory Peck, and our clients are hardly virtuous, so there is little social utility in beating the rap. It's an ethical conundrum, this duty to the individual that conflicts with the rights of society. Do your job well enough and you've returned a killer, rapist, or robber to his chosen line of work. Fail, and you've done society a favor.

On direct examination, Abe Socolow stayed out of the way. He stood at the end of the jury box and asked his questions simply and directly. His witnesses were well prepared, concise, and matter-of-fact. Johnny Fiore, the bartender at Paranoia, used to work at the Delano Hotel, just up the street. He was a short, muscular man in his late twenties with a buzz cut and a black silk shirt decorated with mermaids. Fiore had recognized Harry Bernhardt from the lobby bar of the Delano, where he'd been a regular, and they chatted this last night while Harry drank.

Harry had asked him the time twice, even while checking and double-checking his Rolex.

"Did Mr. Bernhardt appear to be waiting for someone?" Socolow asked.

"Objection!" I was on my feet. "Mr. Bernhardt might have been waiting for the eleven o'clock news. He could have been late for an appointment elsewhere. He could have needed to know when to take his heart medicine."

"Mr. Lassiter!" The judge shot me a look that could have left bruises. Chrissy passed me a note saying that her daddy had never taken heart medication, but I knew that. "Please refrain from speaking objections," the judge ordered. " 'Objection, leading' will do nicely. 'Objection, calls for speculation' wouldn't be bad either."

"That's the one," I agreed.

"Granted."

I was pleased with my clever, lawyerly self for planting the notion that old Harry had heart trouble. So pleased that something didn't occur to me until I sank back into my chair. "Your Honor, I withdraw the objection."

"What?"

"Mr. Fiore has worked several years as a bartender. It is within his area of expertise to determine when a patron appears to be waiting for someone."

Socolow looked at me in true amazement. The judge just shook his head. "Mr. Fiore, you may answer the question."

"Yeah, I suppose he did. I mean, he kept asking the time and looking toward the door."

"And did there come a time when someone did appear and approach Mr. Bernhardt?" Socolow asked, without thanking me for my assistance.

"There sure did," Fiore said, looking toward my client.

"And who was that?"

"A tall lady in a black dress. The lady sitting right there." He nodded in Chrissy's direction, and Socolow pointed a bony finger at her. "For the record, the witness has identified the defendant. Now, please describe what happened next."

Fiore took about three minutes to tell his story. He had been clearing empty glasses from the bar and hadn't actually seen the defendant pull a gun, his view being partially blocked by the patrons at the bar. But he had heard the first shot, looked up and saw her pointing the gun at Bernhardt, heard the second shot and the third, and heard the man gasp, then slump against the bar. No, Bernhardt never fell from the barstool. Just leaned back into the bar, sort of pinned there, blood dripping down his guayabera.

There wasn't much to do on cross-examination. Oh, I had done my homework. I had sent Cindy, my multitalented secretary, to South Beach in her tightest T-shirt, the one that reads I'D LIKE TO FUCK YOUR BRAINS OUT, BUT SOMEBODY BEAT ME TO IT. Cindy learned that Fiore had been fired from the Delano for drinking on the job. I could have asked whether he'd been sipping the Scotch that night. I could have asked how many women in black dresses had been at Paranoia that night. I could have asked if he'd seen a muzzle flash, and if not, I could have implied that someone else had shot Bernhardt. The problem, of course, was that Chrissy had shot him, and a hundred witnesses, both eyeball and forensic, could say so.

"No questions," I said pleasantly, as if nothing could dent my confidence.

The witnesses strolled up, told their stories, and left quietly. Jacques Briere had been sitting at a table twenty feet from the bar. He was a free-lance talent scout playing host to a dozen models, photographers, hangers-on, and wannabees. He heard the first shot and turned around in time to see Chrissy squeeze off two more. One of his guests, the famous Italian photographer Anastasio, had watched Chrissy walk in from the front door and head for the bar.

Socolow used Anastasio to demonstrate, at least implicitly, that Chrissy knew what she was doing, had planned it, and had walked a straight line, literally, to get the job done.

Anastasio hadn't actually seen Chrissy pull the gun. He was admiring her Charles Jourdan shoes and didn't notice anything amiss until after he heard the second shot, having mistaken the first for a champagne cork.

Several others testified, a blur of South Beach's party crowd. At night, in their club duds, they're a flashy group. Today, under the fluorescent lights, they looked pale and out of place. If they'd taken blood tests the night of the shooting, I'd bet none of them could have operated heavy machinery. Abe had discarded the worst of the Ecstasy-popping, cocaine-sniffing, heroin-smoking folks who thought they'd seen a chorus line of dancing hippos. He barely managed to haul in half a dozen citizens who could simultaneously put one hand on the Bible, another in the air, and say, "I do."

My old antagonist was piling it on thick, and I objected once on the grounds of cumulative testimony, but Judge Stanger overruled me. Abe was clever enough to draw one new fact from each witness. No, the woman didn't seem hysterical. Calm. Just shot the man, *pop-pop-pop*.

I kept my cross-examinations brief. Michelle Schiff, a makeup artist, had commented on Chrissy's placid demeanor as well as her tasteful use of eyeliner.

"On direct examination, you testified that Christina Bernhardt had no expression on her face when she apparently shot Mr. Bernhardt?" I said.

"That's right."

"I wonder if you could be more precise."

"I don't understand."

"Well, we always have *some* expression on our face, don't we?"

Socolow bounded out of his chair. "Objection, argumentative." It was a silly objection to a silly question, and

I figured Abe just wanted to stretch his legs.

"Overruled," Judge Stanger said. "You may answer the question, if you can."

"I don't think I understand."

"Let's try it this way," I said. "Ms. Bernhardt didn't look excited, did she?"

"No."

"And she didn't look agitated?

"No."

"Or angry?"

"No."

"Happy?"

"No."

One of the trial lawyer's tricks is to eliminate every snippet of evidence that could be harmful, in order to leave the impression that what is left is favorable. Sometimes it is a tedious task.

"Did she look intense?"

"Objection!" Socolow called out. "Calls for speculation."

"Overruled," the judge said. "The witness can testify as to her observations."

I shot Socolow a dirty look. He was just trying to break the staccato rhythm of my cross.

"Did Ms. Bernhardt appear to be intense, to be focused on what she was doing?"

"Not really," Michelle Schiff said.

"Then what was her expression?" I asked.

Michelle Schiff ran a hand through her hair, which was tinted the color of a copper penny. "I don't know. Her eyes seemed blank. Her face was kind of dreamy. Her mouth was just a tiny bit open. I remember she wasn't wearing lip gloss, and in that light—"

"Blank," I repeated, interrupting her before we sped off in another direction. "Blank and dreamy. As if she were in a daze?"

"Yeah, I guess."

"Or a trance?"

"Sort of."

"Or hypnotized?"

"Your Honor!" Socolow stood so quickly he jostled a file, which crashed to the floor. "Unless the witness is an expert on hypnosis—"

"Sustained. Move it along, Mr. Lassiter."

I paused long enough for the jurors to turn and look at me. "So, in summary, Ms. Bernhardt seemed to be in a daze or a trance when she walked by your table?"

"Yes. I said that."

Actually, I had said that. But I wanted the jury to think she had. "Nothing further," I concluded.

24

Flashbacks

There is nothing worth stealing in my little coral-rock house in the South Grove. Oh, there is the dinged sailboard propped on concrete blocks. It doubles as a coffee table, though the rings on the fiberglass come from beer bottles, not coffee cups. There is a table lamp made from a Miami Dolphins helmet. There is a sofa of Haitian cotton that was once off-white and is now a jaundiced shade of yellow. There are two potted palms, a rusted scuba tank, and an old stack of magazines and football programs.

Which is why I don't lock my front door.

Not that you could open it unless you have hit a blocking sled or two. The wood is humidity swollen, so the door stays jammed shut. My friends know how to get in, but few are willing to suffer shoulder separations.

When I came home that night, there was a red Corvette parked under the jacaranda tree. The downstairs smelled of cigars. The sound of a cabinet door closing came from the kitchen. Then a voice. "Where do you keep the single-malt Scotch, old buddy?"

"I don't drink it except when you're paying, Rusty."

He poked his head out of the kitchen, and I dropped my briefcase on the floor. He was wearing pleated Italian slacks that billowed at the hips and a black silk shirt with an open-mouthed shark crawling up the front. His long red hair was tied back in a ponytail. To my unbiased eye, he looked like a trainee in an executive program for drug dealers.

"And you got shit in your refrigerator," he complained. "Salami and beer."

"The building blocks of life," I said. "As essential to civilization as *Monday Night Football*."

"Nobody eats salami anymore."

"That's why I like it."

"Tofu is in, Jake. Bean sprouts are in. Sushi is in. Salami is so far out, it may come back in."

"When it does, I'll stop eating it."

I sat down on the sofa, kicking off my black oxfords. I hate those shoes. Lace them up tight, feel uptight. Of all my shoes, my favorites were those old black hightops from Penn State. Loved the feel of spikes biting into solid ground, a satisfying *thwomp* you both heard and felt.

Rusty emerged from the kitchen carrying two 16-ounce Grolsches. "Can I buy you a beer?"

"You can tell me why you lied to me."

"Jake!" Sounding wounded.

"You set me up because Guy Bernhardt paid you to. Then you lied to me about it. Now you're going to testify for the state." I took the beer but didn't open it. "Old buddy."

"I'm sorry, Jake. Guy asked me a lot of questions about you, and yeah, he got me to bring you to Paranoia that night. But I didn't know Chrissy was gonna off her old man, and that's the truth."

"Then what did you think was going on?"

He sat down in a chair within a short left hook of the sofa. "I just believed what Guy said. He told me he'd be coming by to see his pop. Chrissy, too. There was some family dispute. Maybe my old friend Jake could help out, be the family lawyer, but I wasn't to say a word to you. Look, if it helps, I'll testify to that.''

''It doesn't help. Your conversations with Guy are hearsay. Besides, Guy could say, 'Sure, I wanted to bring Pop together with Chrissy, but she spoiled everything by killing him.' ''

''It freaked me out, Jake, when she came in and started shooting. But I never figured Guy had a hand in it.''

''And now you do?''

''No. *You* do. If Guy was gonna kill his pop, there'd be easier ways.''

I popped the porcelain stopper on the bottle. ''Not that would get Chrissy out of the way at the same time.''

Rusty swallowed a few glugs of his beer but didn't answer me. I was still wondering why he'd shown up. The offer to testify didn't impress me one bit.

''Here's how I see it, Rusty. You got in over your head, and now you're scared. I figure you're part of some conspiracy without really knowing it. You're not really a bad guy. Dishonest, sleazy, and disloyal to your friends, but in the scheme of things, you're just another guy on the make.''

He looked as if I'd just peed on his shoes. ''Jake, I'm willing to make it right. I'll do anything you want.''

''What do you suggest?''

''Put me on the stand.''

That was the second time he had offered his services. ''What for?''

''I'll tell how Guy paid me to go the club, told me Chrissy was coming, and wanted you there. I'll tell—''

''No, you won't! Guy would say Chrissy had been making threats against their father. That's an admission by a party, admissible at trial. He'd say he feared for his pop's life and wanted two big ole football players there, but we let him down. Because she planned the killing, it's first-degree murder all the way. So you see, Rusty, there's nothing you can do to help. Every time you open your mouth, you hurt us. Guy knows that. In fact . . .''

Sometimes I have to think out loud. I'm not one of the smart guys who can get from A to Z without mouthing all the letters in between. But give me enough time and I'll get there.

''Rusty, you son of a bitch!''

''What?''

''He sent you here. He wanted to sucker me into using you.''

''No. I swear.''

''You're lying through your teeth,'' I said, using my granny's expression.

Rusty's shoulders seemed to slump. ''Okay, okay. Guy told me to try and make amends with you. He didn't say why.''

''You're dumber than you look, Rusty.''

''All right, I made a mistake, but Jesus, Jake, I'm telling you the truth now. I didn't know what Guy and that bald shrink were up to.''

''But you do now.''

''Yeah, I think they fucked around with Chrissy's head. After the drugs and what her old man did to her, it was probably pretty easy. But there's nothing you or I can do about it. Guy Bernhardt's smart, Jake. Real smart. He plays that country farmer shtick, but he's no bumpkin.''

''What are you saying?''

''That you're going to lose, Jake. Don't make it any harder on yourself. Just lay down. It's not like Chrissy didn't pull the trigger. I mean, she's a killer, right?''

''You can rationalize just about anything, can't you?''

''You don't know what you're up against.''

''Get the hell out of here!''

Rusty stood and started for the door. ''I'm sorry, Jake. I was just trying to help.''

''Bullshit! You've never tried to help anyone your

whole life. You were a chickenshit wideout who wouldn't throw a block on a corner 'cause it would muss your hair.''

He stopped and turned. "Jake!"

"Oh, did I insult you? Pity. Maybe Guy will pay a bonus for your wounded feelings.''

He left carrying his beer, and a moment later his Corvette kicked up a spray of pebbles from the driveway and tore off down the street. I resented the noise almost as much as the man who made it.

For once, I knew more than the prosecution. Not that it would do me any good.

Abe Socolow was Sergeant Joe Friday in the courtroom. *Just the facts, ma'am.* He didn't need to know, didn't want to know, every twist and turn in the lives of Chrissy and Guy Bernhardt and their father. I needed to know, but wherever I turned, the answers came out wrong.

"So did that tall glass of gin kill her daddy or what?'' Granny asked me. She had driven up from Islamorada, toting a wicker basket containing conch chowder, white lightning, and jerk chicken. Kip carried a brown paper sack filled with Key lime marmalade, fruit chili, and other preserves Granny had put up.

"Chrissy pulled the trigger,'' I said, sorting through the goodies that now lay scattered across my kitchen counter. "But she was manipulated by her brother and programmed by the shrink.''

"Just like Laurence Harvey,'' Kip said.

"Huh?''

"In *The Manchurian Candidate.* Brainwashed and trained to kill.''

"Yeah, something like that.''

"Can you prove it?'' Granny asked.

"No,'' I admitted.

"Then what are you gonna do?''

I opened a mason jar and sniffed at the rye liquor. "Play

soft defense. Bend but not break. Maybe Guy Bernhardt makes a mistake, and I get lucky.''

Granny gave me her puzzled look. ''You mean Socolow, don't you, Jake?''

''No. Abe's not the enemy. He doesn't even know what really happened. Guy Bernhardt does, and he's the opposition.''

''Chrissy knows,'' Kip said.

''What?'' I was taking a sip of the liquor, but my hand stopped in midtrack.

''I mean, if they programmed her, it's got to be in her head somewhere, doesn't it? Like flashbacks in the movies, where all you need is something to bring them back. I can always tell when someone's going to get one, 'cause there's a close-up of the person's eyes, and the music comes in a rush, and then everything goes to black and white.''

''Flashbacks,'' I said, mulling it over.

''Yeah, like in *Dolores Claiborne,* only there they weren't black and white, just kinda a different color, and Kathy Bates could remember all this really bad stuff that happened to her.''

Granny was looking at me sideways. ''What are you thinking, Jake?''

''Just trying to figure how to bring up the music.''

We started the day with housekeeping matters, both sides submitting proposed jury instructions, even though we were a week away from finishing the case. Judge Stanger granted my motion to exclude Luciano Faviola and Martin Kent as witnesses, ruling that the pattern of prior acts of violence was not similar enough to meet the *Williams* rule, and in any event, there was no question as to the identity of the shooter.

Abe Socolow's direct examination of Rusty MacLean was short and thankfully lacking in surprises. Rusty told the jury that he had been sitting immediately adjacent to a heavyset man at the bar. No, he didn't recognize the man, never saw him before. Mr. Lassiter was sitting right next to Rusty. The jury seemed puzzled by that. No frame of reference. Johnnie Cochran wasn't with O. J. on June 12, 1994, right?

The defendant, Christina Bernhardt, walked in. Sure, he'd recognized her. At one time, he was her agent, but you know how models are. Jump from agency to agency at the promise of better work. She wasn't more than ten feet away when she pulled out a gun and fired three times at the heavyset man. Hit him with every shot.

"What, if anything, did you do?"

What, if anything . . . ? My profession has its little ritualistic questions. Once, in a lawsuit against a dressmaker for a botched wedding dress, the opposing lawyer asked my client, the bride, "What, if anything, were you wearing during the ceremony?"

"I was frozen," Rusty said, shaking his head. "I mean, I never saw anything like . . ."

He let it hang there.

"Then what happened?" Abe Socolow asked in another time-honored question lawyers use to move the story along.

"Jake, Mr. Lassiter . . ." Rusty looked over at me and gave a half smile. He was a boyish charmer until you got to know him. "Jake jumped up and went for the gun, but Chrissy just fainted dead away into his arms."

"Your witness," Socolow said amiably.

There was no need to cross-examine Rusty. Except my need to inflict some pain, preferably not on my client or myself. I stood and Rusty smiled at me, which caused a red-hot spot in my gut to spread to my limbs. I was sweating.

"Mr. MacLean," I began, as if I'd never seen this fellow in my life, "have you ever been convicted of a crime?"

Rusty's smile froze, and he shot an anxious look at Abe Socolow, who merely shrugged. It's a perfectly legitimate question of any witness, but strangely, under the rules of evidence, if the answer is yes, you can't ask, "What crime?" If the answer is no, and it's a lie, you can put on evidence of the conviction to impeach the witness.

"You oughta know," Rusty said finally.

"Indeed I do, but the jury does not." I opened a file and held up a blue-backed legal document, as if examining it. "I ask again, sir. Have you ever been convicted of a crime?"

"Yeah, you represented me. Next time, I'll get a better lawyer."

That drew some laughs from the gallery, and a few smiles from the jury box, but it didn't bother me one bit. Let the jurors think poor Chrissy had a bumbler while the state was represented by the coolly efficient surgeon named Socolow. I am not above a ploy for sympathy. I returned the blue-backed document to its file folder. It was the deed to my house, not Rusty's conviction for fraud, after overcharging models for their composites while making farfetched promises of employment.

"Mr. MacLean, how much time elapsed from the moment Chrissy Bernhardt took the gun from her purse until the last shot was fired?"

Rusty shook his head. "It was quick. I dunno. Less than ten seconds." He stared into space, thought about it, actually brought his hand up as if holding a gun, pulled an imaginary trigger three times. "Maybe six seconds."

"Six seconds," I repeated. "Now, you just testified that Christina fainted after shooting her father?"

"Yeah. I said that."

"So she lost consciousness?"

"She just collapsed, and you caught her before she hit the floor."

"Precisely when did she lose consciousness?"

"Precisely? I don't know."

"Was it a second before she fell, five seconds, six seconds?"

"Well, it couldn't have been six seconds. That would be about when she started firing, and she was conscious then."

"She was?" I tried to sound surprised. It isn't difficult because I often am. "Were you monitoring her heart rate?"

"No."

"Or her blood pressure?"

"No."

"Or her brain waves?"

"No, of course not, but she was firing a gun, for God's sake."

"Which you were looking at, correct?"

"What?"

"The gun, Mr. MacLean. When Chrissy Bernhardt was firing the gun, state's exhibit three . . ." I walked to the clerk's table and picked up the little Beretta. "You were looking at it, weren't you? Your eyes were glued to the gun?"

"Yeah, I guess so."

"Just as you are now?"

Rusty's eyes flicked from the gun to the jury and back to me. "Yeah. It kinda draws your attention."

"Therefore, you weren't looking at Chrissy's eyes, were you?"

He paused a moment, irritated with me. "No, I guess not."

I returned the gun to the clerk. "So you couldn't possibly know if Christina's eyes were open or closed at the time of the shooting, could you, sir?"

The purpose of cross-examination is to eliminate a witness's choices, and just now, Rusty had no choice. "No, I couldn't tell if her eyes were open," he admitted.

"You couldn't see her facial expression at all, whether her face was slack or taut?"

"No."

"And consequently you don't know if she was conscious or unconscious or in some in-between state?"

"Objection! Calls for speculation."

"Overruled, but Mr. Lassiter, why don't you rephrase anyway? 'In-between state' is a little vague."

"Do you know if Christina Bernhardt was conscious at the time of the shooting?" I asked.

"I don't understand the question," Rusty said. He was not going to make it easy for me, especially after I humiliated him with the criminal conviction question.

"All right," I said. "Was she alert to her surroundings?"

"She seemed to know where her father was sitting."

Ouch. I went on without blinking or checking for wounds. "Did she appear to notice you sitting at the bar?"

"No."

"And you were right next to Mr. Bernhardt?"

"Yeah."

"And you were a friend of Chrissy's?"

"Like I said, I was her agent once."

"Did she say hello to anyone in the club?"

"Not that I saw."

"Did she move quickly toward Mr. Bernhardt?"

"No. She kinda swayed over, the way models walk."

"Slowly?"

"Yeah."

"In a languid manner?"

"I don't know what that means."

Neither had I until I looked up synonyms for "faint," "feeble," and "weak."

"Did she seem to be in a trance?" I asked.

"I never saw anyone in a trance," he said, "except in the movies. More like she was real sleepy."

"As if she were sleepwalking?"

"In a way."

"Which is sort of a trance, is it not?"

"Objection! Repetitious." Socolow was on his feet.

"Sustained. Mr. Lassiter, I do think you've mined this ground."

"Thank you, Your Honor," I said, bowing slightly, more to loosen up my back than pay homage to the judge. "Now, Mr. MacLean, did Chrissy try to escape or avoid capture?"

"No. She just collapsed."

"Do you know if Chrissy had any history of blacking out or fainting?"

I expected *I don't know*. Rusty paused a moment, thinking about it.

"Yeah, now that you mention it, she did. On a couple of shoots, she fainted. I told her to go see a doctor, but I don't know if she ever did."

That got the jury to thinking, and I did the same.

25

Turning Out the Lights

"Do I remember her?" the doctor asked, smiling. "Did you just walk through my waiting room, Mr. Lassiter?"

"Sure."

"And what did you see?"

"Half a dozen old guys reading magazines."

"Exactly. A cardiology practice is not usually graced with the likes of Ms. Christina Bernhardt."

I was sitting in the office of Dr. Robert Rosen on Northeast 167th Street. He had a freestanding building within a quick jitney ride of the condo canyons of North Miami Beach. Median age of the neighborhood, somewhere between sixty-five and Riverside Chapel. The doctor had a Salvador Dali mustache and a bushy head of hair. He stared through wireless spectacles at Chrissy's file. On the wall behind his desk was an Impressionist painting of a woman in a garden.

"A lovely girl, Christina," he said, looking at an open folder containing medical records. "Referred to me by her GP for unexplained fainting spells. She admitted to occasional cocaine use, though not within the previous twelve months. We checked for inflammation of the heart, which proved negative. The fear, of course, is transient cardiac rhythm disturbance. That's what killed the young basketball player.''

"Reggie Lewis," I said.

"That's him. Never should have played with his history of fainting. In his case, the heart went into ven fib; he lost consciousness instantly, like turning out the lights. No pulse, no blood pressure. Sometimes the heart goes back on track. Sometimes it doesn't, and the person dies.''

"But that's not what Chrissy has.''

"No. We did the tilt-table test. Raised her upright to eighty degrees. She passed out in . . .'' He thumbed through the file. "Thirty-eight minutes. Classic neurocardiogenic syncope, not fatal. But you can get a pretty good bump on the head, depending where you fall.''

"When she passes out, is it sudden, like with the rhythm disturbance?''

"No. It's more gradual, as the blood pressure and heart rate fall. She'd get woozy.''

"And be semiconscious for several seconds?'' I said. Leading my witness, or the guy who would soon be my witness.

"Yes, I suppose she would.''

I thanked the doctor, who told me to forget his usual three-hundred-dollar consultation fee. I thanked him again, and he said to tell Christina it was just about time for a follow-up visit.

The second day of testimony started with the paramedic, a former Miami Beach lifeguard, who had transported Harry Bernhardt to the hospital. The subject—he used the police term—was bleeding from at least three gunshot wounds and rapidly going into shock. They took his blood pressure, ninety over sixty and falling; gave him an injection of ephedrine to stabilize him; put pressure bandages on the wounds; inserted an IV of Ringer's lactate, a salt solution; took an EKG, then transmitted the strip to the ER at Mount Sinai by portable fax; talked by radio to the trauma surgeon at the hospital; then administered oxygen. Yes, the subject was conscious.

"Did Mr. Bernhardt say anything?" I asked on cross. Which I wouldn't have done unless I knew the answer. Unlike the federal courts and many other states, Florida permits defendants to depose all prosecution witnesses before trial. So I knew the paramedic wouldn't blindside me: *Yeah, the old guy said, "Christina, why did you do this? Why, after everything I've done for you?"*

"He responded to my questions as to the location of his injuries and the medication he was taking," the paramedic said.

"Anything else?"

"He mumbled something."

"And what was that?" Sometimes prosecution witnesses take their instructions not to volunteer anything way too seriously.

" 'Emily.' He kept saying, 'Emily, I'm sorry.' Then I put the oxygen mask on him."

Yeah, I would have preferred him to say, *Christina, I'm sorry. I'm sorry I raped you when you were a girl, and you have every right to shoot me, and if you hadn't done it, I would have done it myself.* But you take what they give you. You plant little seeds, fertilize them if you can, and hope they grow.

"That's all he said?" I asked. " 'Emily'?"

"That's all I heard."

"And Emily was Mr. Bernhardt's late wife?"

"I wouldn't know that."

But now the jury would.

After the paramedic came Dr. Nubia Quintana, the surgeon who had debrided the wounds, inserted a tube through the chest wall to release blood and air from the chest cavity, stanched the internal bleeding, removed the two bullets that had not exited, and given Harry a good dose of antibiotics. She used fancy terms like "tension hemopneumothorax" but clearly gave the impression, which I liked, that the surgery had been no big deal.

"These bullets were twenty-two shorts, were they not?" I asked on cross-examination.

"I'd have to look at the police report," Dr. Quintana said. "They were small-caliber bullets, but whether they were twenty-twos or twenty-fives, I couldn't say." She had done her residency at Jackson Memorial, the public hospital, where the Saturday Night Gun and Knife Club produced significantly greater wounds on an hourly basis.

"And none of the wounds severed an artery?"

"No."

"Or caused extensive blood flow?"

"No."

"In fact, only the chest wound gave you any concern?"

The doctor smiled, a bit condescendingly. "I was concerned about all the wounds. The bullet that pierced the lung was the most serious."

"A bad choice of words on my part," I said humbly. Always admit your mistakes. The jury will like you for your semihonesty. "None of the wounds was life threatening, correct?"

"Not directly, not if treated correctly and promptly."

"Which was done here?"

"Yes."

"And after surgery, what was Mr. Bernhardt's condition?"

"Guarded condition."

"Life signs stable?"

"Yes."

"Heart rate and blood pressure normal?"

"Within normal ranges, yes."

"When Harry Bernhardt was wheeled out of surgery,

you didn't expect him to die two hours later, did you?''

"Objection," Socolow called out. "The doctor's expectations are irrelevant."

"Not to me," I fired back. I was hoping the jury would disregard the judge's preliminary instruction and be pissed off at Abe for cutting off the flow of information.

"Overruled. Doctor, you may answer."

"No, I did not expect him to die."

"No further questions."

Abe Socolow popped back up. He knew where I was going. The element of causation. Doc Charlie Riggs never thought much of my argument, but you never know what will move a jury.

"Dr. Quintana," Abe began, "when you said that the wounds were not directly life threatening, what did you mean?"

"Objection, leading." Now I was doing it, because I knew where Abe was going.

"It's not leading," Socolow shot back. "I'm simply asking for an explanation as to when an injury is directly life threatening versus indirectly life threatening. A man doesn't have to be shot through the heart to die as a consequence of the bullet."

"Now he's leading!" My pitch was a notch higher than normal.

The judge motioned to us. "Come up here. Both of you."

Abe and I circled around the far side of the bench, away from the jury. "Now, Jake, there was nothing wrong with Abe's question. It wasn't leading, and you know it. He's got a right to have her explain the answer she gave you. But, Abe, don't be making speeches in front of the jury, at least not 'til closing argument. The objection is overruled, so get back where you belong."

We retreated to our places, and the judge told Dr. Quintana that she could answer the question.

"None of these injuries individually would likely have killed Mr. Bernhardt. Even together, they might not have killed a younger man or a man with a healthier heart. But the stress of the injuries nonetheless killed him by ultimately causing the spontaneous ventricular fibrillations."

"Nothing further," Abe said, having repaired the damage and then some.

I stood up again for recross. "Mr. Bernhardt had a seriously diseased heart, did he not?"

"He had atherosclerosis, yes. The medical examiner who did the autopsy would be better able to describe the extent of it."

"Can you state with total certainty that Harry Bernhardt wouldn't have died of a heart attack on the night of June sixteenth even if he hadn't been shot?"

The doctor gave me a puzzled look, and I said, "Let me rephrase that one without the double negative. In Harry Bernhardt's condition, he could have suffered a heart attack on June sixteenth or the day after that, or any other day, even without having been shot or undergoing surgery, true?"

"Yes, that's true. He was a candidate for a heart attack at any time."

"Nothing further."

Next came the nurse who had tended to Harry Bernhardt in the recovery room, and then a second nurse who had accompanied him to a private room inside the ICU. Sort of the equivalent of chain-of-custody evidence, as Harry got passed along from Tinker to Evans to Chance.

Harry Bernhardt's life signs were strong when Sylvia Gettis, RN, checked on him at eleven P.M. She'd pulled the graveyard shift and was at the nurses' station when the EKG monitor went off at 11:51 P.M. She raced twenty paces from her station to Harry's room, which was more like a suite for VIPs who were fortunate enough to find themselves in Intensive Care at the plush hospital instead of the county facility. Harry Bernhardt was thrashing in the bed, yelling, in obvious pain. The emergency team— an intern, a resident, an ER physician, an anesthesiologist, a respiratory therapist, and an EKG specialist—flew into the room.

They intubated Harry and forced oxygen into his lungs. They injected him with epinephrine, an adrenaline-like drug, and they started CPR. They checked his blood gases. In the rapid-fire shorthand of physicians, they shouted, debating possible causes of the ventricular fibrillation. Internal bleeding. A collapsed lung. An unseen bullet wound.

Harry's heart was on fire, the muscles contracting fiercely, the organ quivering, shaking itself to death. Then the heart slowed.

"Mr. Bernhardt coded," the nurse told the jury.

"Which means what, Ms. Gettis?" Abe Socolow prompted.

"He flatlined. His heart stopped."

They tried the paddles, jolting Harry's heart with 250 joules of current. *Ka-boom. Ka-boom.* Again and again. Nothing. He was pronounced dead thirty minutes later.

"Did you speak to Mr. Bernhardt before he died?" I asked on cross, realizing she wouldn't have spoken to him after he died.

"No. He was still groggy from the anesthesia."

"And when you responded to the Code Blue, did you speak to him then?"

"I'm sure I asked him questions. He was conscious but in considerable pain. He was not really coherent."

"So he didn't say anything to you?"

"Nothing except sounds, painful cries, that sort of thing."

"Did he have any visitors before the monitor sounded at eleven-fifty-one?"

"Dr. Quintana stopped by. A detective looked in, then left. I told him the patient was in no condition to give a statement. And of course, the family physician.''

I was already sitting down, about to say, ''Nothing further,'' when I realized what she had said.

''The family physician,'' I repeated.

''Yes. Dr. Schein.''

How could I not know that?

I had taken discovery. I had a copy of the ICU log. No mention of Dr. Schein. Of course, he wasn't a treating physician or an investigating cop. Just what the hell was he, anyway?

''What was Dr. Schein doing there?'' I asked evenly.

''I believe he said he was a longtime friend of the Bernhardts as well as their physician. As I recall, he said he was practically a member of the family, something like that.''

Right. This family needed a shrink on retainer.

''When did he arrive?''

She thought about it a moment. ''Just as I was getting back from my break, eleven-forty P.M.''

''You're sure of the time?''

''I was carrying my coffee, and I remember the doctor commenting on the battery acid they serve in the cafeteria downstairs. I always take my break between eleven-twenty and eleven-forty, so that's when it was.''

''Eleven-forty,'' I repeated. ''Which was how long before the patient coded?''

She looked at her notes. ''The monitor sounded at eleven-fifty-one P.M., so it'd be eleven minutes.''

''How long did Dr. Schein stay?''

''I don't know. I was attending to paperwork and I didn't see him leave, but it would have to be sometime between eleven-forty and eleven-fifty-one, because he wasn't in the room when I got there.''

I thought it over. Harry Bernhardt hadn't died of the gunshot wounds. He'd died of a heart attack. What had Lawrence Schein said to him, done to him, in those precious minutes? I didn't know, and I probably never would. But I could use the trial lawyer's best friend, scurrilous innuendo. In a murder case, it's not a bad idea to imply that someone else might have done the killing. Possible suspects can include God with a lightning bolt or vengeful Colombian drug dealers stalking Faye Resnick.

"Did you leave Dr. Schein alone in the room with the patient?" I asked in a tone suggesting this would constitute a grave offense.

"Yes," she said, a bit defensively. Good.

"And he wasn't there when you raced into the room at eleven-fifty-one?"

"No, he wasn't."

"So, apparently, he quietly left the room and the ICU without being observed?" I wanted to say *sneaked out,* but Socolow would have pounded the table, and this got the point across anyway.

"Yes, I suppose he did."

"Did Dr. Schein speak to the patient?"

"I don't know. I wasn't there."

"And I suppose the answer would be the same if I asked whether Dr. Schein did anything to help Mr. Bernhardt."

"Again, I wasn't in the room, but of course, Dr. Schein was not there to treat the patient."

"Why was he there?"

"I'm not sure I understand the question," she said.

"Had Dr. Schein ever visited your ICU before?"

"Not that I recall."

"I'm just wondering," I said. "If Mr. Bernhardt was still groggy from the anesthesia, he couldn't carry on much of a conversation. I wonder what Dr. Schein was doing in there."

"In times of trouble, some people just like to be with those they care about," she said.

"Some people do," I agreed.

26

Lead-Pipe Arteries

I missed the hibiscus flowers in bloom.

Rising early, rushing to court, coming home after dark. The delicate blood-red flowers open in the morning when the sun is up, then close at dusk.

Hibiscus rosa-sinensis, Charlie Riggs calls my flowering bushes. Red, violet, and yellow, they grow in a tangle in the backyard. At dawn, I stood at my kitchen counter, slicing a papaya. The coffee gurgled and dripped through the filter into the pot. Somewhere outside, a cat wailed—an eerie, almost human scream. To the east, orange streaks appeared above the horizon, but in my overgrown yard of bushes, weeds, poinciana, live oak, and chinaberry trees, the world was still painted in dusky grays.

I heard footsteps coming down the stairs. Bare feet padding against the oak. She wore my old Penn State away jersey, the white one with the blue numbers. A faded grass stain on the belly. Had I made the tackle or ended up with a faceful of dirt? Who knows? No jazzy stripes or lightning bolts, no name on the back, no Nike swoosh in those innocent days, just number 58. Plain and simple. Like me.

She came up from behind and hugged me, laying her head on my shoulder. "You talked in your sleep," she said, "but I couldn't make out the words."

"Maybe I was practicing my inauguration speech for the Supreme Court."

"No. You were agitated."

"I was dreaming."

"Tell me."

"I don't remember," I lied.

"Uh-huh."

Chrissy let go and poured herself a cup of coffee. She didn't light a cigarette. I'd been trying to get her to stop. I try to be a good influence on my clients. Don't kill anyone else and please stop smoking.

Outside the window, a bird cawed. I didn't see it, but I knew it was the black fish crow that had built a nest in the live oak tree. Charlie Riggs had told me that the crows are extremely loyal and mate for life. Unlike the black-capped chickadees.

"We used to think most birds were monogamous," Charlie had said, "but we were wrong. The female chickadee will sneak out of the nest for a tryst with a male who ranks above her mate in the bird hierarchy. A queen bee will mate with two dozen drones in a day, and they'll all die when their genitals explode."

"Is there a lesson in this?" I'd asked.

"The mammals are the most promiscuous," Charlie had continued. "Probably less than two percent of the species practice monogamy."

Certainly not ours. In the backyard, the bird cawed again, though it was more like a *cah,* my crow picking up a Boston accent.

I squeezed a lime over the papaya and tried to catch a glimpse of the bird. No luck.

"Jake, what are you thinking about?"

"Nothing."

"That's impossible."

It didn't seem like a question, so I didn't answer.

"I'm frightened when I wake up and you're not in

bed,'' she said. "I always think you've left me."

"I woke up early. That's all."

My dream was still with me. A naked woman. Chrissy? Who could tell? The director hadn't called for any close-ups, and the lighting was bad. I walked into the picture, reaching out, my hands cupping her full, bare breasts. A grinding sound, and then the pain. Her nipples became drill bits, stabbing me, cutting through my palms. It was so damn obvious I didn't even need to call Dr. Santiago for her analysis.

I had awakened in a sweat and crawled out of bed. Chrissy stirred beside me, but I made it downstairs without waking her. I slipped a CD into the player, turned the volume down low, and listened to Sade whisper that I was a smooth operator. Right.

What was I doing? Where was I headed? I am a man without a plan, a defined goal. Careening through life, bouncing off immovable objects, finding friends, battling foes, losing lovers. Drifting on the currents, so near, so far from shore.

In the middle of a trial, there is nothing else. There is nothing that happened before; there can be no life after. All-consuming, this trial more than any other.

Because of her. Now I didn't know which was worse, losing her or letting her down.

The world seemed to be closing in. Abe Socolow was wrapping up his case. Yesterday, a fingerprint expert had testified that Chrissy's latents were on the Beretta that was recovered at her feet. Then came the assistant medical examiner, whose testimony as to cause of death was even more important than Dr. Quintana's because she had done the autopsy.

Dr. Mai Ling wore a white lab coat, a photo ID clipped to her pocket. She was petite and short-haired, prim and fastidious, and it was hard to imagine her elbow-deep in some drunk driver's stomach contents or, even worse, examining the body of an infant tortured by a maniac stepfather. After Abe Socolow ran through Dr. Ling's degrees, fellowships, internship, residencies, and advanced training, he got down to business.

"Now, Dr. Ling, please tell the jury what services you did, vis-à-vis the body of Harry Bernhardt," Abe instructed.

Vis-à-vis? How Continental of you, Abe.

"First, I examined the body. I noted evidence of three recent injuries, all bandaged. I removed the bandages and noted the existence of bullet wounds of a small caliber. There were still EKG patches attached to the torso. I also noted one tattoo." She paused and consulted her notes. "The name 'Emily,' on the decedent's shoulder. Otherwise, there were no scars or disfigurements."

"Then what did you do?"

"I proceeded with the autopsy in the usual fashion. . . ."

Easy for her to say.

"I made a Y-incision through the chest and abdomen, cutting under the skin and muscle to expose the chest wall. I used rib shears to cut through and remove the breastplate. I examined the chest cavity for evidence of blood or other fluids."

"And what did you find?" Abe asked.

"There were traces of body fluids in the cavity, a yellowish liquid made up of water, proteins, and electrolytes."

"Indicating what?"

"Evidence of heart failure. As the heart and lungs gave out, the fluids backed up into the chest cavity."

"Then what did you do?"

"I incised the sac around the heart and took blood samples from the aorta. The blood was sent to Toxicology for routine tests."

Which had come back normal, I knew. No arsenic and old lace, or arsenic and an old shrink.

"Then what?"

"I cut through the pulmonary venous return, the pulmonary artery, the superior and inferior venae cavae, and the aorta. Then I removed the heart and weighed it. . . ." She consulted her notes again.

C'mon, tell us. Was Harry a bighearted guy?

"The heart weighed four hundred five grams, which is in the normal range for a man of his size. I made incisions along the coronary arteries and found evidence of stenosis, a narrowing of the lumen."

"Indicating what?"

"Atherosclerosis. There was both a narrowing and hardening of the left anterior descending coronary artery and the right ascending artery. Probably in the vicinity of seventy to seventy-five percent obstruction in each. Actually, I had some trouble cutting through the arteries and had to replace my scalpel with scissors."

"Why was that?"

"Mr. Bernhardt had what we call lead-pipe arteries. When you touch them, you can actually feel the calcification inside."

"What else did you do?"

"I examined the myocardium, the heart muscle, for evidence of prior heart attacks."

"And what did you find?"

"No evidence of any scar tissue."

"Anything else?"

"I looked for any pale areas which might indicate the lack of oxygen over a prolonged period of time, and found none. I looked for evidence of a thrombus with a superimposed clot, but there was none."

"Based on your examination and the autopsy as a whole, did you reach conclusions as to cause and manner of death?"

"I did."

"What did you conclude?"

"The cause of death was cardiac arrest precipitated by multiple gunshot wounds and the resulting stress to Mr. Bernhardt, all of which aggravated his chronic atherosclerotic heart disease. The manner of death, therefore, was homicide."

Abe Socolow nodded sagely. Then, anticipating my defense, Abe raised a straw man.

"Now, Dr. Ling," Abe Socolow said, "you are familiar with the fact that the gunshots did not strike a vital organ?"

"Yes, I am."

"He did not bleed to death as a result of the shooting?"

"No, he did not."

It sounded a little like cross-examination, but I knew just where Abe was headed.

"Then how can you state that the shooting caused Mr. Bernhardt's heart attack?"

Knocking that old scarecrow down.

"By the process of elimination, for one thing," she responded. "There was no evidence of any other apparent physical cause."

"But you've just told us that Mr. Bernhardt had significant evidence of heart disease."

Again, setting up that raggedy guy . . .

"Yes, but Mr. Bernhardt had no prior heart attacks. There are many methods available to treat his atherosclerosis. Medication, angioplasty, bypass surgery. He could have lived a long time."

And knocking him down.

"Then why did he die?"

"The trauma to the system due to the injuries and the resulting surgery precipitated the incident."

Abe smiled his sincere look, allowed as how thankful he was that Dr. Ling could scoot over from the morgue—

situated comically on Bob Hope Road—and handed me his witness.

I stood up and bowed politely. "If I understand your testimony, Dr. Ling, you believe the injuries caused the cardiac arrest because you can't find anything else that conclusively did."

"In a sense. It is, as I said, by the process of elimination."

"Did you eliminate the possibility that it was just time, that Harry Bernhardt would have suffered cardiac arrest that Friday night, regardless whether he was shot three times or had three shots of bourbon?"

"There was no objective evidence indicating that the heart should have simply failed."

"So you eliminated the possibility because you couldn't find such a cause?"

Dr. Ling smiled tightly. "I couldn't find such a cause because none was there."

"You're not telling us that Harry Bernhardt was a healthy man, are you, Doctor?"

"Healthy, no. But, except for the shooting, Mr. Bernhardt likely would have enjoyed several more years of life."

"And except for the shooting, Mr. Lincoln would have enjoyed the play," I said.

"Mr. Lassiter!" The judge scowled at me.

"Sorry, Your Honor," I said humbly, then turned back to the witness. "How many years?"

"There is no way to determine that. However, I have seen cases where patients lived with far worse arterial deterioration."

"And you have seen cases where persons with less evidence of coronary disease have died of heart attacks, have you not?"

"Yes."

An honest answer. The jury would like her. Still, I was scoring a few small points.

"Isn't it true that Harry Bernhardt could have dropped dead today or tomorrow or next year?"

"We'll never know that, will we, because of your client's actions?"

"Your Honor!" Oh, she was a feisty one. Good witnesses know how to counterpunch. "I realize Dr. Ling has the same employer as Mr. Socolow, but—"

"I object to that!" Socolow bounded toward the podium, but I elbowed him aside.

"The medical examiner is supposed to be an impartial servant of the people," I bellowed. "The defense asks that the court admonish the doctor—"

"All right, all right." The judge waved at us with the gavel. "Jake, you ask questions. Doctor, you answer them simply and directly. Abe, you sit down."

No harm, no foul.

I decided to go off in another direction. "Doctor, what is sudden cardiac death syndrome?" I asked.

She seemed to sigh. "It is the unexpected death due to either too fast or too slow a heart rate combined with respiratory arrest."

"Sudden cardiac death is not an ailment in itself, is it?"

"No, it's a comprehensive term that describes a method of death usually accompanied by ventricular fibrillation."

"As with Harry Bernhardt?"

"Yes."

"And what are the causes of sudden cardiac death?"

"There are many. Heart disease. Hypertension. Certain rare disorders such as Romano-Ward, plus external causes such as electrocution or acidosis as a result of chronic alcoholism. It has many etiologies."

"Including those cases where no objective evidence can be found that caused the heart stoppage?"

She paused. "Yes."

"In other words, if the heart fails in an otherwise healthy person, you might very well determine it was sudden cardiac death syndrome?"

"You might, yes, in certain cases."

"But not in a case where the state attorney has filed murder charges?"

"Objection!" Socolow bounded to his feet. "Argumentative."

"Sustained."

I was thinking about sitting down. I had made my point, such as it was. But sometimes, I try to make it twice. I know better than to ask a "why" question on cross-examination of a state witness, particularly someone experienced at testifying.

"Broadly speaking, how many causes of death are there, Dr. Ling?"

"Four. Natural, accident, suicide, and homicide."

"And you listed homicide as the cause of Harry Bernhardt's death?"

"Yes."

"Though it could very well have been listed as natural, based on sudden cardiac arrest syndrome?"

"That is not my opinion."

"O-pin-ion," I said, tasting the word and finding it bitter. "Defined as your belief, your idea, your notion of what may have happened?"

Socolow's chair scraped the floor. "Objection, Your Honor. Dr. Ling has been qualified as an expert and is entitled to express her opinion without Mr. Lassiter's sarcasm."

"So she is," I responded. "But I am reminded of Justice Bok's classic statement that an expert opinion is just a guess dressed up in evening clothes."

"Your Honor!" Socolow pounded his table this time, and the judge waved his gavel at me, sort of penalizing me fifteen yards for unsportsmanlike conduct.

"Mr. Lassiter, you know better than that," the judge said icily. He turned to the jury box. "The jury shall disregard Mr. Lassiter's last statement."

I didn't mind the instruction. In my experience, jurors forget most everything I say, except what the judge tells them to disregard.

So here I was, the morning after.

Taking stock of my life. And my client's. Wondering how I let myself get entwined with her body and her case. A lawyer must care deeply about the client's fate, but not too deeply. For the same reason a surgeon shouldn't operate on his spouse, a lawyer shouldn't sleep with his client. Too much at stake. Way too much.

"What's going to happen today?" Chrissy asked. She was nibbling some raisin toast she had blackened on the number nine setting.

"The guy from the gun shop will be first. He'll testify you bought the Beretta on June thirteenth, three days before the shooting. On cross, I'll bring out that you used your own name and ID and properly registered the gun. There may be another housekeeping witness or two, but then Abe will rest, and it'll be our turn."

"What about my brother and Larry?"

"Abe doesn't need them. Probably doesn't want them either. Abe's got great instincts. If he senses those two are trouble, he won't call them."

"Are they trouble?"

"Look, even if Schein whispered in your ear that you should kill your father, you're still technically guilty. But jurors do strange things. Look at the O. J. Simpson case. A couple jurors thought he killed his ex-wife but were so offended by Mark Fuhrman that they went along with the acquittal. Part of a defense lawyer's job is to get the jury mad at somebody else."

She moved close to me. A charred crumb stuck to her

pouty lower lip. "So you'll put them on the stand?"

I took her in my arms. "I'll call Schein. His tapes both help and hurt us, but I don't have a choice."

"Will it work? Will the jury get mad at somebody else?"

"Sure," I said. "Probably at me."

27

Bird Spit Soup

There were no surprises. Just the procession of reliable witnesses, Abe Socolow finishing his house, sanding the wood, applying a slick coat of paint and then another. Waterproof, hurricane-proof, Lassiter-proof.

At precisely 4:30 P.M., the witnesses having testified, the last of the exhibits having been identified, marked, and admitted, the judge turned to Abe Socolow and waited. The lanky prosecutor pulled himself out of his chair, dusted imaginary lint from his trousers, stood ramrod-straight, and announced crisply, "The state rests." He made it sound so triumphant, Hannibal crossing the Alps, that I half expected a corps of buglers to accompany him.

"Very well," Judge Stanger said. "We start with the defense case at nine A.M. tomorrow." He banged his gavel and sent us on our way.

The pickup truck arrived at the house just after eight P.M. with its precious cargo: my nephew, my granny, and my doc.

"Jake, I believe that gray-and-white bird in the chinaberry tree is a swift," Doc Charlie Riggs said.

"Uh-huh."

244

"It's too dark to see it clearly right now, but in the morning, I'll check it out."

"Sure, Charlie."

Granny hauled her wicker basket into the kitchen. A checkered cloth covered the goodies, and for some reason I thought of all those movies where the prisoner gets the gift of a pie with a file or gun inside. "Criminy, Doc! Jake's in no mood to talk about birds," Granny said, pulling a sweet-potato pie out of the basket. It was still warm, and I could smell the cinnamon, but I didn't see any trace of a weapon.

"All right, all right," Charlie said. "I just thought I'd look for the nest. It's what the Chinese use to make bird's nest soup."

"Yuck," Kip said, wrinkling his face. "That's gross." He was helping Granny put jars and bowls in the refrigerator. I caught sight of some swamp cabbage ambrosia made with hearts of palm, papayas, oranges, and coconut. If I knew Granny, there'd also be a sour-cream cake; hopping John made from rice, black-eyed peas, and salt pork; and bread pudding. Granny's idea of nouvelle cuisine is draining the fat from the bacon before wrapping it around a scamp steak.

Charlie cleared his throat. "Kippers, bird's nest soup is a rare delicacy. Swifts make their nests entirely from saliva, and if you're ever in Hong Kong, I recommend—"

"Spit!" Kip was carrying a plastic bowl of deep-fried conch fritters. "You eat soup made of bird spit?"

"Don't be squeamish, lad," Charlie said. "In some parts of the world, termite larvae are added to rice for flavoring and protein."

"Gross and double gross!"

"Caterpillar has as much protein per gram as beef, and ten times the iron. Personally, I have tried *Rhynchophorous phoenicis*, weevil, and found it delightful."

"I think I'm gonna hurl," Kip said.

"Not in my kitchen," I advised, then turned to my old friend, the deranged gourmet. "Charlie, if you're finished educating Kip, maybe we can talk."

"We can indeed, but not just yet. I seem to have worked up an appetite."

"You're spitting against the wind," Charlie said, and I wondered if he was still thinking of his favorite soup. We were sitting on the back porch, Charlie sipping at a mason jar of moonshine. I stuck to coffee.

"I've read and reread the autopsy report," he said, "as well as the surgeon's notes, the hospital records, and I've talked to the nurses. There's nothing to indicate Dr. Schein did anything remotely suspicious in that hospital room. The only marks on the body came from the gunshot wounds and the surgery. A heart attack caused Harry's death. You have no proof of anything else."

"Just the knowledge that Guy Bernhardt wanted his father dead and Larry Schein is Guy's errand boy."

"Why? What's the motive?"

"Harry's estate. With Chrissy convicted of murder, Guy gets it all."

Charlie shook his head and tamped some tobacco into his pipe. "If that's true, don't you think they would have kept their distance? I doubt Schein would have shown up in the hospital."

"He had to make sure Harry was dead, and if not . . ."

Charlie lit his pipe, and the scent of cherry tobacco mixed with jasmine from my neighbor's yard. "Do you have the slightest thread of evidence that would support such an outrageous theory?"

"Evidence?" I said, as if I'd just discovered a new word. "That's your job. Mine's to spin the tale of the destruction and death of a rich man."

"Like *Appointment in Samarra*," Charlie said.

"What?"

"A book by John O'Hara. A wealthy man—"

"I know the book, Charlie. I have a college degree that only took five years to earn." I stared off into space before saying aloud, "Appointment."

"What?"

"You're a genius, Charlie."

He grumbled some disclaimer, then said, "What is it, Jake?"

"Harry had an appointment."

"Hmmm?"

"Appointment at Paranoia, Charlie."

You bait different hooks in a trial. And sometimes the lines get tangled. You can say to a jury that dirty cops engaged in an elaborate conspiracy to frame your saintly client, a handsome former running back accused of butchering his wife and her friend. And you can also say that the cops are so woefully incompetent that they can't put the right labels on their little bags of evidence or keep souvenir hunters out of impounded vehicles. It's not my client's blood, but if it is, it was planted, and if it wasn't planted, he cut himself a week earlier when he was carving turkeys for the poor.

To laymen, those poor souls deprived of legal training, the strategy seems contradictory. But to those of us trained in the fine arts of pettifoggery, hairsplitting, and wordplay, it all makes sense. In the first semester of law school, we learn contracts. A man lends a pot to another. When it is returned, it is cracked. The first man sues. The second answers the complaint in the time-honored fashion: I never borrowed the pot, but if I did, it was cracked when I borrowed it.

In Chrissy's case, I wanted to prove that she had been programmed to kill. My *Manchurian Candidate* defense, Kip called it. Chrissy was the guided missile, programmed by the manipulative shrink, launched by the avaricious half brother. At least, that's how I imagined my closing argument, if only I had the evidence.

At the same time, there were the fainting spells. Instead of a hypnotized zombie, Chrissy was an ill young woman who had been semiconscious, and hence without criminal intent, when she shot her father. Not as sexy a theory, maybe, but probably easier for the jury to swallow. In my lawyerly fashion, however, I tried to have it both ways.

Dr. Robert Rosen was my first witness. He smiled warmly at Chrissy and turned to the jury with professional ease and a bit of charm. Doctors are the best witnesses and the worst. When I had prepared Rosen's testimony, Kip was with me in the conference room. The doctor had been blathering on about "classic neurocardiogenic syncope."

"English, please," I told him.

"Yeah, cut the bullshit, Doc," Kip added.

"Kippers!"

"Easy, Uncle Jake. Don't you remember James Mason in *The Verdict*? He's getting this doctor ready to testify, and the doc, who's a total bogon, says, 'She aspirated vomitus into her mask.' So James Mason says, 'Cut the bullshit, Doc. She threw up, and always use her name. *Debbie* threw up.' "

"I didn't care for the movie," Dr. Rosen said unhappily. "Stories about medical malpractice make me uneasy. I did like James Mason, though."

"He was the villain," Kip said. "The Prince of Fucking Darkness."

"Kip!"

"That's what Jack Warden called him. I thought lawyers considered it a compliment."

By the time Rosen took the stand, he spoke in plain English, occasionally fiddling with his mustache while he listened to my questions. He explained that Chrissy's fainting was caused by a gradual decline in blood pressure, and that she would grow woozy just before she fainted.

"So there would be a time of semiconsciousness?" I asked.

"Yes. As the blood pressure falls, there could be several seconds that precede the actual fainting where Chrissy blacks out, sees stars, that sort of thing."

"Would she be capable of processing information?"

"Objection, vague," Socolow shouted.

"Sustained," Judge Stanger said.

"In such a state, would she be capable of forming a conscious thought, carrying out an intended task?"

"Objection, calls for speculation."

Before the judge could sustain the objection, I offered to rephrase the question. "Dr. Rosen, assuming a person with the classic neurocardiogenic syncope is in the preliminary phase of an episode—that is, the person's heart rate and blood pressure are falling and the person is woozy and seconds away from fainting—could that person consciously carry out an intended task?"

"Objection, assumes facts not in evidence."

"I'll overrule it," Judge Stanger said. "It's admissible as a hypothetical question to an expert."

Sometimes judges get tired of sustaining objections and, like everybody else, just want to hear the answers.

"It's a gray area," Dr. Rosen said. "And there's a continuum during which the person loses consciousness. At a certain point just prior to actually fainting, the person clearly would be incapable of performing most tasks."

"Such as aiming a gun and pulling a trigger?"

"Yes. The combination of neural, mental, and motor skills required would not be possible in such a state."

I thanked the doctor and glanced at the jury. I caught a nod or two and nodded right back.

28

Playing the Sap

Sometimes I am so confused, I have to write everything on a legal pad. I draw a line down the middle of the page, scribble what I know on the left side and what I don't know on the right.

Chrissy believed she had been sexually abused by her father. But was it true? I didn't know.

Rusty bearded me for Guy Bernhardt. Why? For money, I was certain.

Guy masterminded Chrissy's mind fuck. He had Schein program her to kill Harry Bernhardt. But why? *Cui bono?* Guy stood to gain. But he would inherit half his father's estate eventually. Why be so greedy, so inhumane, as to want it all now? Why kill your father and frame your half sister? There had to be something more than the estate, but all I had was a question mark on the right side of my pad.

Schein tricked Chrissy into confessing on tape, recording evidence of her premeditation. Or did he? Was Chrissy involved in some double-fake, the legal equivalent of a reverse with a flea-flicker at the end of the play? Was I the patsy for Chrissy, too? Only yesterday, Kip had been watching *The Maltese Falcon* on cable, and I'd heard Humphrey Bogart telling Mary Astor, "I won't play the sap for you."

After I put it all down on paper, I started again, this time ignoring what really happened and trying to figure what made the best story. They don't teach you this in law school; you pick it up in the courtrooms, corridors, and conference rooms along the way.

Okay, take it from the top. Chrissy believed she had been sexually abused by her father. That gave her the motive—but not the lawful excuse—for killing him. Although some jurors might be sympathetic if they believed the abuse actually happened, they would be bound to follow the law. She had not been acting in self-defense or the defense of another, and she was not insane. My argument that Chrissy's fainting amounted to a lack of conscious intent was smoke and mirrors. In other words, no defense, and once Schein hammered me with the missing tape, as he threatened to do if I called him to testify, the element of premeditation would be proved.

So, weirdly, according to my legal pad, we were better off if Chrissy had not been sexually abused by her father. If she had no motive for killing Harry, it *lessened* her blame; it made her programming by Schein all the more necessary to get the job done. If the half brother and the shrink had fabricated everything, it helped me shift the focus to them. *They pulled the trigger, not this poor, confused young woman.*

But was that true? I didn't know. And at the moment, it didn't matter. All that mattered was Chrissy. Which was why I decided to bet the farm on the destruction of Dr. Lawrence Schein.

Lawrence Schein, graduate of Tulane University and the University of Miami Medical School, with an internship at Jackson Memorial Hospital and residency at Massachusetts General, with specialized training in psychiatry, and the author of a few undistinguished papers, did not know where I was going. He didn't know how many cards I held or if I was bluffing.

Charlie Riggs taught me the three essentials of proving that John Doe committed a crime: motive, opportunity, and means. That's also the order of proof. Which is why I started with what Charlie Riggs would call *cáusa* or *ratio,* the reason or motivation for the crime.

"Harry Bernhardt was a friend of yours, wasn't he, Doctor?"

"Yes, for a long time."

Schein smiled as if fondly remembering their get-togethers. He liked the question, was pleased with the answer. After all, you don't go about setting up the murder of a friend.

"When's the last time you had dinner with Harry Bernhardt?"

"Dinner? Well, I don't know. I don't remember."

"When's the last time you were in his home?"

He fiddled with the knot of his club tie. He wore a navy cashmere sport jacket and gray slacks. His shaved head gleamed under the fluorescent lighting. "It's been some time."

"Were you ever in his home after his wife, Emily, died?"

"Not that I recall." Looking puzzled, wondering where I was going.

"And that's been, what, almost fifteen years?"

"Yes."

"Subsequent to Emily's death, did you ever have dinner with Harry Bernhardt?"

"Not that I recall."

"Ever invite him to your home?"

"No."

"Ever go to a Dolphins game with him?"

"No."

"Did you ever pick up the phone and call him? 'Harry, how you doing?' Anything like that?"

He pulled at his goatee. "Harry Bernhardt was not a chatty person."

"So the answer is no. You never called Harry Bernhardt."

"No, I didn't."

"Then I wonder, Doctor, just how you could call Harry Bernhardt a friend."

"Objection, argumentative." Socolow sounded bored, but he was right.

"Sustained," Judge Stanger said.

"Isn't it true, Dr. Schein, that you were Emily Bernhardt's friend, not Harry's?"

"Objection," Socolow sang out. "Dr. Schein is Mr. Lassiter's witness."

"He's a hostile witness," I responded. At the word "hostile," Schein's left eye twitched.

"Come up here, both of you," the judge said, waving us toward the bench. When we got there, he pointed a bony finger at me. "Jake, if I understood your proffer, way back at the bond hearing, Dr. Schein was the treating psychiatrist."

"That's right."

"And he's gonna testify that your client was sexually abused as a child, causing her to lose control or some such thing and plug the decedent three times with a little pistol."

"That's about it."

"So how the hell is he hostile?"

"He's wrong. He's going to insist it happened that way in order to cover up his own wrongdoing. He's hostile now, and by the end of the day, he's going to be downright belligerent."

The judge looked at Socolow, who concealed his glee with a judicious semismile. "If Jake wants to impeach the only witness who can give him a defense, who am I to object?''

''Jake, I hope you know what you're doing.''

''Do any of us, Your Honor? I mean, in the cosmic sense?''

''I'm not fooling around, Jake,'' the judge said, sending a clear warning. ''If you're setting up some incompetency-of-counsel defense, I'll pin your license to the ass of a horse that's leaving town.''

Trying to sound folksy, some judges end up with a bushel basket of messy metaphors.

''Judge Stanger, I assure you, if I'm incompetent, it's purely unintentional.''

''All right, impeach to your heart's content.'' He sent us back to our tables, then turned toward the reporter. ''Margie, please read back the last question.''

The reporter thumbed through her pages, then read in a monotone that didn't do me justice, '' 'Isn't it true, Dr. Schein, that you were Emily Bernhardt's friend, not Harry's?' ''

The doctor cleared his throat and glanced toward Chrissy. She sat at the defense table in a three-piece burgundy outfit: a banded turtleneck, a belted cardigan, and a matching pleated skirt that nearly reached her ankles. Tasteful and refined, but the wrong color. I had forgotten my lecture banning anything that resembled dried blood. ''Yes and no,'' Schein said. ''I mean, Emily was my patient. Her husband was . . . there, in the house. We knew each other, all of us.''

''Cutting to the heart of it, Emily Bernhardt was more than a patient, wasn't she?''

''I'm not sure I understand the question.''

I raised my eyebrows at Dr. Schein, but the gesture was intended for the jury. Then I waited. Sometimes the pause will do it. The silence fills the courtroom. The witness becomes nervous, aware the jury is waiting. A spectator coughs, the courtroom door squeaks open, feet shuffle. A witness in control will wait out the lawyer. After all, Schein just said he didn't understand. I could have re-phrased, but I chose to wait. Ten seconds, fifteen, it seemed like an hour.

"Well, I have become close to a number of patients over the years," Schein said finally. Defensive, worried, shifty.

"I'm not concerned about other patients. Would you please answer the question? Was Emily Bernhardt more than a patient?"

After a pause. "Yes, she was."

"And more than a friend?"

"I don't know what you're implying."

"Yes, you do."

"Objection, argumentative." Socolow was starting to wake up.

Judge Stanger cocked his head. "Actually, there was no question at all. Next question, Mr. Lassiter."

"Dr. Schein, were you and Emily Bernhardt lovers?"

"Objection, irrelevant!" Now, Socolow was on his feet. Caught off guard, pissing off the jury by objecting to a juicy question.

"Denied. This is a murder trial, and I'll give the defense some latitude."

"Were you and Emily Bernhardt lovers?" I repeated.

"No."

I reached into a file and pulled out a faded sheet of paper. "Did you write her love poems?"

His face froze. His eyes were wide. What did I know?

"No."

This time I didn't have my laundry list or my old college letter-of-intent signed by Joe Paterno. What I had was the personal stationery of Lawrence B. Schein and a faded, handwritten note to "My Dearest Emily." I read aloud:

Wild Nights—Wild Nights!
Were I with thee
Wild Nights should be
Our luxury!

I paused a moment, then asked, "Did you write that?"

"No—I mean, yes. I didn't write it, but I copied it, out of a book."

"All right. You borrowed it. After painstakingly copying these breathless words of Emily Dickinson, did you give the poem to your Emily, *Mrs*. Emily Bernhardt?"

He reddened. "Yes."

" 'Wild Nights should be our luxury!' " I repeated. "Were they?"

"I resent your implication. You can't examine poetry as if it were an X ray. Ours was a cerebral relationship, not a physical one."

"Ce-re-bral," I said, as if it were a dirty word. Angling toward the jury, I let my voice fall into a whisper. If you really want them to listen, speak softly.

Rowing in Eden—
Ah, the Sea!
Might I but moor—Tonight—
In Thee!

Two jurors tittered.

"You were Emily Bernhardt's lover, weren't you, Dr. Schein?"

"No! Not the way you mean. No."

"Were you in love with Emily Bernhardt?"

He stared off into space. A vein throbbed in his forehead. "She was the finest woman I've ever known."

"Were you in love with her?" I repeated. Demanding now.

He mumbled something.

"Doctor?"

"Yes, I was in love with her."

"And she with you?"

"Yes."

"To your knowledge, did Harry Bernhardt know of your feelings for his wife?"

"She told him. She didn't love him, hadn't for years. But she wouldn't divorce him. Christina was just a child. Emily didn't want to break up the family, and she wasn't strong enough to fight him." The words came tumbling out now. Maybe he wanted to talk about her. All these years, and no one to tell, to feel his pain, the great unconsummated love of his life. "No one had ever been divorced in the Castleberry family, and Emily was so . . . so prudent in matters like that. She wouldn't pursue her own happiness. Besides, Harry wouldn't let her go. She was his claim to respectability, his entrée to society. And there was something else, too. A mean, sadistic side to him. He liked punishing her."

"You hated him, didn't you?"

"She was so frail," Schein answered, as if he hadn't heard the question. "No strength at all. Like rose petals, an elegant flower of a woman."

"Did you hate him, Doctor?"

"I didn't respect him."

"This man you previously told the jury was your friend."

Softly, "I misspoke."

"And Harry Bernhardt despised you, didn't he?"

"Objection!" Socolow boomed. "The witness isn't a mind reader."

"To the contrary," I protested. "That's exactly what he claims to be where my client is concerned."

Bang! Judge Stanger slammed his gavel down and shot me a look that said I'd better bring my toothbrush to court the next time I made a crack like that. "Mr. Lassiter, please refrain from addressing the jury instead of the court.''

"I'm sorry, Your Honor," I said meekly, "but implicit in my question is the notion 'do you know?' "

The judge turned toward the witness stand. "Doctor, do you know if Mr. Bernhardt despised you?"

Schein's head twisted at an awkward angle, toward the judge above him. Then he swung back toward the jury, unable to decide where he should be looking. "If he did, he never said so to my face. But then he wasn't a man to express his feelings. Subconsciously, who knows? So much lurks there that we can neither control nor explain."

"Isn't that your job, Doctor," I asked, "to explain the subconscious?"

"Part of my job, yes."

"You told Chrissy that her father was to blame for her mother's death, didn't you?"

He seemed to wince. Every mention of Emily Bernhardt tore at him. His fist moved up toward his mouth, shielding much of his face. "It was common knowledge . . . the way he treated her. She was so fine, so fragile and sensitive, and he was this boor. He was insulting and rude. He covered it up with humor, or what passed for humor. But it was always cutting. He couldn't be part of Emily's world so he had to tear it down. He scoffed at culture, at refinement, at everything that made Emily the special person she was."

"So you blamed Harry for Emily Bernhardt's death?"

He looked off again. "Yes. Not with a gun or a needle, but by stripping her of her dignity, keeping her prisoner in the home. He barred me from the house, loaded her with antidepressants and pain-killers. She ODed twice on a mixture of barbiturates and alcohol, and died of heart failure far too young."

"Then how, sir, can you deny hating this man you blame for killing the woman you loved?"

He gripped the armrest of the witness chair and made a truncated gesture with his hand. "No. I knew him for the beast he was. He was a product of his upbringing. He didn't deserve a woman like Emily. But I didn't hate him."

"And Christina," I said. "You resented her."

"Why would I? She was an innocent little girl."

"She kept you and Emily apart."

"I wouldn't fault her for that. That would be irrational."

"Are you a completely rational man?"

"No one is completely rational, but I—"

"Have you ever thought that Christina, innocent as she may have been, was to blame for keeping you and Emily apart?"

He shifted in his chair, arms folded across his chest. "I don't recall ever having that thought. Never."

"What about subconsciously, Dr. Schein?"

"What?"

"Did the thought ever occur in the place where so much lurks that we can neither control nor explain?"

He didn't answer. But then, how could he?

29

The Doomsday Rock

"Killing two Bernhardts with one stone," Charlie Riggs muttered.

"That's my theory," I said.

"You're not biting off more than you can chew, are you, Jake?" he asked, as he gnawed at a slice of garlic bread dripping with butter. "Getting even with both Harry and Christina in one fell swoop?"

"One swell foop!" Kip exclaimed. He was wearing a Deion Sanders jersey just to irritate me. "That's what Peter Sellers says in one of the *Pink Panther* movies."

"Frankly, I never understood the expression, either way," I admitted.

Doc Riggs sipped at his red wine. " 'Swopen' is a Middle English word dating from the sixteenth century. It means 'to sweep.' Therefore—"

"Charlie, we're in the middle of trial, so . . ."

"Actually," he said, patting his mustache with a napkin, "we're in the middle of lunch."

I couldn't argue with that. We were at Piccolo Paradiso, just across the river on Miami Avenue, and I had ninety minutes to finish my rigatoni alla vodka and get back to court.

"But if you want me to dispense with the etymology discussion," Charlie offered, "I shall do so."

"Thank you," I said, motioning to the attentive waiter for a second beer. I never drink during trial, but technically, as Charlie pointed out, luncheon recess is not *during* trial. As a lawyer, I am capable of making fine distinctions.

I had left Chrissy in the care and custody of my secretary, Cindy, and Milagros Santiago. It had been Kip's idea, bless his cinematic little heart. If Schein had programmed Chrissy, the memories should be in her head somewhere, he said. Just bring them back like flashbacks in a movie. I had given the assignment to Dr. Santiago.

Later, I would work with Chrissy to prepare her testimony. Notice I didn't say "rehearse," even though my personal glossary prefers the more accurate, if less genteel, terminology. Clients are customers, referral fees are kickbacks, experts are whores, and bondsmen are bloodsuckers. Client development is ambulance chasing. Pro bono work means getting stiffed for a fee. A retainer means "pay me now for work I may or may not do later." Lawyers' hourly bills are exercises in creative writing, in which our clients pay not only for our time but also for expensive lunches and dinners and the time we spend deciding what to order. Our "research time" often gets us paid to learn what we should have known or to relearn what we have forgotten.

If I sound a tad cynical, let me cop a plea. Guilty with an explanation. With all the garbage and all the games, there are still moments of pure adrenaline-driven exhilaration in what I do. The moment the jury walks in the door is one. I've left a piece of myself in every courtroom I have inhabited, with every client I have represented. Which might prompt me to ask, if I were the introspective type, just what do I have left?

"While I wouldn't want to celebrate prematurely," Charlie said, taking a bite of the bruschetta, "I must say your examination of the slippery Dr. Schein is going swimmingly."

"Swimmingly," I repeated, just because I liked the feel of the word on my tongue.

"Still, you have a distance to go," Charlie said.

"I'm going to crack Schein like a coconut under a machete," I said.

"Broly," Kip said. "Like José Ferrer did to Humphrey Bogart in *The Caine Mutiny*." He rolled some imaginary ball bearings in his hand. "The mess boys stole the strawberries."

"I'll keep Schein on the rest of the day. Then, after Dr. Santiago testifies, I'm going to bring him back."

"Bifurcating his testimony," Charlie said, musing over the possibilities, "which means you expect to elicit something on the first round that will pin him into a corner on the second."

"Just the truth, Charlie."

"*Magna est veritas*. Great is truth. But there's something I don't get. Did Harry Bernhardt rape his daughter or not?"

"I don't know. I wasn't there."

"Jake!"

"I think I can raise a reasonable doubt that he did."

"But why? You'll create incredible dissonance in the jurors' minds. They expect you to prove that he raped her. They may even want to acquit if you prove it. For God's sake, if she's going to testify she was raped when she was eleven years old, why cast doubt on it?"

"She's less culpable if she wasn't abused," I said.

"I'm just a retired coroner, so I must have missed this newfangled development in the law that says you're better off killing someone if you didn't have a good reason to."

"Think about it, Charlie. She had no motive to kill her father. None. She was a pawn in Schein's hands. It's the only way to get around the secret tape. Even if she was abused, the jury will convict her for the cold-blooded plan of revenge all these years later. But if she wasn't raped, if Schein planted false memories and controlled her, then taped what he wanted and didn't tape what he didn't want, he's the only one with the motivation to kill. Chrissy's as much of a victim as her father. Morally, she'd be absolved.''

"But not legally," Charlie said, a bit weakly.

"Not to a judge, not to a law professor," I said. "But jurors are people. They follow a moral compass, not a statute book.''

"Uh-huh," Charlie said, sounding unconvinced. "Isn't it possible the jurors will believe that Schein hated Harry Bernhardt but still wouldn't resort to murder? After all, the motivation for the killing was fifteen years old. Why did it take him so long to seek revenge for Emily's death? And why didn't he ever confront Harry, man to man?''

"Right," Kip chimed in, twisting his angel-hair pasta around his fork. "Like Mandy Patinkin in *The Princess Bride,* when he catches up with the bad guy and says, 'My name is Inigo Montoya. You killed my father. Prepare to die.' ''

"Because Schein's a coward," I said, "who might never have done anything if Guy Bernhardt hadn't egged him on.''

"Many theories," Charlie said, attacking a piece of chicken piccata. "Little proof.''

"I got a little proof this morning before court.''

"Socolow give you what you wanted?''

"Yeah. I didn't specify what I was looking for, just asked for the entire contents of Harry's desk, and there it was.''

"So Socolow doesn't really know what you want?''

"Doesn't have a clue.''

The old buzzard sliced his chicken, then said, "You're quite caught up in this trial.''

"It's what I do, Charlie."

"But are you prepared to lose?"

"What does that mean?"

"Emotionally, are you prepared to go on with your life when . . . if you lose?"

He had that father-to-son look of worry I get only from Charlie. "Okay," I said. "I'm living and breathing this one. It's the most important thing in the world to me."

Charlie sighed and neatly lined up his knife and fork on his plate. "Jake, did you know that at this very minute, the Swift-Tuttle comet, a chunk of rock six miles in diameter, is hurtling through space on a collision course with the earth? On its present course, traveling at sixteen miles per second, it will crash into our insignificant little planet on August 14, 2126."

"Most of Uncle Jake's clients will still be in prison," Kip said.

"What's the point, Charlie?" I asked.

"It's a doomsday rock!" he thundered. "The explosion will be a billion times greater than the Hiroshima bomb. It will create a cloud of dust that will encircle the earth for decades, cutting off all sunlight, killing all crops, destroying the global climate, causing worldwide famine and perhaps the extinction of the human race."

"Holy *Star Wars*!" Kip said.

I polished off the beer. "I get it, but I don't buy it. You're telling me that in the scope of things, what happens in our day-to-day lives doesn't matter. As individuals, we are nothing, and as a species—"

"We're doomed," Charlie said with finality.

"Then why do anything?" I asked. "Why not just hang out at the beach and windsurf and fish and chase women?"

"I like the fishing part," Kip said, his mouth painted with marinara sauce.

"As I recall, you tried that," Charlie said, "and found it unfulfilling. There has to be a balance. You have to find fulfilling work, what Mortimer Adler called play, or what Joseph Campbell called finding your bliss. At the same time, you cannot wager your entire worth, your self-esteem, on something so fleeting as the whims of a judge or jury, not when everything we call civilization can be extinguished in—''

''One swell foop,'' Kip said.

30

Body Language

After lunch, Dr. Lawrence Schein told the jurors that each of us has a secret compartment in which traumatic memories are locked away. "My job is to unlock that compartment, open the gateway to the mind, and release the memories. Only by remembering can we heal."

I kept the questions open and easy and let him talk. I wanted him relaxed and confident. It would make the contrast even greater when I broke him. *If* I broke him.

"All memories are stored somewhere in the brain," he said. "Some are accessible, ready to be called up at any time. Others are frozen, as if in a glacier. I use my training to warm up that glacier, to melt the ice, to let the memories run free as a river in the pristine woods."

He was up to his ass in picturesque wordplay, but I let him continue the spiel. Like a fish on a line, he would run a while before I set the hook. He told the jury about hypnosis, imagistic recall, psychodrama, free association, age regression, and gestalt therapy. He talked about patients in denial and the sensory flashbacks of abuse survivors. The words "remember" and "heal" came up repeatedly, as did the initials PTSD.

"Posttraumatic stress disorder—you may be familiar

with the term," Schein said, with just a touch of condescension, turning toward the jury. "We called it Vietnam syndrome when our soldiers suffered it. Whatever term we use, it means the patient has sublimated the horrors of the past."

He talked about Chrissy Bernhardt's history. The eating disorders, drug and alcohol abuse, destructive relationships with men, the blocks of missing memories from childhood, the feeling of being out of control. He described the differences between traumatic experiences that are remembered in intricate detail and those we cannot remember at all.

"A type I trauma is a short incident that leads to a brilliant, indelible memory," he explained. "A Type II trauma is caused by multiple, repetitious acts and may not be remembered. The mind anticipates the abuse—physical, sexual, or emotional—and represses the memory as a way of continuing to function. Of course, this defense mechanism does as much harm as good. The victim is not spared the agony of the abuse. She only feels it in different, self-destructive ways. Chrissy suffered Type II trauma and hence could not remember it until I unlocked the gate and the healing process began."

"She had no memories of the alleged abuse until you told her she was abused, is that correct?"

"No, not at all. I didn't *tell* her anything." Indignant and better prepared now that he knew where I was going. He gave the jury a little smile that said he was in control of this wily shyster.

"You suggested that her father abused her?" I said.

"No, I helped her remember what had happened so that she could heal. This is a little girl who had been raped, time and time again." He hit the word "rape" hard. An ugly word, and one of the woman jurors seemed to cringe. "To combat the pain and the shame, she had put herself into a trancelike state each time she was abused. Afterward, she told no one. Not her mother, not her teachers, not even herself. She didn't remember because she wouldn't let herself remember.''

He was assured and convincing. He was either a brilliant practitioner of the latest advances in psychotherapy or a complete bullshit artist. I thought I knew which, but could I prove it? Then I played the tapes.

"How old are you, Christina?"

"Eleven."

"Are you a happy girl?"

"Oh, yes. I have everything a girl could want."

The jurors sat transfixed, listening to that childlike voice.

"What do you have?"

"Toys and friends and a wonderful mommy."

"What about your father?"

"He gives me everything."

"Does Mommy love him?"

"I don't know."

"Christina, I'm Dr. Schein. I'm a friend of your mommy's."

"I know. You take care of her. She likes you. She told me so."

"Your mother is a wonderful woman. Tell me about your father."

"He hits her. He hits her a lot and calls her names. Mommy got sick, so she stays in her room. Daddy moved down the hall, next to my room."

"Does your father ever hit you?"

"No. Never. Not even when I'm bad."

"When are you bad, Christina?"

"When I don't do what Daddy says."

"Does he ever touch you in ways that frighten you?"

"No."

"Does he ever come into your bedroom and do things to you?"

"No. I don't remember anything like that at all."

I pushed the Stop button. "Now, Dr. Schein, correct me if I'm wrong, but didn't Chrissy just deny having been abused by her father?"

"Yes."

"After many hours of preliminary questioning?"

"Yes."

"Under hypnosis?"

"Yes."

"Injected with sodium amytal to enhance memory?"

Sure, I knew Millie Santiago thought it didn't work, but I'm a lawyer. I can go the other way if it helps the case, and Schein could hardly disagree after he had used it.

"Yes, I'd given her sodium amytal."

"But despite all of that—the questioning, the hypnosis, the truth serum—you wouldn't take no for an answer."

"I wouldn't accept at face value answers that clearly came from the surface of Christina's consciousness."

"The surface of her consciousness?" I mused, arching my eyebrows. "And where is that located, the cerebellum, the cerebrum, the isthmus of Panama?"

When I've exhausted logic and inductive reasoning, I resort to mockery and ridicule.

" 'Surface' is just an expression," he said through narrowed lips, "but if you must know, the regulator of explicit memory is the hippocampus. Studies show that survivors of childhood abuse often have a smaller hippocampus than normal. The belief is that these memories are stored implicitly in the amygdala, completely independent of the hippocampus."

"Can you prove that? Can we look into Chrissy Bernhardt's brain and find these memories in her—what'd you call it—her hippopotamus?"

One juror snickered. Good.

"Of course not," he bristled. "These are scientific theories about the workings of the brain."

"Theories," I repeated. "The earth is flat. That was a theory, too."

"Objection," Socolow said. "Argumentative and . . . archaic."

"Sustained," the judge said. "Let's get back on track, Mr. Lassiter."

"Wherever these events might have resided in her brain, Chrissy couldn't remember them, correct, Doctor?"

"Yes, but it would have been negligent for me to stop there. Remember, I had tested her. I knew her symptoms, the difficulty she had in relationships and knowing what she wanted, the fear of new experiences, the promiscuity, the sleeping and eating disorders, and several other classic symptoms."

"And these proved to you that she was the victim of sex abuse?"

"They were consistent with childhood sexual abuse. Indeed, they were extremely strong indications of such abuse."

"But why her father? Even if you're right, why not an uncle, a teacher, the gardener?"

He didn't have a ready answer, but he covered up by appearing to weigh the question with utter seriousness rather than terror. He was a good witness, and I hated him. After a moment, he said, "The father is a prime abuser in our society. Parental incest is rampant."

"So, you relied on statistics?"

"Not entirely. I relied on my experience and training."

"And the fact that you knew Harry Bernhardt?"

He nodded before answering. "Yes. I knew Harry. It added a dimension not usually available to a therapist."

"Let's explore that. At the time Chrissy was eleven years old, you were visiting her mother four or five times a week in her home, isn't that correct?"

"Yes."

"And Chrissy was there during those visits?"

"Yes."

"And her father was there, too?"

"Yes."

"Did she run away from her father or seem frightened of him?"

"No."

"Did Harry ever touch his daughter in an inappropriate manner?"

The jurors were all looking at Schein. He had to answer no. If it had been yes, he wouldn't have needed the great, climactic hypnotic therapy to solve the mystery of Chrissy's misspent life.

"No. He was affectionate to his daughter, but there were no overt manifestations of incest."

"Did Chrissy ever display any of the signs of sexual abuse when she was eleven or twelve years old?"

He thought before answering, and I could read his thoughts. That happens sometimes on cross-examination. You know where you're going, and so does a smart witness. Again, Schein was in a bind. If he answered yes, I'd ask what he'd done about the suspected abuse. The answer, of course, would be nothing, and then I'd question both his competence and his credibility. Cross-examination is like chess. You're always thinking three moves in advance.

"No, not that I noticed."

"But this extra dimension of knowing Harry Bernhardt somehow led you to conclude that he had raped his daughter?"

"It was just one factor," he said quickly.

"What else did you rely on, Dr. Schein—the factor that you hated him?"

He ran a hand over his shaved head, then crossed his legs, knee over knee. He turned his body away from the jury box at a forty-five-degree angle.

Body language.

Dr. Les Weiner had taught me all about it for three

hundred bucks an hour. The jurors had never taken any lessons, but they knew. Unconsciously, we all notice the signs. Preening, clenched fists, tightly crossed legs, unnatural gestures are all products of tension. A jerky motion with the hand reveals that the person is trying not to extend too far, and rapid hand movement may mean that the witness is trying to make a point and get it out of the way. Covering the mouth with a hand—psychologically covering up the words—is a giveaway, too.

In the nearly silent courtroom, I heard Schein's feet shuffle. The witness stand was closed in the front, so I couldn't see inside, but I'd give you two to one that he crossed his feet at the ankles beneath, not in front of, his chair. It's a sign of closing down, and I hoped the jurors noticed through the open side of the witness stand.

"No," Schein said finally. "As I told you earlier, I didn't hate him."

"Forgive me. At first you said you were Harry's 'friend,' but no, you then said you misspoke about that. You admit being in love with Harry's wife, writing her romantic poetry, and spending several days a week by her side. You blame Harry for her early death, and now you conclude fifteen years later that he must have sexually abused his daughter, because she was a skinny, unhappy model who slept with a lot of men in Paris and Milan. Is that about it?"

At the defense table, Chrissy sobbed quietly. Schein's mouth moved but nothing came out. He reached for the pitcher, and his hand shook as he poured water into a glass. It took another moment for him to have a sip, then say, "No. My personal feelings had nothing whatsoever to do with my diagnosis."

"Then why, Doctor, even after Chrissy denied that her father abused her, did you suggest that he had?"

"I didn't suggest anything. I continued the inquiry."

"So you did," I said, hitting the Play button.

"Christina, memory is a funny thing. There are memories we recall and some we just feel. What do you feel?"

"I don't know. Strange things."

"Ah, that may be the beginning. Do you know what sex is?"

"Yes."

"Did you ever have sex with your father?"

A sob. Then, *"I don't remember that."*

"But you're crying. Why are you crying?"

"I don't know."

"Christina, have you ever seen the tracks of a wild animal in the woods?"

"Not in the woods, but I've seen turtle tracks on the beach."

"And did you see the turtle, too?"

"Not always. Sometimes just the tracks."

"But you knew the turtle had been there."

"Yes."

"I can see the tracks of the animal all through your life. The monster has been there. I think you see it, too, but you've covered it with layers of dirt. Can we scrape through that dirt, can we uncover the monster?"

"I don't know."

Click.

"What was that, Doctor?"

"What?"

"Didn't you just hit the Stop button before asking more questions?"

He crossed his arms in front of his chest. "No, I wouldn't do that."

I stopped the tape and gestured toward Margie, the court reporter, huddled over her stenograph. "Because that would be the equivalent of the reporter failing to take down some of these proceedings, correct?"

"I suppose."

"Which would create a false record, isn't that right?"

"I don't know if I'd say false, but at least an incomplete record," Schein said.

"And therefore a misleading record?" I do not give up easily.

Exasperated now. "Yes, it could be."

Sometimes the truth comes hard, but as Charlie would say, *magna est veritas*.

Again, I hit the Play button, and after a few seconds, we heard Schein's voice.

"Let's talk about your father."

"I always loved my daddy. Always."

"Good Chrissy. That's a good girl."

"And my daddy always loved me."

"Did he?"

"Daddy told me I was his best girl, and now that Mommy's sick, I . . ."

"What, Christina?"

"I remember now. I remember."

"Very good, Christina. Very good. What do you remember?"

"I make Daddy happy. I pretend I'm Mommy."

"Does he come to your bedroom?"

"Yes."

"Do you have sex with your daddy?"

"Of course I do, silly. I'm his wife."

I shot a look at the jury. Appalled. Disgusted. Compassion for little Chrissy. Which I needed to convert into compassion for big Chrissy, and to do that, I had to prove that something worse had happened to Chrissy than being abused by her father. I had to prove she had been tricked into killing the innocent father she loved by a devious shrink who had implanted false memories in her.

"Now, Dr. Schein, what happened when the recorder was turned off?"

"I have no recollection. I don't know. I could have made a phone call. It could have been anything."

"Anything? Including suggesting to Chrissy—your hypnotized, drugged, anxiety-ridden patient—that her father committed unspeakable acts though she could not remember them?"

"No! I didn't do that."

And I couldn't prove it. But I sure as hell could suggest it.

I played three more tapes, each more graphic than the last. From the anguish in Chrissy's voice, there was no doubt she believed her father had abused her. That was the tightrope I had to walk. She might have shot an innocent man, but she sure as hell believed he was guilty. At the defense table, Chrissy sat looking straight ahead. The jury could see that magnificent profile, a single tear tracking down a cheekbone.

I thumbed through my notes and took a deep breath. All I had to do now was take the damning evidence against my client and turn it around. Finally, I announced, "Your Honor, we'd like to play the last tape, number twenty-seven."

I waited for Socolow, and it didn't take long. "Judge, there's no such tape on the exhibit list," he said. "It stops at twenty-six."

I walked toward the prosecution table and handed Abe a transcript of the final tape. "It's newly discovered evidence," I said placidly, "and there's no prejudice to the state."

"No prejudice!" Abe seemed happy to be angry. "There's always prejudice in surprise. Unless there's a good reason for the failure to discover . . ."

Abe stopped. He was reading the transcript. Then he looked up at me and whispered, "Are you crazy, Jake? You'll be disbarred for incompetence."

"If that were an offense, half our brethren would be selling whole life," I whispered back.

"Gentlemen," the judge interrupted, "would you care to include me in your colloquy?"

"The state withdraws its objection," Socolow said, trying to stifle his smile.

The first voice was Chrissy's.

"I've thought more about what we discussed yesterday."

"The need for goals?" Schein.

"No. What we talked about afterward."

"Oh, that."

"I've made a decision that you're not going to like."

"Maybe you shouldn't tell me."

"But I've told you everything else. I can't imagine not telling you first."

"All right then. But first, let me . . ."

The familiar sound of papers rustling and a chair squeaking and a *click*. Not the internal sound of the recorder being turned off, but the tape picking up the sound of a button being pushed on a different recorder. I hit the Stop button.

"What was that sound?" I asked.

"I must have turned off the recorder."

"So you were mistaken a few minutes ago about never turning off the recorder in the middle of a session?"

He threaded his hands together and twisted them at his knuckles. "Yes, but . . . well, there was the auxiliary recorder, so there was really no loss of information. I mean, the tape we're hearing is from the auxiliary recorder."

"But you didn't turn over this tape to the state, did you?"

"No, it must have been . . . overlooked."

"And you didn't give it to me until the eve of trial?"

He reddened. He had never thought I'd use it. Why would I? It proved the state's case of premeditation.

"No, as I say, I had forgotten all about it."

"And you never told Chrissy about it?"

"No."

I hit Play.

"*Is it off?*" Chrissy.

"*It's off.*" Schein.

"*Well, like I said, I was thinking . . .*"

"*Yes?*"

"*I've bought a gun.*"

"*I thought you were just going to visualize it.*"

"*No. That's not enough. I've got to kill him.*"

"*Figuratively? As part of therapy?*"

"*C'mon, Larry. That isn't what you meant. It couldn't be.*"

"*I didn't mean anything. I raised certain hypothetical actions, all intended to be therapeutic.*"

"*I decided last night. I couldn't sleep. I haven't slept through the night in weeks. I'm having nightmares and migraines.*"

"*It's all part of the process. The pain is coming out.*"

"*No, it's not. Maybe it will after . . .*"

"*After?*"

"*I'm going to kill my father for raping me. I'm going to kill him for ruining my life and for ruining Mom's.*"

"*What would that solve?*"

"*I don't know. But I'm going to do it. You've shown me what the bastard did to me. Now I know why everything in my life has been so—*"

"*You'll be caught.*"

"*I saw on* Oprah, *the other day, a woman who shot her husband after he'd beaten her. She got off.*"

"*I don't know.*"

"*Oh, Larry, don't look so depressed. That's funny, isn't it? I mean, you're treating me, and I say you're depressed.*"

"*You know I can't endorse what you're planning.*"

"*You can't stop me either.*"

"I'm not even sure you're serious. Most people never act on their revenge fantasies."

"You've helped me so much. I'll just be so glad when it's over."

"What, therapy?"

"No, Larry, when the bastard is dead."

The tape ran out, and the jurors exchanged glances. Why's the shyster trashing his case? Just hold on, ladies and gentlemen. There's still a rabbit in the hat.

"Dr. Schein, you knew you were being recorded, didn't you?"

"Yes."

"And my client didn't?"

"That's correct."

"Which is a crime in this state," I said in my best accusing tone.

"I didn't know that," Schein replied.

I moved back behind the jury box. I wanted them to watch the witness. "And this was the fourth therapy session after you suggested to my client that her father had raped her as a child?"

"It was the fourth session after Chrissy recovered her repressed memories of having been raped."

"And this was the last session you would ever have with my client?"

"Yes. Two days later, Christina killed her father."

"If you don't mind, Dr. Schein, we'll let the jury determine just who killed her father." His head snapped back as if I'd hit him with a quick jab. I walked back toward the defense table. Chrissy looked up at me, her eyes misty. I examined a legal pad filled with doodling. I knew the jury was watching, so I wrinkled my brow and studied the pad as if it contained the secret of cold fusion, then resumed my position at the rear of the jury box. Like sex, good cross-examination requires pacing. Start with a little foreplay, build slowly to a crescendo, and wham! Take a few breaths, then start all over again, preferably from a different angle.

"Correct me if I'm wrong, Doctor, but it would appear that on June fourteenth, at approximately four-thirty P.M., Chrissy Bernhardt told you in no uncertain terms that she had bought a gun and planned to kill her father."

"Yes. She said those things."

"You're a close friend of Guy Bernhardt's, correct?"

"Yes."

"Once Chrissy told you of her plan to kill her father, you must have picked up the phone and called Guy Bernhardt."

"No. I didn't do that."

"Then you must have called Harry Bernhardt to tell him that his life was in danger."

"No."

My face reflecting my rehearsed astonishment, I asked, "Did you call the police to warn them of your dangerous client?"

"No. I didn't consider her dangerous."

"Even though you diagnosed her as suffering from post-traumatic stress disorder, the same malady as Vietnam syndrome, in which combat veterans sometimes go berserk?"

"That's relatively rare."

"So you're telling this jury that you didn't warn Harry, you didn't warn Guy, and you didn't alert the police, correct?"

"Correct."

"Then let's see what you did do. Did you seek a court order that would require her hospitalization and testing?"

"No. I tried to talk her out of killing her father."

"How? By saying, 'I can't endorse what you're planning'? Pretty tough language, Doctor."

The judge cleared his throat. "Mr. Lassiter, please refrain from sarcasm."

"Sorry, Your Honor," I said halfheartedly. Sarcasm is

to me what scratching is to a center fielder. I turned back toward the witness stand. "Doctor, where were you on the night of June sixteenth?"

"I had dinner with a colleague at the Hotel Astor on South Beach."

"How did you learn of the shooting?"

"The police called Guy. He called the hotel and had me paged. He told me that his father was in surgery at Mount Sinai."

"And he wanted you to get to the hospital as quickly as possible?"

"Well, yes. Guy was an hour away, and I was much closer."

"Did he tell you who shot his father?"

"Yes."

"Did you, on that occasion, say, 'By the way, Guy, forty-eight hours ago, Chrissy threatened to kill your father. So sorry I neglected to mention it'?"

"No. I maintained the confidentiality of my patient's communication."

"How admirably ethical," I said, and Judge Stanger shot me a warning look.

"By the way, Doctor, why weren't you and Guy at Paranoia with Harry Bernhardt?"

"Why should we have been?"

I opened a little black book so recently produced by the state attorney. "Because, according to Harry Bernhardt's appointment book, he was to meet you and Guy there at eight o'clock."

"I don't know anything about that," he said quickly. "You'll have to ask Guy."

I planned to do just that, but first, as my granny would say, I had other fish to fry.

"What did you do after being informed of the shooting?" I asked.

"I paid my bill immediately, got my car, and rushed to Mount Sinai."

"What time did you leave the hotel?"

"I don't recall. I wasn't paying attention to the time."

I put down Harry's appointment book and picked up another file, pulling out a copy of a credit charge slip. "If you paid your bill at eleven-oh-one P.M., would it be fair to say that you left the hotel in the next three or four minutes, say eleven-oh-five P.M.?"

"Yes."

"At the hospital, did you go to Harry's room inside the ICU?"

"Yes."

"Was he conscious?"

"Semiconscious. He was coming out of anesthesia."

"How long did you stay?"

"Just a few minutes. I went down to the lobby to use the phone. I called Guy, who was in his car, on the way there. While I was down there, I heard the Code Blue call. I ran back to the ICU, but of course, they wouldn't let me near Harry while they worked on him. A short time later, he was pronounced dead."

I put down the police report and picked up the folder containing Schein's reports. He thought we were done. After all, we'd gone through the story chronologically. But sometimes you retrace steps. General George Patton never liked to retreat, saying he didn't want to pay for the same real estate twice. I look at it differently. I'll mine the same ground until I find a precious stone.

"Let's go back to June fourteenth, the day of the threat."

Schein sighed. This again.

"At that time," I said, "Chrissy Bernhardt was suffering from depression, was she not?"

He thought a moment, seemed to figure out where I was

going, then said, "I don't think she was clinically depressed, no."

When they try to weasel out of it, they always make mistakes. Sometimes a simple admission is less damaging than a slippery evasion.

"The preceding month, had you prescribed Desyrel for her?"

"I believe so."

"For what purpose?"

"It has many salutary benefits."

"Why did you prescribe it for Chrissy Bernhardt?"

"For her mental state."

Making me drag it out of him. "For her depression?"

Reluctantly, "Yes."

"And you prescribed Prozac several weeks earlier?"

"I believe so."

"For depression?"

He mumbled something through clenched lips. I wanted one of those dentist's clamps to hold his jaws open. "Doctor?"

"Yes, for depression." Aggravated.

"And Ativan?"

"Yes, for anxiety and depression, Mr. Lassiter."

One of the jurors whispered to another. I didn't think they were discussing the glorious architecture of the courtroom.

"So, Dr. Schein, isn't it true that Chrissy Bernhardt was suffering from depression?"

"Obviously she had some problems," he said, scrambling now, "but she was functioning fairly well. . . ."

And sometimes when they weasel, they just dig deeper holes.

"Functioning fairly well," I repeated. I picked up Schein's medical report and pretended to study it. The important parts I'd already memorized. "What was your diagnosis of Chrissy Bernhardt's condition?"

"Various conditions, but she was making progress."

I turned to the judge. "Your Honor, the witness is not being responsive."

"Dr. Schein, please listen carefully to the question and answer it," Judge Stanger instructed.

I smiled my thank-you toward the bench. A public scolding delivered the message that the shrink was hiding something. "What was your diagnosis?" I repeated.

"Posttraumatic stress order, neurotic depressive disorder, possible borderline personality disorder."

"But she was 'functioning fairly well.' "

When a hostile witness craps on the rug, I like to rub his nose in it.

"She was alert, clean, and well groomed, aware of her surroundings," he said. "Believe me, Mr. Lassiter, I have treated patients in far worse condition."

I'll say this for Schein: He didn't curl up and die the first time you kicked him in the nuts.

"Was she still taking the Ativan, Prozac, and Desyrel on June fourteenth?" I asked.

"Yes, I believe so."

"What else?"

He consulted his treatment notes. "Mellaril to control flashbacks, Xanax for anxiety, Restoril to help her sleep, Darvocet for headaches, and lithium for mood swings."

"Anything else in that grab bag of elixirs and potions?"

He ran a hand over his bare scalp and said, "Not that I recall."

I walked to the clerk's table, carrying a handful of small plastic bottles. "Would the clerk please mark these for identification?"

When she was done with the tagging and marking, I grabbed the bottles and turned toward the judge. "May I approach the witness?"

Judge Stanger motioned me forward and I closed the space between us. I had been in the public zone, the distance strangers give themselves when talking. By moving closer—through the social zone, an arm's length away, to the personal zone, close enough to touch, and nearly to the intimate zone—I increased the stress on the witness. Now, as I hovered over him, leaning on the witness stand railing, I was close enough to let him catch a whiff of rigatoni and beer. His eyes shot from me to the jury to the little bottles. "Can you identify these, sir?" I asked.

Schein slipped on a pair of half-glasses and leaned back in the chair, as if to escape from me. "They appear to be bottles of prescription medication for Christina Bernhardt." He studied them a moment more. "And I would appear to be the prescribing physician."

"Do these medications, these drugs, appear in your notes?"

"No." He anticipated the next question before I asked it, the sign of a nervous witness. "Christina and I had an informal relationship. After all, I'd known her since she was a little girl. She probably called me and I prescribed the drugs for her."

"What drugs, Doctor?" I asked, innocently.

He gritted his teeth and examined the first bottle. "Percodan . . ."

"Which is what, sir?"

"Aspirin with codeine."

"A pain-killer, a narcotic, correct?"

"Yes."

"What else?"

He turned the other bottles over in his hand. "Valium, generic name diazepam, a tranquilizer. Nardil, an antidepressant. And Halcion, a sedative prescribed for insomnia."

"What are the side effects of Halcion?" I asked.

"There are many reported."

"Psychotic episodes?" I asked.

"Yes, but that's rare."

"What else?"

"Oh, everything from nightmares and ringing ears to nausea and fainting."

"Fainting," I repeated, just for the jury. "And Nardil is prescribed for the severely depressed?"

"Yes, ordinarily."

"And the combination of all these drugs, Doctor, what is the effect of that?"

"Well, I'm not sure."

"Because you've never had a patient taking all of them before, isn't that right?"

"I don't know. Some patients are overmedicated just as some people take too many vitamins."

"And Chrissy was overmedicated, wasn't she?"

"I would have preferred her to have taken less."

"Then you should have prescribed less," I said. It wasn't a question, and he didn't answer, so I continued. "Therefore, as of June fourteenth, you knew that Chrissy was having trouble sleeping, was having nightmares when she did sleep, and severe headaches when she was awake. She was distraught from the so-called recovered memory of her abuse, and she was ingesting a cornucopia of pharmaceuticals, which had a variety of serious side effects. She had just bought a gun and told you she intended to kill her father, and your reaction was simply to turn off the lights, send her on her way, and two nights later, you're shocked to learn that she did just what she threatened to do. Is that about it, Doctor?"

"That's not . . . When you say it like that, it isn't . . . fair. You're second-guessing. I didn't know what she would do."

I moved away from the jury box so I could raise my voice without breaking the windowpanes. "But you hoped she would!"

Schein stiffened.

"You hoped she'd do what you wanted to do all these

years!'' Louder now, picking up the tempo, banging on the drums.

"No." He was flushed and sweating.

My voice pealed like summer thunder. "You hated Harry Bernhardt, but you didn't have the guts to do anything about it!"

Schein rose halfway out of his chair. "No!"

"You told her you saw the tracks of the monster where she saw none. You told her she'd been raped by her father though she had no memory of it."

"I helped her remember! I helped her heal."

"You wanted her to kill Harry Bernhardt!"

"No!"

"You prayed for her to kill him! You made her kill him!"

"No!"

"You programmed her to kill and you set her loose."

"No!"

"You took a confused young woman, pumped her full of drugs until her head spun, then you put a loaded gun in her hands and you aimed it and pulled the trigger."

"No!"

"*You* killed Harry Bernhardt! *You* wanted him dead, and *you* got Chrissy to do your dirty work!"

"He deserved it!" Schein shouted. He looked around, realized he was standing, seemed to notice for the first time the jury staring at him, wide-eyed. "But I'm not a killer. I didn't . . ."

His voice trailed off, his knees buckled, and he sank into his chair.

31

Doomed Beauty

The house smelled of tomato sauce, garlic, and melted cheese. I had asked Kip to bring home a couple of pizzas for the nightly war council, so he'd gathered up Tanya from next door, and they bicycled into the downtown Grove. An hour later, they returned with a pizza quattro stagioni (olives, roasted peppers, mushrooms, and artichokes) from Mezzanotte, a pizza musculi (mussels and marinara sauce) from Paulo Luigi's, and a Margherita (fresh tomatoes and basil) from Ats-a-Nice.

"Taste test," Kip proclaimed, carrying the boxes into the house.

During trial, everything tastes like cardboard to me, though I appreciated the theatricality of Kip's gesture. All the pizzas were good, but I'm partial to the basic simplicity of a Margherita. I try to keep both my life and my meals free of excessive clutter. With pizzas, at least, I succeed.

I opened a bottle of Chianti for Doc Riggs and Chrissy, sent Kip and Tanya onto the back porch with a couple of root beers, and popped the porcelain top on a pint of Grolsch for myself.

Chrissy sat on the sofa, her knees tucked up under her chin. She wore one of my old football jerseys, and with her bare feet and no makeup, she looked like a teenager. An unhappy teenager. She had sobbed quietly in the car on the way home from the courthouse, and now she sipped at the wine and stared into space, red-eyed and sniffling.

"I don't know what to believe anymore," she said. "At first, I was so sure. Jake, I could feel it happening, feel his flesh tearing into mine. Even now, when I close my eyes, it seems so real."

Chrissy shuddered, her face filled with such haunting sorrow as to stir something deep inside me. I remembered what she had said the first time we met, how the photographers loved that vulnerable look. Wounded and sexy. Doomed Beauty. I wrapped my arms around her, and she let her cheek rest on my shoulder.

"Regardless of how the trial turns out," she said, "I want you to know how much you mean to me. You're the one man who hasn't tried to use me."

"I'm living inside your skin," I said. "I'd do anything for you."

"You already have. You believe in me, and you're going to win."

"What?"

"Jake, you were brilliant today. You destroyed Larry. You showed what he did to me."

"I proved he had the motive to kill your father. I may have even proved he programmed you to carry out his plan of revenge. But no matter which way we turn, you pulled the trigger."

"What are you saying?" she asked, alarmed.

"We'll be entitled to a jury instruction on the lesser included charges, second-degree murder and manslaughter. A *win* is a conviction for manslaughter."

"Meaning what?"

"A ten- or eleven-year sentence, out in eight or nine."

"Eight years! No, it's not possible."

Chrissy was shaking her head in childlike disbelief. Dr. Schein might say she was in denial.

I cupped her head in my hands. "Chrissy, that's always been the goal. Either hang the jury or get lucky with a manslaughter verdict. If Abe had offered the plea, we would have taken it, but he's always gone after first-degree murder, life with no possibility of parole."

"Eight years," she repeated. "There must be something you can do. Please tell me there's something."

I looked at her, but there wasn't a thought in my head. No plan, no strategy for an acquittal. But I couldn't tell her that.

"There is something," I said with contrived enthusiasm. "I just didn't want to get your hopes up."

"You'll do it, Jake. I know you will. You would never let me down."

I peeked through the kitchen window toward the backyard. Kip and Tanya were stretched out in the hammock, side by side. Kip's hands were behind his head, just the way I lie there. Maybe it's heredity, maybe environment—who knows?—but the little guy is starting to pick up my gestures and mannerisms. I cracked the window just enough to eavesdrop. I know kids are supposed to have their privacy, but I was worried. I didn't have any idea what stage these two were at, so I wanted to know if they were discussing homework or condoms.

"How many movies can you name with the word 'pizza' in the title?" Tanya asked.

"*Mystic Pizza*," he shot back without hesitating. "That's an easy one. Bet you don't know who had her first starring role."

"Julia Roberts, unless you count *Baja Oklahoma*."

"Doesn't count 'cause it was made for cable."

"Yeah, but they showed it in theaters anyway," Tanya said.

Great, the kid had found a soulmate.

They were quiet a moment before Kip said, "*The Pizza Triangle* with Marcello Mastroianni and Monica Vitti."

"Wow! That's a tough one."

I closed the window just as Charlie came into the kitchen and started clearing my counter of a week's worth of fast food. Dried-out burgers, curled pizza crusts, half-empty cola cups.

"You shouldn't make promises you can't keep," he said, tossing some shriveled french fries into the garbage can.

I shot a look toward the door.

"She's sleeping," he said, "but before she nodded off, she told me you had a great, secret plan. Want to share it with me?"

"Nothing to share," I said.

"Just as I thought." He was folding pizza boxes in half, jamming them into the trash. "She's such a frail thing, Jake."

"That's why I've got to win. She'll never make it in prison. Never."

"You're in a quandary," Charlie said. "You've proved Chrissy is a victim of Schein's manipulations, but you can't get around the fact that she killed her father."

"It's not a fact. It's an assumption made by the medical examiner." Getting out of my doldrums, starting to think like a lawyer.

"Unless you have contrary evidence, my boy, it's a *fact*."

"It could have been natural heart failure. It could have been medical malpractice. Larry Schein might have killed Harry in the hospital room."

"Proof, Jake! Where's your proof?"

I thought about it a second. "Schein said a couple of squirrelly things in court today, and they're still bothering me."

"A fine piece of lawyering, Jake, in case I failed to mention it. You built a fine ladder, put your hostile witness on the top rung, then knocked it down. He fell pretty hard."

"Thanks. Did you notice his time line's off?"

"How so?"

"Schein rushes out of the Hotel Astor at eleven-oh-five P.M. He gets to the hospital at eleven-forty P.M. It shouldn't take thirty-five minutes to get from the Astor to Mount Sinai."

"It was a Friday night. You know how slow traffic is on South Beach."

"Only if you go up Ocean Drive. The hospital is a straight shot up Alton. Ten to twelve minutes, no problem, especially if you're in a hurry."

"Maybe someone's watch was wrong. Maybe the valet parkers at the Astor were smoking weed or shooting craps."

"Yeah, and maybe Schein stayed to polish off his Grand Marnier soufflé, but I think it's screwy."

"What else?" Charlie asked. "What else did Schein say that you found 'squirrelly'? An interesting choice of words."

"Why, because he's a rodent?"

"No, because the name is derived from the Vulgar Latin *scuriolus,* which sounds so much like our word 'scurrilous.' At any rate, what did he say?"

"Maybe it's nothing, but it gave me an idea. Can you get a business directory for Miami Beach, one of those books that lists every commercial establishment by street?"

"Sure."

"And go over the autopsy report again, everything from toxicology to the EKG, okay?"

"I'll do it, Jake. But Harry Bernhardt wasn't poisoned; he wasn't stabbed; and he wasn't smothered. He was shot by that poor girl and had a heart attack following surgery. They've got causation nailed down tight. What's the point of attacking it?''

"It's the only way to win," I said.

I finished my preparations for the morning session just after the eleven o'clock news. Now I was lying on my sofa, eyes closed, half sleeping, half thinking, when Chrissy nudged me. She wanted to go out. A vestige of the mow-dell days, parties that start at midnight and end with steak and eggs for breakfast at the News Café.

"I'm too tired," I told her. "I missed my disco nap 'cause I was tied up in court."

"Tell me about it," she said. "Look, if you don't mind, I gotta go anyway. It's an opening, Jake, and they're gonna pay me two thousand dollars."

"You know our rules. No booze, no drugs, no parties 'til the trial's over."

After which there might not be any festivities for a very long time, my lawyerly self might have added.

"Jake, I need the money."

Weirdly, Chrissy had become a local celebrity. While the national advertisers wouldn't touch her, the publicity in Miami had made her a star. A Hialeah garment manufacturer had hired her as the spokesperson for Fem-Gun, a brassiere with a compartment for a .22 pistol. She'd been asked to speak to various women's clubs, including Daughters Against Rape, an incest survivors' group, and Bitches with Balls, a lesbian support group.

Reporters followed her to the courthouse, reported on her clothing, her lifestyle, her garbage (yogurt, torn panty hose, spermicidal jelly), and her reading habits, which consisted of fashion magazines and mysteries by Mary Higgins Clark. So, when a new club opened, it paid to have Chrissy there, along with the likes of Madonna, Sly, and occasionally Jack Nicholson. And if she was going, I was going, too.

The bouncer wore a muscle T-shirt and three earrings, one of which was embedded, like an errant fishhook, in his right eyebrow. His trapezius muscles bulged almost to his ears and bore the telltale acne of steroid abuse. While the plebeians strained against the red velvet rope, my lady and I were waved to the front, Musclehead's dim face showing recognition when he saw Chrissy in her red leather mini.

"Maybe I should frisk you," he said with a leer.

"I already have," I said, and we pushed past him into Quicksand, the newest club about to enjoy its fifteen minutes of South Beach fame.

The throbbing music grated at a decibel level that once induced General Noriega to come out of hiding. Multicolored lasers pierced through a man-made fog that drifted to the ceiling. Some undressed bodybuilders, male and female, frolicked in the pit filled with mud that gave the club its name. On the dance floor, folks of various genders spun and twirled: bare-chested gay boys, their pecs slicked with oil; girls dancing with girls; a few guys with their dates, hanging on for dear life. It was a sea of leather, chains, boots, and bare flesh, each person trendier than the next.

Chrissy leaned close and yelled something into my ear. I couldn't hear a thing. She motioned toward two middle-aged men in double-breasted suits over black T-shirts. A covey of Miami Beach quail hovered around them, and a photographer for *Ocean Drive* magazine snapped off a dozen pictures. One of the men had a ponytail, though he was nearly bald on top. The other had a shaved head, reminding me of Larry Schein. I still couldn't hear Chrissy, but as she moved to talk to the guys, I figured they were the owners of this newest establishment of high culture.

I let Chrissy go do her thing and wandered off on my own. Foam poured into a nearby pit, and several naked revelers dived in and disappeared. A few yards away, a guy/gal in camouflage pants, combat boots, and a pink halter top (which covered his/her small breasts) was pouring pills from a Baggie into the hands of two identically dressed girls who were too young to vote. I took a second look. They seemed familiar. Sure, I'd seen them at So-BeMo auditioning, their mother leading the charge. Somehow they'd gotten into the party scene, if not the modeling scene. One of the girls handed several bills to the transgender Rambo, who kissed them both on each cheek and put the Baggie back into a pocket of his camouflage pants.

I don't know crack from smack, crank from coke, XTC from LSD. Sure, I smoked some weed in my younger days, but now I won't ingest anything stronger than caffeine. I walked over and yelled at the girls, "That stuff will kill you!"

In unison, they stuck out their tongues at me, so I decided to mind my own business. I walked around the perimeter of the dance floor. At the roped-off entrance to one of the VIP rooms, the tuxedoed guardian recognized me. He should have; I'd gotten him probation once on a bad-check charge. He waved me past the ropes, and once inside, I saw several local politicians, a Hispanic soap-opera star, and a few other familiar faces. Softer music played. A spotlight played on a small stage where a naked black woman covered with whipped cream was moving seductively toward a naked white woman covered with chocolate. Though I am inexperienced in South Beach revelry, I figured this was not a cooking class.

The women took each other's hands, then slid thigh against thigh, exchanging whipped cream for chocolate. Then they lay down on the stage, their heads facing in opposite directions, their legs intertwined. Two well-muscled young men appeared. Naked, Caribbean-brown. They placed maraschino cherries on the women's nipples, then lay down next to them, one to either side, the men bent at the waist, their bodies arching into parentheses. All four began moving to the music, and then a young woman stepped from the crowd onto the stage. Applause greeted her.

"There's the artist," someone said excitedly, next to me.

"I call this work *Banana Split,*" she said proudly, and the crowd applauded heartily.

By now I had a headache and wanted to go home. I hoped Chrissy had done her networking and had picked up her check. Her name would be in Tara Solomon's "Queen of the Night" column in the paper, and the pony-tailed Quicksand boys should be happy.

I left the VIP room and found a rest room that had three condom machines. I was bent over the sink, tossing cold water onto my face, when I heard his gravelly voice. "Lassiter, you're making a big mistake."

I lifted my head and saw Guy Bernhardt in the mirror. He still looked like a pig.

"Accusing Larry Schein like that. It makes good press, but it's just a sideshow. The jury won't buy it."

"I'm not done with him yet. Before I'm through, he'll sing a song with your name in it."

"Damn it, Lassiter. You've said the wrong thing."

Then I saw the two guys behind him. I remembered them from the ride through the mango fields. Short, burly Hispanic men owned by their master. Bernhardt took a step back and they came forward. I spun around, flexed my knees, and let my hands dangle at my side. Adrenaline awakened me. I caught the first one with a straight left jab that snapped his head back. I pivoted in time to see the flash of a blade, the second one waving a knife under my nose. I backed up until my ass hung over the sink.

The knife moved closer. It was a shiny switchblade with a black enamel handle. The point was just below my chin when he brought it up and pricked the skin. I felt a drop of blood fall. My head tried to arch backward until my neck hurt. I couldn't move. All I could do was listen to Guy Bernhardt.

"Rusty said you were hardheaded. . . ."

"He doesn't know the half of it."

"He said I couldn't reason with you, deal with you. Apparently he's right. But even a mule, a jackass, can be taught. And today's lesson is that a bigmouth lawyer who points his finger at me is likely to get it cut off. You think you're a tough guy, but you know what? You bleed just like anybody else."

He nodded, and the man dragged the knife across the underside of my chin. A line of blood formed, then began to spill in drops. The man backed off and cleaned the knife on my jacket. His pal stepped forward, and while I had one hand cupped under my chin, he caught me in the gut with a short right hook. I crumpled to the tile floor, coughing and bleeding.

I had two Band-Aids under my chin when Abe Socolow greeted me in the morning. "What happened to you?"

"Cut myself shaving."

"Nervous, huh?" he said, and made his way to the prosecution table.

I had told Chrissy what happened and had grounded both of us for the duration of the trial. Now, we were in the courtroom of the Honorable Myron Stanger, and I was trying to focus on my witness.

The clerk called out her name, and Dr. Milagros Santiago marched to the witness stand, nodded to the jurors, and sat down. She was dressed in a navy skirt and matching jacket, her eyeglasses perched on top her head. She was one of those women who proudly carry twenty extra pounds and to hell what anybody else thinks. Millie gave her credentials and background; then we got down to business.

"The old view of autobiographical memory stems from Freud," Dr. Santiago said. "He described repression as a defense mechanism used to suppress the psychic pain of anxiety, guilt, or shame. We came to believe that every experience of a person's life was stored somewhere in the brain, waiting to be recalled by therapy or drugs, hypnosis or meditation. But now we know it's not that simple. Our memories are constantly being refashioned, and when we dredge them up, it's from a murky sea. There are true memories with false details, and false memories with true details."

She told the jury how historical truth, what actually happened, differs from narrative truth, what we remember.

"We don't store memories like bytes of data on computer disks, ready to be called up with total accuracy at the touch of a keystroke," she said, looking directly at the jury. "Memories are malleable and tend to change and drift with time. When recalled, they're a blend of fact and fiction."

I took Dr. Santiago through her research and that of others. She quoted the work of Dr. Elizabeth Loftus, using her analogy of the memory as a giant blackboard with an endless supply of chalk and erasers. Memory is dynamic, ever changing, susceptible to suggestion, and no one knows where truth ends and the imagination begins. She talked about the personal myths each of us creates about the past, about the dreams we mistake for reality. She told about pseudomemories of past lives and tales of abduction by aliens and satanic abuse.

"The people with these memories aren't lying," she said. "They could pass lie detector tests, and indeed it might be difficult to disprove them. But we know that such memories can be seriously flawed. We confuse dreams with recalled events. As for cases of abuse, memory is weakest at both ends of the spectrum of stress and boredom. Both mundane and violent events actually decrease the accuracy of memory. And, of course, memories can be implanted, either purposely or not, by others.''

As she spoke, I watched the jurors. Rapt attention, some nodding with recognition of instinctual truths. The best expert testimony makes sense to the layman. It fits with reality as we know it. DNA testing, combining genetics and statistics, is a challenge to your average Dade County juror, whose knowledge of English, much less chemistry, is rudimentary. Given a choice between Ph.D.'s dishing out scientific mumbo-jumbo or the visual presentation of a glove that doesn't fit, I'll take the glove every time.

After twenty minutes of listening to Millie Santiago, I wasn't sure I believed my own memories. Had I really seen my father cry that day on the porch when my mother ran out to meet her lover? Or had those been *my* tears?

''Are you saying there is no such thing as recovering repressed memories?'' I asked.

''No,'' Millie said.

On direct examination, just like Socolow, I set up straw men, then knock them down.

''Memory suppression is hardly unknown,'' she continued. ''In one study, researchers found that thirty-eight percent of adult women who had been treated for sexual abuse as children had no memories of the incidents. The difficulty is to recover the memories without contamination by postevent occurrences or suggestions by therapists, whether innocent or malevolent.''

Malevolent. Nice word. I wanted to make it Lawrence Schein's middle name.

''The literature is replete with false accusations,'' she continued, ''such as the former altar boy who accused a Roman Catholic cardinal of sex abuse, only to recant. We now know that many such accusations are therapy driven.''

It was time to move from the general to the specific.

''Have you had an opportunity to examine the defendant, Chrissy Bernhardt?''

"Yes, I examined her."

"Have you reviewed any records in connection with the examination?"

"I read Dr. Schein's entire file, including notes detailing the therapy sessions, his tests and diagnoses, and I listened to the tapes. Additionally, I reviewed as many of the patient's childhood medical records and current records as I could locate."

"Based on your examination and the records you reviewed, are you able to state to a reasonable degree of medical certainty whether Chrissy Bernhardt was sexually abused by her father?"

"No."

The jurors responded with puzzled looks. I had disappointed them. They expected a revelation, and I had none. Yet.

"What could you determine?"

"Christina suffered severe trauma when she was approximately eleven years old, and she repressed the memories of the incidents," Dr. Santiago said. "There are certain indicia of sexual abuse which coincide with the time frame. She had several urinary tract infections at ages eleven through thirteen and also suffered eating disorders, including bulimia. Her schoolwork suffered and she became rebellious at about the same time. These can demonstrate a history of sexual abuse, though they are not conclusive."

"What about the fact that, while under hypnosis, Chrissy revealed alleged instances of sexual abuse by her father?"

"Those statements are as reliable as a witness to a crime who picks the alleged criminal out of a lineup while being coaxed by a policeman. Christina's revelations are tainted by Dr. Schein's overly suggestive questioning and are completely unreliable. In fact, at the present time, they have been recanted, at least to the extent that Christina now states she no longer knows what happened to her.''

"Then how can we determine what really happened?''

"There's no certain way, but with appropriate, neutral questioning under hypnosis, without the use of drugs, there's a possibility.''

I turned toward the judge. "Your Honor, at this time, we call Christina Bernhardt to undergo questioning under hypnosis by Dr. Santiago.''

"What!'' Abe Socolow leaped to his feet. He leaned toward the bench, resembling the bowsprit of a sailboat. "The state objects. You can't put two witnesses up there together and have a tea party.''

"Is that a sexist remark?'' I asked, aiming for the female jurors.

"There's no precedent for this,'' Socolow complained.

"It's an evidentiary demonstration, no different than any other,'' I responded.

Socolow's Adam's apple bobbed above his shirt collar. "It's cheap theatrics!''

The judge motioned us up to the bench. "Let's have a brief sidebar.'' When we got there, he looked at me. "What are you pulling here, Jake?''

"Nothing,'' I whispered. "I don't know what my client's going to say. No one does.''

"Then you're incompetent,'' Socolow said. "First you impeach your own expert. Now this! The court should protect your client from you.''

"I appreciate the state's concern for my client's welfare,'' I said, "but I've fully discussed this with my client, and she wants to do it. She wants to know the truth and wants the jury to know, too.''

"How do I cross-examine a defendant under hypnosis?'' Socolow whined.

"You don't,'' I said. "I don't examine her while she's under, and neither do you. When she comes out of it, she'll remember everything. Then, if you want, ask her questions 'til everybody falls asleep. You usually do.''

"That's enough, boys," the judge said, shooting a look at the jury. "This is a murder trial, and I'm not going to unduly limit the defense. But, Jake, if you start getting into past lives or some kind of witch doctor voodoo, I'll cut it off quicker than Lorena Bobbitt with a pair of shears."

"Judge, I don't know what's going to happen, so I can't make any promises."

"You really didn't rehearse it?" the Honorable Myron Stanger whispered.

"Nope. Dr. Santiago said it wouldn't be proper."

The judge whistled under his breath. "Jesus H. Christ, if they weren't paying me to sit here, I'd buy a ticket."

"That's what I mean, Judge," Socolow said. "Jake's turning your courtroom into a circus."

"Well, if the elephants shit on the floor, we'll just pile on the sawdust," the judge said.

I nodded in appreciation of this gem of judicial sagacity and resumed my position in front of the jury box. Turning to my client with a slight bow, I said, "Chrissy Bernhardt, would you please step forward?"

32

And When Chrissy's Bad . . .

The lights were dimmed. New Age music played from Millie's tape recorder. It sounded like tinkling wind chimes, a flute, and waves pounding a rocky shore. Chrissy leaned back in a recliner in front of the jury box, Millie telling her to relax, to let her mind run free, to approach a brilliant white light. Her body was growing heavy, Millie said; it was sinking deeper and deeper into the chair. Then she had Chrissy count backward from fifty, her voice logy.

I didn't know about Chrissy, but I was getting sleepy. I was also watching her cream-colored Emanuel Ungaro skirt creep up her thighs and hoped it neither distracted the men nor pissed off the women sitting in the jury box.

It only took a few moments before Chrissy was in that never-never land between somnolence and wakefulness. "What is your name?" Millie Santiago asked.

"Christina Bernhardt," she said, eyes still closed, "but on my card, it just says Chrissy."

"What card, Chrissy?"

"My composite. I'm a model."

"Are you a good model, Chrissy?"

"When Chrissy's good, she's very good." She chuckled to herself. "And when Chrissy's bad . . ."

"What do you do, Chrissy?"

"I make scads of money for pouting or cocking a hip or hitting a volleyball on the beach."

"Do you enjoy your work?"

"It's all right." Sounding bored.

"Are you happy?"

No answer.

"Chrissy . . ."

"Sometimes."

"When?"

"When I dream about being married and being a mother."

I liked that. This wasn't just a spoiled, high-paid party girl. Chrissy Bernhardt had dreams of a ranch house with a white picket fence, just like everybody else. At the prosecution table, Abe Socolow was scowling, or was that his version of a smile?

"What do you want from life?"

"I want to eat hot fudge sundaes and get fat."

The jurors smiled. The answers had the ring of normalcy, of truth.

"You mentioned getting married, becoming a mother. Are those goals, too?"

"Sure. But no one's ever asked me. *Ever.*"

"Maybe you haven't met the right man."

"I've met Mr. Wrong a thousand times." The pain in her voice filled the courtroom. "I'm damaged goods. That's what he said."

"Who?"

No answer.

"Chrissy."

"He said I'd always be his, even if I was grown up, even if I was married and a mommy myself, 'cause he was the first. He told me I belonged to him and every other man would know it."

"Is that true?"

"Yes. Everybody knows."

"What does everybody know, Chrissy?"

She sniffled back a tear but didn't answer. I thought of the song that had been playing just before Chrissy shot her father. *Everybody knows that the dice are loaded. Everybody rolls with their fingers crossed.*

"I've fucked a lot of men," she said, and one of the women jurors gasped. "But I've only made love to a few. I fucked men because they bought me dinner. I fucked men because I was bored. I fucked men for no reason at all."

Now Socolow leaned back in his chair and truly smiled, if that's what a shark does just before swallowing a grouper. Judge Stanger was glaring at me as if I were the circus elephant with loose bowels. I was afraid his gavel would end our little experiment before it had a chance.

"I had dreams," Chrissy said. "For years, the same dreams, snakes curling up my legs, underneath my skirt, getting inside my panties, and then inside me."

She sobbed and pulled her knees tight up against her chest. There was no sound in the courtroom other than the wheeze of the ancient air conditioning and the scratching of pen on paper in the press row.

"Tell me about the men," Dr. Santiago said.

"So many men. Always laughing."

"Why would they laugh?"

"Not out loud. Not so that I could hear them. But they laughed at me. They knew. I could tell by looking at them that they knew."

"What did they know, Chrissy?"

"They knew I was dirty." She curled into the fetal position. "Who would ever want me?"

"What made you dirty, Chrissy?"

"So long ago. So long . . . I don't remember." She seemed to drift off.

"Let's go back to that time. Let me help you remember.

I've seen your pictures. You had a ponytail and you rode a palomino. How old are you?''

Silence.

"Chrissy."

"Sugarcane."

"What?"

"I'm eleven and my horse's name is Sugarcane." The little girl voice. "She broke a leg and Daddy had to shoot her."

"That must have made you very sad."

Another sob.

"What else makes you sad?"

No answer.

"Does anything frighten you?"

"The sounds."

"What sounds, Chrissy?"

"At night. In my room."

"What's in your room?"

"He is. The door opens, and he comes in. I can hear the floor squeaking even though he walks on tippy-toes. The bed squeaks, too, but I don't make a sound because he tells me not to. His voice is so rough. He sounds like a pig grunting, and he sweats so much, the bed is all wet. I get scared, 'cause I think he's sick or hurt."

I wasn't breathing. Her anguish cut to my heart. And I was getting what I deserved. After I'd discredited Schein for his methods, he still turned out to be right. Harry Bernhardt had been a slime who raped his daughter. All the fancy footwork and we were right back where we started. Chrissy had the motive, but not the lawful excuse, to kill her father.

"I pull the sheet up over my head so I can't see," Chrissy said, "and I think about an island with green cliffs and high waterfalls. I don't really feel anything until morning, when my peepee hurts. I tell him it hurts, but he keeps coming to my room anyway."

"How many times has this happened, Chrissy?"

"I don't know. Lots of times."

"Who does this to you?"

Another sob.

"Chrissy, who comes into your bed at night?"

A sniffle caught in her throat and she coughed.

"Chrissy, is it someone you know?"

"Yes."

"Someone in your family?"

"Yes."

"Is it your father?"

"My father?"

"Is it your father who comes to your bed and hurts you?"

"No, of course not. Daddy would never do that."

What? In the courtroom, time was frozen. No movement except for dust motes floating in the shaft of an overhead spotlight. A moment of crystal clarity, of blinding intensity, a moment carved into the soft metal of my memory with the forged steel blade of the truth.

"Who does it, Chrissy?"

She didn't seem able to answer.

"Who comes to you in the night? Who frightens you? Who hurts you?"

Unconsciously, Chrissy wiped away a tear with the back of a hand. A little girl's gesture. Sweet and innocent and so painful as to sear the soul.

"My brother," Chrissy said. "Guy hurts me. It's always Guy."

33

Physician, Heal Thyself

Granny was grilling shrimp on the barbecue in my backyard. Fat and juicy, marinated in beer. The shrimp, not my granny, though she was half pickled in her home brew.

Granny was still embarked on a plot to fatten up Chrissy. In the kitchen, duck-and-sausage gumbo was simmering on the stove next to a pot of black bean soup with bell peppers and bacon. Bowls of rice and chopped onions warmed in the oven.

"That girl's gotten skinnier," Granny had whispered to me as she carried the victuals into the house. "I gave her a hug and her hipbones jabbed me like bamboo sticks. It's no wonder she's always fainting, the way she eats."

Granny was right. Charlie Riggs had told me that Chrissy was borderline hypoglycemic and should be eating several times a day, and not just a little tofu. At the moment, Chrissy was curled up on the sofa, purring in her sleep. I checked on her, gently stroked a strand of blond hair from her eyes, and walked to the kitchen where Charlie was making cocktail sauce for the shrimp. I opened a Grolsch, and Charlie hummed show tunes while mixing Worcestershire with vinegar.

In the Florida room, Kip was watching . . . *And Justice for All* on cable. Defense lawyer Al Pacino, half crazed by a legal system run amok, was prancing in front of the jury box while his client, John Forsythe, a judge charged with rape, watched in astonishment. "The prosecution is not going to get this man," Pacino sang out, "because I'm going to get him. My client, the Honorable Henry T. Fleming, should go right to fucking jail! The son of a bitch is guilty!"

I've had clients like that. Most, in fact. But I never gave the speech. And now I had a client I would have done anything to help.

"I did the homework you requested," Charlie said. "Nothing new in the autopsy report, and there won't be if I read it another ten times. I did find something, though. The morgue has started saving ocular fluids from cadavers' eyes. Just freezing them for possible testing later. I've got Harry Bernhardt's."

"And?"

"Toxicology tests are negative. I'll get the electrolyte readings first thing in the morning. Plus, I've got a cardiologist, Dr. Eric Prystowsky, taking a fresh look at the EKG. He's the best rhythm-disturbance man in the country, and if there's something funky there . . ."

Did Charlie really say "funky"?

"Good work," I told him. "I had Cindy check the business directory. There are three possibilities, so we subpoenaed them all."

Charlie wiped his hands on an apron I could swear came from the morgue, but maybe the stains were catsup and molasses. "Were my eyes deceiving me," he asked, "or was that Larry Schein in the front row of the gallery today?"

"That was him. Socolow and I stipulated to waive the witness exclusion rule. It makes sense if I'm going to ask Schein about Chrissy's in-court hypnosis."

"I caught sight of him after your client dropped the bombshell. He turned a grayish yellow, kind of like a beached amberjack."

I took a pull on the beer. "I saw. Complete and utter shock. He didn't know his old buddy Guy was the rapist, I'm sure of it."

"And you're surprised?"

"I was at first. I'd always put Guy and Schein on the same team, but I was only partially right. Guy wanted his pop's money and couldn't care less about Chrissy. Look what he did to her as a kid. He knows Schein hates his old man, blames him for Emily's death. So he tells Schein he's always suspected Dad abused Chrissy. It would explain a lot, and it would make it easier for Schein to take part in something he never would have done otherwise."

"Program Christina to commit murder."

"Exactly. Schein implanted false memories all right, but he thought they were true."

"How does it affect your closing argument?" Charlie asked.

I gave him a preview. "When we began this trial, each of you raised your hand and swore 'a true verdict render,'" I chanted in my speechifying voice. "Now you must be true to your oath. Chrissy Bernhardt is charged with killing her father with *premeditation*. In just a few moments, Judge Stanger will instruct you that premeditation means 'killing after consciously deciding to do so.' But Chrissy didn't decide to kill Harry Bernhardt. Lawrence Schein did. She tried to kill a man who didn't exist, a man with the head of a goat and cloven hooves, a man-beast invented by Lawrence Schein, a devil of his imagination, a man *he* hated, a man *he* consciously decided to kill."

Charlie nodded his approval. "Let's take inventory," he said while spooning minced onions into a mixture that now included chili sauce, hot peppers, plus a secret ingredient

I hoped didn't come from the building with walk-in coolers on Bob Hope Road. "You proved your client really is a victim, first of her brother, then her psychiatrist. That'll win sympathy from the jury, but where are you legally?"

"Simple. The evidence is that Chrissy was defrauded into forming an intent to kill her father. She killed someone who didn't exist."

"Sounds like manslaughter to me," Charlie said.

I drained the Grolsch and looked in the fridge for one of its brothers. "Socolow thinks so, too. On my way out of the courtroom, he offered me a plea. Eight years. Says he'll go below double digits 'cause we're such old friends."

"Which means she'd be out in six years and a few months with gain time," Charlie said, dipping a finger into his cocktail sauce, then tasting it. "Mmmm. So much better than tired old catsup and horseradish."

"I turned it down."

Charlie raised his bushy eyebrows.

"I can win, Charlie. I can win this case."

"Manslaughter's a win. You said it yourself. She killed a man. Regardless whether she was tricked into believing he had raped her, she killed him. The jury will have to find her guilty of something, and manslaughter's a lot better than first- or second-degree murder."

"They like her, Charlie. I can feel it. You're getting too hung up on the law, on technicalities. They're looking for a reason to acquit. I can feel their emotion."

"Theirs," Charlie asked, "or yours?"

This time, Dr. Lawrence Schein was ready. Pale, baggy-eyed, and haggard, but ready. He had brought a lawyer, who sat in the first row of the gallery. I liked that. This isn't Los Angeles, where everybody from Rosa Lopez to Kato Kaelin (whose English isn't as good as Rosa's) brings a lawyer, an agent, and a publicist to court. Jurors, blessed with common sense, distrust anyone who needs a mouth-piece. I planned to hang a neon sign on the lawyer at the first opportunity.

Schein took long pauses, weighing each question before answering, his eyes flicking to Jonas Blackwell, an aging medical malpractice defense lawyer who knew his way around a courtroom.

"You understand that my client has repudiated your conclusion that she was sexually abused by her father?" I asked.

"It was not my conclusion, it was hers," Schein said smugly.

"Under drug-induced hypnosis?"

"If you want to call it that."

"And suggestive questioning by you, Doctor?"

"I wouldn't characterize it that way. But I will concede this. Recovered-memory therapy is as much an art as a science. I quite correctly diagnosed your client as having been raped as a child."

"Unfortunately, you nailed the wrong perpetrator."

"Had I been right, we'd likely be here to discuss the murder of Guy Bernhardt," Schein fired back.

Ouch. A finely scripted answer, the handiwork of Jonas Blackwell, I was sure. I could have objected and moved to strike the nonresponsive answer, but that would have simply underlined it. Instead, I plowed ahead.

"Prior to yesterday's testimony, did you have any idea that Guy Bernhardt was the person guilty of raping Chrissy?"

"No, of course not."

"You find it hard to believe, even now, that your friend Guy is a rapist, don't you?"

"I believe the testimony is credible, but yes, it comes as a complete shock."

"Whereas you had no trouble believing that Harry Bern-hardt, a man you hated, was guilty?"

"I thought he was guilty. Apparently I was wrong."

"When Chrissy was in your care, did Guy Bernhardt ever tell you he suspected his father of abusing Chrissy?"

He hesitated. "No."

Of course not. He'd already testified he hadn't discussed the therapy with Guy. He couldn't contradict that lie by telling the truth now.

"Who's that you're looking at?" I said, my voice just a notch below a holler.

"What?" Startled now.

"There, in the front row, the man in the suit taking notes." I pointed toward Jonas Blackwell as if he were a purse snatcher.

"That's my lawyer," he said softly.

"A law-yer!" Making it sound like a loathsome disease. "If you've sworn to tell the truth, why do you need a lawyer?"

"Objection, argumentative," Socolow said.

"Sustained," the judge said. "Mr. Lassiter, you know better than that." He turned toward the jury. "A witness is entitled to have a lawyer present in court, and you are not to infer anything regarding the witness's credibility from the fact that he does have a lawyer."

No problem. I'd already made my point.

"At any rate, Doctor, you now acknowledge that Chrissy Bernhardt was not raped by her father?"

"Yes, that's correct."

"But last June, you believed he was the worst kind of criminal, a man who would rape his own child."

"Yes, I believed that."

"Just as you believed he was responsible for the death of his wife, Emily, the woman you loved?"

Schein blinked. "Yes, he destroyed her life. Your client would agree with that."

"So as you drove to the hospital on June sixteenth, you were convinced that Harry Bernhardt deserved to die?"

"Objection, irrelevant," Socolow said. "The doctor's not on trial."

Not yet.

"I'll tie it up, Your Honor," I responded.

"Then I'll overrule for now."

"I'm not God," Schein said. "I don't determine who should live and who should die."

"Let's back up a bit, Doctor. At eleven-oh-five P.M. on June sixteenth, you left the Hotel Astor, rushing to get to the hospital, correct?"

"Yes, I believe I testified to that."

"And you arrived at the ICU at eleven-forty P.M., where you encountered Nurse Gettis?"

"That sounds about right."

"You drove up Alton Road to get to the hospital?"

"Yes."

"And it took thirty-five minutes to get there?"

"It was a Friday night. Traffic was heavy."

"If I told you a test drive we've done the last four Friday nights, never exceeding the speed limit, averaged twelve minutes, what would you say?"

He didn't say anything and neither did I. If I really had time to do test drives, all my exhibits would probably be in color-coded binders, too.

"Where did you stop on your way to the hospital, Dr. Schein?"

"Nowhere!" The answer was too quick and too loud. It surprised even me, but I was beginning to discover that the doctor was a bad liar. Most basically honest people are.

"I'm going to ask you again, Doctor, and if you want to consult with your lawyer before answering, I have no objection."

In other words, if you're going to lie, at least do it right.

"I don't need to consult anyone," he said, eyes flashing toward Jonas Blackwell, seeking support.

At the prosecution table, Abe Socolow watched intently. He loved to win, but deep down, he was a lot like me. He loved the truth even more.

Chrissy sat at the defense table, dressed in a short mint-green jacket with silver buttons over a matching A-line dress, her hands folded together in front of her. She chewed at her lower lip. Scared, confused, trusting me with her life. She didn't know where I was going. I hadn't told her. Early this morning, she had asked what I was doing as Cindy and I pored over a stack of prescription forms just delivered to my house from three pharmacies. Playing lawyer, I had told her. Now Cindy sat in the row of straight-backed chairs between the defense table and the bar separating the lions from the Christians. Her fingernails were painted black and embedded with silver stars like the nighttime sky. Toenails, too, judging from the planetarium view of a big toe sticking out of a straw sandal.

Thanks to Cindy, I had the ammunition, and it was time to start throwing hand grenades.

"Dr. Schein, isn't it true that you stopped at the Beach Mart Pharmacy on the way to the hospital?"

His mouth was locked tight, and the muscles of his jaws were doing isometrics. This time he didn't look at his lawyer. He looked directly at me.

Wondering.

How much did I know?

"I don't recall that." Hedging his bets.

"The pharmacy's located on Arthur Godfrey Road. It's open twenty-four hours. Does that refresh your recollection?"

"Not really."

Cindy had cased the place, and now I wanted to make it sound like my second home. "Just a little hole-in-the-wall. Sunglasses up front, Russell Stover candies on a rack by the register, and a pharmacist behind bulletproof glass in back."

It wasn't a question, so he didn't answer. He was waiting, and I wanted him to wait some more. To sweat, to worry. *How much does the shyster know? I know it all, Schein, and I can prove most of it.*

I continued, "There's a pass-through counter in the glass wall that they hand the prescriptions through. On the inside of the counter sits a time stamp, so every time a prescription is filled, they stamp it, isn't that right?"

"I don't know." His neck was blotched with red, and I'd bet his heart was racing. Hook him up to an EKG and the stylus would draw the Himalayas.

I made a big production of going back to the defense table, opening files, looking for something, seeming to have lost it. I felt his eyes on my back. Let him sweat some more. "Ah, here it is, Doctor. Perhaps this will refresh your memory."

Sometimes I bluff, and sometimes I really hold the aces. "Your Honor, may I approach the witness?"

The judge waved me forward. On the way, I dropped a copy on Socolow's table, then handed the little rectangular form to Schein. He grabbed for it. "Can you identify that?" I asked.

He nodded.

"You'll have to answer audibly."

"It appears to be a prescription form from the Beach Mart Pharmacy."

"And that's your signature, isn't it?"

He studied it, as if trying to decipher the Axis war code. No answer. Wondering if he could deny it. Hoping for a miracle that would keep the sky from falling.

"Perhaps you remember the pharmacist as well as he remembers you," I prompted. Bluffing now. The pharmacist was on vacation in Barbados, not in the corridor waiting to testify. I hadn't been able to reach him.

"That's my signature," he said at last.

"KCl," I said. "What's that?"

"Potassium chloride." His voice was a whisper.

"What's it used for?"

"Many things. Making fertilizer, for one."

"You weren't doing some gardening that night, were you, Doctor?"

"It's a harmless substance," he blurted out. "Potassium and chloride. Both are found naturally in the body."

"Really? Then I suppose if someone was injected with potassium chloride, it wouldn't show up in a toxicology test?"

"I don't know anything about that."

"What's potassium chloride used for, Doctor, besides making fertilizer?"

"It's used in heart surgery."

"And what does it do?"

His eyes darted to Jonas Blackwell and back to me again. "I'm not an expert. I mean, I'm not a surgeon."

"Oh, don't be so modest. The drug is injected into the heart to stop it during open-heart surgery, isn't it?"

"I'm not sure."

"You weren't performing open-heart surgery that night, were you?"

"No, of course not."

"But you wrote a prescription for one hundred milliliters of potassium chloride, which you picked up at eleven-twenty-seven P.M. on your way to the hospital, didn't you?"

He didn't answer.

"Doctor?"

"Yes."

"Thank you," I said. I returned to the defense table and let him hold on to the prescription slip. He looked like he wanted to swallow it. "Dr. Schein, do you remember, the other day, I asked if you blamed Harry for Emily Bernhardt's death?"

"I remember."

"And do you recall your answer?"

"Not verbatim."

"Well, it struck me as a little odd, so let's just take a look at it." The jurors leaned forward in their seats. I had them. I had Schein. I had the whole damn world just where I wanted it. Cindy handed me the daily transcript, provided efficiently by the stenographer for a sum equal to the gross national product of a small Caribbean nation.

"I asked you this question: 'So you blamed Harry for Emily Bernhardt's death?' And you answered, 'Yes. Not with a gun or a needle, but by stripping her of her dignity, keeping her prisoner in the home,' et cetera, et cetera. Now, what did that mean, 'Not with a gun or a needle'?"

"It's just an expression. It means, not with a weapon."

"Then wouldn't the expression be 'a gun or a knife'? Where does a needle fit into this?"

"Knife, needle . . . They sound alike."

"But you were thinking of a needle. So it made me wonder, Doctor, what would Freud say? Why were you thinking of a needle? What memories were lurking in your subconscious?"

"I have no idea."

"Going back to the night of June sixteenth at the Beach Mart Pharmacy, you also purchased a fifteen-gauge hypodermic needle, didn't you? If you like, I'll show you the store's cash register receipt."

A vein in his shaved scalp seemed to throb, but it could have been my imagination. He stretched his neck out of his shirt collar, then answered. "Yes, I sometimes inject tranquilizers into patients, and of course sodium amytal during hypnosis, as you know. I was out of syringes, so I . . ."

He drifted off.

"On the way to see Harry Bernhardt, who had just been shot and operated on, who was in the ICU, you stopped off to do some shopping—is that your testimony, Doctor?''

''Well, yes.''

''Now you don't inject potassium chloride into any of your patients, do you, Doctor?''

''Of course not.''

''What would happen if you were to inject potassium chloride into someone not undergoing surgery, someone not on a heart pump?''

''It would short-circuit the electrical activity of the heart.''

''There'd be a rhythm disturbance, wouldn't there, Doctor?''

''Yes, I believe so.''

''And the heart would go into ventricular fibrillation, then stop, indicating to all the world that the person died of cardiac arrest?''

''I didn't do that!''

''I didn't say you had.''

''I've seen the autopsy report,'' Schein said, though no question was pending. Good. Let him run his mouth. ''There's no indication of anything like that.''

''No, there aren't even any unexplained puncture marks on the body, are there?''

''That's right.''

''But if the potassium chloride had been injected directly into Harry Bernhardt's IV tube, it wouldn't leave any unexplained marks on the body, would it?''

''I suppose not.''

''Is that how you did it, Dr. Schein? Did you pop a dose of KCl right into the IV?''

''What are you saying! No!''

''Doctor, when the man you hated . . .''

Motive.

''. . . was lying flat on his back, semiconscious and sedated . . .''

Opportunity.

"... you took that fifteen-gauge hypodermic needle and injected his IV tube with a massive dose of potassium chloride, didn't you?"

Means.

"No!" He looked toward the judge for help but didn't get any.

"When the potassium chloride hit his arm, he started thrashing. Even coming out of the anesthesia, he could feel the sting of the KCl, couldn't he?"

"No! I don't know."

"Doctor, if I told you that the ocular fluids removed from Harry Bernhardt's eyes showed elevated levels of potassium, would that surprise you?"

"Not at all," he said, licking a bead of perspiration from his upper lip and calming down. He relished the question, had a ready answer. "Potassium levels increase after death. It's not an indication of hyperkalemia."

"To what level would they increase?"

"I don't know exactly, but they could easily double or more, say from five milliequivalents per liter to ten or fifteen."

"So if the test showed two hundred milliequivalents per liter, what would that suggest, Doctor?"

Good old Charlie Riggs.

"I'm not sure. But you can't prove ..."

He let it hang there.

"And if a cardiologist with special expertise in heart rhythm disturbance comes into this courtroom after examining the EKG of Harry Bernhardt and identifies a widened QRS duration and subsequent ventricular fibrillation, indicating probable potassium poisoning, what then, Doctor? What do you say then?"

The swinging gate in the bar squeaked open, and Jonas Blackwell rushed through. "Your Honor, I request a brief recess."

"Denied!" the judge shouted. "And sit down."

The lawyer stopped in his tracks, looked around, and took a chair next to Cindy. Judge Stanger turned toward the witness. "Dr. Schein, there's a question pending. If you wish, the stenographer can read it back."

"I've made a ter . . ." Schein mumbled, his voice trailing off.

"What's that, Doctor?" the judge asked.

"I've made a terrible mistake," he said, his voice barely audible. "I believed Guy. I never would have done it had I known. I swear . . ."

Jonas Blackwell was on his feet. "Your Honor, my client invokes his Fifth Amendment rights. I request that the questioning be terminated."

"I said, sit down!" the judge thundered. He leaned close to the witness stand. "Doctor, your counsel suggests that you rely on your right against self-incrimination. Do you wish—"

"No!" Schein waved off the judge with a stiff gesture that reminded me of Richard Nixon on the day he quit. "Harry Bernhardt was an evil man. Maybe he didn't abuse Christina, but what he did to Emily was a crime. He knew we were in love. He could have let her go, but he was so cruel, so inhumane. And Emily was so beautiful and frail. She lost the will to live. It's Harry's fault she died, not mine."

That puzzled me. "No one said it was your fault."

"He killed her," Schein said, "maybe not with a gun or a needle."

There it was again. What was he saying? We weren't here to talk about Emily. Or were we?

"How did Emily die?" I asked.

Socolow stood up, seemed to think about objecting, and sat down again.

"I begged her to leave him." Not exactly responsive, but why not let him ramble? "I told her how I'd take care of her, protect her, but she couldn't do it. She wasn't strong enough. He snuffed the life out of her. She begged me to do it. . . ."

Lawrence Schein stared into space. Abe Socolow and I exchanged looks. He shrugged his shoulders, telling me it was my ball, run with it. At the defense table, Chrissy's eyes were filled with tears.

"Do what?" I asked.

"End it. We made a pact. I'd poison her while she was sedated. Then I'd kill myself."

Omigod.

A rumble of astonished voices swept through the courtroom.

Judge Stanger lifted his gavel, but never brought it down. Miraculously, the noise stopped, no one wanting to miss a word.

"With potassium chloride," I said, all the gaps filling in. "The *needle*. You injected Emily Bernhardt, but then you chickened out. You killed her but not yourself. You're a killer and a coward."

His head bobbed up and down. "At her first spasm, I knew what I did was wrong. All these years, and I still see her pain, even with the sedatives. I've carried it with me all this time. That's why I had to do something."

"Why?"

It's a question you're never supposed to ask on cross, but this time I knew the answer.

"Because I'd killed the wrong Bernhardt. I'd carried the guilt and shame for so long, it had nearly driven me insane. I had to kill Harry Bernhardt. I had to heal myself. It was *my* therapy."

34

The Defense Rests

Judge Myron Stanger shed his black robe and tossed it across the sofa. He loosened his tie, opened a door of leaded glass on his credenza, and grabbed a bottle of Jack Daniel's.

"Let the record reflect that we have reconvened in chambers," he said. "Counsel for the state and defense are present, as well as the defendant."

And the court stenographer. She never gets mentioned, but there she was, banging away at her little machine. I could hear the commotion on the other side of the door, the judge's secretary fending off reporters like a blocker picking up the blitz. Britt Montero's angry voice came through the door, something about the First Amendment and access to the courts. Chrissy and I sat next to each other in chairs facing the judge's desk. She looked confused and frightened. I patted her hand and winked at her.

"Let's go off the record, Margie," the judge said, and the stenographer straightened up and cracked her knuckles. "Goddamnedest thing I've ever seen in a courtroom, and I've tried more cases than the two of you put together. What the hell do we do now, boys?"

The judge hadn't opened the bottle, wouldn't until the

hearing was over. He pulled a Cuban cigar out of his desk drawer, a stubby four-inch Entreacto that would have looked good on Edward G. Robinson.

"I'd like to make a motion," I said.

The judge simultaneously lit his cigar and nodded to Margie, whose fingers were poised over her keys the next instant.

"But first, the defense rests," I said.

The judge exhaled a pungent puff of white smoke and turned to Socolow. "Any rebuttal?"

Socolow said, "The state waives rebuttal."

"The defense moves for a judgment of acquittal," I said, opening the rule book. "Under 3.380, no view which the jury may take of the evidence favorable to the state can lawfully support a conviction. The undisputed evidence is that my client simply did not kill her father. A third party did, and hence . . ."

Did I really say "hence"?

". . . there is no basis on which a jury could find her guilty of murder of any degree or of manslaughter."

"What about aggravated assault, Jake?" the judge interrupted, while studying the red-hot tip of his cigar. "If Abe here asked for it, I could charge the jury on ag assault or maybe attempted murder."

"Respectfully not, Your Honor," I said. "She hasn't been charged with aggravated assault, and under *Perry* v. *State,* the charging document can't be amended now because of a variance in proof. Additionally, attempted murder is not a lesser included offense, because it's possible to commit each offense without committing the other, and each contains elements the other does not. Therefore, under the rule, the court has no choice but to render a judgment of acquittal."

There are occasions—not many, I grant you—when I almost sound like a lawyer.

The judge puffed on his stogie, if a thirty-dollar cigar

can be called a stogie. "Abe, sounds like your buddy's done his research. You got anything to say?"

"Jake's wrong about one thing," Abe said, looking at me with a tight smile. "The evidence isn't undisputed. The medical examiner testified that the cardiac arrest stemmed from the shooting. Dr. Schein seems to think he killed Harry Bernhardt. Technically, therefore, it's a jury question. It's—"

"Judge, the EKG and the electrolyte test make it clear what killed—"

"Jake, don't interrupt me!" Socolow stood and paced to a window overlooking the Miami River. "I said, *technically* it's a jury question. That doesn't mean the state wants it to go to a jury. We'll be in front of the grand jury this afternoon and we'll have an indictment for first-degree murder against Lawrence Schein by dinnertime, maybe another against Guy Bernhardt for conspiracy. It'd be pretty damn embarrassing if we charged a man with murder the same day a jury convicted someone else of the crime. I'm not sure what killed Harry Bernhardt. Maybe your client did it; maybe Schein did it; maybe God said it was time. But I know this. There's a difference between moral culpability and legal culpability. This young woman's been victimized by her brother and her doctor. I'm not going to add to it."

Socolow turned back to us. I thought he was looking at me, but he gave Chrissy a rueful smile. "The state does not oppose the entry of a judgment of acquittal."

"Motion granted," Judge Stanger said, happy to close another case. "The defendant is forthwith discharged. Bond is released. Ms. Bernhardt, the clerk will return any possessions that may have been seized by the state." The judge looked at me and grabbed the bottle of whiskey. "Anything further? I think I see a special setting on my calendar with a Mr. Daniel."

"Judge, I'd just like to say one thing," I told His

Honor—lawyer-speak for intending to say several things. "I've known Abe Socolow for a lot of years, and he's busted my chops more times than I can remember, but he's always been honorable, and today . . . well, today, it just reaffirms my faith in Abe the man. The system doesn't always work. Hell, it doesn't usually work. But Abe is living proof that if you care more about justice than merely winning—"

"Shove it, Jake!" Socolow was turning red, embarrassed to be considered a human being instead of a cold-hearted prosecutor. "Next time you come in here with one of your typical lowlifes, I'll kick your ass from here to Sopchoppy."

"I love you, too, Abe."

Charlie Riggs was cutting the heads off a mess of mullet, slicing down the backbone and through the ribs. He removed the gizzard and liver, scraped away the gray membrane of the stomach cavity, then used a garden hose to rinse away the blood. He moved quickly and efficiently. No wasted motions with the knife.

"You've done this before," I said.

"Twenty thousand autopsies is pretty good practice for cleaning fish," he replied.

He laid open half a dozen corpses and slid them into the bottom tray of Granny's smoker, a homemade contraption that looked like a little shingled house on top of a fifty-five-gallon steel drum.

"Aren't you going to scale them?" I asked.

"Not for smoking, Jake. The scales and skin insulate against the heat."

Charlie asked me to get the melted butter and a paintbrush, so I headed into the kitchen where Granny was making a strawberry pie. As usual, Kip was watching TV in the Florida room. *Ferris Bueller's Day Off*, about a smart-ass kid playing hooky. I could hear Kip talking back to the tube, saying Matthew Broderick's lines. " 'They bought it. Incredible. One of the worst performances of my career and they never doubted it for a second. How could I possibly be expected to handle school on a day like today?' "

I made a mental note to check on Kip's number of sick days.

"So where is she?" Granny asked. "Can't have a celebration without the guest of honor."

"Said she had a stop to make and would be along later, Granny."

"That poor child. She's not healthy, Jake. Dark circles under her eyes, looking so sad today, even after you won. And I swear, she's skinnier every day. Just skin and bones."

"Flesh and bones," I said, absentmindedly.

"What's that?"

The phone rang before I could answer her. I walked into the front hallway. The phone was an old black model with a rotary dial. When Kip first saw it, he laughed and asked if Granny had stolen the props from *Dial M for Murder.* But it wasn't Grace Kelly on the phone. It was Abe Socolow.

"Where's your client, Jake?"

"Right about now, I'd say she's on Useless One, headed down here. Granny's throwing a party. You want to come?"

"That would be inappropriate."

Inappropriate. A perfect Socolow word. Though it was after six P.M., I knew old Abe still had his suit coat on, his tie knotted snugly at the neck.

"Jake, I think you ought to keep a close watch on her for a few days."

"I intend to. Maybe for more than that." There was an uncomfortable silence. "What is it, Abe?"

"Maybe nothing. People get strung out in trial, I can

understand that. But your client caused a big stir in the clerk's office when she got her stuff back. I wasn't there, but the head clerk said she was pretty near hysterical when they couldn't find the evidence file. It was still up in the courtroom, so it took a few minutes, and your client cussed up a blue streak, started crying and shaking, that sort of thing. Finally, they gave her the box, and she was rooting around in it, frantic like. She tore through all the exhibits, the medical records, her papers, the dress she wore the night of the shooting, the purse, everything. Then she ran out of there with just one thing."

"What, Abe?"

"Exhibit three, Jake. She took the gun."

35

Stolen Waters Are Sweet

I raced north on U.S. 1 from Islamorada. She would have been headed south from Miami. The farm in Homestead was closer to her.

I prayed I wasn't too late.

I was doing eighty, occasionally ninety, passing RVs on the two-lane road, staying in the passing lane where the road widened every few miles. Flying past the shell shops, convenience stores, and telephone poles topped with osprey nests. The Olds 442 had stiff springs and a rear stabilizer bar, a 400-cubic-inch V8 throwing off 350 horsepower, and shitty brakes for a muscle car. It didn't matter. I wasn't going to slow down until I got there.

The top was down, and the wind tore at my face, bringing tears to my eyes. At least I told myself it was the wind.

I stayed on the highway, ignoring the Card Sound bridge, and slid onto a gravel road just before the turnpike entrance south of Homestead. The engine was roaring, the tires kicking up a tornado of dust as I pulled into Bernhardt Farms just after seven o'clock.

As soon as the engine died, I heard the sweeping whoosh of the irrigation towers in the field behind the farmhouse. But no other sound. The house was dark. A

Land Rover and two Jeep Wranglers were parked in the driveway. So was Chrissy's Mustang convertible, the hood still warm.

The front door of the house was cracked open, and I headed inside. Down a darkened corridor, past the kitchen, through the living room, down another corridor. A light shone through an open doorway from a room at the rear of the house, the side facing the mango fields. I walked toward the light and I heard her voice.

". . . going to kill you," Chrissy Bernhardt said.

A man's gravelly laugh. "Don't think so."

I walked through the open door. Same varnished pine walls. Same boar's head on one wall, a rack of antlers on another. The jalousie windows were open; the paddle fan whirred overhead. Chrissy stood to one side, ten feet from me, another ten feet from Guy Bernhardt, who sat on a leather chair.

She was holding the Beretta 950 in a shaky hand. Her hair was a mess of tangles, her dress wrinkled, and her eyes puffy. She was the most beautiful woman I'd ever seen.

Guy Bernhardt was holding a bourbon in one hand, a 12-gauge shotgun cradled across his knee with the other. The barrel was pointed at Chrissy's midsection.

"Glad you're here, Lassiter," he said, without taking his eyes off his half sister.

"I want both of you to put down your guns," I said. "You first, Guy."

He laughed again. "Me first? With this homicidal maniac pointing a gun at me? I don't care if you did get her off. She shot Pop, *tried* to kill him, even if someone else finished the job."

"You're going to take the fall for that," I said.

"No way, Lassiter. I had nothing to do with it. How was I to know crazy old Larry Schein was a killer? Twice, in fact."

"Bullshit! You put him up to it, first with Chrissy, then you told him to get his ass to the hospital and finish the job."

"Prove it! You think I'll crack like that fruity shrink?"

"I remember everything now, Guy," Chrissy said. "Every detail, the way your voice sounded, the smell of your breath, the pain, the nightmares. Over and over again." She sobbed. "I'm going to kill you."

"No, Chrissy!" I shouted, taking a step toward her.

"Stay back, Jake!" She wheeled the gun toward me.

I stopped, and she swung the gun back toward Guy.

"As I recall," Guy said, "Sis is not a very good shot. And that peashooter holds what, twenty-two shorts? Whadaya think, Lassiter, should I let her get off the first one like the good guy in a western?"

"You're not a good guy. You're a bucket of slime."

"Or should I just splatter her guts on the wall? I've got a right to defend myself, and I've got my witness. This deranged woman shows up at my house, waving a gun, threatening to kill me. I know her propensity for violence. What's a man to do?"

"You kill her, you'd better kill me, too," I said.

His eyes flicked toward me. "Ah, chivalry. Chrissy, here's a man who didn't run out on you. That's a first, isn't it? You see, Lassiter, Sis has trouble holding on to men. Freaks out sooner or later, and they take off. Pop always thought she was high strung. But we know the truth, don't we Sis? You're wacko."

"You ruined my life," she said, eyes filling with tears.

"You had every break, so don't blame me," he said bitterly.

"I don't get it, Bernhardt," I said. "Why'd you set her up? Hadn't you done enough to her?"

"Fuck you! You don't know how it was. You don't know how Pop spoiled her. Nothing was too good for little Chrissy. And her mother was even worse. I was a barnyard animal to Missus hoity-toity Emily Castleberry Bernhardt. While she was having high tea, I was up to my ass in manure. But Pop's the one I couldn't forgive. His only son, his own blood, and he treated the migrant workers better than me. My hands would bleed from cutting cane, while darling Sis was on the beach with her rich friends, making fun of me."

"I never made fun of you. Never."

"Shut up! Pop tried to make it up to me later. Brought me into the business. What else was he going to do with it? But I always remembered. Every insult. Every abuse. And I'd already made Chrissy pay, hadn't I, Sis?"

"Why did you kill him?" Chrissy cried. "You would have gotten the money anyway."

"Pop couldn't see the future with his bifocals. I gave him the facts. The well fields are running dry, and there's no other answer but to desalinate. I'm building the biggest reverse-osmosis plant in the country. Hell, with advanced membrane technology, I can turn brackish water into drinking water cheaper than a conventional system, and I can sell it for whatever I want. If you're dying of thirst, Lassiter, how much will you pay for a glass of water?"

"That's why you're dumping all the water into the bay," I said. "You're trying to dry up the South Dade wells."

"Supply and demand, Lassiter."

"Daddy never would have gone along with it," Chrissy said.

Guy barked a laugh. "You're right. The damn fool wouldn't. Didn't think it was right to get rich selling water. Be like some Arab sheik, he said, only worse, selling water to his fellowman. Quoted Isaiah to me: 'Every one that thirsteth, come ye to the waters, and he that hath no money; come ye and eat.' That old hypocrite. I told him I knew my Bible, too. What about Proverbs? 'Stolen waters are sweet, and bread eaten in secret is pleasant.' "

Still pointing the shotgun at Chrissy, he sipped at his bourbon and said, "I've had my secret bread, haven't I, Sis? Now it's time for stolen waters. Hell, it's all free, seven hundred feet down. All the water you want. And I can turn it into dollars. Hundreds of millions of dollars."

"What about the brine?" I asked. "What do you do with millions of pounds of salt laced with mercury, arsenic, and heavy-metal ions?"

"I'll be a son of a bitch," Guy said. "You've been doing your homework. We could use deep well injection, but it's expensive as hell. We could dump it in the ocean, but the EPA would be all over us. Or we could buy every politician in Tallahassee and just dump the stuff."

"Where?"

"Limestone quarries, swamps, anywhere."

"That's crazy. It would pollute the groundwater."

"So then they'd need us pulling up water from the Floridan Aquifer even more than before, wouldn't they? A nice symmetry there, don't you think?"

"You're out of your mind," I said. "You'll never get away with it."

"Oh, we'll make some show of lining the dumps, do some solar evaporation, play around with some new techniques to keep the boys at DERM happy. But if I were you, I wouldn't want to drink any well water in the county once we get started."

"You're nothing like Daddy," Chrissy said. "He was a good man." Shakily she raised the gun, then steadied it with both hands.

Guy's drink crashed to the floor and he raised the shotgun until it was pointed at Chrissy's head. "You're a witness, Lassiter. She's gonna shoot me!"

"No!" I shouted.

Neither said a word.

Total silence except for the whir of the paddle fan and the whoosh of the irrigation towers in the fields.

Chrissy's hand shook.

A sly grin spread across Guy's face. "Sis, you may be crazy, but you're still the best piece of ass I ever had. Tight and juicy."

"You bastard!" she cried.

The gun danced in her hand as she sobbed.

The rest took just a few seconds.

Guy Bernhardt steadied the shotgun with both hands.

I watched as his finger tightened on the trigger.

I took two steps and dived for him. Startled, he swung the gun in my direction.

The first explosion was soft, a car backfiring behind me.

The second explosion was a mountaintop exploding with volcanic force.

I ended up on the floor, the discharged shotgun in my hands, a hole the size of a cantaloupe in the knotty pine ceiling. I looked up at Guy. His eyes were open. Dead between them was a dime-sized black hole. Behind us, Chrissy was saying something, but my ears were ringing. I turned in time to see her eyes roll back and her knees buckle. I caught her just before she hit the floor.

36

Committed to the Truth

"You can't be her lawyer!" Charlie Riggs thundered. "You're a witness."

"Socolow said he wouldn't object to my representing her in front of the grand jury," I said.

He harrumphed and packed his pipe with cherry tobacco. He was pacing on my back porch. "If I were you, I wouldn't take that as a compliment."

"Haven't we had this conversation before?"

"Lord yes, and I thought you'd have learned your lesson."

"Abe's gonna let me testify in front of the grand jury and represent Chrissy, too. I'll tell my story, she'll tell hers, and we'll try to head off an indictment. If they indict her, I'll get Ed Shohat to handle the trial."

Charlie aimed some smoke in my direction. "Let's take inventory," he said as usual. "She went to the house with a loaded gun, intending to kill her half brother, correct?"

"Yep."

"Guy armed himself with a weapon of his own?"

"Yep again."

"Which he had every right to do, correct?"

"Under the doctrine of self-defense, sure," I said.

"She stated she would kill him, didn't she?"

"Sure did," I admitted, "but he threatened her, too. And he tried to provoke her."

"Oral provocations are no defense to murder."

"That's true, Charlie."

"Two shots were fired, one by each of them, right?"

"Right again."

"Then it seems to me," Charlie said, "that your client is innocent only if she didn't fire first."

"Go on, Charlie."

"Well, if she had backed down from her threats and Guy became the aggressor, she would be justified in using deadly force to defend herself. But if she fired first, well, she just assassinated him, and it would be first-degree murder."

"You may be right," I said.

"So which way was it?" Charlie demanded.

I didn't answer.

"Jake! The grand jury's going to ask you, so you might as well tell me. And don't forget you'll be under oath. I always taught you to be committed to the truth."

"You also taught me to do what I believed was right."

"That advice was not contradictory," he said.

"Charlie, I've always sought the truth. I've never lied to the court."

"And never will?"

It took me a moment to answer. "Charlie, have you ever had a situation where the truth and justice don't coincide, where the truth will do more harm than good?"

He pointed his pipe at me. "That's not for us to judge. We speak the truth and let the system handle it."

"The system doesn't work, Charlie."

"Balderdash! It just worked. You walked your client out of a murder charge when it seemed you had no chance."

"You think I can do it twice?"

"That's not my concern. The truth is the ideal we strive

for. The truth is all that matters. *Veritas vos liberabit*."

"No, Charlie. Sometimes the truth will imprison you."

Chrissy wore an ivory linen suit with a fitted jacket and fabric-covered buttons. The pleated skirt stopped just above the knee. It was an innocent outfit if I've ever seen one.

The clerk of the grand jury asked if I promised to tell the truth, the whole truth, and nothing but the truth, so help me God.

I allowed as how I would. My palms weren't sweaty and my nose didn't grow. Lightning didn't sound in the distance and the wind didn't rattle the windowpanes.

I sat on the witness stand and marveled at the different view, looking toward the gallery. Abe Socolow approached me and asked a bunch of preliminary questions, including whether he could call me Jake, inasmuch as we'd known each other all these years. I said he'd called me a lot worse, so he got down to business.

"And when you entered the home of Guy Bernhardt the night before last, what did you find?"

"Guy Bernhardt was aiming a shotgun at Chrissy Bernhardt, and she was aiming a Beretta 950 at him."

Abe had me identity the two weapons, the massive shotgun and the little pistol.

"Did either party threaten to shoot the other?" Abe asked.

"They each threatened the other," I said.

"What did you do, Jake?"

"I asked Guy to put down the shotgun, and he refused."

"Then what happened?"

"Two shots were fired, one by each of the parties."

"Who fired the first shot?"

Chrissy looked at me with haunting green eyes. Seeking, pleading. Abe Socolow stood a foot away, his hand resting on the witness chair. Twenty-three grand jurors, solid citizens all, waited for me to answer.

So I did.

I followed Charlie's advice.

Half of it, at least.

I did what I thought was right.

Red-Hot Thrillers

featuring pro linebacker-turned-attorney Jake Lassiter
by PAUL LEVINE

FLESH & BONES
72591-6/$5.99 US/$7.99 Can

"An enjoyable, breathless thriller."
Atlanta Journal Constitution

FOOL ME TWICE
72590-8/$5.99 US/$7.99 Can

"Wildly entertaining...a blend of raucous
humor and high adventure"
St. Louis Post-Dispatch

SLASHBACK
72162-7/$5.99 US/$7.99 Can

"Jake is great fun"
New York Times Book Review

MORTAL SIN
72161-9/$5.50 US/$7.50 Can

"A definite must-read"
Larry King, *USA Today*

Buy these books at your local bookstore or use this coupon for ordering:

Mail to: Avon Books, Dept BP, Box 767, Rte 2, Dresden, TN 38225   G
Please send me the book(s) I have checked above.
❏ My check or money order—no cash or CODs please—for $_____is enclosed (please
add $1.50 per order to cover postage and handling—Canadian residents add 7% GST). U.S.
residents make checks payable to Avon Books; Canada residents make checks payable to
Hearst Book Group of Canada.
❏ Charge my VISA/MC Acct#_____Exp Date_____
Minimum credit card order is two books or $7.50 (please add postage and handling
charge of $1.50 per order—Canadian residents add 7% GST). For faster service, call
1-800-762-0779. Prices and numbers are subject to change without notice. Please allow six to
eight weeks for delivery.
Name_____
Address_____
City_____State/Zip_____
Telephone No._____   PL 0198

Edgar Award-winning Author

LAWRENCE BLOCK

THE MATTHEW SCUDDER MYSTERIES

EVEN THE WICKED
72534-7/ $6.99 US/ $8.99 Can

A LONG LINE OF DEAD MEN
72024-8/ $5.99 US/ $7.99 Can

THE DEVIL KNOWS YOU'RE DEAD
72023-X/ $5.99 US/ $7.99 Can

A DANCE AT THE SLAUGHTERHOUSE
71374-8/ $5.99 US/ $7.99 Can

A TICKET TO THE BONEYARD
70994-5/ $5.99 US/ $7.99 Can

OUT ON THE CUTTING EDGE
70993-7/ $5.99 US/ $7.99 Can

THE SINS OF THE FATHERS
76363-X/ $5.99 US/ $7.99 Can

TIME TO MURDER AND CREATE
76365-6/ $5.99 US/ $7.99 Can

A STAB IN THE DARK
71574-0/ $5.99 US/ $7.99 Can

IN THE MIDST OF DEATH
76362-1/ $5.99 US/ $7.99 Can

EIGHT MILLION WAYS TO DIE
71573-2/ $6.50 US/ $8.50 Can

A WALK AMONG THE TOMBSTONES
71375-6/ $5.99 US/ $7.99 Can

WHEN THE SACRED GINMILL CLOSES
72825-7/ $5.99 US/ $7.99 Can

Buy these books at your local bookstore or use this coupon for ordering:

Mail to: Avon Books, Dept BP, Box 767, Rte 2, Dresden, TN 38225   G
Please send me the book(s) I have checked above.
❑ My check or money order—no cash or CODs please—for $_____is enclosed (please
add $1.50 per order to cover postage and handling—Canadian residents add 7% GST). U.S.
residents make checks payable to Avon Books; Canada residents make checks payable to
Hearst Book Group of Canada.
❑ Charge my VISA/MC Acct#_____Exp Date_____
Minimum credit card order is two books or $7.50 (please add postage and handling
charge of $1.50 per order—Canadian residents add 7% GST). For faster service, call
1-800-762-0779. Prices and numbers are subject to change without notice. Please allow six to
eight weeks for delivery.
Name_____
Address_____
City_____State/Zip_____
Telephone No._____   BLK 1297